PRAISE FOR *PSYCHOPOMP*

"Maria Dong's *Psychopomp* is science fiction at its best, exploring questions large and small about how we structure our society, extract resources from nature, and survive as individuals. It's propulsive and twisty and atmospheric as hell. Get in the space elevator, loser. We're going for a ride."

—Yume Kitasei, author of *The Deep Sky*

"*Psychopomp*'s compelling protagonist doesn't know who she can trust or believe—least of all herself—and I was thrilled to watch over her shoulder every step of the way. Maria Dong weaves in tension thread by thread until the story is taut and ready to snap. This is a smart, sharp book whose dark vision of the future feels mirror-perfect to our current system."

—Aimee Ogden, author of *Emergent Properties*

"Flawed characters, mystery and paranoia. Secrets unravel piece by piece in this richly drawn and complex sci-fi thriller."

—Ai Jiang, Nebula and Bram Stoker Award-winning author of *Linghun*

"An unflinching, brutally honest dive into heartache, depression, and resilience. Dong pulls no punches with her protagonist, who is determined to get the better of the monsters that haunt her. Claustrophobic and intense in ways that invoke Daniel Kraus's *Whalefall*, *Psychopomp* is a riveting story about courage and self belief."

—Eliane Boey, author of *Club Contango*

"A carceral mining operation; a tethered moon; a main character who isn't sure she can trust her own tortured mind. *Psychopomp* pulls you into a world of secrets, lies, paranoia, and hallucinations, but it also thrums with moments of transcendent beauty. This is a book that will have you helplessly reading deep into the night, burrowing into its pages like the protagonist burrows into the moon."

—Jennifer Hudak, short fiction author

"A riveting page-turner. Dong is clearly a master of the craft, skillfully infusing science fiction with the harsh realities of work exploitation and mental breakdown. I kept thinking about the story's protagonist long after I finished the book."

—Renan Bernardo, Nebula and Ignyte award finalist author of *Disgraced Return of the Kap's Needle*

"A cinematic sci-fi thriller that cleverly combines action with tension, and certainty with doubt. A cast of complex characters propel the reader along a journey of secrets and self-discovery."

—Catherine McCarthy, author of *Mosaic* and *The House at the End of Lacelean Street*

"*Psychopomp* is a gripping deep-space thriller packed with tension and inhabited by complex characters exploring how to live in a world designed to oppress and use them. Along with main character, Young, readers will hurtle headlong through this story, not knowing who to trust."

—Angela Sylvaine, author of *Frost Bite*

"Who can you trust if you can't trust yourself? Mining the personal and mental toll of surviving in a system built on lies and exploitation, *Psychopomp* is brutal, intense, and breathtakingly introspective. Beautifully written and full of cosmic emotional gravity, this shadowy sci-fi world comes alive with vast twisting secrets and darkly intricate characters. A gritty, unforgettable meditation on the strength it takes to believe in yourself inside a world engineered to deceive you."

—Amanda Cecelia Lang, author of
Saturday Fright at the Movies

"In *Psychopomp*, Maria Dong breathes new life into the classic science fiction elements of corporate-state dominance, the corruption of the natural world, and the repression of a people, to craft a tale of the irresistible power of truth and connection. Intimate and epic in equal measure, this book won't let you go."

—Patrick Barb, author of *Helicopter Parenting in the Age of Drone Warfare* and *JK-LOL*

"Haunting, atmospheric, gloom-tinged with a crystalline beauty. A gut-punch illuminating the weight of power, desperation, loneliness, and survivalism, *Psychopomp* is a fever dream and a pioneering science fiction triumph."

—Belicia Rhea, author of *Voracious*

PSYCHOPOMP

CONTENT WARNING

This work explores many themes in depth that represent potentially triggering content, including abandonment, parental trauma, infidelity, self-harm, mental illness, sexual manipulation, emotional abuse, drug use, homelessness, financial anxiety, debt slavery, vomiting, violence, and suicidal ideation.

Please take a moment to consider if reading these themes would present you harm, and if so, please consider saving this book for a different day—or reading a different book. Nothing is worth your mental health.

Edited by Marie Croke
Proofread by Maddy Leary
Book Design and Layout by Rob Carroll
Cover Art by Katerina Belikova
Cover Design by Rob Carroll

Library of Congress Control Number: 2025932485

ISBN 978-1-958598-52-8 (paperback)
ISBN 978-1-958598-79-5 (eBook)

darkmatter-ink.com

PSYCHOPOMP

MARIA DONG

*For Justin and June,
who pull me through the darkness
and float me into the light.*

Some say the world will end in fire,
Some say in ice.
From what I've tasted of desire
I hold with those who favor fire.
But if it had to perish twice,
I think I know enough of hate
To say that for destruction ice
Is also great
And would suffice.

—Robert Frost

1

I EYE THE torn corner of my glove, sure testament to the fact that I am a fucking disaster.

"Well? What's your vote?"

At Adda's question, I jam my hand behind me, as if into a back pocket. Dumb because *one,* regulation Annie suits don't have pockets, and *two,* whipping your hand behind you is the universal symbol for having something to hide.

Adda raises her eyebrows: two thin, black arches over frosted irises that are only a few shades darker than the quartz-like piezanite we're here to mine.

Back planet-side, blue eyes are rarely found outside of Ur-Lapla, a city on the eighty-fifth parallel—one so far north, it's almost on the pole. But light eyes often feature in the old fantasy books my sort-of boyfriend keeps begging me to read. When Adda looks at me like this, it's like she knows they're magic, like she's casting a spell of silence.

"Young. *Vote.*"

I glance at the rest of the crew, but they haven't turned their helmet projections on, which means I can't see their faces. Just three curves of mirrored glass, glinting in the light from the Pomp drone. Including myself and Adda, the Fore, there are five of us. The divergence vote is split two and two, which means I'll break the tie.

It's too much pressure—especially since I know things they don't. They're relying on the Pomp, a guide that conveys crackling recommendations through the piece jammed in Adda's ear. *Take this fork. Mine at a ten-degree uphill grade.* The information is comfortingly specific, unless you've gone through, say, 93.3 percent of the 240 circadians of training necessary to become a Pomp before flaming out. If you had, you'd know that these recommendations are just educated predictions modeled from penetrating radar data. They try to calculate potential crystal load and tunnel stability of each side of the fork, but it's guesswork. It's often wrong.

And when it comes to voting on which direction to take in a Cable tunnel divergence, there's a lot unaccounted for: someone's sneeze. A son-chem drill that loses calibration ahead of schedule. An unmodeled structural defect that could make the tunnel collapse, trapping everybody inside—everybody that isn't killed by the blast produced when a ton of rock crust and Cable suddenly compresses one of the piezanite crystals.

After washing out as a Pomp, I've somehow managed to go a full 105 circadians as part of a general mining crew without being the tie-breaker in a vote. In fact, my first thirty circadians, there wasn't any voting at all: If the Fore and the Pomp picked the wrong tunnel and everybody died, well, that was on them. Have fun filing a complaint.

After I tried to kill myself, I got transferred to Adda's unit, but the Pomp's recommendation was always strong enough to garner a consensus—until roughly two minutes ago when the Pomp suddenly couldn't choose. More crystals to the west, but the tunnels might have less stability. Less yield to the east, but the crust-rock looked better. Our safety at risk, Adda brought it to the crew.

I finger the hole in my glove. More rubber crumbles away. Maybe there's already cancer growing underneath, clumps of fat, black tumors. Then again, we're miles underground, hidden from the sun and the poisonous gases that cling to Hib's surface like a skin. And the truth is that nobody knows what, exactly, causes Miner's Rot, so we just follow the mantra: *The gear you're supposed to wear, in good repair.*

I bite my lip. "You should just vote without me."

Adda's snort is clear, but a crackle mars her reply. "Young. Do you not understand how voting works?"

I wish she'd just decide for us, but Adda believes in giving people a choice about their own safety—which is kind of funny, given that we've all been sentenced to mine an explosive substance on the freaking *moon* until we somehow manage to pay back the cost of our imprisonment. Then again, at least for me, this place is a step above the Equatorial prison I'd been rotting in before my trip up the Elevator, sewing shoes and bags until my hands bled.

Someone in the back sniggers—Oye, maybe—and the pressure starts, a spring winding in my chest. Fuck. I know they're all staring from behind their helmet-glass. I can't breathe. I'm going to snap right here in the tunnel. "I have to piss."

Oye groans. "Young, gross. Why can't you just piss in secret like the rest of us?"

I shrug. "Sorry." I shuffle away, backtracking to the last tunnel bend. But as soon as I lose sight of them, I stub my toe and go sprawling forward.

I throw out my hands in time. A jarring shock, and half of my glove evaporates into dust as something hot vibrates through my palm. A vague thought leaks into my brain: *We're going to have to suspend operations until I can get a new glove—*

Something flutters in my vision, light-dark, as if I've just taken several slow blinks. I try to roll onto my knees, but I'm woozy and unclear about which way is up. I fall forward, splay against the ground spread-eagled, and try to breathe.

My fuzzy vision falls on my hand, pressed up against the rock of the tunnel floor. In the gaps between my fingertips, I spy small flickers of silver embedded in its surface. I follow their dance as they braid together and sink below, far past where I should be able to see.

They merge into a thick band—now, I can tell it's Cable. I can trace the band's flow, the way it rises from underneath, wrapping around the tunnel until it hangs in the ceiling overhead before breaking into a V-shaped fork.

Oh, no. I'm—I'm seeing things. This can't be real, but I *recognize* it. That fork is the divergence that we stopped to vote on—but I'm not just seeing *it*. I'm seeing *into* it, deep into the east branch of the fork: a silver river of Cable studded throughout with fist-sized loads of piezanite. The crystals are sparkling tumors, all waiting for painstaking extraction with the son-chem drill.

I can even see the crust-rock above the Cable, feel through its surface to the smooth, dense interior: a single, solid mass, one confident in its own stability. Even after the Cable has been hollowed out, this rock ceiling will hold.

I back up—not in the tunnel, where I'm still flat on my back, but hurtling backward in my mind to the point of divergence. I take the west branch and my lungs collapse. This is a fucking mother lode of piezanite, the crystalline structures flaring so bright in my mind's eye, my jaw vibrates—but the crust-rock above, it feels…wrong. Damaged. Crumbling, like my glove.

And just like that, I can't hold on to it. My vision snaps back into the dark of the tunnel.

"Young!" Adda's voice is sharp. "We don't have time for this. Get back here!"

I scramble onto my feet and come face-to-face with the Pomp's drone. The bird-sized piece of machinery has floated in here—which is fucked up, because who watches people take a piss? I glare at its camera before remembering the operator can't see my face.

I hurry back, dreading what I'm about to say. Except for Gyu, Adda is the only person who has treated me like a human being—at least, ever since they scraped me out of the dunes right by the colony's door despite having walked hours away before I'd lost consciousness. I've heard the jokes, that I couldn't even die right, but Adda never brings any of it up.

She voted for the west tunnel. I want to agree with her, to give her realness and her kindness more credence than a momentary hallucination that just hijacked my brain.

But I can't shake the dread. "I vote east."

"Outvoted." Adda points her chin at the group. "We got updated data from the Pomp. Says there was an error in the reading and that both tunnels look equally stable. We're going west."

"Right." I bite my lip. How did the Pomp figure that out when their drone was with me? Or did I just make that up, too? *In fact...*I glance over my shoulder. I don't see the drone anywhere. Almost as if it was never there.

I want to argue with the data—you can't say the tunnels "look" stable because you can't just *see* crystals in the vein or faults in crust-rock. It's all just probability. CPI—nobody knows what the letters stand for, anymore, although my guess is that the "P" is for "prison," and that the company would really like it if we all just forgot that—has poured a planet's worth of resources into solving that problem, and people like me and the rest of this crew were the best they could come up with.

Except that I *did* see it. Which can only mean I'm sick again. I just hope it goes away before anybody finds out. "Sounds good."

Adda nods at my glove. "What about—"

"I'll get a new one before the next shift. I'm okay with it if everybody else is."

She nods, amusement pinching the corners of her mouth. She's impressed by my bravado—or maybe just my stupidity.

We get into formation. The son-chem drill is heavy enough that it takes four people to operate, the head sending waves at just the right frequency to vibrate the sprayed solvent into the fibers of the Cable. The Cable will unfurl slowly as it dissolves, looking for all the world like a lock of silvery hair caught in a flame, exposing loads of piezanite beneath.

We all keep a sharp lookout for the emergence of any crystals. The drill's wavelengths are too tight to set a reaction off, but if someone doesn't spot the piezanite, birthing its way out of the dissolving Cable like an earthworm poking from a hole, it could free-fall to the floor.

Piezanite produces energy when subjected to sudden pressure. A hunk the size of a baseball, if quickly squeezed with the amount of force generated by a human fist, could blow us all sky-high. It's an incredible source of energy, and the one mine discovered planet-side has long been tapped out. Hib is the only place you can get piezanite, and piezanite makes the whole world run.

When I first got to Hib, I thought we'd be mining from above, the drill pointed under us, but some property of Cable has led to the natural formation of tunnels underneath it, leaving it exposed. From below, you just shave it off with the son-chem drill until you reach the piezanite crystals contained inside.

But if you want to top-mine, you've got to first painstakingly chip away layers and layers of crust-rock to expose the vein. If that crust is too unstable and breaks apart, your ministrations could make an entire length of Cable fall into the tunnel underneath it. If there's any piezanite sticking out of the Cable's insulating body, you're fucked the moment it hits the floor. Decades ago, before the invention of the son-chem drill made top-mining obsolete, one of the very first crews on Hib blew a crater the size of a small city into the moon's surface.

For just a second, I close my eyes and imagine the piezanite emerging, the team uncovering it with the precision of an archaeologist's brush—

"Fucking pay attention," shouts Adda, and I snap into the rhythm of the drill.

2

BY THE END of the day, nothing's happened, which makes me feel better *and* worse: I'm glad for our safety, but even more sure that I hallucinated.

I can't go to Medical. I can't tell Adda or Gyu. I've just got to keep my shit together and hope a good night's rest will fix all of this.

It helps that the group is in good spirits. We've excavated about two kilograms of piezanite—a small load, but promising. Split five ways, with a little extra for Adda's portion as Fore, it's probably enough to buy a week off our sentences.

We ride the tram up to the surface of the mine. As soon as we emerge, though, I've got to jam my hand in my armpit. With so little air, there's no perceptible wind to disrupt the endless dunes of gray sand, but the unending dark means the air temperature is always far below freezing. Frostbite would equal a trip to Medical—which I need to avoid if I'm going to keep the fact that I'm losing it under wraps.

We scurry back to the shuttle: a massive vehicle designed to tackle changes in grade with ease. The area around this mine is mostly flat, with a preponderance of small sand dunes, but a lot of Hib's surface is mottled with deep craters or fingerlike, rocky projections that were created when the moon first split off from the planet. For obvious reasons, CPI tries to place mine entrances in flatter, more easily accessible areas, although sometimes the overland shuttles we take to work each circadian are forced into circuitous routes by random crevasses and craters.

I know from previous runs there isn't much to see between this mine entrance and the colony, but the last mine I was assigned to required cutting into a narrow pass. And because of how dark and small Hib is, it always felt like the two sides of the pass just materialized on top of me, threatening to crush me between their jaws.

The shuttle's hinged body heaves as its powerful engine propels its massive treads over the sand. Normally, the erratic movements don't bother me, but a headache hits me halfway back to the station. The pain's torture, but it makes me feel better. Maybe I'm not nuts. Maybe I'm just getting sick with some nasty fever. You'd think colds would be uncommon on a moon, but viruses made it to Hib as soon as people did.

We arrive, and the front row of seats disembarks. I wait my turn and stand up to file into the aisle, but Adda grabs my wrist. "You should come with us this time."

I look at my boots, hiding my face from Adda and the three people now trapped in my row, even though they can't see through my helmet-glass. Whenever the crew has a decent haul, they go to Rikki's, check their balances, and knock back a few cold ones. Adda invites me every time, but I've never said yes.

The guy next to me gives up and squeezes past, his ass brushing my pelvis. The other two follow suit.

The spring winds tighter in my chest. It'll be torture to sit at a bar, pretend that everything is alright. I'd rather go to my hatch. Alone.

"Come on," she says, patting me on the back. Her touch is muffled through Annie's thick rubber, but it's there, and it makes my guts ache in a way her grabbing my wrist hadn't.

I'm suddenly aware of the weight of the charm around my neck, lying warm against my breastbone. A reminder of my biggest and oldest failure, of the many things that are wrong with me.

She mistakes my silence for assent. "Great!" she says, like she really means it. She grabs my wrist again and pulls me forward off the shuttle, down the path, and through the airlock. Everybody starts stripping as soon as the blowers kick on, sensors already having registered the change in the oxygen content. Like most moons, Hib's got the barest trace of an atmosphere, but the gases are all wrong, and the dome over the station protects us from those and the radiation and who knows what else.

We keep our boots on, of course. The magnets in them are attracted to a plate buried under Hib station. Hib's a lot smaller than Ung-Nyeo, the planet it orbits, but it's a lot denser, too, which means it's got enough gravity to keep you mostly in place. But without the magnets, walking through the station feels like trying to tiptoe through neck-high water, even after 330 circadians.

There's too much fog on the helmet to see well, but I still take it off last. I usually wait until my crew's gone to expose my face, but I can't do that today, so I rip it off like a scab, stash all my gear into my locker, and turn around. Some people wear their Annie suits home, but most leave things here to get picked up after taking advantage of what Leisure has to offer.

Adda is looking at me, her short brown hair mussed into a bird's nest. She's alone.

"Where did—"

"They're going to meet us there," says Adda. "Get us a seat and order us a beer, all that."

The brief reprieve from the crew's presence doesn't relieve the pressure in my chest, but it keeps it from winding tighter.

She starts walking. I settle in behind her, but she slows her pace and falls back so that we're shoulder to shoulder.

"I'm glad you finally decided to join us," she says. "I feel like we don't know anything about you."

I wince. There's one thing *everybody* knows about me. Suicides on Hib aren't unheard of, given our circumstances, but failing at them does make you an interesting subject of conversation—apparently even seventy-five circadians after the fact.

"Yeah," I say, trying to sound gruff, but I just sound constipated. "What do you want to know?"

"Like—where are you from?"

"Ung-Nyeo." I use the Hangan word for our planet to throw her off the trail, but she just groans at my joke.

"What a funny *coincidence*, Young. So am I. Which part?"

"The terminator band."

She rolls her eyes theatrically at my non-answer. The terminator band, where Ung-Nyeo's dark and light sides come together, is a dim strip sheltered within the cradle of the giant wind-walls our ancestors built. These walls encapsulate all habitable temperature zones on the planet. In areas like the poles, where the merciless beat of the sun is attenuated by the curvature of Ung-Nyeo's surface, the path of the wind-walls expands far enough into the light that you can actually see a true day—or so I've heard. Ur-Lapla, the almost north-pole city on the eighty-fifth parallel, is a bastion for the rich, full of crops that grow without artificial light cycles and radiant skin that requires no vitamin supplementation. It's not exactly welcoming of people like me, and Vrinka on the south pole is no better. Most of the world's poor reside near the equator, competing for the limited space inside of the wind-walls' thinnest part, where the strength of the sun's heat pushes the line of habitation even farther into the dark.

I can't help but notice how blue Adda's eyes are.

"*Where* in the band?" Her voice is growing tense.

Assholery is my preferred method of shoving people away, but there's no sign that she's being malicious. I'm just wearing out her patience.

I look reflexively at the top of the tunnel, imagining the sky behind its riveted, industrial curves. From Hib's dark side, you can only see Ung-Nyeo's light side, a shining tan and blue circle the size of my thumbnail, and only if there are no clouds to block the view, which is rare. "Tenth," I finally say. With the ninetieth parallel being the north pole, and neg-ninetieth being the South, she knows, now, that I'm basically from the equator. I would have told her that I was from Li'Airet, but I have no idea if she'd recognize the name of my city or not.

I answer the next question before it comes, defiant. "East Band." Now, she'll ask.

The two bands, east and west, are just the two sides of the terminator band as it encircles the light side of the planet. I have stereotypically Hangan features—a flat nose bridge, epicanthal folds, sharp cheekbones, a strong jaw. These all mark me as West Band, despite the fact that I've never been. And my skin is dark, my hair wavy enough that I have to be careful how I comb it. Before going to prison, I'd never left the slums of Li'Airet—but even people I saw regularly liked to ask me where I was from.

Her smile takes me by surprise. "We're from opposite sides of the planet, then. I'm tenth, too, although I'm West Band."

I blink. I'd guessed she was from Ur-Lapla itself, her blue eyes marking her as someone good enough to be from the north pole. Only now do I realize how stupid that is—if she really was from Ur-Lapla, she wouldn't be serving her time here on Hib. Our prison station is a veritable sea of ethnicities, all mixed together—but there are limits. Nobody here started out rich.

She laughs, reading my expression. "Yeah, I know. It's the eyes. But the truth is that you can find blue-eyed people anywhere." She shrugs. "I guess we both just don't look like the places we're from."

I TRY HARD to think of a way to get out of going to the bar without pissing Adda off, but everything I can come up with makes me sound like a bitch. By the time we've made it down the tunnel, around the ninety-degree bend, and through the second airlock into the main dome, I've got nothing.

The tunnel walls fall away. The clear dome of Hibiscus station is expansive, the contents it shields, claustrophobic—although, after the close confines of jail, the tram to the planet-side anchor of the elevator tether, and the packed ride up the elevator in a cargo container, seeing the station for the first time felt like the endless vista of salvation. It reminded me of Li'Airet, the same frenetic busyness, the same crush of buildings and machinery and people blocking your view.

But within a few circadians, the similarity passed. Hib station is clean. It's still noisy, but there's no wind to drown out the conversations; it feels like you can hear everything in the world at once. It isn't nearly as crowded. The dome was built large enough to accommodate the crews in a way the slums have never managed, with all of us getting private housing. You can walk down the spoke-paths and back alleys without getting picked up and carried by a crowd of people, can lay down at night without your walls reverberating as your upstairs neighbor trips over his drunk feet and slams into the floor while a family full of crying children squabbles downstairs.

Unlike Li'Airet, Hib station is also intuitively organized. We walk from its outer edge, down one of the main spoke-paths that lead to the exchange hub in the center. The spokes cut the station into hexants that perform separate functions, although some areas have grown or shrunk based on demand, spilling over into other hexants.

Hexant *Internal* caters to the business of running the station itself—things like medical, sanitation, etc. *Storage*, *Mining Operations*, and *Lodging* are self-explanatory. *Provisions* revolves around oxygen and food production, although a lot of food is just brought up via the elevator. And then there's our current destination, *Leisure*, an oblong area that has managed to swallow over a quarter of the station. It's much closer than the hour's walk to Lodging, which I can't help but think is purposeful because it's hard to pass the cafes and arcade bars and movie theaters and massage parlors without stopping. Whatever you spend gets billed to your account, added to your penal debt and the cost of your transport. You can't leave until the tab is paid off.

Most people never plan to. They'd rather stay here where they have access to food, medical care, hot water, where you work five half-circadian shifts and get two circadians off despite how mind-numbing and dangerous the work is. It's better than starving in the street or dying of an overdose. It's better than being shoved out of the wind-walls into the bright Desert or the dark Ice.

Even if I wanted to go home, trying to kill myself probably removed that option. Medical and rescue are both horrendously expensive. Despite the gnaw in my stomach, I haven't checked my balance since the attempt seventy-five circadians ago.

On our walk over, Adda asks me questions: about growing up, about my family, about what I did to get locked up. It's my worst nightmare, and I skate around her inquiries the best I can, but the same questions are going to bubble up again once we're all seated at Rikki's.

I feel like I'm going to vomit.

Adda puts a hand on my shoulder. "Listen. It's important for crews to bond. You let these people in, they'll defend you from the wolves."

I know what she's saying, but I'm not sure if I believe it.

We cut our way through the restaurant cluster, each one a shitty version of a different ethnic cuisine on Ung-Nyeo. I see Hangan, and I have to swallow for a second, but the lump of longing in my throat passes.

Too soon, we're outside Rikki's door. Two miners burst into the street, staggering and slurring their words. I don't understand how they managed to get toasted that fast—the shift just ended. They must have been in the very first row on the shuttle.

"Ready?" Adda says.

My throat is too tight to speak, so I just nod. She guides me in, helping me weave through the dim. There are three bars on Hib station—one fancy, one somewhere in the middle, and then there's Rikki's. The floor is sticky enough to make the magnets in my boots optional. Something wild and distorted crackles on an overhead radio—from neg-thirtieth parallel, based on the raucous beat. I trip on an uneven threshold and marvel. This entire station was constructed by engineers, which means that someone included a janky floor in their meticulous planning just to give us a little taste of home.

The crew is squeezed into a booth like rats. There isn't really room for two more. Kola and Stomp give half-hearted nods, but Oye doesn't bother with the effort.

"Hey everybody. Where's Hannah?" Adda says.

It takes me a second to remember that Hannah is Adda's girl-friend. Adda has mentioned her often enough in the tunnels, but the idea of meeting a new person on top of everything else makes my stomach churn harder.

"Bathroom," says Oye.

Adda shoves me into the booth next to Oye before scooting in after me. We're basically in each other's laps, and to top it off, I'm trapped.

A glance at Adda tells me this isn't an accident. She smiles. "So, Young and I were just getting caught up. She's apparently from the tenth parallel—"

"So, you failed out of Pomp training?"

Heads snap up at Oye's question. Including mine. She's staring me dead in the eyes, a smile barely curling around the corners of her mouth.

This was how it was going to be then. "Yeah."

"Wow," says Oye, her eyes going wide in a shitty imperson-ation of innocence. "You pissed the bed on that one."

I grit my teeth. "It wasn't *deliberate.* I did fine until the final simulations, but I couldn't manage to—"

"Is that why you tried to bite it?"

"Oye!" barks Adda, but it's too late. The question's out there, laid bare for everybody to goggle at. Tension hums between us like piezanite, waiting to fall and consume us in an explosion.

"Yeah," I finally say. "It's not the only reason, but it's one of them."

Adda's eyes go wide—for real. She hadn't expected me to tell the truth.

"What was it like?"

The low voice is one I haven't heard before. My heart almost stops as I roll my gaze over to the corner of the table. The entire time I've been on the crew, Kola's never said a single word in front of me.

"You don't have to answer that," says Adda, her voice almost a growl.

A raw spot opens in my chest, bright with heat. This, *this* is why I never come to Rikki's with the crew. It's all unfolding exactly the way I thought it would.

I stare down at the table. Somebody has painted on a wood grain, fake as shit. As if there were trees still around, waiting to donate their bodies so that we could build crap out of them.

My next words are as fast and angry as a rivet gun. "What was it like? Well, I fucked it up. I disconnected the locator beacon instead of smashing it because I thought I was strong enough." I lick my lips. "And then I ran out of air. My chest was burning. I got desperate. My mind was screaming at me the whole time to just let it go, to just *die*, but I hooked the fucker back up anyways."

Nobody says a word. I look up at drawn, pale faces. Jaded or not, there's good luck and bad luck, and giving them this kind of blow-by-blow is a way of inviting that bad luck right into the tunnels with us. There's a vicious flicker in my guts at Oye's expression I can't help but savor—she looks like she's going to faint.

"When your suit senses your oxygen is that low, it mists you with a chemical that shuts your body functions down. It puts you in stasis—buys you five, maybe ten minutes. But it's a fucking nightmare. It comes with a little residual puff of oxygen for the inhalation. I had five seconds where I was so relieved, I almost peed my pants, and then the air was gone, and I started suffocating all over again."

Someone gasps. They all look sick. This is too much for them—I've taken their morbid curiosity and turned it against them. They don't really care what it felt like—they just wanted to play their fucking game of *poor, sad Young.*

I start talking faster, my voice jovial, quick, like I'm back on Ung-Nyeo and waxing poetic to my ex, Brin, about how sexy his new haircut is. "You know what the worst part is? It's shit like this. It's waking up, every circadian, knowing every single fucking person on this station knows what happened, that every fucking person you'll see for the rest of your miserable fucking life will stare and try to figure you out. *Were there any signs you were about to blow? Are you parents crazy, too? Did your performance get shitty in the mines, lately?* Mine did, in case you're wondering." I laugh uncontrollably, so stilted and harsh it sounds like I'm barking. "*Mine*, get it? *Mine*."

"Young, *shut it*." Adda is reaching for me, but there's a roar in my ears.

I whip my hands away before she can grab them, still talking. "—and now, everybody is looking down on you, not because you're suicidal, but because you didn't have the presence of mind to smash a *fucking beacon*, because you didn't get it right—"

A woman arrives at our table. Recognition hits me like a tunnel collapse. My throat closes up.

She's gorgeous. Her makeup is expertly done in subtle and complimentary shades, her sloppy clothes somehow elegant on her petite frame. She leans over to kiss Adda on the mouth, one of her pigtails swinging forward to obscure her eyes, some trick of the light making her sharp cheekbones gleam underneath her dark skin. She's a blend, like me, like Gyu, a product of population movement around the terminator ring. She's even got my nose—pert, small, the bridge so flat it can't support a pair of glasses.

It's *her*. The girl I ran into the circadian I failed out of Pomp training. The roar and throbbing beat of Rikki's fades as it merges with the clink of glasses and the twang of guitar-music from Willow's, the middle bar on Hib.

She pouts as she walks up to grab her drink, her inebriated slur doing little to mask her flat city accent. She sounds like Li'Airet.

Later, I'm in the bathroom, crying and hurling at the same time. There's a knock at my stall door.

"Hey, are you okay?" That accent again.

My throat burns as I answer. "Yeah, I just—I fucked up. I'm so fucked. I don't know what to do."

As if she's able to watch me replay the memory here in Rikki's, Hannah's face—because this has to be her, the one Adda has talked so much about—twists in recognition, connecting me with her past even as I connect her face and name.

In my ears is her laugh, high and floating. *"You're hilarious. This is a fucking penal colony. We're all slaves for the rich bitches raping the world—but what are you going to do, die? Pull your shit together." The door creaks. The floor groans as she walks out.*

A three-second conversation. Not really advice, but it had planted a seed.

My chest tightens like a spring, such a massive jerk that it doubles me over.

I can't be here right now. I can't.

I grab a glass and slam it down in front of me. Beer splashes out. Oye and Stomp fling themselves back to avoid the spray, but I'm already crawling under the table. Once clear, I bolt for the door.

"Hey, wait—" yells Adda, and I can hear someone—Oye—say, "What's her problem?" before I burst through and sprawl out into the street.

Right away, I feel better. The pressure in my chest eases as I scramble to my feet. For a second, Gyu's face flashes in my mind—he's got my mom's golden skin, more than I ever had it. Even as the thought surfaces, my brain screams—*It's the wrong thing to think right now. Why are you so fucked up—*

I could find Gyu. He'd welcome me. Instead, I turn on my heel and run to where I should have gone in the first place, the only spot on this entire forsaken moon I feel safe. The hatch.

I sprint across Hib station to the dome-lock. The next minutes pass by in a blur, and I come to fully suited, already down the tunnel, watching as the final airlock whooshes open.

Someone hollers my name. I look back—Adda is waving frantically, her mouth forming an "o" as she yells. She's not suited, though. She can't follow me out.

I turn and bolt toward Hib's desolate surface.

3

LIKE ALWAYS, IT'S cloudy out. Without light reflected from Ung-Nyeo to help me find my way, I have to switch on my helmet-lamp as soon as I clear the station.

I've never seen anything as flat and featureless as this part of Hib's sandy surface, shrouded in eternal dark. Even in the parts that have craters, dunes, or rocky hills, Hib's overall aesthetic is so bleak and depressing that any change is an improvement—be it the brilliant white illumination of the lights inside the colony bubble, the glint of a mineshaft, or the long sprawl of a fence that encircles one of the many areas miners are not allowed to access.

But despite Hib's desolation, I don't understand the people who stay inside the station their entire sentence, playing pinball and cards and drinking tea. There's no freedom there because there's no place to be *alone*. Our lodging doors don't even lock, as if to remind us we're actually prisoners.

A raw spot opens in my chest. I slow down and glance back, the beam from my helmet swiveling around in a wide arc, but there's no sign of movement.

I didn't really think Adda was going to follow me out. I just hope she hasn't panicked and called Enforcement. I could smash the locator beacon, but I need it to find the hatch, plus I don't want a repair added to my tab.

In my mind, a third, darker reason to leave it alone bares sharp teeth. There's always the chance that I'll give in to temptation. Walk out and wait until my lamp battery dies, and I'm submerged, airless, in the dark. This time, there would be no beacon to save me.

That would shut my crew up, I bet.

I picture my Annie suit slumped around my inert body, somewhere far from the borders of Hibiscus station. It should be creepy, scary, *something*—but I just feel blank.

I don't know how many bodies it takes before they send out a collection. They probably just do it when they run out of suits.

I bet somebody already died in this suit, I think, and *that*, at least, jostles something loose. I get moving, fast enough that the charm bounces against my chest, rapping out the same dirge it has beaten for the last five years—*failure, failure, failure*—and glance down at the oxygen canister. There's a little jump of anxiety, but then I realize the gauge is upside down. The tank's nearly full.

I'm relieved.

I'm disappointed.

The terrain is changing now, the flatness broken up by a series of small dunes that grow as I progress. I scramble over one, and the way the sand has fallen on the other side—like the curve of a girl's hip, combined with the sinking compression in my chest, the way I can't breathe—it transports me, and not to my ill-fated airless walk. Instead, I'm on a beach.

(*Are these hazy images real? Or are they the residue that's left over when you've had a thought so many times, you've reformed it into something new?*)

I am small. Someone has put my thick hair into pigtails, which are now soaked through, their heavy weight pulling on my scalp. It's bright here, as if we're somehow in Ur-Lapla and not the sixty-third story of a skyscraper my parents have broken into after hours.

I know it's fake, but I can't help marveling.

The water is cold, but the air is colder, so I alternate between staying submerged and jumping up to splash. Freezing air hits my shoulders as I cast glittering diamonds from my finger-tips. As young as I am, I know I will never get another chance to play on a mostly deserted beach—that it's reserved somehow for people who are different from us, although I don't yet understand the distinction. That my parents have done something naughty getting us here.

Something in the light changes, darkens—or maybe, I hear a roar. I can't remember why I turn, and the vagueness in my thoughts sends a shaft of frustration through grown-me, long-striding through an oasis of sand.

The wave climbs up, a monolith, blocking out my view of the sky. A brilliant sheen reflects where the curve of its body catches the light. The top breaks into white foam. I wait, breathless, as it descends on me, and I'm knocked off my feet by the crash.

(*Was it really the monster that I remember?*)

Outside, I'm running, a bounding rabbit in low gravity.

Inside, I'm drowning.

I go deaf as my head is pushed under the water. In the murky quiet, I float, vague and formless, as raspy seaweed brushes my limbs through brown scattered light—and this, this is familiar, akin to the twilight that greets me every time I step outdoors. I can't swim. I've never seen a body of water larger than a bathtub—but I know I'm supposed to move my arms and legs, and so I do, kicking and flapping hard, not knowing if I'm going in the right direction.

Wait, am *I going in the right direction?* I have to stop, consult Annie. A map reflects off the glass inside of my helmet, the navigation indicating the coordinates I saved.

I change my course, angling toward the hatch.

I found it the circadian they released me from Medical—where I'd spent every sleeping period wondering how it was possible the crews had reached me in time when I'd spent the hours before my air ran out walking away from the station. And then the doctor told me that the patrol had scooped me up ten minutes from the dome-lock—that I must have just walked in a big circle.

It didn't make sense. I tried to retrace my steps over the sand, an awful pilgrimage of obsession. I never figured it out—but I *did* find the switch, unburied by a rare, chance wind.

I'm holding my breath. The spring in my chest is so tight, I half fear that if I try to inhale, no air will come in. My skin writhes with the feeling of being watched, of being shamed.

I'd been brave. I thought I wouldn't be afraid of asphyxiating, but the truth is that dying on Hib isn't like drowning. There's no sudden, painful yank as someone grabs you by the arms and hauls you out of the water, the quiet chased away by a world overbearingly loud and bright. You'll never dangle, gasping and coughing, like a prize-winning fish.

Somebody laughs, but I can't remember if it was my mother or my father. Timelines crash together. Even as I think the words, *I can't breathe*, I can hear my own gasps, loud and rushing inside of my helmet, like the roar of a hungry wave.

I freeze. The hair goes up on the back of my neck—someone is watching me.

My legs give out. I fall to my knees and swing the beam of my headlamp back and forth in a wide arc, but, of course, there's no movement except the sand I've kicked up, because none of this is happening. I'm not dying. There's nobody here.

Earlier today, in the mines, I saw something I couldn't have possibly seen. No meds, no drugs, no implant this time, which means that if I really am cracking up, it's my own fault. That it's real, and there might not be any coming back.

I crawl forward a body length, and Annie dings, letting me know I've reached the switch's location. I stuff my gloves into the sand, scoop out handfuls like a dog.

It's got to be here. It's got to—

And there's the button, glinting like a jewel in the light of my headlamp. I flip open the cover. The button clicks under my finger as I push, and then something rumbles below me, a monster threatening to devour, one I call forth with every fiber of my being. A cylinder rises up from the ground. Sand dances across its surface, vibrating like grains of rice on a speaker, before sloughing off down the sides.

Everything freezes and goes silent. I'm alone again, with only the rasps of my breath. The cylinder has come up as high as my knees, the flat surface on the top still half buried in sand. I brush it off, grab the handle, and flip it open, before slipping into the belly of the beast.

4

IT'S A SHORT drop to the bottom. The hatch door closes automatically behind me.

"Annie, turn off my lamp." My suit complies, plunging me into darkness. For one, brief, hyperventilating second, I fight the reflex to turn my lamp back on. I try to take slow breaths, to ignore the demons hidden in the darkness.

Five breaths, ten, and the black fades to the hatch's shadowy angles, backlit by dim green. As with the hatch and everything else in it, I'm not sure where the running lights that trace its inside perimeter came from or how they work—although I think they might have some kind of bioluminescent bacteria in them. Up close, the long tubes look like they're filled with liquid.

My pulse slows as I examine the square room. It's small, the available floor space's length and width each just a bit shy of my height, and I can barely sit up without bonking my head on the low ceiling. Two metal-lined tunnels lead away from the room.

One is a long, thin shaft, so claustrophobia-inducing that I had to have three beers to work up the nerve to crawl the three minutes to the end. It leads up to the surface through a kind of one-way flap—at least, if there's a way to get back in through that side, I haven't figured it out. An escape exit, maybe.

The other one took me three circadians to break into. The door has a puzzle on it, one with black and white tiles that slide back and forth. I recognized it almost instantly—my parents used to give me similar puzzles. The goal is to get all the black tiles on one side and the white tiles on the other. I worked on it obsessively when I wasn't in the mines, a task that kept my mind off of failing out of Pomp school, of almost dying. I'd imagined the door led to a hidden cache of riches, but once I finally solved the puzzle, I found it just opens up to a small room filled with provisions: dusty packages that looked like they contained water, dented canisters of liquid oxygen, some brown, formless masses that *might* have been bags full of de-hydrated food.

Every so often, I scramble it again, solve it again, and try not to think about my parents asking me to do the same thing.

I lean forward and press the small button on the wall in the corner. Something clicks above me.

Locked. I've come here at least once every time I get my double circadian off. It's the only place on Hib where I have the authority to bar myself in against the world, where I have the freedom to do absolutely *anything I want*—cry, fart, sing, masturbate—without worrying that somebody is going to walk in on me. Where no one will ever give me a knowing look or a searching glance.

And after seeing that girl—Hannah, her name is Hannah—in Rikki's today, I need it.

I lay supine, feeling the hard rim of the dome against the back of my head. Some intrepid person—maybe one of the very first miners on Hib—designed this place. It could've even been the legendary Jimmy Kang, if he'd ever existed, though I doubt it. Jimmy's just a fable; nobody escapes Hib. Even dying just gets you recycled.

Still, it's fun to think about him throwing this place together out of pieces of scrap metal and stolen hydraulics—and then leaving it for me to find.

I say a silent word of thanks and let my thoughts drift, but they keep trying to turn to today's events, to almost drowning at the beach, to the day my parents—

No. I know I'll soon shine a light on that darkness—but not yet. Not like this.

I press my palm against my chest, to the spot where the charm rests. I take a full breath and start with a scale, trying my hardest to concentrate on a thousand variables at once: full timbre, lifted palate, good resonance. Don't gliss up or down between notes. Eight up, eight down, a major key that's full and happy.

I cycle through the modes, letting my voice warm up. I'm impossibly loud in the dome of my helmet. The spring in my chest unfurls, a bent-paperclip's worth of tension at a time with each new scale.

Something hot and wet starts to leak out of the corners of my eyes. The break is coming.

Once the creaking and the sand has gone out of my voice, I switch to actual songs. I start with something catchy, almost a century old. I press my limbs into the hard metal of the hatch floor, pinning my suit in the thin space between us. I float between modern and classic, borrowing from the different cultures of the terminator band like the world's best thief—which I'm not, I am definitely the worst—and in the middle of a folk song about making bread out of tears, the tension finally breaks inside of me like a dam, and I start to sob.

My chest rises and falls in huge swells. I roll to my side, curl up into a ball as the spirit that possesses me tears out with incredible fury.

It's over fast. My head and body tingle, scooped clean of everything but a curious emptiness. Like I'm one of the many vacant way stations on Hib's surface: the mine tapped out, the building slowly being buried under gray sand. Like the spring has been ripped from my chest, leaving a gaping hole.

And now? I'm free of the tension—for a little while. I'll be able to float through some portion of my day. I'll be able to drift through my mind, no matter how dark the thoughts are, because the part of me that's *me* is dead, at least for a bit.

Weariness descends on me, hangs off my bones. If I broke my beacon now, they'd *really* never find my body, never get this suit back. Somewhere, some CPI asshole would apply a formula for my missed work and add sums to my sentence until it was longer than the life I'd already given up.

At that, I can't help but chuckle.

MOST TIMES, AFTER the anxiety is purged and I'm nice and numb, I return to the moment my parents left. It's the only time I can handle it, and although it aches, I can't help myself. I poke at the memory like I'm trying to break a loose tooth free of its decaying roots while trying to ignore that it feels like going home.

I started to think about dying before I had my first period. Not wanting it. Just thinking about it. I knew it was a weird thing to do, but I've always been a very curious person—and at first, it was just little flashes here and there, something you note in the same idle way as the breeze picking up. We'd walk by the train, and I'd wonder—what would it be like to throw myself into the tracks? Was there a way to do it so that I was the only casualty? I'd imagine the pain—but that it would be over fast. I'd picture the funeral, people crying for me. Sometimes, at that part, I'd get a little stab of guilt.

But the thoughts grew until they followed me around all of the time, background music that never faded. I'd catch myself looking at the top of a tall building or a particularly sturdy bit of rope, and I'd feel a raw, scraping anger—but then that faded, too, and what it left behind would be frightening if I could feel anything.

It's hard to describe: like floating in a river, knowing the rapids are coming, but you just can't muster the energy to fight your way to the bank. It's easier to let the river take you and feel nothing—and nothing, really, was what I felt, all of the time.

And still, the thoughts grew for years until I woke up one

day and they weren't questions anymore, but *advice*. A refrain that spoke clearly, crisply, telling me that I wasn't good for anything. That I didn't have to feel like this all the time. That nobody loved me, and that I should just die.

I did something, then, that I now pull away from in my memories. I move instead to what happened after one of the times I came home from the hospital.

My parents weren't the same. They paced a lot. They waited until my back was turned to converse, arguments in flurries of emphatic gestures. Maybe they thought I didn't know they were talking about me—but I could hear the swish of their arms on the fabric of their shirts, catch flashes of their signing in reflections.

Once, I got angry and started yelling at them, covering my mouth the whole time so they couldn't read my lips. I just wanted them to know I was screaming, without them knowing why. I wanted them to feel confused. To hurt.

I don't blame them for what happened next.

It wasn't very long after, I think—although it's hard to tell because, by then, I was sleeping all of the time.

It started with us moving. My dad decided I'd recover better if it was quiet around us. If the air was cleaner. He broke into one of the houses in the Uptown neighborhood and smuggled in the three of us. There was a hedge that provided a measure of privacy, so that we could come and go without being observed.

That house was like an entirely different world. For the first time, I had a room to myself, a bed so soft that even my aching body didn't protest. There were no neighbors upstairs or downstairs. The temperature inside was always perfect, and everything was clean.

My mother told me not to get too attached to it. The owners had just gotten married and decided to travel to Ur-Lapla for their honeymoon, but they'd be back.

Some time after we moved in, she came to my new bed, sat down, and smoothed my hair, and even as dead as I felt, I had to wonder at that gesture, so tender and full of affection.

She waved at me to let me know she had something to say. It

took me a long time to turn my face enough to see her.

We're going on a little trip, she signed. One of the brown bandages on her arm had come loose, the end of it flapping.

I waited while she fixed it, rubbing on the little piece of tape that kept it fastened to her elbow. "To the beach again?"

Her face tightened, her mouth pulling into a thin line. She shook her head. *No, not back there. Somewhere else fun. Somewhere farther away. Daddy is working out the details.*

I rolled my eyes. It was clear, even then, that she didn't understand. I'd never be able to get away from myself. And I liked it here, where it was clean, and quiet, and soft.

She stroked my head some more. I fell asleep, and the next circadians passed as if in a dream. Every so often, I would wake up to the noises of her packing, moving things. Being deaf made my mom terrible at sneaking around.

Once, I woke up, and there was a bag on the edge of my bed, clothes packed in neat triangles and tight rolls. They weren't my clothes. When I opened my eyes again, the bag was gone.

I'd awoken because I'd heard something—but I wasn't sure what it was. A cry? A slam?

Underneath the numbness was a cloying pulse, like the light of a flare finally fizzling out in the dark. *Something is wrong, wrong, something is wrong.* But I didn't want to get up.

I waited for a long time. Any moment now, my mother would come swooping in and ask me if I needed help going to the bathroom. The door would creak open as my father peeked in, checking on me. But nothing happened.

I stared at the wall. I could feel, even through the lethargy that filled my body, a tiny, vibrating whisper of wrongness. It took everything I had to roll over, to somehow get myself seated at the edge of the bed. My limbs moved in slow motion. Was that from how I felt, or from recently being in the hospital, or just lying down for so long?

I didn't want to peel myself out of this bed. But I had to know. I wobbled to the door, to the stairs. My muscles struggled to bear my weight.

At the silence, I grabbed the rail, and wobbled down.

My bag was sitting in the middle of the living room floor, its cheery flowers bringing back an argument at Jang-mun market. My mother had wanted plain, undyed fabric, because it was cheaper. But my father had managed to convince her. *It makes her happy. She doesn't ask us for very much. And we're not going to pay for it, anyways.*

But—what was that? Sitting on top of the bag, half buried in the fabric, something gleamed. I reached in and plucked it out—a little metal tab like a charm, shaped in a crescent, with some numbers and letters on it.

I held it up to my eye, and then I noticed the impressions in the rug. Two other bags had been here, large circles where the fibers had been pushed in a different direction.

I stood there for a long time, watched as they unbent, until all trace of the weight that had pushed them down was gone.

I went to the bathroom. Made a snack. Sat by the window, over and over, like a dog, waiting for their return. I watched as the food dwindled, little by little, a silent clock that marked the time by its absence.

And when it was all gone, I had to face it. They weren't coming back.

5

REALIZING YOU WERE so insufferable to be around that even your parents bailed on you without preamble is a heavy burden. I didn't try to kill myself again until I failed out of Pomp training—at least, not all at once, although there are a lot of ways to kill yourself a little bit at a time.

The time directly before waking up in Medical is cloaked in fog. I'll probably never fully remember it, but I don't need to. I know the track my mind takes when logic starts to unravel, and I've spent countless hours staring at the ceiling instead of sleeping, untangling the mess from what came after. I'm pretty sure it goes like this: Becoming a Pomp made it seem like everything else that had happened—being caught and kicked out of that house, sleeping rough, learning to steal, rising to a tiny bit of fame as someone who had a knack for telling a real jewel from a fake, being arrested and threatened with eviction into the Desert or the Ice—all of it had coalesced together into a meaningful path. My past was no longer a series of desperate stopgaps, attempting to stave off the panic. I'd taken a test and shown I had an *aptitude*, one that made me a candidate for the kind of job that garnered respect and helped save lives while earning fast enough that I might not die on Hib.

And then I failed out and realized I was wrong and that Hibiscus station was the end of the line for me.

At some point, you have to ask yourself what you're waiting for.

I turn and check my tank. Half full; I've spent too much time in my secret hatch. Gyu will be waiting, and if I don't get back fast, he'll start asking questions. Long absences make him worry about my state of mind.

Once outside, I hit the button, and the hatch sinks beneath the surface. Part of me still can't shake the feeling that someone's watching as I fly across the sand. Every so often, I click off my headlamp, risk stumbling in the dark so I can run unseen.

I make it back to the station, through the airlock and the tunnels, and hoof it toward Lodging. This time, I keep my suit on. I have to clean and charge Annie, and if I don't have my helmet with me in the morning, I could get into a lot of trouble.

Lodging reflects a level of planning and intelligence I don't usually expect from a massive corporation. Instead of shared dormitory-style housing, the sector is formed of a mess of tiny, identical modular huts all nestled so tightly, you sometimes have to hold your breath to scrape between two of them. But they're individual, a fact that allows CPI to advertise that transferring your debt to Hib will net you a "private house." *House* is a generous word, and they neglect to mention that none of the huts lock, in case Enforcement ever finds it necessary to walk into a space that you don't own—because you won't own anything ever again, not unless you somehow find your way back to Ung-Nyeo.

Mine is in the very back, and before it pops into view, I hesitate in an alley. Once I get there and Gyu sees me, I'll have to make a choice. I want to be alone, bury myself in my bed, and pretend that the incident at Rikki's—and my whole life here—never happened.

At the same time, I have to admit I'm scared. Sitting alone with the lights off tends to lead down winding corridors, places that Gyu can ward against. He's like a Pomp-drone spotlight that drives back the dark.

Gyu will leave if I ask him to. But what if I need him here?

By the time I pop out of the alley, I still haven't decided, though the frantic energy of my run is gone. I spy Gyu, squatting outside of my door, his lips pressed into a thin gray line, his face sagging and his dark eyes glittering with worry.

When he sees me, he stands and rubs his lower back. "Hey. I thought your shift ended at—"

"I had something I had to do."

Gyu's cheek twitches. He never says it directly, but it's always there: *I'm afraid that you've decided to kill yourself again.*

Then again, I could be wrong. Maybe he's just thinking, *This shit is fucking annoying.*

Gyu bridges the gap between us on floating steps. He's got magnets too, and yet, he always moves like that, as if hauling his body around is a boon instead of a burden. His jaw bobs, and I catch a flash of something that makes my stomach turn—*this is more worry than normal, there's something wrong*—but then he's kissing me, the softness of his lips rubbing against my chapped skin like silk over scuffed metal. He smells like mint. It reminds me of our first kiss.

It felt then like it does now, like he was gluing fragments of me together. "I missed you," he says, and something shifts in my stomach, the sudden feeling of falling. *Liar.*

But his brown eyes are warm and earnest. Gyu's one of those honest people that is a little boring, but mostly good. I have no idea what the hell he's doing with me. He just showed up, a few circadians after I tried to bite it, hanging around like a neighborhood cat that realized a little more time spent at the back door of a restaurant will make him fat.

It was easy to start sleeping with him. Maybe it's because his face echoes mine, a mixture of features from each band, like someone just picked them at random from opposite sides of the world. It makes me feel like we belong together. Stupid, but it's working so far.

"I missed you, too." It's a lie, a reflex—but as soon as I say it, it somehow isn't.

"So. Are you hungry? I can make you something." His smile is tentative, but it's there.

I'm not hungry, but I'm too tired to protest. I nod and turn toward the door, and that's when I notice—there's something off about the angles. There's no gap, but I still reach out, pull on the handle, and the door catches and clicks.

I'm sure I shut it completely. I always do. I hate myself for asking, but I ask, all the same. "Gyu—did you go inside?" I can't even look up at him. There's a pinprick boiling behind one of my eyes, making my throat hurt.

He coughs. "I brought you some perishables. I didn't know you'd be late. I didn't want them to go bad."

Of course. It's logical. I can picture him standing on the stoop with a carton of frozen red-bean cream, a surprise for me purchased with actual months of his sentence. The sticky melted liquid slowly dripping between his fingers, spurring him to step inside.

It's the exact thing he *should* do, and yet I hate that he entered my space without asking. Even if there wasn't a way to get ahold of me.

I throw the door open and step into the hut's single room. I rip Annie off and jam the suit into the cleaner. As I plop down onto the bed with a *thunk*, I feel vulnerable, but also defiant, like a cornered snake.

The door clicks, so soft I barely hear it.

A flash of panic—*he left, he's so fed up with my shit that he's just left me here*—and a helpless surge of rage. *Even Brin left—*

"Young," he says, clearing his throat. "Look at me, please?"

My face is hot, my eyes stinging. I turn and glare at his stupid face, at the clothes I know are enviously clean, despite the fact that I can barely see them in the dim. Gyu doesn't toil over a drill in the mines; he works for Engineering. I don't exactly know what that means, except that he takes measurements and writes reports that are eventually sent back to Ung-Nyeo. I read part of one once while he was sleeping. I understood some of it from Pomp training, but it was still so dry and boring that my eyes glazed over.

There's something in the set of his shoulders that makes the hair on the back of my neck stand up. He's absently cupping his hand over his pocket, almost as if protecting his leg.

He notices me staring and brushes off his pants. I look away, as if my curiosity has been satisfied, but I'm pretty sure there was a small bulge in his pocket. Is he hiding something from me?

"Hey." He sits on the bed next to me before leaning over and giving me a side hug. My skin crawls, but I sink into his shoulder, deepening the embrace. I hate myself for wanting it, but I do.

He lays me down and crawls into bed behind me, shaping himself around my legs and back. Firm and gentle, like being suspended in a hammock. He gets hard, but he doesn't mention it. He just holds me like that. The raw ache in my chest grows, through my guts, my limbs, and the next thing I know, I'm crying again.

"Hey," he murmurs. "It's okay—"

"It's not okay." I sound like a snotty child, but I'm right. It isn't, because it's never been.

He clears his throat. "Do you want to talk about it?"

My parents' charm has fallen forward under my shirt, the yarn that I've wound around it rubbing on my skin. I *do* want to talk about it, tell him about the mine, about Rikki's with Adda and Hannah, about the hatch.

I want to tell him I'm worried I'm cracking up again.

But I can't get his pocket out of my head. The way he put his hand in front of it, as if protecting a secret. When I open my mouth, what comes out is, "Why are you here?"

He stiffens behind me. "Why am I what?"

"Here. With me. In my bed. Right now."

"I just—" He lets out a breath. "I just want to be here. Isn't that enough?"

Please let it be.

But my heart is beating faster. I try hard to shove the fear down, to just be in this moment, in Gyu's embrace, but the shine has gone off it. By the time he gets up and flips on the light, the spring in my chest is back, winding tight, and it fucking *hurts*.

The truth is that Gyu and I don't have a real relationship. We've never talked about monogamy or responsibility or the future, which means he's well within his rights to do whatever the fuck he wants. Sometimes, I think about screwing other people, and if the opportunity came up, I probably wouldn't say no.

Gyu would. He's just not that kind of person.

His pocket is needling at me, making it hard to take a full breath. I could find out. I could get him to stay the night. Wait until he's asleep, sneak whatever it was out of his pants. He always just leaves them on the floor.

A warning blips in the back of my mind, but I shake it off, and it's gone.

He starts sautéing some onions in a pan. The fragrance fills the room, and despite being wonderful, it turns my stomach. I have to stop thinking about it. I should just remove the temptation completely. Him leaving isn't him abandoning me, not if I ask for it. Right?

There's a tight, leaden spot in my chest, and before I know it, I stalk across the room. I take the pan out of his hand, set it on the stove. Press my mouth against his, shove my fingers in his hair the way he likes. There's a moment of tension, a dam holding back the force of a flood as he tries to pull away.

"Young, are you sure? You seemed so mad."

I'm sorry, I think, and I mean it, enough that I almost pull back—but I don't. I kiss him deeper, and he breaks. I guide him to the bed.

When it's over, I roll off him. Gyu moves to take me into his arms, but my insides itch, and I get up. He grabs my wrist again, this time gentler, an echo of what just happened.

"I'll be right back. I just want to get cleaned up."

He relents. I go into the bathroom, find a washcloth and wet it. Look at myself in the mirror.

Straggly hair. My mother's eyes, my father's lips. A face that just can't seem to decide—does it want to be thin or fat? West half or east half? Ugly or interesting?

Exhaustion hits me like a wave. I try, but it's hard to get clean. When I can't delay any more—when I know he's going to be thinking, waiting—I crawl back into bed. He pulls toward me immediately, and I flip over. I don't want to be pressed chest to chest, the charm trapped between us.

"Is anything wrong—"

"No." There's a flicker of guilt for lying to him. "I just wanted to make spoons."

"Okay," he says, with a happy grunt. He pulls me close.

It's nicer than I expected. There's something familiar in it, something that makes me fade a bit. I can feel him settle too, feel his breath deepen. I wait for the right moment to get up.

I can't stop thinking about my plan, the way I'm going to act when he leaves later. There's a voice reminding me: *You don't have to do this; it's still not too late*—but it's just an echo, lamenting a failed cause. I imagine myself, breath held, crawling on the floor. The sliding of the fabric as I pull the bulge out of his pocket. My stomach flops with anxiety, with guilt—and the growl is so loud that Gyu jerks awake in bed next to me.

"Shit, Young. Is that what I think it is?"

Fuck. No wonder I got caught stealing.

"No," I say, but he's already rolling into a sitting position. Before I can protest, he pulls his pants off the floor and buttons them around his waist, then ducks back into the kitchen to finish cooking the aborted meal.

What am I going to say? That my guilt sounds like hunger?

He makes noodles and sets two bowls in front of us. I'm deep in my thoughts, trying to figure out how long it will be before I can access his pocket, when he looks up.

Shit. I've been staring at him. He smiles at me. I blush and glance away, slurp up a noodle of my own, *hu-ru-ru-ruk.*

Gyu's too good for me. I want to tell him everything, want to exist in a world where I could confess what I'm really like without him leaving me.

He slurps down another noodle. "You know, it's not so bad, being on Hib."

I almost drop my spoon. "What?"

"Yeah, I know. We're prisoners, we're stranded, our bodies sold to scrabble fortunes out of the dirt—I get the arguments against it. But think about it. You get by. You have a nice little place here." He gestures at the walls of my shack, and I try to see it through his eyes. The pot simmering on a small warmer. Solid walls, privacy, a real bed—all things I haven't had since the owners of the house my father broke into came home.

He mistakes my silence for argument. "There's a real shower in the bathroom, one that will actually spit out hot water. You can rent a hov and cruise to the other side of the moon. You can eat and eat and never be hungry. It's better than dying in the street or being sent out of the wind-walls."

All for a price, I think, but I get what he's saying. I agree, even. And yet, I can feel that little gear tightening in my chest, cranking tighter and tighter, making it hard to breathe again. I focus on his pocket. What is Gyu hiding from me?

"Of course, there are options, if you hate it so much. You could still be a Pomp," he says, stopping me cold.

"What the fuck is wrong with you?" I can't help the sudden venom in my voice, the flare in my chest.

But he stays level-headed. "I could get you an authorization to take the last level again. You're close enough that it wouldn't be a stretch—"

I snort and put down my spoon. "What's the point?" My appetite's gone again, this time for good. "Earn a little bit more? I'm still not leaving here before I die." *And I'll just fail out again, anyways.*

But in the back of my mind, something glimmers, vibrates, buzzes. Angles of sound, smatters of light, a hallucination of threads and crystals. If anybody finds out that I'm seeing things, I'll be locked in a basement somewhere—or maybe just ejected into space. There's no point in keeping around a miner who is also a safety risk—and there's definitely no way you can make that person a Pomp.

He clears his throat and stares down at his plate. For a second, I think it's just sadness—but there's something else in it. The hair goes up on the back of my neck. "What is it?"

"It's not just a little bit more. If you worked your way up the right track, it's a lot more. You could pay your way out of here fast—maybe five, ten years." He looks up at me, and his eyes are shining, eager. "You could get out of here young enough for it still to be worth something. Figure out a new existence. Marry someone, have kids, whatever. You don't have to die on Hib."

My pulse pounds. My hands are sweating, but that's nothing compared to the way my thoughts are bouncing around in my head, like the red light of a spitting flare flying down a mineshaft.

Five seconds ago, he was telling me how great it was here. I can't tell if that was a lie, or if he's just changed tactics when his attempt to lift my spirits failed, but if he knows what's good for him, he won't say anything else. He'll just keep quiet because I'm quiet, and that should be enough—

"You're smart, Young. Don't you want your life to be something more?"

The light in his eyes dies as he realizes what he's just said. I try to hold myself back, but it's too late. Something inside of me snaps like a piece of dry kindling. "Shut the *fuck up*, Gyu."

He pulls back as if I've hit him, but I'm not through. "What are you, stupid? I don't want *something more*. I don't want to exist at all. And I don't expect someone like you to understand. I'll bet you went to some fancy school, had parents that greased your way through life. You didn't have to figure out your own way in a slum. You didn't have to—"

"That's not fair—"

I steamroll over him. "Just because we're both prisoners doesn't mean we're the same. I don't know what you've done, and you don't know what I've done, and we can never be the same. Now, get away from me. Get out—"

His face crumples. "Young, you can't mean that—"

"I mean it! I barely *know* you. You're just some piece of shit that likes your girls crazy, that smelled some tail you wanted to bang, and now that I don't want to hear your bullshit, your feelings are hurt. Get *out*."

Inside, I'm screaming. Every single action, word, and movement triggers a giant branching network of future events that raises like a specter in my mind. I'm hurting him, I know I am, but I can't hear anything over the *thump-thump-thump* of my own blood in my ears.

"Young—"

"Do you think you're so much better than me? That you can *save* me? Well guess what, you asshole. I don't need to be *saved*. People like me stay broken. If you want to fix something, go find some machinery. Now get *out*."

It feels like my entire world is collapsing, like I'm caught out in the dark again without any air, and I need him out of here.

He looks like he's going to say something, but he leaves and shuts the door behind him, and everything bleeds out of me at once.

I'm sorry, I think, but I'm not sorry, not yet. I can't feel anything but panic. I'm shaking, and I've grabbed the little charm in my hand, rubbed my finger over the yarn—

A flash of pain. I look down and discover I've pulled the yarn aside, somehow managed to cut myself.

I'm repulsed by my blood, by this piece of my insides, pulled out. The metal of the charm peeks through its layers of once-white yarn, now all flecked with red.

Something snaps inside of me, and then I'm not me at all. Outside of my body, I'm centered. Calm. Sure in what I have to do.

I run out into the street. He's there, walking away with his little floating steps. He hasn't gotten far.

I chase him down, grab his hand.

"I don't think..." he starts, his voice gruff. He doesn't look at me.

"Please." The words burn, but I force them out. "I'm sorry. I want you to come back. Stay until the next shift starts."

But he won't, because who would. He'll run away, like all—

He turns and embraces me, and my heart dies. "I'm sorry, too. I shouldn't push like that."

It's ridiculous, him apologizing to me.

He grabs my face and pulls it up to meet his. "I don't think I should stay, though." His eyes are wet, glistening. I've hurt him, and I *want* to care about that, but his secret is pounding in my head, as big as a pulse, laughing. It's about to get away.

I'll never know. I can't deal with not knowing.

I nod and drop my hands, making the movement big. My heart is screaming in my chest as I shift forward, tuck my head under his. I pat his side hard with one hand, a distraction, and slide my fingers into his pocket with the other. *This is crazy*, I think, but then there's something flat and thin between my first and second finger. I clench them together, getting a grip, as if around a fat cigarette. *He's going to notice, he has to feel the pressure there—*

He turns away, the movement pulling the thing out of his pocket. I crumple my hand into a fist, hiding it, but he's already walking down the path that will lead him back to the hub of the wheel.

And then he's gone.

It isn't too late to throw this thing away. To be a better person than the one I've been my whole life. To be someone who isn't ashamed of people finding out what she does when they're not looking.

I creep back into my room. I almost open Gyu's secret on my bed, but part of me is terrified he's going to come bursting through the door, furious with what I've done, so I go into the bathroom, and then into the shower, and I shut the door.

The panel blinks on, asking me if I want to add a *luscious, hot shower* to my tab. There's no price listed, of course.

I open my fist to unveil a crumpled piece of paper—real paper, not like the discarded wrappers miners scrawl messages on. I smooth it against the wall. The handwriting is neat, spidery, somewhat feminine. I don't recognize it. It's not what I expected—no declaration of love, no coded message about some covert meeting.

Gyu is watching you.

I don't know what to make of it. Why would he have this? He obviously didn't write it to himself.

I thought I needed this, that I needed to know. But now, looking at it, I can't parse any of it—who wrote it, where it came from, what it means.

I crumple the paper back up before sinking to a squat in the stall. I want to hold on to it and pore over it for clues—but what if he decides to come back, and he catches me here, holding the evidence of my treachery?

The world spins. My head is pounding by the time I tear up the paper into pieces and throw them into the toilet. It *whoomps* each time I activate the suction cycle, but the flecks of paper are light, and I have to push the button over and over again, until they're all finally gone.

6

WHEN I FINALLY fall asleep, my dreams are strange, full of angles. Dark tunnels. Crystalline vibrations. The sensation of motion, of spinning in place like a top.

And then, I'm floating high above a familiar scene. A children's playground, this one nestled in the middle of an oasis of sand—as if I've just walked out of Hib and found one abandoned not far from the exit.

It's dark, the only light from a huge yellow globe shining in the center of what looks like a merry-go-round. After a moment, I notice a child: a little girl seated on the outer edge of the giant metal disk. She holds a teddy bear up toward the globe, straight-armed, as the merry-go-round starts to spin.

Where have I seen this before? Is it a forgotten memory? A captured image I once saw on a screen?

As she spins, faster and faster, I notice the glint of the silvery threads in her sleeves. The way she never lowers the bear, so that part of her face is always cast in shadow, even as the hair surrounding it shines.

It's us, I think, recognition making my scalp tingle. The light is the sun, the girl is the planet Ung-Nyeo, the teddy bear is Hibiscus. The girl's silvery sleeves are the tether: a fat strand that stretches between the planet and its moon, one that has existed since long before human history on our planet can remember, and that makes our home unique in the universe.

There *are* other planets that orbit their sun in the same way as ours, so that one side is always cast in darkness, and one side is always light. Moons that orbit the same way as Hibiscus does: a near side always facing the planet, the far side always away.

But only we have both. A planet locked to a sun; a moon locked to the planet. A bright spot on either is forever bright, a dark spot forever dark. And between planet and moon stretches a braid stable enough to build the elevator on, flexible enough to connect two planetary bodies, stiff enough to hold them apart, strong enough to never break.

Old myths about the tether hint at it being spun by gods or the same unknown founders that created the ancient wind-walls, though scientists have firmly established that only nature could create such a thing. But that's hard for me to believe because the whole arrangement has always felt *wrong*, somehow. Like Hib is somehow Ung-Nyeo's captive, both of them forever condemned to hide pieces of themselves from the light. I don't know that nature makes that kind of mistake.

I stare at the playground far below me for a few more minutes, and that feeling of wrongness pervades—and yet it calls to me, too. I recognize the siren's song of destruction: mine, the planet's, the moon's. I do not care.

I stretch my arms up until they ache, and then I dive, hurtling through the air until I hit the sand below face-first. Instead of impacting, I go *through*. I swim all of the way toward a giant pearl in the center.

Circadian, I think, the word connected to nothing at all.

I wake up to a low beeping. I'm disoriented by seasickness, the feeling that I should be rotating still. Instead, I'm sitting slumped over. At some point, I crawled my way out of the bathroom to the bed. Even wrapped in the mystery of Gyu's note, it had been almost impossible to keep my eyes open.

Or maybe it wasn't just exhaustion. I started sleeping a lot before I tried to kill myself. More than once, the suit beeped to warn me that I was late for work—although it hasn't happened in a while.

The beeping accelerates, as if Annie is aware that she just graced my thoughts. It's a pretty clear *fuck you*. If I don't put my suit on and cross the perimeter in time, I'll be subjected to BANS—Benign Auditory Noxious Stimulus—so I fumble it on.

I've only been hit with BANS once, right after I got out of Medical. I still didn't care if I lived or died—or have the energy to report for my new work assignment. The beeping accelerated until it was a flat whine, and then came a sudden, ear-splitting groan. It felt like the world was tearing me apart. I couldn't tell which way was up. A moment later, I was on the floor, vomiting in my suit, listening to Annie *whir-click* on and suction everything into the waste compartment. Then came the panic, because there wasn't any air until Annie filled the suit again.

BANS alternates the signal with a brief reprieve to give you time to get to work. And there's not really any escaping it. You can't leave Hib station without your suit on, and someone else's suit initiates BANS as soon as it senses you're the wrong occupant. If the suit goes into BANS and you're not in it, Enforcement will send someone to pick you up and put you in solitary—where you'll be subjected to an entire cycle's worth of BANS without warning, just random moments of vomiting in the dark.

And BANS doesn't just affect you. Anybody in range of your suit gets hit with it, which means that you can look forward to friendly visits after hours, the kind sure to leave you a souvenir.

Which is another way I know the Jimmy Kang escape story is bullshit. It doesn't matter if he supposedly slipped into a cargo container or if he climbed the tether, hand-over-hand, all the way back to Ung-Nyeo—he needed to wear a suit, and once he was late for work, it would've rendered him helpless.

My balance is off as I stumble out of bed. My head thumps madly, and my mouth is dry, as if from a bender.

On the second transport over to the tunnels, the beeping has sped up enough that people edge away from me. I can't see their faces through their helmets, but I can imagine their rage—they're on time for their shifts, so why can't I be on time for mine?

I realize I'm still missing a glove. I hide my exposed hand in my armpit. I should have gotten that straightened out before going home yesterday.

By the time I reach the perimeter line, the beeps have reached a frenzied climax, the spaces between shrinking until there's just a single, vibrating note.

I cross into silence. Panting, I bend over and rest my hands on my knees while sucking in air. A blower kicks on as Annie senses the increase in oxygen demand, and the cool breeze brings a wave of relief. I guess some fears die hard.

I straighten up, and additional blowers activate: Annie has sensed my perspiration and is attempting to maintain homeostasis. The sudden chill gets me moving, but after twenty steps, the adrenaline fades, and the colors bleed out of my world. I slept like shit, and I'm exhausted. There's a layer between me and everything, one heavier and thicker than Annie's plasteel rubber.

I shuffle up to the door and wait for Annie and the lock to exchange keys. The metal shield in front of me splinters open into silvery flower petals, and I pass through, into the first tunnel. At the sudden dark, I give Annie the command to light my headlamp. There's a pause, and then a beam spills through the black, glinting off the rounded walls. They're fairly rough-hewn, but easy to follow.

I make my way down onto the platform and into a small room whose only opening is the door I came through. My feet become impossibly heavy, a function of the magnet built into the floor, and I clank across in awkward stomps, like a person trudging through sucking mud.

The canister is like the hatch—closed. Secure. I hate it, though, because I know what's coming next.

The door closes behind me. I hold my breath.

Something above me hisses and rattles, and then the ground lurches. The canister flies down the pressurized system, a screaming fast descent that drops for too many heartbeats before suddenly changing angles. The grade is never so sharp that you'd fall on your ass, but without any view, any windows, any hint that it's coming, it's still somehow awful. I hate doing this part alone. I hate doing it with other people even more.

This process takes long enough that apparently some guys find a way to use the time and all the adrenaline. Somehow, I've never thought to pass it that way. If there's anything good about the drop, it's that it keeps me from thinking about what happened with Gyu—until it doesn't. Before long, the little cog-wheel starts to tighten in my chest, a spring *clink-clink-clinking* with each breath of new weight.

I imagine an air jet failing to kick on as I approach ground level, neglecting its duty to redirect the canister toward the next bend of the shaft. If the canister just slams into the bottom, and I'm magnetically fastened to the floor, what happens to my body? Do I fold up like an accordion or stretch out like a piece of elastic?

I was never any good at physics, but I can tell my bones would shatter either way.

My stomach churns as the canister decelerates, a soft *whoomp* and jerk as jets and blowers check its movements. After all that, the last few hand widths of the tube are achingly slow. We come to a stop, the door opens, and I shuffle out into the next tunnel.

BEFORE THE TUNNEL transitions into its final forks, there's a hanging board littered with paper trash that holds a variety of scrawls. The truth is that it's both unnecessary and a badge of pride. You can leave notes through Annie, either setting them to play right away or as soon as a person crosses a specific threshold. Messages like that, though, are only free if you're in someone's chain of command and it's specifically for work, which has led to a vibrant culture of *trash-ives*—notes written on food wrappers, flattened package containers, discarded pieces of rubber—all pinned up on a board.

I don't get a voice memo, which means that although Adda has never written me a note, I know there's probably one there. She's not the kind of person to leave someone hanging as to their fate—and at this moment, it can go one of two ways. Either she's taken my spot on the drill— so that the operation continues forward and everyone gets paid the same despite my tardiness—or she's decided it's not safe to proceed with her distracted. In which case, they're all sitting there, stewing until I show up so that they can whip my ass at the end of the shift.

I don't really have time to stop and look for a note, but I can't not do it, either. I scan so quickly, I almost miss the huge rice-cake wrapper, fat marker warped by Adda's tight script.

> *Young, you late bitch. Hurry up and get here before my dainty hands get tired.*

I let out a breath. Adda didn't have to do that. She could have just as easily alerted Operations and turned me in, billing me for everybody's time.

The odd vibration of the drill echoes through the tunnel. It's hard to gauge how far away it is—the sound-head itself doesn't make any noise that the human ear can hear, but the drill's engines emit a low thrum that vacillates between a high-pitched whine and a low metal groan. All of that is overpowered by the echoes of rock falling, starts and stops, the shuffling of feet—things could be right next to you or twenty feet away, and they might sound the same.

I tuck my exposed hand into my armpit, shielding it from view, and vault down toward our worksite. Despite the smooth floor, I stumble over something, fall forward, ass over elbow. There's a brief, spinning flash of curved metal—somebody's Pomp drone, lost or getting maintenance—

And then there's something else. A mind's eye glimpse of something dark, angular, full of square structures, sharp sides, a tiny star with the power of a supernova—

An explosion.

And I'm airborne. The sound and heat hit me a second after the shock wave. Annie's blowers kick on, but the inferno is a maelstrom of fire and pressure, angry demonic fingers that immediately start fusing my suit to my skin.

Annie fills instantly with foam. It stinks of chemicals, like the time I bleached my hair under a bridge, the ammonia scent making my eyes water—and then it fills my lungs, and I can't breathe.

I'm lying on my side. I'm coughing, almost laughing, because of course, this is how it ends. Suffocating in my suit, as if I were underwater.

There's a fresh blast of air as the foam is suctioned out. My head is ringing, and there's something in my fist. I hold up my hand to see the food wrapper fused to the outside of my glove. It isn't until I look at the other hand, the skin red and angry despite being tucked under my body, that the memory comes back.

Adda.

I can barely tilt my head up—the rubber at my neck has melted, reformed. There's a flash of the Pomp drone out of the corner of my eye, and then it floats away, but *oh*—

In front of me, there's no tunnel anymore. Everything has just collapsed, as if wiped from the earth.

7

EVERYTHING THAT HAPPENS next comes in flashes, as if I've been nodding off at random intervals. I half-dream of the explosion again and again—the boom, the flash, the rubble of the tunnel closing. Flying backward through the air, landing on my back. The long pause, and then people grabbing at my arms.

I'm somewhere. Medical, I think. The man in front of me is short and balding. He's wearing glasses and a vest over his regulation gray civvies, an outfit as bored as his flat expression.

He must not have been close to any of my crew.

He's talking to me, but my hearing keeps cutting in and out. The whine in my ears suddenly gets louder, but his mouth isn't moving anymore.

I shake my head, slowly—my back and neck are starting to stiffen up—and point at my ears. The movement is nauseating, as if my skull is filled with jelly and banging on top of my neck bones. I have to sit still for a second before I try to speak. "I can't hear you. You have to talk louder."

He rolls his eyes. My hearing clears suddenly.

"*I said—*"

I flinch at the yell, but I can't go back now.

"*There's something wrong with your labs. Are you sure you haven't been using any drugs?*"

I almost crack up. By now, he's already checked my balance and seen every charge on it. Yes, some people try to get stuff smuggled in, especially since you can't use on the clock, but it's a lot cheaper and easier to just to buy it direct from CPI and shoot up off-shift.

Plus, after Brin overdosed, I stopped doing drugs. And that feels like it was a very long time ago. "I'm sure." My voice sounds like it's underwater.

He nods, but the look he gives me drips with doubt. *"You're very lucky. The burn isn't bad. Your hand should heal pretty well without much intervention, although we can't guarantee that you won't get cancer down the line. There's been a lot of exposure."*

I look at my hand. Compared to the other one, it's obviously swollen, the fingers like fat sausages.

"I'm going to wrap it!"

His scream is so loud that I can't help flinching. He rubs some kind of ointment on my arm, and it instantly feels better.

When he pulls out the bandages, my heart stops. They're tightly woven, brown, about as wide as my palm. I've seen them before, wrapped around my mother's left arm, a barrier against the world as obvious as an armored gauntlet. She never left the house without them. "What are they?"

He follows my gaze, and his mouth tightens into a firm line. "I realize these aren't optimal, but burn dressings cost extra. If you're worried about the friction, I'm going to put some loose gauze underneath—but tape costs extra, padding costs extra. Even the ointment isn't free." His dark look burns with defiance. "These are expired, and so I thought we could use them up instead of throwing them away. I'm just trying to save you some money."

I swallow. I don't know what it's like to be tasked with saving people's lives, much less how it feels to charge them for it. CPI breathes down all our necks at every turn.

He's waiting for an answer.

"No," I say. "I appreciate it. I've just seen them before and was wondering what the primary use is."

He nods, but he clearly doesn't believe me. "They're for swelling." He puts a thin padding over the ointment and wraps my arm.

Mom, why do you wear those every day? I asked countless times, but she never wanted to talk about it. I'd seen her bare arms before, after she got out of the bath, while she was still wrapped in a towel. Her skin was perfect, as even and flawless as paint. No burns or scars.

When he's done, my arm feels better, the pressure comforting despite the sting. There's a moment of silent relief—and then I remember Adda. The way her hair stuck out on one side as she extended her invitation to Rikki's. Me, running away from her girlfriend at the bar. And in the background, a series of jagged edges, a tunnel chock-full of piezanite.

I'd voted against taking that branch—felt something there, as dangerous as a waiting viper. But had that been real? Or was this accident just a coincidence? If it *had* been real, I should've pushed harder to take the other branch. And if it hadn't, I'd still have been late to my shift. Adda was at the drill, distracted by its operation instead of directing the flow of the work while keeping her eyes on the ceiling. And that distraction is probably what killed her. What killed them all.

So either way, this whole thing was my fault.

The man is talking again. I nod, but I can't hear anything he says.

I FINISH AT Medical and turn in my burned suit to a technician at Equipment. The bored woman tells me there's little chance of fixing Annie, but I hope. She saved my life, and the idea of losing anybody else—even a suit—is more than I want to deal with right now.

The technician stamps my card. Her gaze lingers on me a moment too long. "It says you're due at Engineering next. Probably going to get a new crew assignment."

I reel from the comment, but she's already turning away, taking her suspicious appraisal with her. Her statement is impossibly heartless, a complete erasure of the events that have just transpired. I'm still covered in dust and dried foam, baked in the smell of burnt rubber. Is some fleck of the debris on my skin the fingernail of a crew member, burned to ash and blown through the hot currents of the explosion?

She couldn't have been clearer if she'd spit on the ground and made a protective warding sign with her hands. Nobody will want to work with me now. Either I'm the cause of the tragedies around me, or I've got the kind of luck that it would kill you to be around.

And yet, despite my pain, by the time I walk out of the door and make my way to Engineering, the technician's face has already faded into blotches, swirls of abstract paint and color. Nothing sticks in there, nothing but Adda's face and the faces of Oye, Stomp, Kola. My crew. A blink, and I nod off. Another blink, and I'm in front of Engineering's main building.

I've never been inside. Engineering has trade secrets about piezanite in it, the kind that convince rival entities to try to sneak *into* a prison on the moon. At least, that was the justification for the extra security, for the exit debriefing—and now, even if you somehow manage to pay off your debt, you can't leave until CPI finishes a background check on you, one that takes almost two hundred circadians as they crawl through every part of your life on both Ung-Nyeo and Hib.

And of course, they charge you for it.

The simple metal placard above the door looks laser etched: *ENGINEERING*. I don't know how much money it cost to bring it up on the elevator. It couldn't have come up on a load like the one that brought me up, because every inch of that cargo container had been jam-packed with sweating bodies.

I don't want to do this. But if I leave, they're going to find me and make me do it anyways, so I knock on the door before spotting the intercom button and pushing on it. A speaker crackles.

"Can I help you?" The voice sounds female, surprisingly pleasant.

"I was sent down here to—"

"Name?"

"Young. Young—"

"Yes, I see you on the schedule. Come in."

The door clicks. Nothing moves, but I grab the handle and pull, and it opens outward, the lock disengaged.

I step inside. The ground under my feet clangs—some kind of metal grate—and I'm immediately hit with a current of warm air from above.

"Sorry—" The woman's voice disappears in a sudden roar. She steps out from behind the desk and points at the blowers on the ceiling. Her skin is olive, lighter than mine or even Gyu's, but her hair is a tight afro that curls around her head like a cloud of stardust. Her clothes are ornate to the point of being ridiculous. I can't hear anything she says over the fans, but I catch something in her glance: a wary fear. Suspicion. It's everywhere.

But then the blowers shut off, leaving only a minute breeze that flutters the starched collar of her dress, the ruffles on its hem. When she holds up her hands, palm-up, her face is open and inviting. "The blowers keep out the dust. It's noisy, but effective."

"Right," I say. Out of all the places I've been on Hib, this is the only one with a system like that. You'd think Medical could use one, but I guess not.

"So." She taps one expertly painted finger against her lips, the ruby polish a blazing luxury that I can't help but stare at. If she's a prisoner here, she's like Hannah—not planning on leaving. "You're here because of the tunnel collapse."

Maybe it's her smooth, emotionless voice. Maybe it's just the glaring contrast—this clean, made-up woman whose appearance screams like a beacon against the compiled visual memories of three months of gray sand and dark skies. Whatever the reason, something inside of me shuts off, and I can't feel anything at all.

It's a lie. Somewhere, trembling behind a wall I can't see, I'm sure my feelings are still there. Ready for their resurrection. But it's a relief that they're gone for now. "Yes. The tunnel collapse."

"There will be an engineer here to interview you any moment now." She peeks behind me as a door on the wall opens. Her eyebrows go up. "Oh, there he is—"

I turn. At Gyu's face, the wall inside of me crumbles.

8

I WAIT, BUT Gyu is silent. His gaze dances between me and the other woman. There's something there—a twitch at the corner of his mouth, or maybe the outside of his eye, something so fast that I get the feeling of it more than actually perceive it—and then he points at the hallway he emerged from. Before my brain can piece it together, he turns, leaving me to stare at the back of his crisp white shirt, at pants that cling to his ass.

"Be careful."

I flinch at how close the woman's murmur is. She crept up, noiseless, until she was right over my shoulder—but when I spin around to look at her, she's already walking away.

A whiff of her scent stays behind, clean and mildly antiseptic in a way that gives lie to her ruffled dress and ruby polish. I've smelled it before, somewhere—

"Young!" The gruffness in Gyu's voice shocks me. He's paused in the hallway, although he hasn't turned around.

I run after him, trying not to stare at his ass, trying to avoid thinking about the fact that I've seen it naked. That he's seen me naked. It's hard not to think about it.

We get lost in a byzantine series of hallways. Every so often, there's a door he has to badge through. Two have retinal scanners, and at those, he pushes my face forward into the eyepiece before taking his turn. I'm angry, until I remember who I am, and where I am, and the anger dies away.

Finally, we pass into a square, featureless room with a table in the middle. The lights above are dim. Half of them are out, giving them a kind of alternating pattern in the ceiling, *on-on-off-on-off-off-on*, like piano keys.

"Some of the bulbs are out," he says.

I look back down, and of course, he's staring at me. There's a hint of a blush on his cheekbones.

"I didn't say anything—"

"We haven't replaced them because we're moving toward bioluminescent lights in the next few months. They'll run off of some of the station's excess methane, because—"

"I don't care."

He shuts his mouth, his lips so tight their edges turn white.

Should I not have said that? I just want this to be over with. There are two giant elephants in the room: the tunnel collapse and our fight from earlier. Both of them things neither one of us wants to talk about.

I feel like I'm hanging on the edge of something, waiting to fall. I've felt this way before.

Sometime in the months after leaving the house my parents abandoned me in, I started sleeping on the flat roof of a dilapidated apartment complex. It had been condemned and slated for demolition, but until then, it was a place for people to fuck, shoot up, and get out of the rain. Without the buffer of my parents, just being inside made me hyperventilate. But once I got to the top floor, I could climb out of one of the windows onto the roof. Perched up above the seething city below, I finally felt safe, like an eagle in its aerie.

Until the day I stood up and turned around, and came face-to-face with a kid.

"Hey," he said. When he talked, the sore at the corner of his mouth seemed to move of its own accord.

I followed the line of his gaze to my bag. Before I could say anything, he grabbed it and shoved me hard.

I lost hold of the straps and windmilled at the edge of the roof for a moment before giving up and just letting myself fall.

Maybe Gyu wants to talk. Maybe I want to talk—but not as much as I don't want to talk, not as much as I want to just tuck in my arms and let whatever is going to happen, happen.

He leans forward until his face is inches from mine. His expression changes, the hardness melting out. "Young, are you okay?" he whispers.

The sudden tenderness makes me dizzy. "What's going on?"

He coughs under his breath. "I have to interview you. The camera in this room is broken, which is why I wanted it to be here. I'm not—" He clears his throat. "If CPI knows we're together, they'll assign someone else to do your interview. And they could make things really hard for us down the line."

He runs out of words. Turns his hands up, a helpless gesture. *This* is why he gave me the cold shoulder in the lobby. The woman's warning—*be careful*—suddenly makes sense. He must have asked her to stay quiet about us.

I feel like such an ass. "What do you need me to do?"

He nods, his relief obvious. "Just play it cool and answer the questions. Act like we don't really know each other that well."

I nod.

He looks at the lights and their piano-key pattern, and then he pulls a file from the corner of the table. After his whispers, his next words are startlingly loud. "Please confirm your identification number—"

"Can we skip that part?"

His eyes widen. He shakes his head, leans forward and whispers again. "Someone could be listening outside. We have to do everything by the book."

I nod. "Prisoner number 1253459."

He confirms my birthdate, my name. His expression is flat, almost wooden. In my mind flickers a glowing moment post-fuck, his smile so warm it makes my chest ache—but there's no trace of that man here now. "Is it true that you were late to report to this shift?"

"Yes. I…I'd gotten in a fight with someone. After my last shift." I suddenly feel naked. Has he checked his pockets? Does he know about me tearing the note into confetti and flushing it down the toilet?

"You said a fight. Was this a physical altercation?"

"You *know*—"

His look is sharp.

"No." I shake my head. "Just verbal. Maybe a fight is the wrong word. It was just a misunderstanding."

"What was the nature of the argument?" His gaze is too intense, the facade cracked. *He wants this*, I realize. He wants me to tell him the things that I never say outright. To apologize. To explain. To give him a chance not to leave me.

A raw spot opens up in my chest. "I can…I can be kind of stubborn, sometimes. I'm not good—" I look up at the ceiling, *on-off-off-on-off*. "—at letting people in."

It's lame. I know it's lame. It doesn't help that it's true.

I wait, but he doesn't respond to my olive branch. "So, because of this altercation, you were late?"

"Well, no. I just…"

I want to tell him. What it was like, in that dark and suspended moment before I pulled the note out of his pocket, how close I came to being strong enough to walk away. The vise grip that clamped across my heart as I dragged myself into the bathroom, the dark hole that opened after flushing the tattered strips of paper.

I don't say any of that. I can't. I shouldn't even be thinking it, after what happened to my crew. "I was tired, after the argument, and I overslept."

"Ah." I can't tell, in that one syllable, if he's sympathetic or not. If he understands. "And then what happened?"

"I ran straight to work. Annie was beeping. By the time I was on the shuttle, it was going into overdrive. I barely managed to cross the perimeter in time."

His lips purse with worry, echoing the dread in my chest, because soon, we're going to get to what comes next—and all at once, I feel like *such a fucking idiot* for pushing him away in the first place. I deserve to be punished—for what I did to him, for what I've done to Adda—but I don't want to face my cowardice.

He nods. He knows what I'm thinking. "And what happened next?"

"I started down the tunnel, but I didn't get very far. There was a boom—" *A flash of something falling, of angles, of crystals.* "—and then it was, you know, too late."

"Right." He nods. "So you didn't see any of your crew in the tunnel."

"No. I didn't—" I cough. "I didn't have the chance."

"And what was the last time that you saw them before that?"

"This is stupid, you already—"

He shoots me a warning glare.

For just an awful, selfish moment, I want to start screaming, but I shove that down. "My last shift. At work."

"Did anything strange happen during that shift?"

Something weird hums in the air between us. I could be imagining it—but even though we haven't been dating long, I feel like I *know* Gyu. I've broken bread with him, watched him sleep, complained to him that I never know when my cramps are coming because I stopped getting periods after the implant went in. I'm sure there's the tiniest hint of strain in his voice, and it's enough to make me wonder what I'm missing. "What do you mean, strange?"

"Strange. Like, did anybody behave in any way out of the ordinary?"

My stomach flutters. "I don't know what you're getting at."

"Okay. We can come back to that. So, the last time you saw them was at work."

I should correct him. He doesn't know about the bar—unless he does, and he's waiting for me to lie. Trying to trap me with my own words.

The rivulet of guilt I feel is nothing compared to the torrent of suspicion that absorbs it. *Stop it.* But I won't. I can't. Everything is knocking around in my head.

He waits, and when it becomes clear I'm not going to respond, he nods. "Let's back up. Why don't you describe what happened that shift?"

"We came to a fork, and we took a vote on the tunnel path."

"Yes?" He leans forward, ever so slightly, but he's not looking at me. He's looking down at his hands, at the clean, pink-tan nails, the corners filed square. There's a smudge of pencil lead in the crease of one of his fingers, and it shimmers in the odd fluorescent light.

"And the vote was kind of split, and then I had to go pee, and when I came back—"

"When you came—"

"I like privacy when I pee, even if it's in a suit." The snap in my words is too harsh, and I take a breath to calm myself. "And when I came back, Adda told me she'd gotten a new transmission, and that it said the east tunnel was a better choice, so she was changing her vote. And that meant I was outnumbered, three-to-two."

"An updated transmission," he says, and there it is again, that flicker that everything isn't quite right. I could be imagining it. But maybe—

If Adda had lied about that, then why? To get us to follow her own hunch?

"And then what happened?"

"And then, nothing. We found a small load, four kilograms I think." *He's going to ask about the bar now.*

But he just nods. "Did she seem—odd in any way? Worried? Like she was—"

"Like she was hiding something?"

His eyes flash open, just a quick flicker, but I caught it. "Maybe," he says, as cool as can be, but he's fishing for something.

"No." I look him in the eyes. "It was like any other shift."

In the back of my mind is another glimpse. Shadows. Angles. Then light.

And then it's Gyu's face again. Even his skin looks tired, his eyes wet with concern. *Fuck,* what am I doing? Do I really think Gyu is lying to me? Or is this just me, not trusting myself, because I'm coming apart at the seams?

I shouldn't have lied to him about the note. It's poisoned me, and I can't pick out truth from my own stupid fuckery.

"Alright," he says, and he nods. "Do you have any questions?"

His eyes warn me to keep my mouth shut, that I can ask things later, when we're alone. I ignore him. "The guy at Medical. He said there was something wrong with my labs."

Gyu's face tightens, but he nods. "Yes. There was a trace amount of some drugs in your bloodstream—" He shakes his head, mouths *it's okay*. "—but we've determined it was most likely caused by the explosion itself. A lot of chemicals were vaporized into the air. It's probably throwing off the lab values with some false positives."

I nod. From the way he's checking his watch, the interview is coming to a close, but something is gnawing at me. In my mind is the explosion again, the angles, the light.

I want to know if my vision of the Cable divergence was real or if I am just going crazy. The fact that the tunnel *actually* collapsed could be coincidence. I try not to think about this need to sift through the ashes; it feels an awful lot like the compulsion to steal the note out of Gyu's pocket. A *sick* behavior, in more than one way.

"There was a Pomp drone," I finally say. "Next to me, during the explosion. Did it record anything?"

He raises an eyebrow, but he rifles through the folder. "I didn't see anything about a nearby drone." He flips through the papers a few more times. "I can run a report, if you really want to know, but it will take me a moment."

He wants me to say *no*, but I can't. "I'll wait."

He steps out the door.

The folder, unattended, looms large. *Don't touch it.*

But the itch starts in the back of my mind, penetrating through my cells, like the call of an addiction. Five breaths go by. Ten.

It's almost a relief to reach out and slide the folder across the table. The sheaf of papers is about as thick as my little finger.

I leaf through half of it, comforted by the presence of droll engineering jargon—

But then there's a whole section of papers about me. Laboratory work. A medical report regarding the explosion. I scan through it the best I can, but it feels as dense as the pages that proceeded it—like I'd need years of training and a translator to make any sense of it. There's a single line that leaps out at me, a notation in the "abnormal findings" column—trace amounts of UNKNOWN COMPOUND, LIKELY SOPORIFIC, which someone has amended with LEVELS TOO SMALL FOR CONFIRMATION, PRESUMABLY ARTIFACT OF EXPOSURE DURING EXPLOSION.

After this page follows a different kind of report. Ten or fifteen sheets that illustrate the worst parts of my life in terrible, vivid colors.

Under CHILDHOOD FACTORS, there are entries for FAMILY STATUS, including the subheading PARENTAL ABANDONMENT. Under MEDICAL STATUS, there are records going all of the way back to when I was a child, entries that read SUICIDE ATTEMPTS and DEPRESSION and one last one that makes me hold my breath: PSYCHOTIC BREAK.

I make it through a few words of that entry before I have to stop. I shuffle the pages into a neat stack, slide them all back into the folder, and push that back into Gyu's spot across the table.

My mind replays the interview with Gyu, only this time, it feels like the constant darkness that surrounds Hib station has leaked into the dome, into this room, snaking black fingers between the seams until I'm swallowed in their chill.

Gyu has read these reports. He knows all about my deepest, darkest secrets. He knows I'm not to be trusted. That somehow, I killed Adda and the rest—as if there had ever been any doubt.

Inside, there's a storm raging, but the wall is back up, containing everything somewhere safe. Somewhere I can't feel it.

9

GYU RETURNS TO confirm there was no drone near me before the explosion, and then there isn't anything left to interview me about. When he states I can go, the tension between us dissipates, but it leaves behind something that feels both final and inexplicably heavy, like the weight of the charm around my neck or the *clunk* of my magnetic boots. I slide out without meeting his eyes.

He follows me down the hallway. Every so often, I get lost at an intersection, and he takes a step or two forward past me until I set off in the direction he's indicated, walking fast so he can't see my face.

The woman with the curling cloud of hair isn't there when I finally make it back to the lobby. Gyu hangs back as I exit. It feels like he's going to say something, but he doesn't, and the door closes behind me.

I've been hallucinating, and it isn't safe to think about that here. I'll go to my hatch, lock myself in, and try to figure out what to do.

I set off briskly, but my legs turn to lead. The distance between me and that elusive capsule of safety seems to multiply with each step. Twenty paces, thirty paces, and then the realization hits me. It's too far. I'll never make it.

It's crazy. My legs are the same as they were the day before—except now, there's the weight of Adda and the crew and an explosion and the weird interview with Gyu, all pushing down on me, and there's no way I'll haul myself across the sand without collapsing.

What would happen even if I did, once I climbed inside and let these feelings out? I can picture myself collapsing, an inert, dead shell, no battery left to power it. I turn around, but I don't go straight home. I drift through the wheel's spokes like a jellyfish. Which is exactly what I am: aimless, spineless, formless.

If only I were instead a bee. Bees have industry. Purpose. Bees don't walk off into the sand in a suit with a disconnected locator beacon, only to wake up in Medical. Bees don't wonder if the flowers they remember are in fact figments of a broken imagination.

Eventually, I look up to find my feet have taken me back to my hut, and that Gyu is waiting outside. There are wrinkles in his shirt, in the corners of his eyes, dirt on the hems of his pant-legs. He looks as dog-eared as a well-read book that's been stuck back on the shelf to gather dust.

I come up, but I don't say anything. He doesn't either, and I finally turn toward my door. Maybe he went inside, maybe he didn't, but at least it's been shut all the way.

He puts a hand on my shoulder. "Young, wait—"

I glare at him, and he whips his arm back like he's been burnt.

I don't know. I feel guilty, but I just—he shouldn't touch me without asking.

He presses his lips together. He turns to go.

My guts leap into my throat. It's easy to be the one closed off. It's harder to be the one being walked away from.

"I don't know what you want from me," I say. It's almost a whisper, but he hears it and stops.

"I feel the same way."

I rub my hand over my arm, feeling the catch of the edges of the bandage under the pads of my fingers.

We've played this game before. Today will end the same way our last encounter did. Him making dinner. A fight. Me sleeping alone.

I almost say *no*, because we can't do that again, but maybe I'm wrong. Maybe things will be different this time. "Do you want to come in?"

I stand to the side, let him through the door. He goes toward the kitchen—but then he catches himself, turns back, rolls his fingers into fists, over and over.

What if this is the way he always feels, and he's just hidden it until now? Maybe he actually hates cooking. Maybe he just does it because it gives him something to do when he's with me.

The idea—that my presence is not enough hurts.

"There's going to be a holiday," he says, and then he shuts his eyes. "That's the wrong word. I mean that…CPI's going to give us a few days off. So that we can, you know, honor your team and everything."

I snort. There's no written guideline governing which deaths result in days off and which don't, but nobody on Hib thinks it has to do with remembrance. The collapse changed the tunnel structure. CPI needs to run new simulations and rebalance the teams. And despite their legal authority over us, they know anybody close to crew will be drunk for a few days until we can finally sweep our grief under the rug and get back to the drill.

"Okay."

"The funeral's tomorrow."

My throat seizes up. I look down at my fingers.

He shuffles behind me, all the way into the kitchen. The air fills with the scent of hot plastic, the conduction plate heating up. Out of the corner of my eye, I catch fragments of Gyu's chef-ballet, his artful spins as he chops onions.

I crawl into bed. The air fills with a hiss, with the *tsk-tsk-tsk* of beating eggs, and then the sizzle crescendos into a roar. The almost-grandeur of it makes me feel like a voyeur—like I've been sleeping, awoken by his bustling around the room. Like I should announce my return to consciousness by stretching and yawning theatrically.

But this is my house, so instead, I lay on my side, facing the wall, my hand wrapped around the charm and its yarn.

My mind fills with Adda's face, her cocky half-smile as she asks me if I want to go to Rikki's—

Not that. Anything but that.

I push it away, and instead, it's the empty spot my parents' bags left, the creases in the fibers of the rug. The old-paper scent of that house, buried behind the aroma of Gyu's cooking—and those smells stir the memories of other meals made for me, presented on the foot of my bed like an offering to the dead. Dancing fingers, a flurry of signs: *You can't stay in bed all day. You have to eat.*

A bowl of seaweed soup. Slivers of garlic cut like fingernails, floating on thick lily pads of dark leaves. The tangy, savory scent of the broth.

Something easy to eat. Something my mom thought had superstitious healing properties, if only I would slurp it down.

I dip spoonfuls of soft white rice into the broth like submerged boats. It smells like the ocean breeze from the fake beach at the top of a skyscraper, and I wonder where she got the seaweed. I doubt the couple who owns this house kept it in the pantry—

"So, I brought you your reassignment papers."

Gyu is still in the kitchen. His voice was light, but tension wrapped each word, like the thin membrane on a bead of a water. He's waiting for me to stick in a finger and break it, to send it trailing down the glass.

I roll over and sit up on the edge of the bed, and my head fills with fog. "Oh? What do they say?"

"I don't know. I didn't read them."

Immediately, I know two things. The first is that he is absolutely, positively lying to me. The second is that as much as I hate him for it, I wish he was sitting next to me on the bed.

Gyu turns and beams me a smile, his teeth sparkling against the backdrop of his light-brown skin. In some ways, his face echoes mine. "Are you hungry?" He sets two plates on the table.

"No," I say, but my mouth waters. Eggs are hard to come by, and he's whipped these up with ham and green onions, none of that prefab, mixed, masticated shit that they pack into bags for the journey up—these must have cost him dearly. He's done them up really thin, and brown oil glistens on their surface like sweat.

I sit down at the table. Still standing, he picks up a plate and hands it to me. "I made this one first. No ham in yours."

My cheeks flush like fire. I don't know why I lied to him about not eating ham. Fucked up, but it's too late to undo it.

I cut off a piece with my fork. Even without the ham, it's still pretty good.

He makes a circle of the kitchen, comes back with his arms laden. He sets down a bottle of tomato sauce, and it rattles slightly, before finding its balance. There wasn't any tomato sauce in my fridge.

"I thought we could try something different," he says. He awkwardly maneuvers the next items from his arms onto the table. Two bowls of fried rice, their contents dyed reddish-brown. "Have you ever had omurice?"

My throat closes up. *Mommy-rice.* When I was a kid, I'd messed up the pronunciation, confused the *eomma* of "mommy" with the *omu* of "omelette." I didn't realize until I was fifteen and met some other Hangans, true West Banders. They weren't mixed. They could tell the vowels apart.

My head aches again, a sudden pressure like a storm front— and suddenly, I'm crying.

"I'm sorry," he says, as he puts a spoonful of rice on top of the eggs. "I know this isn't the right way to make it."

And just like that, I'm laughing. He laughs with me, and the tension between us is sucked away like gas into a vacuum. The sadness is still there, hanging over my head like a sword, but now, Gyu's created a little bubble here at this table, as safe as the hatch.

I eat while he makes idle conversation. Before I notice it, I'm chasing the last spare grains of rice around the plate.

He clears his throat. "So, about your reassignment. You don't have to join another drill team, you know."

I put my fork down. I know what he's going to say next. "No, Gyu. I *can't.*"

He reaches for my hand across the table. His touch is light, but it somehow pins my wrist to the wood. "I wouldn't say this if I didn't think it was good for you. Shouldn't you at least try?"

"Adda just fucking *died*—"

"I know, and I'm sorry. It's terrible. But there isn't time to wait on this. Once you're reassigned, it's a lot harder to pull the right strings. You might not have the option anymore."

The pressure in my throat, my chest, it hammers down like stone. "I failed, Gyu. I'm not meant to be a Pomp." I don't have to add the rest, that failing almost killed me. That I'm losing my fucking mind. That making me responsible for a crew's navigation and safety is essentially asking them to die, too.

"I don't agree. You're *smart*, Young. I think—" His voice cuts off, an odd note, as if he is choking.

I look up. He's biting his bottom lip so hard it's turning white. I wait, but he doesn't meet my gaze.

"Young, if you'd been the Pomp, they never would have gone down that tunnel."

Something bright flashes in the back of my mind. In my lap, my burned hand suddenly aches under the bandages. "You don't know that. That's a...that's a stupid thing to say."

"Is it?" His look is sharp. Curious. The hair goes up on the back of my neck. There's no way he could know about what I saw. Right?

Fuck. I can't tell what's real, and what I'm just reading into. "Yeah," I finally say. "It's stupid. If I'd have been a good Pomp, I would have passed the final simulations. That's the long and the short of it."

"Not everything can be measured in a simulation," he says quietly. "We like to think all this data is enough, that these tools are enough, but the best Pomps run on instinct. I think you have the right instincts."

The back of my head tingles with new possibilities.

Instinct. What if I'm not losing it? What if seeing the Cable was just some intuition my shitty mind made into something bigger, something that I could break down and understand?

"And then you wouldn't have to worry about fitting in with a new crew, because they wouldn't know—"

Hope turns to rage in a heartbeat, but I manage to keep my face calm. Of course. That's what this is about. He's afraid for me, afraid I won't gel with my new crew, not once word of my *instincts* gets around. And while he's probably right, I don't need *him* to rescue me from that.

My mouth floods with copper bitterness.

He sighs. "I'm sorry," he says, reaching for my wrist again—but he stops himself before he makes contact and puts his hand back in his lap. "Look, there's—I have to tell you something."

A lump forms in my throat, sticking like grains of rice. The cryptic note I stole from his pocket flashes in my head, brighter than the light from a drone. My bandaged arm is still aching. "Okay."

"I realize—I realize that this is fucked up. This whole situation. It's fucked up in every way it could possibly be. You and me. Adda and your crew. Everything that happens here on Hib, everything that happens down on Ung-Nyeo. Believe it or not, I even get why you are the way you are."

It feels like he's peeling the flesh off my ribs. Of course he thinks he gets it. He's read my file, the worst moments of my existence. And what do I really know about Gyu, about his life before he came here? Almost nothing, that's what.

Underneath the table, the bandages pull tighter as my hand curls into a fist.

He rubs his face. "I'm doing this all wrong. Look. Do you ever—do you ever think about the future? About what you want, once we're out of here?"

I can't help the laughter that bubbles up, slow and dark like oil. "No," I finally say. It's honest. I don't. "A few months ago, I was ready for all of this to be over. To tell the truth, I'm not a hundred percent past that. So no, I don't think about the future."

Gyu runs his fingers through his hair. "Well, look. I do, okay? I think all the time about what I'm going to do when I get off this rock. And the truth is that if things keep going the way they're going, it might not be much longer."

In my confusion, I'm having trouble marking time. Was it just last night that he was trying to convince me that Hib wasn't so bad? Before pushing me to be a Pomp? "Congratulations for you—"

"I want you to come with me."

It feels like he's just slapped me across the face. I can't even breathe. "What?"

"When this is over. Isn't that better than whatever else you were planning? Are you going to languish here until your body gives out and you die? We could have a place. Maybe a family—"

A chill. "I'm not sure if I want—"

"Fine. No family. It doesn't matter. Look—I know you're fucked up. Like, really fucked up. But the truth is that I'm really fucked up, too. And maybe as two fucked-up people, we can make a little fucked-up life for ourselves. We can stand each other. We can *understand* each other. But we can't do jack shit if one of us is here and the other one is there, and it's too much to ask for me to stay behind when—"

"I'd *never* ask you to stay—"

"Can't you just try?" He grabs my wrists. His eyes are burning brighter than the white-hot spark of the sun over the Desert. He waits, searching my face for something he doesn't find.

Part of me is here, in this room. Another part is floating through the corridors in my mind, a thousand other *can't you justs* echoing around me like my life's refrain.

"I've never been able to *just* do anything," I say, but I'm not really talking to him.

He slumps back against the chair. "Just…think about it, okay?"

The little safe bubble that he's created pops. The spring starts in my chest. My thoughts swirl together in violent disagreement.

Yes, I want that, too.

Please don't ever leave me.

How dare you?

And another loop, one that is almost laughter in its cruelty. *I can't be a Pomp, Gyu. People will die.*

I'm trapped. Trapped in here, trapped with him, trapped in the one place in the entire colony I should feel safe.

I turn and leave without a word. He doesn't come after me.

WHEN I'VE WORN myself out playing jellyfish some more, I return, too exhausted to keep treading water.

I open the door to emptiness: The house is empty, I'm empty. Gyu and his offer are gone. This was my last chance.

It always goes this way. I desperately drag people into the black hole of my emotions…until they get too close. Then the fear hits, cold and prickly, and I switch polarities, shove them away as hard as I can. The most patient partners, like Gyu, come back—until they run out of forgiveness.

In the end, I'm always stuck with myself. I thought my ex, Brin, would be an exception—because he was like me, vacillating between desperate to be close and desperate to be alone. When I found his body, blue-lipped from an overdose, I almost laughed despite my horror; it was like the universe was grinding the point in, making sure I understood I wasn't meant for anything other than solitude.

I take a breath and step into my room. It hums with a familiar loneliness I can be thankful for, even though it hurts. Everything seems in its rightful place—Gyu has even washed the dishes we used, put the tomato sauce in the fridge, wiped the table down. Spotless. Neat. As if he was never here, except that I never keep things this clean.

Against the tidiness of the kitchen, the crisp, white paper of a thick envelope on the counter glares at me. The flap faces up, its point looking as torn as I feel, and I imagine Gyu sealing it, only to reopen it to fix whatever was inside.

My heart beats faster, spurred on by a swell of hope. What if this missive is a final, desperate message, a paper plane thrown off the top floor of a skyscraper? I have to keep my hands from shaking as I reach for it and flip it over. Maybe this is Gyu telling me I haven't fucked all of this up after all—

The tight, square text is too perfect to be handwritten:

```
PARK-SMITH, YOUNG.

RE: ASSIGNMENT.
```

I sag, as if the only thing holding me upright is my bones. Of course. The crew assignment. He'd said that he'd brought it for me before he made his offer. Before I ruined his plans for the future.

I almost open it to look, but even that feels like a lot right now. And I'll find out soon enough.

I put it to one side, and my gaze falls on another, smaller envelope. It must have been under the first. Did Gyu leave this for me too?

This one just says YOUNG, the name handwritten in a looping scrawl. It's not Gyu's penmanship or the spidery letters from the note I stole. Several other names above mine have been blacked out, the envelope repurposed to deliver this missive.

The card that I pull out from inside looks expensive—another two weeks on a sentence, maybe more—and it doesn't make sense until I turn the lettering right-side up, and I realize that the date neatly printed across the top is tomorrow's.

It's from Hannah. She's invited me to Adda's funeral.

10

I ALMOST DON'T go to the funeral, but Adda and the crew deserve better than my cowardice.

That doesn't make the hours leading up to the evening service any easier. It's like my body is split between two brains. Even as my muscles atrophy into a mush too weak to push me off my bed, my legs bounce and my skin crawls. Those parts are anxious, ready to go and be done with it, for better or for worse.

As further proof of my body's incoherence, my arm has swollen up while I was asleep. I'd left the bandages off, certain the extended compression wouldn't be good for me—only to wake up to puffy, shiny skin, tight with fluid. When I check in the bathroom mirror, it doesn't seem too bad, until I hold my elbows up to compare them. My elbow looks like a plum.

Fuck.

I change the gauze. It hurts to wrap it, but I do, making the bandages tight. Once I'm done, the aching fades, and I go back to bed. Before long, the bandages loosen and roll down.

I get up and check in the mirror again. My elbow has started to wrinkle, which I take as a good sign. I try to rewrap my arm, but halfway through the last bandage, I drop the roll, and it runs a circle around the sink before wedging itself behind a pipe.

I bend down. With a raking motion of my fingers, I just manage to grab it. When I stand up, there's a jerk at the back of my neck—something on the sink has caught on my chain. Water splashes and gurgles in front of me.

I rush to turn the knob off, but a tinkling chime informs me the water charge has already been added to my account.

I check the panel. Shit. It's more than a bad shift's wages, and I've already been billed for the next two minutes.

Well, fuck it, then. I've already paid.

I wash my face in real water for the first time since making it to Hib. I don't have any soap—skin is sanitized by a quick blast of UV, the radiation fine-tuned to prevent cancer—but it's still better than nothing.

I realize that I don't have anything to dry my face with. I pull off my half-soaked shirt. I rub my face until it's mostly dry—and then I see the reflection of the charm around my neck. The chain isn't broken, but the yarn that I've wrapped it in has come loose, and it's sopping wet.

It feels like a bad omen.

I finish up in the bathroom. Sit back on the bed, expose the charm. Its surface is tarnished, oily patches of black spilling into the embossed numbers and letters across the front, a code of gibberish I've never been able to decipher. I haven't seen it in a long time. It hurts too much to look at it and think about the way I found it, lying in unfurling carpet fibers once occupied by a bag.

Except that today, it doesn't hurt, because I'm too hollow to feel it. So, maybe that's good.

I cut a new piece off the yarn I keep stashed in the drawer by the bed. There are probably easier, less time-consuming ways to hide my shame, but I've done it this way since I was a kid. There'd been a white ball of yarn in one of the cabinets in my new bedroom. It and the chain I used to hang the charm around my neck were the last things I took before leaving that house, the only things I had time for as new, strange voices wended their way up the stairs.

My mom always maintained that white was the color of death. So, when that yarn ran out, I started using green, and then brown, and then whatever else I could find—but never white. If I had any, I might do white today, given the circumstances, but I don't, so I won't.

After a few minutes of winding, its surface is hidden again, the tarnished shine occluded behind an orderly bird's nest of green string. It feels right, that deep within the belly of this soft, vibrant thing, is something hard and covered in black.

RIKKI'S IS CROWDED, the floor sticky as ever, although someone's made an effort to wipe down the tables. Little beads of moisture cover their lacquered surfaces.

It's almost disgusting—so much money to ship the furniture up the elevator, all to create an atmosphere of fake cheap that misses the mark. After all, the tabletops and the furniture all match, which is more than I can say for any place I ever drank at or broke into for the night, trying to get out of the wind—but the designers of Hib station never consulted people like me.

I'm standing in the back nursing a drink when Hannah arrives. She's cut her hair short, with blunt bangs that run straight across her eyebrows, setting off the sharp angles of her cheekbones. She's rubbed something red on them that makes her look embarrassed.

Or angry, I think, as her gaze finds mine. My brain is clouded from the alcohol, but I can still parse that the situation doesn't make sense—why invite me, if she doesn't want me here? But there are lots of rules on Hib, established over two decades of mining, and as an outsider, I'm not privy to most of them.

I almost spit in surprise when she crosses the room and sidles up next to me. "Hi, Young."

There's no time to prepare myself before the embrace. She smells amazing, like citrus and flowers—*nobody's skin smells like that.* By the time she tears herself away from my rigid form, her slim curves leaving echoes on my skin, my pulse races from shock and more than a little shame.

I rattle like a piece of metal. Only an awful person would get aroused at a moment like this, drunk or not. I take a breath and push that energy away.

Her eyes go wide. Something glints in them, setting off a muffled alarm in the back of my mind.

"You were there, right? At the end?" The glint deepens as her eyes fill with tears. "Did she—did Adda say anything?"

The vertigo is instant, stunning, like being hit with a hammer. "I don't…I was too far away." In the back of my head is Hannah's laughter, looping together with Adda's smile, with the explosion, with wondering: When Hannah found out I tried to kill myself—did she also remember laughing at me the night before?

She leans in for another hug. I back out of her reach, my feet less steady than I thought they'd be, but she closes the gap between us, lithe as a snake. "People are saying she did it on purpose."

Another hammer blow, even as she places a petite hand on her chest, the pink in her nail beds echoing the pink on her shirt and setting off her skin, rose lights against night skies. She's shockingly beautiful, and I have to take a deep breath before I can answer her. "I don't think she would ever do something like this on purpose."

"I don't either." Hannah puts her hand in mine. Her fingers are warm.

My ears are burning, my face is burning—*I'm* burning. I scan the room as she grabs my arm and pulls me closer. "You worked with her. And *you'd* know."

Her unusual emphasis throws me. Hannah means that I'd know if Adda wanted to kill herself. Because I tried to kill myself. As if there's some kind of telepathic exchange between people who are actively fantasizing about death.

I want to snap at her, but she's mourning. Her grief has stretched her skin like a kite, so tight over the frame of her bones that you can almost see through her.

"It was definitely an accident." The answer is not even close to what Hannah deserves. What Adda deserves.

Hannah pivots before theatrically collapsing into herself. I lunge forward. She's heavy, and it's hard to hold her up—with each sob, she heaves us both, and between her motions and my unsteadiness, we teeter between standing and falling to the ground, rocking as if on the shuttle to the mine. She bawls, a sound so loud and harsh, I cringe. Her grief is too raw for me to look straight at.

I glance around the room for rescue, but everyone is silent. Staring. And the four faces I keep expecting—they're all absent.

And it hits me, then, in a way it hadn't yet. That Adda is not coming back. That none of them are coming back, that they'll be dead, forever and ever, and it's probably my fault. This isn't even like my parents, who are running around somewhere thinking about how stupid I am, how glad they are to get away. Adda and my crew have left all of us for good.

And to my surprise, I start crying, too. Suddenly, Hannah's the one who has to hold me up, because I'm the one who's screaming.

THINGS CHANGE AS we approach the viewing.

Of course, there isn't anything left of the crew to see. Instead, Hannah and two funeral-goers she indicates with a pointed finger move to the back and stack two tables. On the top one, they put four personal tablets, already cued up to static photos of our lost brethren. From the graininess, Adda and Oye's photos were shot in low light: a lover's work. Kola and Stomp are both immortalized in a joint picture that shows them with their arms linked, simultaneously throwing back huge steins of beer at the bar. You can tell from the creases in their eyes, rising over the rims of their glasses like four suns, that they're smiling. This certainly isn't a side of them I've ever seen, including that last night at Rikki's—but then, they had something else to focus on.

Every so often, one of the screens goes dark, and someone reaches up and gives it a tap. I flinch when I see that. It feels like waking the dead.

The bottom table becomes the altar. We approach one by one with our offerings. Flowers made out of food wrappers. A handwritten note, rolled into a thin strip and tied into a knot. Someone has actually paid to have a picture of Adda, Kola, Stomp, and Oye printed onto glossy paper, before cutting their faces out and sticking them onto a pastoral scene that no doubt represents some rural variation of an afterlife.

On either side of the table are a series of mismatched cups. I can smell their acrid contents from my place in the back. Somebody has taken it upon themselves to defy CPI's regulations and brew their own shine, stealing money out the corporation's pockets—it gives me a thrill. Adda would've liked that, at least. When the Pomp drone wasn't around, she'd taken to calling CPI an *"iniquitous den of selfish murder-pigs."*

By the time we get to my turn, the table looks like a garden made out of trash, like some forgotten heap left after a group of explorers had come and gone.

All eyes are on me. I try to just act *normal*, but Hannah grabs my hand and refuses to let go of it. I pull, but she's got me tight, and the way she tugs on it—it almost feels like she's flirting with me.

Another glance around the room shows that I'm not the only person with this idea. I'm not part of this group here to mourn. I'm on display.

I need to say my goodbyes and leave before I have a total breakdown. "I think I have to do this alone."

"Oh," says Hannah. She pouts, her face contracting like an affronted squirrel's, before she sighs and pulls her hand away. "Yeah, I understand. Just, don't leave without telling me, okay? I need to talk to you…about Adda."

Her words are strained and clipped, the pauses between speaking volumes. Her behavior has nothing to do with me. She just doesn't want to be alone. Perhaps more than anyone else on Hib, I can understand that, can make peace with being her cheap stand-in.

I sway on my walk up to the little altar. My note is crumpled in my hand like a secret stolen out of a pocket—and like that other note, my vague lines about *working hard together* and her *being such a great Fore* hide more than they give away. If I were being honest, it would say things like:

I'm sorry I was too much of a chickenshit to tell you what I saw in the tunnels.

I'm sorry that I'm a fuck-head who was late yesterday. This is all my fault.

Thank you for being the only person who didn't treat me like a plague after I tried to kill myself.

I tuck the note in, under a little hand-drawn picture that I can't make heads or tails of. I made notes for the others, too, but my thoughts on Oye, Kola, and Stomp are just echoes, reflections of the things I want to say to Adda. I don't put them in.

I turn, but the alcohol has finally caught up with me. I have to throw my hands out onto the altar to keep my balance, and I knock several objects to the floor. A cup falls, smashes into dust, the hot scent of shine vapors engulfing me like a mist.

Even my vision is disjointed. My gaze finds an empty spot on the ground before my brain finally pivots my head to locate the cup shards. In the wet patch on the ground, something glints.

People are moving behind me, rushing up in a series of murmurs as their shock wears off, but I'm picking up the piece of silver metal before I can stop myself. Did my charm fall, somehow? Did Hanna rip it from my neck? What happened to the tarnish?

But when I hold the charm up to the light, my eyes focus on the stamp. I make out two characters—*XH*—before the charm is ripped from my grasp.

"Young, what the fuck is wrong with you?"

The pressure in my chest threatens to crush my rapid heart into stillness. "What is that?" I sputter.

Hannah checks the charm over thoroughly before gently putting it back on the table. The chain pools around it, a small galaxy around its star. "It's Adda's. It *was* Adda's."

She whirls, presumably to snap at me, but I'm already on her, a thousand questions screaming through my head on winds as fierce as the ones that blow against the walls of the terminator band. My chest burns as if the yarn-wrapped charm has recognized its twin, ignited with magic at their pairing. I grab her shoulders, shake her before I can stop myself. "What is it? The charm? Where did it come from?"

The punch is swift, just a firecracker of pain that throws me backward several staggering steps. Miraculously, I stay on my feet. I sway in circles.

"It's a Fore tab, you damaged fuck."

She's not laughing, not like she did in the bathroom at Rikki's, but it feels the same. "It's a what?"

"A Fore tab?" She rolls her eyes. "From the first Fores on Hib? They used to give them out. It was her mom's—"

She shakes herself, as if out of an impending sleep. "Look, Young, I think you need to leave."

"But I need to—"

"Get out. *Now*."

I want to argue, but nausea surges through my stomach, my throat, and when I spin away, the world lurches on its axis. Someone reaches for me, but I push them away and bolt through the crowd, shoving until I make it to the door, and then I'm running.

Without a suit, I can't flee to my hatch. I run headlong through the station, stumbling, getting up, stumbling again, tea shoppes and pinball arcades swirling around me—their neon signs advertising pleasure, none of them honest enough to tell you how many more weeks on Hib you'll have to pay for each sip, each momentary thrill.

I bolt to Lodging, then down to my house, run inside. I almost make it to the bed before I realize the door isn't shut. I turn again. My luck runs out, and I fall.

I crawl on all fours like an animal, shut the door with my hand, and then I'm too tired, too hot to make it to the bed. Instead, I lie there on the floor, as the spring in my chest snaps in half.

The wail that comes out is agony itself. I pull at my hair, scratch at my face, and then I'm just sobbing, even as I pull the charm—my charm—from between my breasts, still wrapped in spring-green yarn.

A Fore tab. Where did it come from? Why did my mother have it? And why did she leave it behind?

I should have stayed. Should have asked what it meant, because I don't know. All I know is how much it hurts.

11

THE KNOCK AT my door isn't a surprise. I was kicked out of a
funeral, and half of Hib has seen me, crying and staggering
drunk through the street. I could just not answer it, but the
off chance that it is Gyu, that I haven't blown our whole thing
completely to shit, gets me crawling out of bed.

Oh, look at that. Some of my steps are missing the ground.
I don't know how long has passed since the funeral—but I'm
obviously still half-drunk.

I crack the door. Light leaks in around a tall, male frame,
penetrating into my bubble of dark. A flicker of irritation
answers it, snaking fingers through the pounding in my
forehead. This brightness has sullied a place that wasn't
meant to receive it.

"Hi," Gyu says. He's holding a huge box, one he can barely
see over.

I'm too afraid to respond. This hole is too deep, the sides
threatening collapse.

He sets the box on the ground. He runs his fingers through
his hair, blows out a sigh. "Look. I came to check on you."

The yarn-wrapped charm—*no, the Fore tab*—is in my hand.
Has it been there the whole time?

I turn away, drop it into my collar. Every movement feels like
pressing through primordial sludge. "I'm fine."

What a lie. And I have no idea what to say next.

He teleports across the distance between us and grabs me by the arm. "Why didn't you let me know you were having trouble? I care about you, and when I heard the way you left Adda's—"

"Don't."

We hang there in stasis, me half turned away, his hand on my arm. Neither can see the other's face.

He clears his throat. "Look, I'm sorry, okay?"

His apology injects every muscle in my body with plastic. "What?"

I wait, stunned, as he continues. "I said I'm sorry. I shouldn't have pushed you about being a Pomp like that. It was a real asshole thing to do. I'm just—I'm just worried. And I really see us together. I *need* you."

My ears pick his words out of the air, conduct them down the right canals—but once they're in my brain, they just rattle around and around, like a cat with its head stuck in a bag. I've been awful to him. Manipulative. Hurtful. Reactive.

And here he is, standing in my doorway, blaming himself. It's like he's addicted to chaos.

The tab around my neck threatens to drag me to the ground.

Gyu comes in and steers me to the bed. While I'm in his arms, my steps are steady, balanced. He helps me sit before taking a seat next to me. "I'm sorry. I know I'm not what you see for yourself."

I almost laugh, but I can't. It hurts too much.

"I won't push you about being a Pomp anymore. Just let me be here for you."

In my head is a wash of forbidden faux ocean water, golden snakes of light slithering through an endless sea without up or down. The shine of a newly polished crescent charm in the middle of an offering table. They feel like one and the same.

I can't make words. I just nod.

"Okay," he says. His voice is light, the weight of a boiling ocean escaping in a hiss of pressure and steam as something shifts between us.

He reaches for my hand, pats it like an old lady would. "Do you want to talk? About Adda? About us?"

I don't. I want to pull out the charm around my neck, unwrap it. Puzzle over it another time.

But it will always be there. Gyu won't. Why give up a person that hasn't left, for the detritus of those who did?

I just need all of this to stop. If he says one more word, if I have one more thought, I'll be pulled apart.

My mouth is on his before I can stop myself, my body already engulfed in an aching fever. Before he can react, I've pulled up his shirt, exposing the golden-brown, taut expanse of his abdomen. I trail my mouth up and down over its surface as if my very touch could breathe life into his flesh.

He cups the points of my jaw, pulls my face up to meet his, and his hesitation stabs through my lust. Behind the grim line of his twitching mouth, his eyes are hungry.

I wait as if suspended above us. He'll tell me *no*, now. To stop this. That I'm drunk, that I'm not in my right mind. I've heard all this before.

Instead, he bites his lip, and the motion stirs up the embers of my greed. Finally, he swallows. "Are you sure?"

I surge on top of him, cover him like a wave. There's a fever-breath of hesitation, a firmness in his muscles, but the torrent of my heat melts it away. We tear off clothes as something rough and angry and painful and ecstatic builds in my chest. I'm ready for him within seconds, pushing him into me, fighting my way to the top.

I don't stop, even when it feels like drowning.

GYU SLEEPS OVER.

It's not what I want, but once the heat of our union evaporates, it leaves only a nagging pull, the feeling that I've sinned—against him or myself, I don't know.

But there's no way to get him to leave without hurting him, and I've already done that enough.

Once his breath turns soft and unwavering—once his body is in my bed, but his mind floats far away—I finally start unpacking the question that has lodged itself in my head.

I spin it around and around, trying to make it point this way and that, but it's like trying to control the float of a leaf on running water. It goes where it wants.

Asking why my parents left after this long—it's digging up a grave. Something tells me that if I breach that top layer of soil, there will be more, layers upon layers like rings of a tree, each one years in the making, and that all of them will hurt. Because the truth is that my parents' abandonment is just the outermost layer, the dark, muddy shell of a geode that hides crystal-bright years of pain underneath.

I could leave it alone. I could open my crew assignment envelope, start again on the drill, and let the years pass until I get cancer or die in a cave-in. Or I could accept his help. Become a Pomp, keep my head down, and earn my way off this rock. Gyu's a hard worker, and with his skills, he'd get paid decently. We could find a place in Li'Airet or one of the more temperate cities. It would be tough, but manageable. Maybe we could even have a family—

But these visions are all lies, no more than mirages in the Desert. My plans collapse like the buildings I carved in the sand during our trespassed trip to the artificial beach. The vision of Adda's Fore tab looms, white-flash bright, swinging in the back of my head.

If I were a Pomp, I'd have access to information. Not just things like rock density and projected crystal growth. I could open personnel records, comb through people's pasts, things that would give me clues to the mystery of the note I found in Gyu's pocket, the stamp on Adda's tab.

I wouldn't be able to stop myself. I'd try to figure out what makes Gyu tick, how much he owes, how many lovers he's had. And then I'd get caught, like I always do, and Gyu—Gyu, who stuck his neck out for me to pull me out of failure—would be in trouble.

And I failed out of Pomp training the first time for a reason. Adda, Oye, Kola, and Stomp all just died. I'm afraid to peel back the layers, to find that underneath is a trash-board missive that proclaims it was all my fault.

But, what about the instinct?

The thought comes unbidden, a flame that shrivels the tangle of spiderwebs in my mind, whispering about the day before the explosion, the crystalline angles right before the vote.

The weight of ghosts presses me into the bed in the dark. I drift backward through time, to when my parents left, and then before, to when I almost drowned. Back, even further again, back to the first time I figured out my mind was a liar. That I would never know for sure what was real, ever again.

In my ears is the soft rattling of someone flipping through a sheaf of paper, piano-key lights above, off-on, off-off-on. A page with a titled section halfway down the middle: PSYCHOTIC BREAK.

12

ME GOING TO the hospital, us coming back to discover what I'd done to the house—that would all come later. The beginning was my mom finding me in the closet, door shut, hiding in a nest I'd made of a grown woman's winter clothes. The sweaters were musty from six months in a cardboard box. Fear had driven me to unbury them and haul them out into the light, to sacrifice their chance at hiding for my own. The closed door had trapped in their stale smell and my panic sweat, and even then, backed against the corner, the cool wall pressed against my skin, I was shaking.

This was a long time before we stayed at the Uptown House, the one we'd borrowed from the honeymooning couple. My parents had found a job cleaning for a rich woman who was never home. They would take me with them and put me in another room with some toys while they worked.

I don't remember why I felt like I had to hide. If it had happened before or just the one time—but I remember crying, and thinking I'd never be able to stop. That my hands were too small, too clumsy to make the signs needed to communicate in my mother's world. That even with my voice, I didn't have the words to explain what was happening to me. Instead, I pulled at my skin, my hair, over and over. Tugs of pain, fire-hot, like ant bites, whispering that I was real.

My mom called for my dad. When he saw me, he dropped his bucket, soapy water arcing across the floor. It feels like I fought him as he dragged me through into the street, but I don't trust my memory on this, because there are no pictures for this part in my mind. Only sensations, flashes of pain and hot and cold—and then we were at a hospital.

I'd never been to a hospital. Too expensive. I waited while they scanned with a giant machine, silver and plasteel edges glinting and vibrating as they tried to contain its monstrous roar.

People in uniforms talked in front of me, but never to me.

It's not a brain bleed.

No signs of seizure activity.

A list of things it wasn't, but nobody said what it was.

I fell asleep, then. Some medicine, an injection. When I woke up in bed, there was a new bump on my forearm. It itched. I wanted to claw it out—it was different, my body was different, there was something *in there*—but my mother held my hand and shook her head.

"Just wait," she signed. "*It will be okay.*"

MAYBE SOME OF that isn't true. Memories of that part of my life are all fuzzy, just flashes of color.

After the hospital visit, I was tired all the time. The exhaustion just kept getting worse until my mom had to dress me before school: rolling me in bed to get my clothes on, washing my face for me, helping me stand up. All five floors of our apartment building shared one bathroom, and they had no patience for me and my turtle pace. They'd bang on the door while I nodded off on the toilet, until my mom would come in and take me back.

We shared our one-bedroom apartment with another family and an old person, Mx. Ya. Mom, Dad and I all slept in the living room. Mx. Ya slept on the floor of the kitchen, and I remember mom dragging them up and begging them to call the hospital, because it didn't have the kind of phone that would let her sign, and it was too hard and too expensive to get an interpreter. She'd written her questions down, but Mx. Ya couldn't read well. Still, they relayed what the hospital said. It was normal, a side effect that would pass. They glanced at me nervously while they spoke, as if they didn't trust my mom's ability to parse the meaning of their words from their lips alone.

My parents had fought hard for me to keep going to school. I'd dropped out several times when their work dried up and the fees were too much, only to come back months behind when the funds came back. Now, their money was truly wasted. Every class, someone would shake me awake to shuffle off to the next one. When my dad came for me at the end of the day—sometimes hours late—I'd be sleeping on a bench in front of the building, and he'd carry me home on his back.

Until my parents gave up. They came in and told me I didn't have to go to school anymore. I woke up later to find them gone—presumably at the market to get something for dinner if they could find it cheap enough. Mx. Ya was out, pushing their little cart on the street to gather trash. We hadn't seen the other family who lived in our apartment for at least two circadians. They'd skipped out.

I remember waking up, a strange thought stealing over my brain. It was *good* my parents were missing because I had a very important mission, and if I didn't get it right, everyone was going to die. I was on a *quest*.

I wish I knew what it was, but there's nothing after that. Nothing until I woke back up at the hospital with a mask over my face. I remember cracking my eyelids to my mom, her eyes red from crying, my dad's haggard expression as they leaned over me.

He's grown a beard, I thought, although it was more of just a two-day stubble. He hadn't had that when I'd seen him last.

My arm hurt, hot and aching. I pressed over the tape, and the bump was gone, the space suddenly flat.

I spent the walk home picking at my arm. When we'd made it up most of the stairs to our apartment, my mom's face tightened. *Wait here.* She boarded the last flight by herself, my Dad staying back to stand with me.

But on the staircase was a small, silver coin. As soon as I saw it, a switch flipped in my mind—and I *remembered*. My quest—not what it was, but that I'd had one. That something bad had happened.

Only now, I knew that there was no quest. And something terrible waited for me inside, something that was my own doing—and I needed to know what it was.

I shot past my mother. She grabbed at me, but drug-addled, poorly-slept, hospital-room me was still too fast. I made it to the door, threw it open—it wasn't even locked—and through that square of wood, I spied a picture frame, the painting upside down. Mx. Ya's family portrait.

I stepped into the house. Into another world.

My parents' steps thundered after me, but I'd already seen everything. The pictures, all upside down. The garbled writing on the walls in lip paint, some of the letters up so high I must have climbed counters, windowsills, boarded the sparse furniture. The buttons and beads on the table, grouped by color and ordered by size—and with that came flashes of memory about my mission, single frames glowing bright in the dark. It'd been important, tied into the very fate of the world.

It'd been a lie.

My mom caught up with me then, swept me up in her arms, but over her shoulder, I saw the open stove, pillows and blankets crammed inside. *Shutting them out,* came the whisper in my mind, although I couldn't remember who I'd barricaded the stove against.

I tapped on her shoulder to put me down, and she relented. I studied her face: the upward sweep of her black eyes, the full lines of her mouth, the strong jaw and the high forehead, the low hairline.

"It's okay. We've been robbed, but we'll manage everything. We just forgot to shut the door, how silly—"

She was lying. I'd done this. "I'm crazy, aren't I?"

She shook her head, and the lines of her face collapsed, like a dam that had given way to a powerful sea. *"No, I'm sorry, I'm sorry."* And then she was wailing, a sound I'd never heard her make.

My dad laid his hands on my shoulders and kneeled in front of me. *"It's not you. It was the medicine,"* he signed. I thought he was talking about the hospital until his gaze flicked toward my arm, toward the missing bump.

My whole body tensed up, ramrod-straight. "They took it out. Why would you let them put it in me in the first place?"

"We're so sorry. We thought it would help you."

They hugged me. I didn't want them to hug me, didn't want their tears wetting my shoulders, didn't want their apologies. I wanted my closet in the rich person's house—although we would never be able to go there again. Because of me.

I breathed, but it was like a big machine had taken over my insides, filled my lungs and my organs and kept them pumping because my brain had gone away.

They picked me up. They put me to bed. How many times did they tell me they were sorry?

It didn't matter, because my thoughts were caught, spinning like a coin on its side, trying to give words to a feeling I was too young to understand.

I thought that feeling would stop haunting me once I'd gotten old enough to name it, but I was wrong. How can you forget a broken trust? It wasn't just trust in my parents. It was in everything—the world, myself, my own mind. Because the truth is that your mind can lie to you about what is real and what isn't. Now, when it comes to choosing between those two possibilities, I'm never sure.

GYU TURNS IN the bed in a groan of springs and rustling sheets, and although I never fell asleep, it feels like I've just woken up. The last vestiges of my ethereal memories are filled with a dream's haze.

I feel soft pressure on my still-closed eyes, and with it comes a whisper of a clean, almost minty scent. The touch draws across my eyelashes, inside to out, chasing away a tear.

"Hey," says Gyu. "Are you okay?"

I could do this. I could just curl up in Gyu's embrace. Throw away my parents' last offering to me. Leave it all alone. Let these buried pains stay in their grave.

And then what?

Take Gyu's offer. Become a Pomp.

I sniffle through a nose-full of snot. I'll tell him the truth—at least, as close to the truth as I can get. "I'm worried that if I take this job, I'll fuck everything up."

He wraps his arms around me, and it's the most amazing feeling in the world. His lips find my forehead, soft, a lingering impression that drags me up through the depths and into the light. "You won't. If you make a mistake, we'll figure it out. But everything is going to be okay, Young. I'm sure about that."

I want to believe him more than I've ever wanted anything in my entire life, but there's one word holding me back, its single syllable louder than the beat of my own heart. *Why.* "Why are you so nice to me? Why are you doing this for me?"

He closes his eyes. "Because I know what it's like."

Underneath my body, the bed spins. What is he talking about? The feeling of being *unmoored*—it rocks me with its anger. Powerful, even if it is irrational. I bite back a flood of epithets. "What do you mean?"

He sighs, rubs his face. My crying woke him, but he's still tired. "Sad. Hurt. Lonely. Anxious."

They're good words, but they're too small to encapsulate the feelings that swirl in the back of my head, the constant, running commentary on how awful I am, how much better my absence would leave the world.

He rubs his arms, then mine, but he doesn't pull me closer. "Sometimes, it feels like—" He closes his eyes, searching for the words. "Like my thoughts are a red flare, bouncing and spitting down the shaft of a mine. Did you read that book I loaned you? The ghosthook book?"

I shiver with recognition at his description, but I shake my head. Gyu is always loaning me books and asking me to read them, but I never do. I don't even know which one he's talking about.

"Ah. Well, it's about a girl that's been part of some bad magic, on a jungle island. Their world is a turner—"

"A what?"

He shrugs. "A *turner*. The planet and its moon don't have a tether connecting them. Instead, they both turn, but at different speeds. Every spot on both of them alternates being light or dark depending on if it's facing the sun or not."

Something is crawling up the back of my head. I try to imagine the colony bubble, bathed in light, but I can't.

He presses his lips into a line. "It's interesting. You should read it. Anyways, there's this girl, and she makes a bad choice, and a ghost sinks a hook in her chest. For the rest of her life, no matter how far away she travels, she can always feel it there, piercing and pulling, waiting to drag her back into the ghost's clutches. It's like the ghost has become a part of her."

My skin ripples with electricity—with recognition?

"You don't have to be that girl. You can take out the hook. I can help you, if you let me." He sighs. "I'm sorry. I said I wouldn't push—"

"No." The pressure in my chest squeezes, erupts, fades: a sequence so fast, I can barely track it. "I'll do it. Hook it up, and I'll take the job."

His arms tense around me, whispering promises. His voice is thick. "Ah, Young. I'm so, so relieved. Really! You won't regret it." He tucks my head under his, and for a moment, I've again stolen a quiet evening on warm, golden sand.

But then it gets too warm. "When can I start?"

"Well, operations aren't supposed to resume until the shift after next—"

"Is there a way to start earlier?"

I don't say the next part, that I'm afraid I'll change my mind, but he must figure it out, because then he says, "Alright. We can start first thing next shift."

I nod and fold myself back into him. *I can make it that long*, I think, but there's no conviction in it.

It's when we're both drifting back to sleep that the question floats to the surface—and once it does, I can't let it go.

I hate to wake him, but it's better to ask now, before it festers. I'm starting over. I *won't* be myself anymore: the one in the middle of a crying fit, begging him to fend back the demons I've built up in my own head. Not when a few words could have prevented it all.

"Gyu?"

He snorts awake, but he couldn't have been too far gone, because he replies almost immediately. "Yeah?"

"What happened? To the girl?"

"I—what? What girl?"

I blink in the dark. "With the hook in her chest."

"The—*ah*." He finds my meaning. "The ghosthook." He yawns. "They got it out. She lived happily ever after."

Somehow, I can tell he's lying.

In the last vestiges of the sleep cycle, my dreams are full of crystals. Dark angles. Laughter that turns circles around me, the feeling of going home.

13

I WAKE TO the murmur of a river, the tinkle of chimes. Custom alarms are the kind of extravagance I never waste money on, and I'm annoyed that Gyu doesn't trust me to get up on my own—but then I see the box on the table. A present, with a note on top. It's real stationery: a small, pink card about the size of the palm of my hand. Ten times as expensive as the pleasant alarm sounds.

Meet you at Engineering.

<3, Gyu

P. S. Look in the box.

P. P. S. I'm proud of you.

I melt as I cover the heart with the pad of my little finger. We've never used the word *love*, but the affection in this note is obvious.

Although the present calls to me, I ignore it and drop the card into my desk drawer. I'll find somewhere safe to put it later, but I need to get ready. Pomps work inside of Hib's bubble, which means that although they need a visor with display in order to interpret readings and interact with the Conduction's virtual interface, they don't wear full protective gear, like Annie suits. For the first time since I started mining, I'll have to pick out an outfit to go to work in.

Before I failed out, my classmates used to debate what they'd wear once they graduated. When you're a Pomp, nobody sees you outside of the projection that you choose inside of the Conduction, but each person was so intent on finding a style to signify who they were on the inside. Stripes, bold colors, pastels. Nobody ever asked me, and I was glad, because I couldn't choose.

I still can't. Now, I own six outfits, and they're all the same. Neutral colors and soft, stretchy fabrics designed to lay well under my suit and make it easy to get around. I pick the one that has the least wear and lurch into the bathroom.

This is stranger still, like unearthing a ritual I haven't performed since long before I got arrested. I used to paint makeup on like armor, but prison and Hib took that away. After I came up the elevator, the sight of my naked face made my chest prickle with anxiety.

But then I met Gyu. He stroked my cheeks and called them beautiful. Kissed my eyelids, the curve of my lips. After that, it felt wrong to long for makeup, as if even the desire to go back to my old face would break my luck.

Maybe that's wrong. Maybe my face should just be mine.

I give it a good scrub. Comb my hair and pile it at the top of my head. I don't want to pay extra for anything else, and when I look at myself in the mirror, I feel unfinished—like I've missed steps in a recipe—and now my appearance will come apart like deflating bread.

In the back of my mind are my mother's signs, her hands darting like sparrows as she tells me how thick my hair is, how much I'll appreciate it when I get old and it starts to fall out—

I am not going down this road. Opening this door again has to happen bit by bit, breath by breath, like easing my way into cold water. And right now, I have things to do.

And suddenly, my naked face—the same face that required no adornment since I came up the elevator—looks pathetic and vulnerable, and I can't leave like this…but I don't have any makeup to change it.

I decide to pretend. My cheeks burn as I pucker my lips in the mirror. I run a finger over the curve of my bottom lip, the notch on the top, while picturing deep-red lip paint spreading in its wake. I pinch my cheeks to make them blush, massage the bags under my eyes, visualize their disappearance. I hold on to that image, best I can, and even though I know it isn't real, the spring in my chest lets out a little bit. By the time I've attended to my teeth and my flyaway hairs, I'm as ready as I'll ever be. At some point, I've shifted from preparing to delaying, to buying time.

Even so, I take a moment to open the present and peek in the box. He's tucked the flaps to keep it shut, leaving a small hole in the middle. I stick my finger in and yank, and the flaps pop open, groaning as they release each other's hold.

My breath catches in my throat. Some parts have been replaced. Others are charred, sooty, stained. But it's my Annie, at least in part.

I wonder if he's replaced the glove.

I give her a last, longing look, and I step out of the door.

The feeling is immediate. Invisible spiders climb the back of my neck, and I *know*—someone is watching me.

I search the alley. Try to creep up on whoever it might be, my heart beating like the vibrations of the drill.

But just like back at the hatch, there's nobody—not even a wind, because there's no wind inside of Hib station. Just my conscience, my fear, drawing intention out of random movements.

Or maybe it's trying to delay my walk through the station. I haven't ventured out since Adda's funeral, and the dome will be packed with throngs of people enjoying the good fortune of their time off, despite the grim circumstances of their origin.

I keep my head down as I make my way toward the center, into the crowds, but that doesn't stop the conversations from waning when I get close, as if I'm surrounded by a bubble that sucks nearby sounds into nothingness. People stare, only to look away as my gaze catches theirs. I can feel the weight of their eyes on my back, so intense it shreds my clothes to ribbons.

At first, I think it's just because of how badly I embarrassed myself, but I catch narrowed eyes and lowered brows. Suspicion.

I should've predicated that even without the details, people suspect me of having something to do with Adda's death. There's a surge of gratitude in my belly that Gyu made his offer, that I accepted. If I can somehow manage not to embarrass myself and fuck things up for him, maybe I won't have to crawl into this den of tigers. I feel like I can hear their thoughts, slipping through my mind like shadows.

She sensed something, you know. But she didn't say anything.

It's a shame her suicide didn't work out. With someone else on their crew, Adda might still be alive.

The closer I get to Engineering, the faster I walk. By the time I make it to the door, I'm out of breath and covered in sweat. There's a pause before the voice comes over the speaker, but when it does, I want to collapse with relief.

"Hang on, I'll buzz you in," Gyu says.

The door opens. The blowers kick on as I step in, and the same immaculate woman from before is sitting there, her hair perfectly coiffed, her skin shining.

Something warm rolls through my stomach—until I glance down at my hands, the nails jagged, the palms callused from the vibrations of the drill.

When I look up again, she's staring, but she drops her gaze, her face melting into an expression that reveals nothing.

Despite his voice coming over the loudspeaker, Gyu is nowhere to be seen. I swallow through the lump in my throat. "Do you know if—"

"He'll be right out." The words have an edge to them, the slightest flicker of a warning. Did I do something last time, offend her in some way?

The portal door that leads to the bowels of Engineering flicks open with a *snick*. Gyu steps out, his outfit immaculate as always. "I'm glad you're here." His words are warm, but his voice is tight.

I almost laugh—I have nowhere else to go—but behind me, the woman snorts, stealing the mirth from my mouth. "Right. I'm sorry I'm late."

"No, it's perfectly fine. First shifts are tough. Young, have you met Celeste?"

I don't have time to reason through the odd distance in his tone before he waves at the woman. Celeste gives me a smile, tight as rivets, before she goes back to tapping at something on the computer.

"Yes. She was here when I came in for my interview." And then it hits me—we're back in front of the gaze of others, and the previous rules still apply. *Don't act like we're romantically involved.* I fight like mad to stifle the urge to wink. "I'm excited to get started, sir."

My cheeks flush. *Shit.* The old-fashioned honorific is so heavily gendered, it feels like it's straight out of a historical drama. What if that pissed him off, if—

"Great." He beams. "Let me show you around."

After the door closes behind us, Gyu explains that we'll start in his personal office.

I swallow. I hadn't even thought about space. Most Pomps in training visit the galley for their simulations, a giant room packed with terminals for communal use. Once proficient, they move to a personal pod. Instead, we're going to his office.

My stomach clenches in titillating greed. I imagine shoving a stack of papers off his desk in a sudden cascade. Would we be able to stifle every sound, every rattle? Or would a little groan escape—

"Here we are," says Gyu. "It doesn't usually look like this. I had some things moved around."

Seeing the room is like being dunked in a barrel of frigid water. There's no desk—no furniture at all, actually. Unless we're making love on the bare floor, my flight of fantasy isn't coming true.

The only thing that breaks the room's flat planes are the few windows in the far wall. They frame a view of the outside, lights bouncing off the foreground of the dome. Behind the transparent barrier is empty gray sand that darkens with every passing foot, until there's nothing but black. I don't know what direction we're facing, but we must have walked all the way through Engineering, all the way to the outer border of the station. And although I've fled into that endless darkness what feels like a thousand times, something about my vantage point here in Gyu's office suddenly reminds me of my suicide attempt, of being found afterwards, my memories missing.

What happened out there?

A shiver goes down my spine. "Wow," I say. "A room with a view." Gyu doesn't know it, but I'm changing the subject on myself.

He clears his throat. "I thought it would make sense to find out what you already knew somewhere kind of private. Lower stress."

"Right," I say.

"And I think views are important. They can put you in the right headspace for Pomp duties."

I stare through the window and picture myself walking off into Hib's emptiness again. This view isn't doing much for my headspace.

Gyu presses a button somewhere on the wall, and a panel opens to reveal two standard-issue Pomp headsets. They're both black, with dual ear covers for auditory transmission. Unlike the ones we used for school, the microphone in these is hidden.

"Here," he says. He hands one to me. "Put it on and get ready."

I comply and flip the visor strip down over my eyes. My world fades to black, leaving me blind. My heart beats faster. I've been in Conduction before. I know what comes next, but even so, the moments before Con fully loads into visual space press the walls in on me—and I'm suddenly back to that fateful solo excursion in the sand with my air gauge on empty and my lungs full of fire.

"Ocean," says Gyu, and rippling bands of light fill my view. There's a roar in my ears, and I can smell and taste the salt. The panic is immediate—I'm drowning again, I can't find *up*—

But I can't let him know any of that. "Not this one," I finally choke out.

"Sorry," says Gyu. This time, the black is heaven-sent. "What about this one?"

At once, everything is green. A heavy line of trees blocks us in like a cage, and the confinement, the way it shuts off so many possibilities of movement—it instantly feels safer.

"No? I can—" he begins.

"Yes," I say, before he can change it again. "It's great."

"Great," he says. "Hang on. I need to check some notes."

There's a long pause. I wait, but it makes me nervous. I let my gaze trail over the leaves, shiny with the virtual moisture that the Con has hung in the air. The air feels cool, but at the same time, the humidity is already calling sweat to my skin.

I shouldn't do anything, but I'm curious. I rotate my fingers in space, a flickering gesture that calls up the specifics of the Con visualization. Words scroll in front of my eyes: JUNGLE CONDUCTION, VERSION 2.54, CREATED—

I make a fist to cut off the rest. *Jungle.* The place where the ghosthook girl from his story lives. *So, this is what that looks like.*

"Sorry," Gyu says. "I'm just making sure I haven't missed anything. It'll only be a bit longer."

I take a few more breaths and try to relax. As far as I can tell, we're not connected to any mining groups—so it probably won't hurt anything to see if the lookup is online.

I lift three fingers and drop them in a sweeping motion, and a book appears in my view, floating eye-level off the ground. It's set to the defaults: high contrast, one hundred percent opacity, so it blocks everything behind it completely. I rub my fingers together in a soundless snap, and the book becomes mostly transparent. *Much better.*

I almost say *jungle* out loud before I remember that Gyu is working—and I'm not sure if I'm supposed to be doing this at all.

My hands still at my sides, I quietly type in the word *jungle.* Unlike most of my peers, I don't have to hold my hands up to type—in fact, I doubt someone who wasn't also a Pomp would even notice the slight quivers of my fingers. Towards the end, I was getting to the point where I could do this without moving at all, but I'm already rusty.

The lookup returns a series of entries, and I select the first:

AN IMAGINARY ECOSYSTEM, POPULAR IN CERTAIN KINDS OF ALTERNATIVE HISTORY FICTION, DESCRIBING AN AREA, TYPICALLY IN THE TROPICS, OVERGROWN WITH DENSE VEGETATION AND CHARACTERIZED BY HEAVY SEASONAL RAINFALL.

As a definition, it leaves more holes than it fills. I look up *tropics*, and *vegetation*, and none of it really makes sense until I stumble somehow, entry by entry, to the *revolving world hypothesis*. I have time for only a few sentences of that before Gyu appears in the space to my left.

"What are you looking at?"

I clench my fist, and the book disappears before he can get a real glance at it—as if he can't just look up my last action. It was a reflex, but now, I feel like I've just been caught stealing again. "Nothing, really. I was just occupying some time."

"Okay," he says. "Let's get started."

THE FIRST FEW exercises Gyu wants to try are just reviews of basic manip skills. I try not to be a bitch about it—and there *are* one or two rusty gestures that I have to repeat a few times, until my fingers remember the movement—but the truth is it's all there, almost as good as the day I failed out. There's an art to communicating with the interface, an intentional way of moving that's also listening, like looking for the knot in a tight muscle or tasting for the missing ingredient in a dish.

"That's really impressive," he says, and I can't help but feel vindicated, even as I know that the standard of comparison isn't quite fair. Not every Pomp had the benefit of deaf parents. By the time I made it to Hib, I'd written volumes with my hands.

In fact, I could do even better if it wasn't for the bandages on my arm, which squeeze tight every time I try to bend my wrist. After I get home, I'll unwrap my arm and leave them off while I sleep. The officer at Medical didn't tell me how long I was supposed to wear them for, but my skin has already started to flake off, revealing new, pink growth underneath.

I really did get lucky—it's basically a sunburn.

WE SPEND A quarter cycle blazing through different content areas, and the order in which the topics are introduced is familiar—it matches basic Pomp training. Time starts to blur, and as hard as I try to concentrate, Gyu's questions also send me down long hallways of buried memories.

When he asks me about the function of the equipment, the son-chem drill and its capabilities, I'm suddenly back in the classroom, a stifling box scattered with desks and matching chairs. It's filled to the brim—and if it wasn't for our age, our shaggy hair and scruffy clothes, you wouldn't know that this was a room full of convicts. It's early in the training still, and we're all overflowing with excitement, secure in the knowledge that we've somehow ended up at the top of a food chain, that instead of dragging around a heavy drill and chipping away at our debt, we'll be blasting through it with a vengeance. Each morning started out with a sweater, a barrier against air that was cooler than the Jungle Con—but by mid-morning, the warmth of so many bodies packed in one room had us glistening like pigs.

When Gyu asks about the nature of piezanite, about the characteristics that are relevant for us as Pomps to know, the group project comes to mind. The memory's a bit more painful—at ten circadians in, it was already apparent that I was not going to be best friends with any of my peers— but the memory is still a good one. After my parents left, my hiatus from school became permanent. I never got the chance to discover if I'd have been good at advanced studies or not—and there I was, doing my own work and the work of my peers. I should have hated them for it, but I couldn't. I was having too much fun: analyzing, synthesizing, making connections.

Pomp school is short. At that point, I often wished it were longer.

When Gyu asks about group dynamics, about why the psychological profiles and team backgrounds are so important—it's then that my stomach starts to turn. We are getting close to the end.

We'd been inside of a simulated Con a few times, and it was there we met the final instructors, the ones whose job was to push us through practical knowledge, to find a way to boil the thousands of facts we'd crammed into our brains each cycle down into the sweetness of performance.

It's easier said than done, and I concentrated so hard on that part that I hadn't realized, at first, how much my new instructor hated me.

I never saw her face. Those exercises were all with visor, all inside the Con. She always used a representation that had a glow attached to her helmet, so no matter where you were standing in the tunnels, you could find her easily—but she never turned her display on.

In fact, I'm not sure she was a *she* at all. Her voice was gravelly, distorted by some kind of machine. Maybe I just assumed *she* because the woman I called Instructor became something fearsome, overpowering like the presence of a ship: a giant, foreboding structure.

I'd asked a classmate—one of the only people who bothered to speak to me at all—about why our final instructors didn't give us any names or faces. Were they trying to scare us?

She pouted her lips and rubbed on some lip stain. She'd been smart enough to bring it up with her in her one allotted box of possessions—in fact, her whole box had been makeup. She'd paid off a quarter of her debt before she even started Pomp school, just hawking the contents of her box.

She blotted her lips on a food wrapper. "Even if someone doesn't do well, CPI waits until the final skills tests to fail them out, because there's always the chance that they're just bad at test-taking or something. So the final instructors hide their identities. We're all in desperate straits, here, and they don't want to run the risk of one of us coming after them for a failing grade."

Was the anonymity the reason Instructor felt bold enough to pounce on every misstep, every hesitation? She drilled me so fiercely that she entered my dreams at night, literally eviscerating me in front of an awed group of classmates. It only took seven circadians before I started to fall apart.

"Young? Are you ready or not?"

My memory snaps like a clipped thread. "What?" I'm breathing hard, and I try to reanchor myself. A simulation. We've been running a simulation.

"Are you ready?"

Fuck. I hadn't been paying attention. "I'm sorry. I couldn't hear you for a second—visor artifact, maybe. Ready for what?"

He hums to himself. "That's strange, I'm not detecting a vi—"

"*Gyu*. Ready for what?"

"Let's try something live."

No. *No,* I am absolutely *not* ready—because this, this was where everything fell apart the first time. My heart gallops. I can't feel my fingers.

But this is it, isn't it? Gyu is giving me my last chance. I have to do it—and *Instructor* isn't here. This is Gyu, and Gyu will help me.

At least, I hope he will. "Yes."

"Great."

Next to me, the fingers of Gyu's avatar sweep and fly, as if he's holding an argument with himself. I stare at one of the trees, at the green of its leaves, at the grooves in the bark—anything to keep my mind off what is coming. It's hard to breathe.

A panel blinks to life in front of us, white lines curving against the dark green of the jungle, criss-crossing over the top of the view. Those are Cable—the silvery veins of metal, thicker in diameter than a person's height, that wrap through this moon's crust. Each one is bordered by a hollow tunnel underneath, and some of them hold chunks of piezanite inside, ready to be broken free like pearls from an oyster.

Looking straight at it makes me a little dizzy, so I don't. Instead, I concentrate on one corner of the display, where five dots blink. Four are light green. One is red, to stand for the Foreperson.

"Alright, you're loaded in. Why don't you take the reins from here?"

"I—"

"It's okay. Just start from the beginning. You can have as much time as you want. The crew has been informed that there's going to be a delay. What's the first thing you want to do?"

I shut my eyes. There isn't a right answer to this question, exactly. It's up to a Pomp what they want to investigate first. The fearless ones jump immediately into crystal loads, figuring out where the computer thinks the best paydays are, and working backward from there. Conservative Pomps try to decide what they are comfortable with before letting themselves get tempted. They start with the tunnels, checking the stability of the rock crust and the probability of a collapse or failure. In the end, it boils down to personal style, to the way your mind works.

"I like to start with the people," I finally say. It feels stupid—out of all of the things I need to know *right this moment*, it seems the least important. Some Pomps don't even bother to check the personality profiles, the background information, the records. One of my instructors even said that the performance of those who didn't was better than those who did—that they'd found it led to slightly riskier behavior, but with better rewards—which meant your mining crew was happier with you overall. *After all, dead crews can't complain, and it's not like your next crew sees your record. Just don't kill all of them, all the time.*

"Oh," Gyu says. "Can I ask why you want to start there?"

I clear my throat. My ears burn, and of course, the sensors in my helmet are catching every second of it, reporting it to Gyu. There was a Pomp once who had a stroke in the helmet and gave some pretty terrible advice, and CPI has been careful ever since. "They're putting their trust in me, their lives in my hands. They deserve for me to see them."

"Ah," he says, his tone carefully neutral.

For a moment, I flutter, no longer sure I'm right—but sure I'm about to die of embarrassment.

"I think that's admirable," he finally says. "Well, do your review, and then we'll lead them into it."

Quickly, I sign through the sequence of gestures that brings up their profiles, their histories, their lives. For the first time, though, it feels like more than my due diligence. It feels *invasive*. Little echoes of the interview I had with Gyu ripple through my head. Me, watching as someone read the worst moments of my life in front of me. Nobody has a right to these things.

But we're prisoners, so they do. And now, at least for this moment, I do. And if I want my chance at this job—my chance at the life that Gyu has talked about, as impossible as it sounds, I need to do this.

I find out that the Fore and two other people on the team have children. That four out of the five are here for debt—one is here for assault, though, and I make a note to be careful not to stress him out too much until I see how he gets along with everyone. One of them actually has an advanced education, and I think, *Maybe he'll be able to give better input into the tunnel*—but no, he went to music school, and it doesn't look like his family was independently wealthy. No wonder he wound up in debt.

I comb through their lives, little by little, as quick as I can, until a sense of them fills my head. This is them: my brood. My responsibility.

"Okay," I say. "I'd like to do tunnel safety and construction next."

"Sounds good," says Gyu.

I indicate my target with my gaze as I rotate my hands, smoothing them over the surface of an imaginary globe. The simulation zooms me in, as if sensing my desires. I manipulate the view—rotating it, peeling away layers, checking density. Every so often, the computer flags areas that stand out in its probability calculations—this bit is *likely stable, eighty percent*, that one is *projected highly unstable, seventy percent*. Sometimes, it marks things that are so probable that there is no doubt to them, and these, it layers below everything else in transparent view, letting me know where it thinks the sure bets are.

It's a deluge of information. The first time I looked at a view like this, I felt like I was drowning again, like I'd never know which way was up. But even as I fell apart over the seven cir-cadians I spent with Instructor, the prediction map got clearer and clearer, until I could glance at a layout and visualize the pattern it was supposed to represent, like looking at an embroidery diagram, stitches marked in symbols.

The picture in front of me depicts a fork. On the east is a tunnel that is safer; the west looks both more profitable and more dangerous. The familiarity makes my heart ache—and I want to steal a glance at Gyu, even though I know that movement, too, will be tracked—but he isn't doing this on purpose. He couldn't be. The similarities are coincidence.

Eighty percent of the decisions that Pomps make don't come down to *mine* or *don't mine*, to *yes* and *no*. CPI has already chosen *mine* for us, already decided that we will push ever-forward. The Pomp is just there to provide suggestions and feedback. To guide at the splits.

It'd be nice, though, if this split was *up or down, north or south*—anything but what it is.

"Okay," I say, when I've got what I need. "I'm going to pull the loads now." Another flicker of my hands, and I sweep them across my body, pulling the structural overlay out of the way. I'll put it back when I'm done, taking the composite view, but in this moment, I just want to look at the crystals themselves, see if the prediction map speaks to me in some way.

If the structural overlay is like a pattern, the crystal overlay is like being on the wrong side of the fabric and trying to discern the exact placement of each stitch on the other. It's a nearly impossible task. The computer helps the best it can, but we've all heard that the best Pomps can do this part almost by feel. The instinct that Gyu was talking about.

After a few seconds, I tell the computer to load everything in 3D space instead. I close my eyes. The transition makes me nauseated.

When I open them, it's there, waving in front of me, clouds of stardust like some distant nebula, areas of probability that range between dark and dense to soft and light. None of them are homogeneous. In the middle of the lowest projected density, there's a bright spot—a low chance of a very high crystal load, but only in this one specific location. Here is a cluster of medium probability, medium load bits, the translucence almost a perfect fifty percent of either stark value. And here—

I'm getting lost in the details. It's the wrong way to go about this. So instead, I lean back a bit, unfocus my eyes ever so slightly, imagine my lids getting soft—

Soft eyes. Left foot heavy. My mother's signs, instructing me during one of the few sessions I spent with her in her routine meditations—

And it's like something clicks into place. I know which way I want to go, even if I could never put it into words. "We're going to start with the west fork," I say. "Do you want me to alert the team now?"

"No. I'll convey your instructions, just for continuity's sake. I'm a hundred percent certain in your capabilities, but I don't want the crew to realize you're still in training and get nervous—and I also don't want any banter to distract you. So for right now, I've turned off the audio feed in both directions."

"Okay." I don't know if that's normal or not. I never made it to the live part of training.

He relays the message, and the little dots on the screen, the ones meant to represent the crew, take up a formation. The four light-green dots form a box, the shape of a crew on a drill. At its head, the Fore's dot blinks twice, a signal sent by her tapping on the button on her vest.

Ready.

15

AFTER THE DECISION on a split has just been made and the crew is working, a Pomp's input really isn't needed. Once someone is a full Pomp and has been doing the job long enough that it doesn't scare them anymore, that time is their own. Some Pomps use it to avail themselves of their free access to the lookup—a perk of their position—and do research on a topic that interests them. Others sit down and read a book, or watch a show, confident that they'll make back the cost by the end of the day.

I'm still a student, though, and terrified—and I've got Gyu here, looking over my shoulder, so there's no way I'm going to take my gaze off the screen. But as the shift stretches on, I can't stop my mind from occasionally wandering, though I bring it back every time I catch it.

Somewhere at the quarter-shift mark, I remember when Instructor taught me something new about myself.

Every Pomp student goes into their first Con with predictions about what it will be like. Sometimes, we imagine ourselves, hands flying, crystals pouring over us so quickly we almost can't catch them all—so lucky that we pay off our entire debt in one monster day, one that goes down forever in the history books as the *largest load ever recorded*. I once dreamed I'd found a load so fantastic, it literally changed Ung-Nyeo's economy. Crystal prices crashed, energy became cheap—and then the dream got away from me, devolving into nonsense about being cast into the dark Ice and skating my way over frozen lakes.

And sometimes, the fear gets to us, and we imagine our first attempt will end in heartbreak. Loss. Explosions. We'll make a simple mistake—one, that it turns out, is an extra-criminal offense, one so bad it's literally its own class of crime, and we'll be given the ultimate punishment. Blasted out to space in a capsule engineered just for this purpose. The airlock doors open, and we watch as vacuum tears our organs apart.

It doesn't matter that the crime and capsule both don't exist. That we don't know if vacuum even works like that. The fear is there, and it's real enough.

Most of the time, we just hope that we'll get through the first shift. Everybody says the first live shift is the worst, and it usually happens on your seventh circadian of full-immersion simulations. Which, of course, was the one where I flamed out.

I cough and glance at Gyu, but his helmet projection shows his expression is soft. He's thinking, too. I ping the computer for updated projections. It makes no sense to have all of the data shift in front of you in real time, given how slowly a mining crew progresses—it's a tremendous pull on resources. Still, you can request the computer re-run the projections before schedule if there's something you want to check on.

Gyu's voice crackles through my earpiece. "Everything okay?"

"Yes. I just…I was just being thorough."

His chuckle is good-humored. New Pomps are so legendary for pinging too often that it's the punchline to a number of well-known jokes.

What smells like ham and goes ping-ping-ping?
A newbie working up a sweat.
Why did the newbie stop pinging?
He crashed the entire system, hang on, we're all gonna die.
Some are funnier than others.

Jokes aside, I can tell Gyu thinks I'm doing well. Even if I didn't know all his tells by now, he's not trying to hide his opinion. Every so often, I make a choice, and he nods or *hums* appreciatively to himself. Once or twice, I catch the eyes on his helmet projection flicking back and forth, as if reading text, and I know he isn't even paying attention.

It feels like I've been raised on a breeze of warm air, wafted up toward the stars. Gyu thinks I'm doing well. He trusts me with a live crew. And I can tell, in the free, easy motions of my fingers, in the way I keep finding exactly what I expect as I go, that I am *rocking* this—and that means, that maybe, just maybe, he was right. Maybe I have the instinct. Maybe it really was just a bad day, a cold coming on that never materialized, an electrical hiccup in my brain that having worked itself out, won't happen again.

Nobody's perfect. And I don't have to be perfect. All I have to do is not fail. Instead, I'm tearing through this exercise like I was born to do it. It feels like it did that third cycle of simulations, where everything suddenly knitted together at once, where the entirety of my pathetic existence melted away, to reveal me sprinting my way up a mountain—stumbling, falling, but still leaving the others in my dust. I never knew I could feel like that—which made it all the worse when Instructor sent me tumbling down.

And this isn't even a simulation. This is *live*. I'm doing it. I'm Pomping a crew.

I'm looking at a unique configuration in the Cable when the display in front of me freezes. A bright yellow ring appears in the center of the screen, indicating a high priority—and confidential—call.

My pulse speeds as my brain fills with the image of someone from on high taking my chance from within my clasped fingers—but I can't ignore the call. I make a fist, and the ring disappears, but I don't hear anything.

It takes a moment before I put it together. Of course. This is Gyu's private space, which means the call is for him. He's probably not authorized to share it with me.

I wait. With the display frozen, I can't research the tunnels or keep tabs on the crew. This seems as good an opportunity as any to use the lookup. I make a sequence of gestures, fast enough that when the book appears, it's already translucent.

I glance at Gyu, but he's still standing there, his helmet projection now off.

I want to pick up the threads I was reading before, the ones on the *revolving world hypothesis*. But it feels weird to look that up in front of Gyu—

"Hey, Young?"

I jump as Gyu's voice pipes into my headset, but I manage to stop myself from closing the lookup. I don't need him thinking I'm trying to hide something from him. "Yeah?"

"There's something I need to take care of. It's important." He sounds distracted—even a little anxious, maybe.

Something tells me our training is up for now. It's hard to bite back my disappointment. "Yeah. Sure. I totally get it."

"So I'm just going to have you go home and we can pick back up next shift—"

"What about the crew?" The words come out of my mouth before the thought is even fully formed, and it takes a me a moment to continue. "You can't just leave a live crew without a Pomp. They've already been deployed, and they aren't even close to making up their drill rental for the day." If we'd been short a Pomp, and they couldn't have been sent out because of that, they'd at least have a zero balance—but this way, they'll wind up owing. *Because of me.*

The silence that follows is terse. "We'll have to get someone to fill in—"

"Are there any Pomps not occupied right now?"

He clears his throat, but we both know the answer. This poor crew that was assigned to me and Gyu, that had to start late because of a *technical issue* that never existed in the first place—now, they'll get less than nothing for their labor.

I think about the front two drill operators. They both have families—families I bet they miss every day. They deserve the chance to make a dent in their debt, but instead, my training has added to it.

Gyu makes a frustrated noise. "Young, it's not…you can't take this personally—"

"I know," I say, but we both know that I do.

Another long pause. "Okay. I have an idea. Hang on."

I wait. This time, I'm too nervous to do anything but stand and rub my fingers together. The lookup flicks on, off, on.

The Con fades to a black screen. I flip my visor up to see Gyu. He's already got himself mostly unhooked. "Okay. Here's the plan," he says. "Celeste has some experience as a trainer, so she's going to sub in for me until I get back, okay?" His voice is tense—it doesn't sound like Celeste liked this proposal.

The idea of working with somebody else—of having to show somebody else what I can do—for a moment, it sends me hurtling into an abyss. But within seconds, I'm clawing my way up, dragging myself out. This is okay. I just proved that I know what I'm doing. My team was progressing fine. And Gyu wouldn't leave me with someone else if he didn't think I could do it.

I give him my bravest smile. "Sounds great."

He nods. "Good. Just make sure—"

The door behind us flicks open. Celeste steps through, her visor in the up position. "Okay," she says.

Gyu glances at me. "You sure you got this?"

I nod. "I got this—"

"Yes," cuts in Celeste. "I'm sure she'll be great."

And with a final nod, Gyu disappears out the door. It makes my stomach turn a little that he doesn't look back.

"Visors down," says Celeste.

IT FEELS LIKE the cards have been sorted against me.

I can't help it. Celeste's first move is to change the Con back to ocean. Right away, it's harder to breathe—but I promised Gyu I'd do this. And I can do this. It's not a real ocean, just like the jungle before wasn't a real jungle.

She doesn't load in an avatar right away. In fact, she spends several long moments not doing or saying anything. *That's okay, too. She's stepping in on the middle of the shift. She's just getting caught up.*

"Okay." Her voice is so harsh, the vowels so clipped, that I have to swallow hard. "Well. This is interesting," she says, the strict directive suddenly fading away. Instead, she sounds... *amused.* "It looks like, seventy feet back, you chose a north branch at an uphill grade, versus the recommended downhill grade. Justify that choice."

The phrasing makes my skin crawl. Her way of asking questions—instantly putting you on the defensive, as if the working assumption is that you already fucked up, and here, she just wants to know why—it's so like Instructor's style that I have to take several deep breaths before answering.

"I could tell that given the stability of the crust-rock on the bottom-left corner—"

"You could tell before the computer," she snarls, and my skin tingles in recognition. A bright helmet. A faceless avatar. *No. This isn't possible.*

"I'm not saying that, I'm just saying—"

"What about here? Why did you advise the crew that the east fork is the best one to take, when the south fork has a much better projected crystal load?"

"Given the stability prediction—"

"Fifty percent stability is within acceptable margins—"

"*Yes.*" The word comes out louder than I intended, so loud it's almost a roar, and my gut clenches. "Yes," I say, more muted. "It *is*, but given the combination of mineral types and the noise in the signal in the bottom-left corner, I—"

"Fine," she says, her tone as flat as lake ice. "Let's move on. According to the instructions that Gyu left, I'm supposed to convey all of your orders to the crew. So, what's your next order?"

I swallow. "Can I please see the crew again?"

The overlay pops down, gray against the background of a flickering ocean. It's a horrible contrast, and I move my hands in the gesture that will increase the illumination—but nothing changes.

"Sorry," says Celeste. "I like it this way. It's easier on my eyes." She laughs to herself, a single, chuffing grunt. Two facts slam into me with absolute certainty. The first pisses me off—she's lying. This projection can't be better for her than one that is *easy to see*. It's complete and utter bullshit.

My rage, though, can't do anything to warm the cold pit in my stomach, because I'm working right now with a live crew, meaning that any mistakes could endanger the safety of a breathing group of people. And the safety valve—the person next to me, overseeing my work, making sure that I don't make a dangerous mistake—is the one person that made it her personal mission to ruin my life not so long ago.

Celeste and Instructor are the same person.

"Hurry up," she says. "Let's get this over with."

LIKE CABLE BEING eroded away by a son-chem drill, everything unravels, exposing the danger underneath.

I'd suspected before that Instructor—no, *Celeste*—had read the details of my file, but now, I'm positive. The little jibes she drops here and there reveal far too much knowledge, too much targeted hurt to be just random chance.

What's the matter, Young? Why can't you follow an order? Are you deaf?

With those graceless hands, you're lucky you're not a thief. You'd make an absolute shit thief, Young.

Keep fucking up like that, and you'll be homeless.

Alone, each cut could be random chance, a lucky blow by an instructor used to shit-talking all her students. But taken together, it's obvious—she's not only read the summaries of my life, she's also managed to feel between the cracks in the words and rip out the weeds underneath.

I can't help it. It gets to me. I call out *east* when I mean *west*. I doubt my ability to read the probability projection of crystal density—is that really a shaded area, or is my vision swimming? Everything starts to blend together and become cloudy, like tailbone soup broth, and my calls stop making sense. Celeste takes me to task, viciously, for each wobbly decision. *Justify this choice.* And I try, but my words are abandoning me.

At one point, I forget to double-check a grade reading, and after Celeste relays my command, the Fore actually pings us. Only Celeste can hear him, of course, and it's in the gravelly voice of Instructor that she conveys the response. "The rock slopes up. The Fore wants to know why you didn't make a recommendation as to dig grade?"

Hearing that voice again, it hits me like a blow to the gut. I can sense the amusement in her tone—amusement I always suspected was there, but couldn't quite be sure of because of the mixed voices of a roomful of students clogging up the audio feed. Here, now, it's just her and me, and her delight in my failures is obvious. *She knew I forgot to check, and she didn't say anything.* She's going to watch me fail, hang me with my own rope.

And despite the voice in my head whispering I deserve this, I still can't understand why she hates me so much.

A quarter shift passes, and in that progression of time, in each rapid beat of my heart, the knowledge that Gyu isn't coming back to save me swells, growing and billowing up over me like a fog. I'm drenched in sweat, and without Annie to help me regulate temperature, the foreign feeling of my clammy skin is like a portent of terrible things to come.

The signal pauses again, like it did during Gyu's call, but instead of freezing or fading to a black screen, an ocean fills our view. Celeste's avatar is gone, leaving me underwater and alone, waiting for her to finish her call.

When the cover wiggles over my ear, I almost jump out of my skin. I reach up for the visor, but a strong hand grabs my wrist and holds it down. The spring in my chest has taken on its own fury, clawing like a caged animal. I try to rip my wrist away, but even now, some part of me holds back a piece of my strength—if something happened, if I hurt Celeste, even in my own defense, I could spend a long time in solitary, and I'll definitely lose my chance at this job.

"You should have just done it," says Celeste. Her voice, no longer filtered by her replicator, is a murmur, but she's so close to my ear that the words are almost deafening. "You should have just ended it—and if you couldn't do that, you should have kept your head down."

I *should* just take this. But the spring in my chest snaps with a *ping*, and in that wash of unleashed force, I muster some reserve I didn't know I had and push her violently away. Before she can grab me again, I flip up my visor.

"Why are you doing this?" The words come out quieter than I wanted, their bravado dying halfway into the sentence, but I cling to them as if they're life itself. "I was decently good at the simulations. I—"

"You." Her eyes narrow into a squint. Between pairs of thick, full lashes, hot embers glow. "You are such a liability that—"

"And you can't do this, anyways. There's a *crew* down there." It's one thing to take a call from on-high. Neglecting Pomp duties to have a personal chat is not only a policy violation, it's a big offense—one that I'm sure Celeste isn't exempt from.

I wait for the eruption. Instead, Celeste laughs, the sound more vicious than a slap. "Oh. Your crew." She flicks her fingers in front of her, and the display changes. Words appear at the bottom: SIMULATION 43, VERSION 1.56A.

The feeling of falling. She's got to be faking this. Gyu wouldn't do that, tell me something was live when it wasn't. He wouldn't—

The cavalier way he answered the call. The way he was ready to just walk away to attend to an errand, never mind the crew down there—the way he just had Celeste step in.

I'd thought it was because he'd gotten some important order from on-high, but now, looking at it, this explanation makes more sense.

No wonder he'd monopolized the audio feed. There was no one asking questions of their Pomp. No one to send orders to. He didn't care about the crew, because they never existed.

But *no*. It's Gyu. He wouldn't hurt me like this. "There has to be a reason—"

"Gyu doesn't trust you with a live crew. It's a smart decision." Celeste smiles, and it drives in the knife.

It takes everything in me not to sob, not to break down in front of her, not to let her know how effective her assault has been. My vocal cords have turned to stone.

She loses the mocking tone. Instead, when she speaks again, there's a softness to it, as alluring a lover's. "Just give up. Go back to your job in the mines. People will forget your fuckup, soon enough. And if you just keep your head down, before you know it, they'll be shipping you back. It's better for everyone—especially for you."

I look up, and her face shocks me. Her eyebrows are up, the corners of her lips dipping ever so slightly. She looks… concerned. *Kind.*

It's so far from her previous expression that I know one of them—one of them *has* to be false—but now, I don't know which. The cruel Instructor? The kind Celeste? Or maybe it's just me, cracking up again, paranoid in the face of everything.

It feels like someone has pulled the ground out from under me. I sink down into a squat. "I can't," I say, and the ache in my chest—*Gyu's a liar, Gyu's a liar, Gyu's a liar*—it's counterbalanced by the feeling of the note I stole from his pocket between my fingers, by the crackling *rips* of paper as I tore it to shreds and cast it into the toilet like a handful of sand. This is what I deserve.

"You have to." She takes a step in closer, but when I flinch, she backs up again. A kindness.

I don't understand her. I don't understand anything.

"You have to let go of this insane decision. You're going to kill people, Young, and when that happens, how much longer do you think you'll survive—"

"*Celeste.*"

We both look up at the hissing "S" sounds, the whip-crack at the end.

Gyu, his face a mask of rage, is standing in the door.

He's come to save me, like I hoped he would, but he's just too late.

I don't know how much time passes before any of us speak. The silence between us hangs with no sign of detente, marked only by haggard breaths from all three of us.

Eventually, Gyu is the one to break the ice, each word falling slow and separate from the others, spreading ripples in their wake like skipping stones. "What—in the hell—do you think you're doing?"

"My job," says Celeste. Against the hot rage in Gyu's voice, Celeste's is cold steel. "I'm doing my job."

Gyu shakes his head. Pity leaks out from behind the rage. "People gossiped about why you were pulled as an instructor, but I never would've imagined…"

Gyu's words ring hollow. Instructor had been *pulled*? If I had gone to Pomp school a few circadians later, would I have made it through without ever meeting her in the first place?

I imagine that alternate history. One where I was never pushed to the point of doubting if my own existence was worthwhile, if my failures could ever be overcome—but of course, I can't fully blame Instructor for that. It's not like it was the first time I'd tried.

Still. Gyu had known that there was something wrong with Celeste, and he'd let her train me, had put her in a position of power over me while I was still alone and vulnerable, a headset strapped to my ears, my vision filled with data. She could have stabbed me in the back—in the *front*—and I would have never seen it coming.

Celeste finally breaks the new silence. "You knew she would never make it. That's why you put her in a simulation, instead of taking her live—"

"I put her in a *simulation* because I've never seen her work. Because somehow, her performance files up until the day she was removed—"

"She failed out, you mean—"

"—have all been obliterated. *How*, exactly, did that happen, Celeste? How did a number of files that only a few key instructors and their superiors have access to suddenly delete themselves for one person only?"

Celeste turns her face away. "I don't know."

"I think you do," he says, and his voice is colder than I've ever heard it. It's so cold that it makes the back of my neck tingle, that it sends chills up and down my spine.

Gyu did this on purpose. Setting me up with Celeste. He *wanted* to see her push me, wanted to set a trap and figure out if his suspicions about Celeste were real.

But even as I have the thought, it rings hollow. He wouldn't do that to me…would he?

"If you're accusing me, just do it, Gyu." She turns back to look at him, and her eyes are again embers, but there's no other trace of emotion on her face.

"Alright, Celeste. Here's another question. Why is it, that in the middle of training my new student—"

She scoffs at the word, and it feels like a needle pressing into my chest.

"—I get an urgent call, stating your credentials have been used to access the next shipment down the elevator?"

A flash of expression, and then her face turns passive again, but there was no mistaking the slack in her jaw or the widening of her eyes. The way her eyebrows flew to her forehead, before coming back down again. "I don't know."

"Interesting," he says. "Because the only way to use those credentials is with your security codes. Except that security feed shows that you were *here* when that call came in. So, if someone used those codes, you're guilty of a serious security violation—"

"I didn't give my codes to anybody," she says, and her face is so earnest that my stomach turns.

"If that's the case, I think you'd better go investigate, don't you?"

"I—"

My brain is finally starting to catch up. Most miners don't have credentials, other than the ones we use to make purchases, linked to a passcode or an instant retinal or thumb scan. But people who work for Engineering—managers, higher-ups—they have multiple redundant security systems to verify what they're accessing. ID cards, passwords, all necessary before they're able to look up certain information, give instructions, or enter secure areas.

I don't know Gyu's password, although I once came out of a bathroom and caught him typing the first letter on his tablet. It looked, maybe, like a "G." Or possibly a "C."

Even if Celeste hasn't given out her code and somebody hacked her, she's still at fault, because it means that she left her key card somewhere it could be cloned.

She presses her lips together. "I'll go figure out what this is all about."

When she leaves, it's like opening the lid on a boiling pot. The pressure, the steam escapes, but the heat is still there. The room is as tense as ever.

Gyu starts. "I'm sorry—"

"A simulation? You really didn't think I could do it." I should watch my mouth—we're still here, deep within the bowels of CPI Engineering, where anybody could overhear us. But just like in the interview room, my world has narrowed down to a point, to this moment and my anger, and there's really no controlling it.

"That's not true," he pleads. "Try to see it from my side, okay? I've never seen you in action, never worked with you before. I wanted to give you the best chance of making it, and I can't help you if I don't know where your strengths and weaknesses are—"

"Maybe I don't *want* your help." Even in this moment, I know it's ridiculous—I can see the logic in his words. How exhausting I'm being—I'm even exhausting *myself*. It feels like I'm running on a giant spinning disk, like one of the ones used to rotate crops across the terminator band, into and out of the light. As if the second I finally made it all the way to the end, it would gyrate just far enough to put me back where I started.

"I know you don't need it. I know you can do this without me. But I really did want to help."

His voice is so soft that I have to stay quiet to hear. Is that honest? Or an emotional tactic, designed to manipulate me?

"You left her here with me. You knew she'd torture me—"

"All I knew is that Celeste was always rated as a very compe- tent instructor, until very recently, when she started to show some signs of stress. They pulled her from her Pomp-training duties at that point and just kept her here in Engineering full-time. But in the entire time I've worked with her, I've never seen her like that."

I scoff, but already, my resolve is breaking, each desperate word like a worm, pushing its way up through dark soil.

"You have to believe me, Young."

Suddenly, I'm too tired to stay angry. Instead, exhaustion rolls through me like a thousand lengths of Cable have wrapped around my ankle and are dragging me down to the moon's core. "Why?" It's not a complete thought. I want to say *why lie to me*, and *why is this happening*, and *why did I ever think I could do this in the first place?*

Instead, he answers the question he hears, the one that proves he doesn't understand me at all. "I think it's because we used to sleep together," he says quietly.

She hates us for sleeping—oh, used to. *Does this mean he doesn't want to sleep with me anymore?*

And then pronouns and tense click into place, as if pulling up a rock to reveal a squiggling mass of worms underneath. He doesn't mean me and him. He means him and *her*.

"You used to sleep with Celeste." I wait. I need to hear him say it, need him to confirm that the cold stake that's driven itself through my chest is real. Because I shouldn't jump to that assumption—

"Yeah," he says, finally, and there's real shame in his voice. "It was a long time ago. She didn't used to be like that."

Before he can say anything else, I'm making my way out the door.

17

I KNOW IT'S wrong to act like this. Gyu's relationship with Celeste likely happened before he even knew I was alive. Still, my legs are speeding toward the exit, towards *out*, towards *escape*, and I don't think I can stop them.

"Young—" he calls after me. "You can't just leave. Don't you realize—"

"I'm sick," I say, and in the narrow hallway, my voice is far too loud. I fake-cough into my fist. "I'm sick and I need to go to Medical."

"Alright," he says, but he steps in and grabs my wrist. I struggle, but he's stronger than me, stronger than Celeste was. "But there's a form we need to fill out in my office first."

I've never hated him more than in this moment. He pulls me forward, his arm held down stiff at his side, so low I have to stoop to keep up. I try to drag my heels until I realize that's just going to send me flying onto my face.

Once I'm in, he shuts the door behind him. And then he slumps against the wall.

"God," he sighs, mostly to himself. "That was fucking close. Young—you can't act like that here. They'll put you in solitary—"

"Maybe I want to be in solitary," I say, even though the thought makes my insides cold. Solitary is rough on anybody, but on someone like me, who already isn't quite sure of what's real, it's an extra-special nightmare. I've only been there once. I made it a circadian before I was having conversations with people I'm only half-sure I was making up.

"You won't be able to become a Pomp—"

"I don't want to do that anymore. Send me to the mines."

"Please, Young. Just *listen* to me for once, and then you can do whatever you want, okay? I'm trying—"

He cuts off, suddenly, and it's the smartest thing he's ever done. If he'd said those next words—*I'm trying to help you*—I'd already be out the door. Still, my wrist is throbbing, a reminder of the eroded trust between us.

Although truthfully, was it there in the first place? For the first time, I feel justified in what I did with the note I stole from his pocket, but it's a hollow satisfaction.

"I didn't set you up. I was suspicious of some of her actions lately, but I thought—" He runs his fingers through his hair. "I thought she was stealing, because some of the resources that have been going down in shipments have been disappearing. And then last shipment, there had been an *extra* item in the cargo. Rocks, if you can believe it. Some big, heavy rocks. I still don't know if it was her or not, although her badge had just been used, and when I got there, there was another big rock. I think she might have an accomplice, but I don't know what their angle is."

I almost laugh. I've never asked Gyu what he did to get himself placed on Hib, but now, I'm sure it was just simple debt-crime. It certainly wasn't theft.

I became a bad thief when my ex, Brin, died. I didn't feel like I cared, but I couldn't seem to stop myself from stealing bigger, bolder things, things I didn't even need. Before that, I was a pretty good thief, but even a bad thief can tell the rocks were a test. They might be trying to figure out how much weight can be slipped down before someone notices, how closely the cargo manifests going *down* the elevator are checked, or how long before an aberration is caught by the system.

It wouldn't be too hard to have an accomplice try to steal the rock sometime after the elevator finally made it back to Ung-Nyeo. And if that person got caught, well, it's just a rock. They're just some kid playing a prank, and certainly not a mastermind that just verified if something the rough size and weight of a large lump of piezanite could be smuggled. It's still a huge risk, because CPI is no doubt wise to that sort of thing, but a crystal that size is enough to buy several lifetimes of secure, easy living in the terminator band. If they didn't get caught, and they didn't set off any alarms, they'd know their plan was tight.

Celeste would know, I think, and I feel a reflexive moment of solidarity for a fellow thief, one so bold as to try to steal something huge right out from under CPI's nose—and then I remember who she is, and what she did to me, and I hate myself almost as much as I hate her.

Gyu takes my hands so gingerly that his touch doesn't aggravate my already bruising wrist. "Young, you have to understand—I *never* in a million years thought she'd do something like that. And if you had told me that Celeste would be so petty as to bully someone I was in a relationship with, I'd never have believed them."

For a second, it's just white noise—until I hear *a relationship*. And then I hate myself ferociously for letting my thoughts get trapped by a single, stupid word. This isn't a *relationship*. We're just fucking around, and he—

He put a lot on the line, trying to get me back into Pomp training. I can hate him as much as I want, but that part is true. "So," I say, keeping my voice gruff. "What now?"

He nods. "It's up to you, Young. If you want, I will try to go after her for attacking you—what she did doesn't break any specific policy, but given the aberrations we're already finding with her credential use, anything else is fuel for the fire. She'll most likely be punished, but—"

"But?" I want to hit him for even *thinking* she should be offered any kind of leniency. I almost *killed myself* because of her—

"But she'll drag our relationship out into the light, and in order to keep everybody satisfied, we'll probably have to end it. I might be able to convince somebody to do me a favor, and continue your Pomp training, but I can't promise that." He puts his head in his hands. "Actually, no. I need to be honest with you. I can try, but nobody is going to agree to that. So, if you do pursue her, I will support you, but for Pomp training, it will be the end of the line."

"So those are my options."

He nods. "Unless you can think of any others. I can try, too. We can give it some time."

I swallow. Something's nagging at me like a loose tooth, but it isn't until I glance around the room and see the headset that I realize what he's asking me to decide.

On one hand is Celeste. The way she tortured me, broke me down until I was a mess. There's Gyu's betrayal, too, of leaving me alone with her.

But in the other hand is my way out. The future that Gyu talked about with me—even if I am not sure I want it, I don't want someone *else* to make my choice for me.

And pointing down over all of it, like a giant sword suspended from the ceiling, is my performance today. The way I found my groove, only to choke at the end for the second time. There's the explosion, proceeded by a vision of two tunnels and an ass-load of piezanite. The fact that I still don't know whether what I saw in the tunnels before Adda's death was real or not.

I don't know how I'm supposed to decide. "If I choose not to go after her, what happens next?"

He nods, quick, almost eager. Like he's *hoping*—and his hope is a crushing weight in my chest. "Okay. I think—Young, the truth is you're amazing. I think you can do this job. But I don't want to put you in a live-fire situation right away. Not after that—at least, not alone."

He swallows, nods. He's working himself up to something, pushing through his own fear. It's almost comical. What's he afraid of?

"So, here's what I came up with. It's…it's only if you want to do it, okay? It's just one idea, but I had to get clearance to see if it was even possible, which is one reason I was gone so long—"

"Spit it out."

He bites his lip. "I was thinking that we could start live next shift, but as a team. Like, instead of just a final test, we can do it—" He groans. "I'm fucking this all up. I mean I'll be there, but just for emotional support or in case you feel stuck and want to run stuff by me. Other than that, I'd stay in the background. And it would just be for a little bit, to prove to CPI that—"

"You mean you'd babysit me," I say, the words bitter in my mouth.

His face crumples. "It's a compromise. It's just one idea. I'm open to anything—but I know CPI is open to this idea, too. We've talked about how the current Pomp education model might be missing really promising candidates, because not everybody flourishes in that kind of environment, and…"

His words peter out. I guess he can tell I'm not listening to him anymore.

I don't think about the future. The house somewhere on the outskirts of the terminator band, an apartment in Li'Airet. Instead, I'm thinking about the next shift. About what just happened. About what I can live with, what I can get through—because thinking farther than that tends to lead me down dark roads, and I can't do that right now. "So I go home, go to bed, come back freshly rested. What should I expect when I come back?"

"The new location will be familiar. The data from the simulation—it's real data from a projected site that CPI has been itching to get started on. I fed in all the readings we had. I thought it might, um, give you an edge." He rubs the back of his neck, clearly hoping that I don't connect the dots—that *edge* here could easily be interpreted as *crutch*.

"And the people?"

"We'd move into position in your planned team. It's actually the same team you were going to be assigned to as a miner, we've just subbed one person out to take your place.

We thought it would be best for you to be working with a new team, because sometimes the dynamics—"

I hold up a hand. I know what he's talking about. When everybody is new, it's actually easier on the Pomp. Everybody is still feeling each other out, giving each other a chance to make an impression. If a team loses only their Pomp, there can be a lot of hostility against the replacement.

And a newly-formed team is also less likely to gossip or share observations—which means it would take them longer to put together the pieces and figure out who I am.

"Do I have to answer you right now?"

His jaw is stiff, but he shakes his head. "No...we could push it a little while, maybe—but I need to know long enough before the next shift starts that I can get everything processed."

"Okay," I say, "but I would like to go home now."

He lets out a stiff sigh. "The shift's almost over. Can you wait just a few—"

"No."

"Right." He swallows. "It would make my job a lot easier if you stopped at Medical later and just made up some kind of illness—maybe the stomach flu or something. I'll reimburse you for any fees—"

"Yeah," I say. "I can do that." I won't.

He hasn't actually given me permission to leave yet, but I do, because I know he isn't going to stop me.

WHEN I MAKE it home, I pause for a second outside the door, but of course, Gyu isn't here. There's no way for him to beat me home—and I doubt he'd come here anyways, not after the shift we just had.

I push in the door. A rat runs out, and I jump backward— how the fuck a rat got up the elevator, I have no idea, but it raises its lips and hisses at me, and as disgusted as I am, I'm also kind of impressed. It somehow survived the trip up, made it through Hib station, and into my shit.

It scampers off. I turn to go inside, but then I freeze. It looks like a windstorm has hit my room.

Everything is in disarray. Drawers are pulled out and thrown aside, the contents dumped out and pawed through. The mattress is off the bed and leaning against the wall, a huge rip in the side. Every cabinet is open, every one of Gyu's books off the bookshelf and piled in a messy heap on the floor. There are exploded packages of instant noodles everywhere, their contents crumbled and scattered on the ground. Even the refrigerator, empty though it was, wasn't safe. Except for when Gyu makes food, I've never seen it open.

I walk over, close its door. The panel dings to notify me that I've been charged for its use, and that chime finally penetrates my mind, restarts my thoughts: *Someone had been here.*

It feels like my unknown visitor stripped me naked and ran their hands all over my body. I've never felt as safe in my lodgings as I did, say, in the hatch—but it was still something. It was mine, and it has been violated.

I don't know where to start. There's no obvious place, no thread to pull that will unravel this mess. Eventually, I pick up the books that Gyu has loaned me and put them back on the shelf. It takes a lot of stooping to get them all up. Half the covers are bent, including the book about the ghosthook girl, which causes me a pang of guilt.

I work on the drawers next. I find the letter with my new crew assignment—*my* new crew, if I choose to take the job— and pick it up to put it on the drawer, but I stop when I see what was underneath.

Adda's funeral invitation. It's been torn in half.

It could have been an accident; everything in here is just strewn around. But it feels personal, deliberate, because she was my Fore. Because Adda was ten times the woman I'll ever be, and some idiot Pomp made a bad call and blew her sky high, and I gave up the one chance I had to prevent it from happening by oversleeping.

It's too much. I sit down on the bed, curl into a ball—and it's not until then, Adda's invitation slowly crumpling in my fist, that I realize I have no idea who did this, or why. Who would hate me this much, to devote this much time to taking my whole life apart?

Gooseflesh pops on the back of my neck. *Celeste.* Who else? After what she did to me today—and then her getting caught by Gyu? Jealous because Gyu left her, she came to my house. And the explanation feels as full of holes as gauze, but it's the only one I can come up with.

And finally, *finally*, a ball of anger grows in my stomach, pushing its way through my organs. Because no matter how pissed she was, she had no right to do *this*. This was my space. This was mine, and she came into the place I eat, the place I *sleep*, and turned it all upside down.

Fuck her. I'm going to report this. I'm going to let Station Enforcement take her down and stick her in solitary for this, for what she's done to me—

And then what? And then it'll be my word against hers. And Gyu and I will definitely be over, regardless of if I want that or not. People will dredge my suicide attempt to the surface like a body hidden in bottom-sludge.

And then I won't become a Pomp, and I'll never find out if the shit I saw in the tunnel that day was real.

And *that's* the key to this. The key to everything.

I look around for the letter, wading through the ocean of trash, before remembering I put it on the drawer. I pull my assignment out of the envelope for the first time. There it is, the list of my new crew members—at least, all of them except for one, the one that they will sub in for me.

At the bottom is the location. It's just like Gyu said: a newly discovered vein of Cable that CPI wants us to start with. Coordinates, including depth. Judging by the prefixes, the site isn't connected to the primary mine, but instead, some auxiliary one I've never been to.

It feels like a new beginning, like those few moments where the wind that always wails outside of the wind-walls of the terminator band suddenly dies, and then everyone inside cracks a smile to say, *Ung-Nyeo had to take a breath.*

When you sing, you find ways to hide the breath. Slip it into natural pauses or at the end of phrases. But that's not what I want. I want to breathe fire.

I'm not going to let Celeste take this from me. Not the Pomp training, not Gyu, not my chance to get off of Hib.

I've crumpled the letter. I smooth it out again and make another note of the coordinates.

Before I do anything else, I'm going to find out if what I saw was real.

18

I TRY TO run through a plan, but it's useless. All I have is a mixed bag of things I know and things I need to know, and no pieces fit with the others. Everything hangs on if I can see something outside of the new mine location, and if it mirrors what the crew comes across when they're live with me and Gyu.

I feel like the penultimate player at a table, waiting for my final opponent to reveal their hand.

And I probably won't even be able to get into the tunnel. CPI is a massive, multifaceted machine, dedicated to extracting the most precious material in the world. They've got security—and even if they didn't, I know from experience it's *this* kind of sloppy impulse that gets a person caught, a big-ass jewel in your hand, before being deported to the moon.

I can't afford to make that mistake again. And my need for this makes it dangerous. As a thief, you're never safe, but it's when you're too invested to walk away that you run the worst risks.

From the coordinates, I can tell it will take me half the time I have before my next shift just to get there and back. I'll be dead on my feet during my first live Pomp experience.

I'll let future Young handle that.

I'm almost out the door before I remember Gyu. He *probably* won't come, but I can't be sure. And if he sees the place destroyed, he won't suspect an intruder. He'll think I've done something crazy.

It takes me a little bit of searching under various piles before I find a scrap of paper wrapper large enough to write on. I fold it in half and scrawl a message on the outside in big, bold letters:

GYU.

On the inside, I write:

> *I've got a headache. Please don't wake me, because I took a sedative and I need the rest. I'll take the sign down if I wake up.*

I put on a two-gloved Annie, scorch marks and all, and slip out the door, shoving the note into the crack so it sticks out like a flag. Then, I wing it through Hib station until I get to the outer edge of Leisure. There's a kiosk for personal vehicle rentals, and although I've never gotten one, I've seen it done, and even rode on one once. My class, newly arrived and flush with freedom, had been more than ready for a drink and a joyride.

I cue up the cheapest model available. The price—five thousand credits a quarter circadian—is staggering. By the time I make it back, it'll be four weeks on my sentence, if not more.

But there's the crew tomorrow. Five human lives, each one inextricably tied to another crew: four dead people who no longer have the chance to earn off their debts.

I hit accept. The machine asks for my pass code to confirm—no chance of claiming you hit the wrong button by mistake—and I hesitate before entering it.

I go back to the options. Add a navigation unit, cycle through, and this time, I put my code in.

The doors on the machine open. A low shelf slides out with the vehicle on it. The hov's bottom is a giant, inflated tube, like a big rubber boat. There's a fan underneath that drives air downward, which makes it float off the ground. Another giant fan on the back provides propulsion. It's the best way to get over the shifting landscape of the dunes.

Once I make it out the dome-lock and into the darkness, I idle in place so I can get situated for the ride. I cue in the coordinates on the craft's autopilot before pulling the wire that will disable Annie's locator beacon. Hopefully, if Gyu stops by and realizes I'm gone, having to track the craft instead of my suit will buy me a little extra time. I don't want to be interrupted before I figure this out.

Once I'm certain I'm ready—oxygen levels double-checked, destination correct—I open up the throttle. The hov roars to life, throwing me backward with the force of its movement and kicking up a monster cloud of sand. Every part of me vibrates. I pull away from the station without looking back.

I give Annie the command to turn down the background noise, but I don't switch on my headlamp. The clouds are heavy right now, but the smokelike hints of light diffusing through their joints tells me that somewhere buried behind them is Ung-Nyeo's light side, shining like a star, giving me just enough light to make out the undulating shapes of shadows within the constant fog-cloud of sand being kicked up around me. It's still flat, but before long, the surface will break into soft dunes. After that, it could be anything from rocky chasms and craters to small, jagged peaks—but though I should keep an eye on the terrain, especially with no lamp on, my gaze is drawn upward.

Right now, my parents are there, somewhere, making a meal or tucked against each other in sleep. Maybe they have another child, one they didn't abandon. One who isn't falling in with the wrong people and fucking up so much Enforcement takes them away.

I'm terrified of where I'm going, of what I'll find when I get there, but I'm also exhausted.

I can't tell how much time passes before the craft decelerates.

THE VEHICLE SLOWS to a stop. "Annie, headlamp."

The beam flicks on. I scour the sand for the entrance. As a new auxiliary mine opening, it won't be as obvious as the well-established one I use for my normal daily shifts—a massive portal surrounded by tracks from the over-surface shuttle treads, the rapid change in grade that leads down to the descent tram—but a mine entrance has to have *some* infrastructure to keep it stable and secure. I should be able to spot it easily, but my headlamp doesn't catch anything but sand dunes.

I can't use my helmet navigation, because I disabled Annie's locator beacon, so I pull the coordinates from the assignment letter up on the hov's autonav screen instead. The map glows green as I zoom in as far as I can. In the corner sits a little Y-shaped symbol, marking the structure that stabilizes the tunnel opening—far enough away that in the dark, wandering through the sand, I would have never found it by random chance.

I shut off my head lamp and kill the craft's engines. The fans die, and the giant rubber barge sinks into the ground. I've gotten lucky, for once—the clouds aren't as compact here, and once my eyes adjust, there's a thin trickle of light that bounces off the soft dunes. It's just enough to proceed forward without stumbling.

Annie is still blocking background noise, so my footsteps are perfectly silent, my thoughts too loud. Is this what it's like to be ejected into space, seconds before your organs fly out in explosive decompression?

I tell Annie to turn atmospheric sounds back up to normal levels. I pick up speed while trying not to bounce. After a bit, I think I've meandered off in the wrong direction—but then I catch a gleam of thin light playing off the metal of entry doors and an entrance's stabilizer frame. There's something else, too, something that glows red.

By the time I can make out the security devices that have been set up around the entrance, I'm out of breath. The locks are engaged, the word ARMED written up at the top in bright red. There are also a number of small, squat machines that sit around the stabilizer. I'm not sure, but I think they're used for invisible laser perimeters—usually connected to some kind of security system.

In other words, I'm not getting in this way. And while I don't see a guard, that doesn't mean one isn't waiting somewhere right inside the entrance. Suicides on Hib aren't uncommon—but every so often, people decide that they want their death to burn a giant hole into CPI's pocket, and they try to take part of a mining vein with them.

I could have gone out that way, maybe. Then again, I almost did—it just wasn't my intention.

A memory of the smell hits me: the burnt chemical tang, hot rock and cooking flesh. It's like I'm there again: on the border of the collapsing tunnel, Adda and the crew inside, the roar of the explosion rattling inside of my helmet.

I'm suddenly on my knees, doubled over and gasping, the fans in my suit kicking on as sweat prickles cold all over my body. I fight the urge to rip my helmet off and take great sucking gasps of the thin atmosphere.

A minute goes by, maybe, before I'm calm enough to stand again. And with it comes the realization that this plan—stealing out to an auxiliary entrance in the middle of the night when all my shit is strewn around my house like garbage? To what? See if my "visions" in the tunnel were real? Even if they *were*, this is idiocy.

I turn around and hike toward the hov. I'm climbing on before Celeste suddenly appears in the back of my mind like a specter, only doubled into twins. On my left, she's as she was when I first saw her behind the desk: the nice clothes, a cloud of hair floating around her head like a halo. On my right is her as Instructor, the reflective display of her Pomp visor showing me only my own scared face as she barked orders at me. I am suddenly *one hundred* percent certain that my place is trashed because of her. That I failed out of Pomp training because of her.

And whether this plan is idiocy or not, I *can't* let her *win*.

But what are my options? I take a few deep breaths, close my eyes as I try to figure something out. I can't approach the mine entrance, that's for sure. Any other entrances that speckle Hib's surface are likely guarded the same way.

I sit down on the ground and close my eyes. Even if the vision in the tunnel was real—if there's some kind of essential instinct that I was tapping into that let me see the Cable—I don't know *how* I did it.

But a good first step is probably getting *closer*, right? I hesitate for a moment, but then I turn around and walk back until I'm just right outside of the entrance, a stone's throw from the perimeter. It's a little too near for comfort, though, so I back up a few steps until I'm tucked behind a tallish dune, and then I sit down and close my eyes again.

I feel oddly exposed, like I'm being watched—but when I open my eyes, there's just the semi-darkness. I try to ignore the feeling and sink into the sounds of my breath in my helmet, the echoes of the waves in my ears.

After a while, I think I catch something—a quick flicker— but it disappears. I wait, and I wait, but it doesn't come back.

Shit. Shit, shit, shit. Of course nothing is happening. Did I really think I was some kind of chosen one? That after a lifetime of being a complete fuckup—that I was just going to, what? Prove everybody wrong?

I crawl to my feet and imagine going back, getting drunk. Maybe I'll have a big, screaming fight with Gyu. Throw him out and revel in that white-hot moment of power, before the darkness sucks me back in. Maybe I can figure out where the drugs are on this forsaken mess of a moon.

I lose my shit. I repeatedly stomp on the ground, as if some-how, the puny force of my legs could reach all of the way down through the crust-rock and the silvery veins of Cable, down to the little pieces of piezanite within, compressing them with such fury that everything starts to explode at once—

My foot doesn't land right—the ground isn't where I think it's going to be—and there's a white-hot flash of pain in my ankle, so intense that I overbalance and fall, my face knocking into my helmet.

Fuck. I hope my ankle's not broken. I crawl up, try to stand, but it's too painful to put any weight on it.

What the hell just happened? I turn on my headlamp. The sand looks—like sand, like it always does, smooth, softly undulating. I brush it aside and dig with my hands.

A few breaths later, I've uncovered something strange. I don't know what to make of it.

The sand is shallow here, and somebody has cut a hole in the crust-rock: a perfect square, each side about the length of my forearm. I dig the sand out, the sensation muffled by my gloves.

Eventually, the hole's as deep as my arm. I can't reach any farther. Just as I decide to get up, my gloves rub up against something hard and flat, right at the end.

I shine my beam down. Half buried in the sand, a matte, silvery square flickers in the light. A vein of Cable. I've never seen one run up so close to the surface.

I lean back to sit on my ass, hissing as the movement puts pressure on my forgotten ankle. It must be some kind of survey hole. Someone cut through the rock, likely to insert an instrument, and discovered this band of Cable, and that's why they put the auxiliary mine entrance nearby.

I've got to leave soon if I don't want to be late for my first shift with Gyu, but there's literally a vein of Cable right under me. I close my eyes and try to picture the vein, try to evoke what I felt the day Adda asked us to vote, but nothing happens.

Then the memory comes to me: my glove fraying away into dust.

It's dangerous to take safety equipment off up here. Besides the poisonous atmosphere, people say there's a lot more radiation at surface level. But cancer seems very far away, whereas tomorrow is right on top of me.

I pull off my glove. Unwrap my arm, the bandages peeling off like a scarf unraveling. I lie on my belly and roll halfway onto my side, before extending my arm as far as I can down the hole. The air's impossibly cold, a biting chill that I know I won't be able to stand for long, but I stretch down to make contact with the vein—

And in an instant, everything changes.

My vision swims. Heat races through my arm. The blowers in my suit go full throttle before their sound fades away as an empty space opens up in my head. I drop down into the tunnel, run through the vein like I've been caught in a fast river and it's dragging me with it. Forks of Cable break apart in front of me—up, down, this way and that. They climb and fall, bend and straighten, and as I go flying past, I'm aware of the piezanite, each chunk as bright as a teardrop made of white fire, each singing with a voice as distinct as a face. I can see the places where the crust-rock runs thin, fractures spreading as the song of the Cable seeps out.

I don't direct the flow. Instead, it's like the Cable is deciding what it wants to show me. Where it wants me to go. And when I feel like I can't stomach any more, when my head is churning and my ears are ringing and it feels like the body I have left might melt into waste and seep into the very sand itself, the Cable pushes back and throws me out.

It's everything I can do to pull my arm out of the hole, to roll onto my other side. I feel like someone has opened me up and drained out my blood, removed my organs and replaced them with wax. My arm aches, my ears ring, and my head is on fire.

But my heart is singing, my face covered in tears.

SOME TIME GOES by before I crawl to my knees and push the sand back in the hole. I feel drunk, losing and finding my thoughts in waves. At first, I think my headlamp is flickering— but then I realize the flashes are me blinking, that my eyelids are moving so slowly, my brain can't process the change.

I wrap my arm as best I can and put on my glove. I crawl into the hov and set the path back to the Hib station before engaging the throttle. It's not until I don't hear the blowers kick on that I realize I've gone deaf—but my ears are ringing, and already, hints of sound are sneaking in.

The hov takes off, everything shifting and sliding below me, a raft that bears me back to life.

I did it. It's real.

There's another thought, one so new it's foreign, so delicious that it unmakes me. I am *special.* I can do something I've never heard of. It doesn't matter how messed up I am, how badly I'm fucking up with Gyu, how much Celeste and everyone else on Hib station hates me. I can do this job better than anybody else on Hib, because I have an ability that nobody else has.

And what happened to Adda, Kola, Oye, and Stomp, never has to happen to anyone else, ever again.

And as soon as I have that realization, I'm asleep.

WITH THE HOV bouncing so hard underneath me, it's no surprise that in my dreams, I'm floating. *A boat.*

But when I look down, I'm greeted by a vision—not of wooden planks and rope or of steel and rivets, but instead of gray-blue flesh. A gleaming creature, as slick and wet as a peeled grape, so massive that it forms its own island beneath me.

We're facing each other, this creature and me. I could reach down and lay a hand on the giant, black-pupiled eye.

I should be afraid, but I can sense the intelligence of the behemoth beneath me, the quiet in its soul. It fills me with a rare peace, to be here in its presence—the knowledge of my smallness in the universe epitomized in a functioning monument of muscle and bone and brain and lungs.

The creature's thoughts rain over me like the fat, warm drops of a wind-wall storm.

Do you know what the word "circadian" means?

I nod, but the creature laughs at me, as if I've just told a joke.

Would you like to dance?

I would like to, and somehow, the creature knows it, and its flesh rumbles underneath my feet.

Up, I am pushed *up*, up toward a brilliant sun that is no longer burnt orange, but instead, a piercing yellow-white. It flourishes with the light of a thousand fires, and when I look down, there are holes in my vision, as if part of my gaze has been burned away in a flare of religious glory.

The creature shifts again. We start to spin—a leap, as it pirouettes like a dancer, mist glistening off its great bulk as it rises sparkling toward the sun.

IT'S THE FEELING of deceleration that awakens me. I can't separate the hov's movement from the creature's revolving dance, and for a moment, I'm stuck lying on my back, a foot in two different worlds.

My eyes open to a darkness that is already brightening into dim. I sit up, and Hib's colony bubble rises on the horizon, a brilliant spot that is the fragile ghost of the sun in my dream.

Already, I can tell the nap did me a world of good. I shake my head, content in the sounds of my breath inside of my helmet—I can hear again. My head no longer swims, and my sense of *up* remains steadfastly lashed to the dark sky above me. My arm still aches, though. It feels strangely heavy, almost like it's fallen asleep.

And then, we're outside of the dome-lock. I set the hov into neutral and try to stand. The instant my foot hits the deck, I'm slapped by a pain so thick and deep that the utter *wrongness* of it makes me want to hurl over the side of the craft.

I hadn't noticed the bulge in the dark—but here, in the reflection of Hib's colony lights, there's a warp to the shine of Annie's skin over my leg. My ankle is so swollen, it's literally pressing out on the rubber.

Fuck. I hope it isn't broken. And I've still got to get the hov back.

It's an absolute bitch, shoving the hov while hopping on one leg, but I somehow manage to get it to the kiosk. Annie's blowers are going full bore, but I'm still drenched in sweat.

The machine receives it and asks me if I want to know my balance.

I select *no*.

And then I continue, hopping on one foot down Hib's spokes. And although I *see* the other miners around me, it feels like they're not really there—like I'm prowling through a ghost-town, aware for the first time of the passing of the spirits around me.

When I make it back to my door, I have to pause. I know what I'm going to see when I open it, the violence contained inside, tainting everything I own.

But there's nowhere else for me to go, and more than that, I'm fucking tired—so I shove it open. Strip off Annie, put her in the cleaning unit.

For one dark moment, I consider tidying. Everything's a mess except for the books, neatly filed on the shelves, the little hole in front of the desk, and the reassignment letter that sits on top.

Fuck it.

I crawl into bed.

19

AT THE SOUND of the door opening, I sit bolt upright.

It's got to be Celeste, back to fuck me up, because tossing my place wasn't enough—

The light flicks on. It's Gyu.

"Holy fuck." I flop backward onto the bed, jostling my ankle that aches with the threat of more pain to come. There's a little hammer tap-tap-tapping behind my forehead.

The sterile light chases back the shadows in the room and tries to bleach out the memory of my trip to the mine entrance, but it can't fight through the wall of my exhaustion. Now that the eminent threat of being stabbed in my own bed by Celeste is gone, I'm just too tired to give a shit.

"I'm sor…" His words die as he looks around the room, at the piles everywhere. "*Young.* What the fuck happened here?"

I swallow as my gaze follows his. When I was little, I played with a statue in a market and broke it. I shoved it behind a basket before my mother could see, but in my guilt, the sweep of her gaze emanated the heat of a roaring fire. This feels almost exactly like that, me silently urging his eyes to pivot away.

Just like then, I cough and offer a sorry excuse. "I lost something. I had to find it."

His eyebrows draw together. "Young…are you in trouble? You know you can tell me if you are, right? You can trust me."

He comes up to the bed. His expression is so concerned, so tender, that it single-handedly builds a bridge between us.

I want to reach out for his face and tell him my triumphs in stunning detail. The strange hole I found and the way I journeyed down it, through the Cable, dizzyingly mapping my way through everything below.

He takes another step, his gaze darting like a nervous mosquito from my arm, to my face, to my ankle. The edge of the bed sheet has ridden up, and it looks like there's a purple fruit attached to the end of my leg. My foot is twice the size of the other one.

He scans the piles of my things, all of it torn and thrown about—

A flash of a room, the walls scribbled on in lip paint, Mx. Ya's family portrait upside down, a pillow stuffed in the oven—

I suddenly see myself the way he must see me, right here, right now. Like the sick child my parents ran to the hospital, too frantic to even shut the front door.

I look down at myself. At the dirt and sand all over me—I was too tired to get cleaned up, although I sorely regret that now. I look like I've been digging graves—no, like I've just crawled out of one.

"Young. I just need to know. Are you really okay? I know yesterday was a lot—"

His voice fades to a buzz. There's a question hidden under his question, a benign and yet painful suspicion under his concern. He wants to know if I'm about to hurt myself. And held up to the lens of his scrutiny, of his compassion, of his worry, I have to wonder—*did any of that happen? Maybe I got out there in the hov, in the sand—but what really transpired when I stuck my arm down that hole?*

All of the joy, the raging triumph that buoyed me through the journey home, through my fantastic dreams of dancing with sea creatures and a brilliant sun—it all turns to ash in my mouth. Because none of it can be shared. Even if he would believe me—and he wouldn't, he *shouldn't*—it's a risk. If he thinks I'm weird now, what is he going to think when he figures out what I can do?

And more than that—what will CPI do?

I see myself in a laboratory, shackled to a cold table, my abdomen open as they pull out my organs. It's not a pleasant experience.

"I know how this looks," I finally say, because the first part of convincing someone you aren't crazy is admitting that you look crazy. You have to validate their assessment of you. "I was so upset yesterday, after what happened with Celeste—and then I realized I'd lost something important."

"Lost what?"

The charm burns against my chest, an obvious answer. "Something my parents gave me."

It's a lie, of course. The charm's right there. And yet, somehow it isn't a lie.

"Oh," he says. His face relaxes the tiniest bit—he's still guarded, but he's willing, practically begging me to make this entire scenario make sense. To make this all okay. "And your headache?"

The note for Gyu I stashed in the door, like a flag. Fuck. It wasn't there when I got back.

I clear my throat, buying some time. "I think that whatever I took really knocked me out. I just feel like shit, you know? I have a bad reaction to a lot of drugs."

"Did you—" He holds his breath, lets it out. "Did you have anything to drink?"

It hurts so much I can't answer, at first, and his face falls with disappointment at my silence.

"No," I finally say, my voice hoarse. "I didn't. You can test me if you don't believe me." Even as the words come out of my mouth, I'm suddenly terrified, because I've bluffed without meaning to. There was no sedative, and if he tests my blood, he's going to catch me in a lie.

"I'm not going to *test* you, Young. I trust you." But his voice is thin, almost reedy.

The second rule to convincing people you aren't crazy is to martyr yourself with righteous indignation at some small detail, one that you can pull apart, thereby making them doubt the fabric of their whole experience. There's a brutal sort of irony in it. "You should test me anyways," I say. "I don't have anything to hide."

He wavers, and for a second, I panic again, but he shakes his head.

When I look up again, he's gotten closer. He reaches out slowly, tentatively. He's afraid of getting bitten.

When he embraces me, I don't lean into it, but I don't lean away, either. This isn't to comfort me—this is the cautious moment of poking your fingers toward a ghost, waiting for them to slide through. I have to convince him that I am real, and solid, and so I wait, straight without being stiff, while he strokes my hair. I can't help the way he puts the fires out under my skin, one by one. I can't help but feel, despite the mess between us, that it's nice that he's here—

And that thought ruins the moment. "Why are you here?"

He bites his bottom lip.

The third rule to convincing people that you aren't crazy is to go on the defensive. In this case, his appearance isn't truly rational—most of the things that people do aren't. There's always some chink in the armor.

"You never told me about your decision. I thought I should just let it go, maybe—not push you, but..." He takes in a breath of air, deflating as he lets it out. I can almost see the fog of stress blow off him. "I wanted to try to convince you that you should take the job, because—"

"I'll do it. I'll take the job. Even with the babysitting."

His eyes widen. He'd expected a fight.

I shouldn't have acquiesced so soon. It's suspicious. "I just— you're right about everything. And maybe it would be good to have someone looking over my shoulder for the first few weeks." That last bit is a thorn in my heart, but I ignore it. It doesn't matter if he's there or not, because the truth is that I *can* do this. That I have the ability to reach down into the veins of Cable and pull out their secrets.

Either that, or I've cracked completely, and none of this matters, anyways.

"Okay," he says. "Well—our shift is going to start soon. I'll go first, and you can get cleaned up and meet me there."

His blank expression throws me. Shouldn't he be happy? Isn't this what he wanted?

And then I see the room again as he sees it, and the thorn pierces a little deeper. Of course. He's worried about me, and that's sapped the joy out of my acquiescence.

It hurts to swallow. I know, all too well, the feeling of getting something you longed after—only to find out it was poisoned the whole time.

Before he makes it through the door, I'm on my feet. The sudden pressure on my ankle feels like a gunshot, so painful I have to gasp as tears mist my vision.

He turns, and his eyes are so morose that I want to rip them out of his head. Anything to stop him from looking at me like that.

"Gyu," I say. "Come here."

He approaches slowly, but I limp back over to the bed.

"Ung-Nyeo's piss, your ankle—" he says, but by then, I've already pressed my hands into his thighs, letting my weight fall hard enough to throw him back onto the bed. The jostle is like a fire in my ankle, but there's one starting in my belly, and I can't feed one without feeding the other, so I just try my best to ignore it.

I crush my lips into his neck, as if I could drink away his fear and his grief. "I know how all this looks. I had a really, really rough time after the shift—"

He gasps as I make my way to his earlobe. He's still not moving, still a prey animal held in the gaze of a predator, but next to my hand, I can feel him stiffening.

"—and I lost it for just a little while, but I needed that. Needed to lose it, to *grieve*—" My hand finds the hardness against his thigh, and he gasps again. "—to be okay with making this decision. Please tell me you can understand—"

And then it's like the fuse has been lit, like the flare is red and spinning down the shaft—once thrown, it can only go down, lost to us now and forever. He surges back over me, tenderly maneuvers me against the bed. His face is so hot his cheeks look like twin suns, redness trailing down his jaws, his neck. I sit up enough to bite at it, and the growl that rumbles out from his belly sets my insides quivering in response.

"I understand you," he says, a gasp that ends in a moan, like an ecstatic prayer. "But we don't have a lot of time—"

"We can be quick." I won't be defied. Not now. The spinning, the loss of control, the searching, fearful glances he's given me since arriving—I'm going to burn them all away. This is ground I know. This is ground I *understand*.

And there is nothing like it for convincing him that I'm intent on staying alive.

AFTERWARD, GYU DEMANDS I go to Medical to get my ankle looked at before reporting to work. He tells me he'll come up with some excuse. His expression is tight, but before I can ask him how he's feeling, he's gone.

I clean myself up, get dressed, and set out. As I peel through the spokes, there's something tense in that final moment with Gyu that unravels me, a victory slipping out from between my fingers.

I try to tease it out, but it feels like a loose tooth, every poke painful and itching. Before long, the world spins, and my ears are ringing again. I feel hot and dizzy and like I might throw up, but I finally know why: It's because I'm using Gyu. I've *been* using him all along, trying to patch over old wounds. I should give up this job. I should let him go, and maybe he can find someone who will treat him better, who can love him in a way that isn't broken.

But I won't. And the finality of that knowledge, it pushes the thorn back through my heart until it pierces through the fleshy walls of each chamber and surges out the bottom.

I need him. I need this job. I need this chance to prove that my parents weren't justified in walking out years ago.

I can do better, I think. *I will do better.*

I push in the door to Medical.

I'M ASSIGNED TO the same officer who treated me after the explosion, but when our eyes meet, I can tell he doesn't recognize me—until he pulls my file up on his tablet and his face goes white. When he speaks, his voice is tight, but perfectly even.

"What do you—"

"I'm here for my ankle," I say. I don't want to make this weird for either of us. I bend my knee to lift my foot, slide up the fabric that has grown tight during the walk. The swelling is getting worse.

"Ah," he says. "This shouldn't take long."

Hib doesn't have access to all of Ung-Nyeo's different medical advancements. If you've got some chronic disease, one where it would cost more to ship up the medication than it would to ship up another one of you, you usually get sent back. And because nobody has heard from anybody that got sent back for medical reasons, people tend to hide shit.

But hiding things doesn't make them go away. If you manage to make it to the end of your sentence, once you're back on Ung-Nyeo, you'll still need the procedure or the medicine or whatever—so you commit another crime, and then you just wind up back here. There's no escape.

I look down at my ankle, and relief whispers through my body. An ankle, even if it is broken, is simple. Orthopedic. Reset the bones, fabricate the splint, inject some cells that will make you heal faster and reknit everything from the inside out. If I were in the mines, I'd be back to digging with a week— limping a bit, most likely, but still productive. At the very least, it isn't something I need to hide.

The scan is over before I realize it. "It's not broken," he says, and he turns his tablet toward me. I can see the bones, gray-white and tightly aligned, like puzzle pieces, but the image doesn't really mean anything more to me than that. "It's just sprained. I think we can just wrap and splint it for now—"

"What about the injection?"

His lips are tight. "We're running low on stock until the next elevator comes up, so we're only supposed to use it for necessary cases. And it looks from your file like you're temporarily assigned to desk duties—"

"Right." He doesn't have to explain anything else. I don't need my ankle to do my new job. CPI has time to wait for it to heal on its own.

"Just stay off of it. No weight through it until it heals."

"Sure," I say.

He's pulling the scan away when I catch something out of the corner of my eye: a white mass at the very top, embedded in a ragged dark patch. It's almost perfectly round, like a pearl. "What's that?" My knowledge of anatomy isn't great, but it just looks—*off*, somehow. Like something that can't naturally exist.

He follows the trajectory of my finger. His eyebrows pull together. "It's an artifact," he says. "Just a mistake of the computer. It isn't really there."

His voice is completely even, but I can feel tension bow-stringing underneath.

"A mistake?"

"We get shitty equipment," he says, and it's almost a joke. Like, of course, Medical gets second-rate everything.

I remember my arm. "I was here before," I say, and he nods, because, of course, he remembers me by now. If he didn't, there's my file in front of him, detailing the explosion—plus the time I spent in Medical before then. "I've been wrapping my arm with the bandages you gave me, but it feels like sometimes the swelling gets worse. This morning, my arm felt really heavy, and the bandages didn't seem to go as far up my arm as—"

"I'll get you more bandages."

"That's not…I mean, it looks like the skin is doing okay. Do I need to keep wrapping it? It seems to help the swelling, but… is the swelling going to go away, or—"

"I can't know anything without doing a scan, and this wouldn't be an authorized usage of one. There's no visible injury this visit."

"What about the scan you did before? When I was here?"

"I didn't scan your arm."

The memory of him rolling the wand over my arm and chest pops into my mind. "I could have sworn—"

He makes a show out of scrolling through the record, clicking on different files and pulling up the notes. Like the reports in the interrogation room after Gyu walked out, I can barely makes sense of them. He leafs through them, quick, but there're no pictures. Just words.

"No scans," he says. "And no authorization for one."

"How do I—"

"Maybe," he says, clearing his throat. "You should wait before pursuing this. They'll bill your account almost forty thousand credits for a scan, and—"

"Ah," I say. I take the bandages he's offering with his other hand. Forty thousand credits is months of service—not worth it unless I'm dying. "Thank you," I say, and I walk out before he can say anything else.

20

WHEN I GET to Engineering, I have to pause outside the door to gird myself before hitting the button—but it's Gyu's voice that answers, not Celeste's. And after the door slides open and I step through the windstorm of the fans, it's clear that the room is empty.

Gyu busts out of the back room. He glances down at my ankle—it's still swollen, but I make a show of it, taking a few steps in a circle as if modeling a new outfit. I try not to let on that it hurts like a bitch. "I'm ready for this."

"Great," he says, although his face doesn't match his voice. He turns to lead me down to his office, where he gets me set up. The silence is uncomfortable, but I don't know how to break it, so I settle into the work instead.

Gyu waits while I cycle through cons. As soon as Jungle flashes over the screen, with its misty, green trees, I feel soothed—but I also want a fresh start. In addition to the imaginary biomes, there are some more realistic ones in the con that reflect the terrain on Ung-Nyeo, and I try those first.

DESERT is impossibly bright, and when I turn down the ambient lighting, it just looks like Hib, so I skip it. ICE is shrouded in darkness, a mess of cold, howling wind—but then I adjust the lighting and the temperature, and the scene that greets me is both completely unexpected and impossibly beautiful.

A sparkling sea of white that glitters like diamonds. The snow's surface is perfectly flat and unbroken. It feels like it would be a good omen.

I glance at Gyu. He hasn't turned his projection on yet. Maybe he really is committed to the idea that this oversight is all for show, a matter of procedure that CPI has decided on. So far, he hasn't given me any guidance and seems content to just watch, so I do my crew review. There's been a change overnight, one of the members subbed out due to an after-hours accident. I read the file, but it all turns to jelly in my nervousness, and when I can't waste any more time with that, I hold my breath and bring up the simulations for the mapped area.

I wish I hadn't turned my visor projection on. It seems impossible to keep my face calm, to hold my expression at a time like this. Almost *everything* on the predictions of the crust-rock stability is exactly the way I saw it when my hand was in the hole. Only a few areas vary slightly, the computer unsure of how much certainty to give individual structural pieces.

Every part of my journey through the veins of Cable is still there in my mind, in almost perfect clarity, ready to be played like a recording. I close my eyes and fly through the veins again, looking for the hot-white explosions that can only be the signature of the piezanite. Last shift, I felt pulled to them, as if by magnetic attraction.

I bring up the crystal prediction overlay. This doesn't match as well, which makes my insides twist a bit, but I concentrate again on keeping my anxiety off of my face.

I make the first call, and the crew gets to work.

THE FIRST HALF of the shift passes in almost perfect synchronicity. I make commands, knowing full well what the outcome is going to be before the action is performed. In a way, I'm just coasting—and without the stress of feeling like this entire endeavor is a house of cards, ready to collapse at a breath in the wrong direction, I suddenly can't help but love what I'm doing. I'm in control.

Every so often, Gyu makes a satisfied *hmmm* next to me. Once, a prediction I verbalize—that despite the grade change anticipated by the computer, the crust-rock is going to only shift slightly, and we should continue digging straight—comes true, and the gasp he makes in our private channel gives me an almost sexual thrill of delight.

I'm in control, and I can do this—at least until about half-way through the shift, right before the meal break. That's when things go sideways, and not in the way I expected.

It starts with something innocuous: a variance in the drill that doesn't make sense until I check the settings through the central console. A warning flashes at the bottom of the screen: LOOSE COUPLING.

By the time Gyu shifts forward, about to give me some direction for the first time, I've already opened the crew communication line—the shared channel between the entire crew, Gyu, and myself. "Hold drilling for a second," I say. Through the drone, I watch and listen as the Fore repeats the command. The crew stops, the roar of the drill suddenly fading to a background throb.

"Standing by for orders," says the Fore.

I swallow. Something feels off. "Equipment check. Check coupling fasteners and report abnormal values."

Each of the four people on the drill check the gauge nearest to them. One by one, four different voices echo through the Pomp drone's acoustic sensors.

"Normal."

"Normal."

"Normal."

And then the back right. "Normal."

Gyu flicks his fingers, opening a private communication channel. "It's probably a false reading. Sometimes the dust from the drill gets into the sensors and messes them up." He says this like I've never worked a drill.

I check the display reading from the sensor again, the words LOOSE COUPLING lit up like a red beacon. After a moment, I bring up another schematic, one that shows the real-time data as it comes in, the variances recorded before the computer does us the favor of interpreting the information into words. Designed to be read by true Engineers, the numbers are as meaningless to me as any other Pomp, but I can sort of grasp the shape that all the data together forms. The back of my neck tingles.

"Requesting secondary visual confirmation from the Fore," I say.

Next to me, Gyu stiffens, a movement that is mirrored by the entire crew in front of me, Fore included. Gyu flicks his fingers together, opening a line of communication between the two of us. "You should be careful," he murmurs. "You don't want them to feel like you don't trust—"

"Please reply," I say in the crew channel.

After a few moments, the Fore nods. "Order received." She turns to look at her crew and shrug, as if to say, *Well, this Pomp's an asshole, what are you going to do?* After another moment, she walks over to the drill, and checks each of the couplings herself in turn.

When she gets to the back right, she freezes. She reaches out, her body blocking my view of her fingers—but then the message on the bottom of the screen, LOOSE COUPLING, turns bright green before disappearing.

"What happened?" I say into the crew channel.

"Nothing," said the Fore. "I just jostled it for a second, but the reading looked good. Maybe there's some dirt in the sensor."

"I see," I say.

Her voice was normal—no tightness in it at all, and it takes me a moment before I realize how much that bothers me. There should be *something* there, some minor emotion trembling under the surface—annoyance. Frustration. Worry. Unless she's trying to hide something.

But that sounds crazy, too. And it's clear Gyu doesn't see that there's anything wrong with this picture.

Even so, I briefly debate asking Gyu about the procedure to discipline her. One of her crew members got sloppy, and by covering it up, she runs the risk of encouraging further safety issues down the line. At the same time, so much of crew management—especially in the early stages, before everybody is woven together enough to know each other's strengths and weaknesses—comes down to trust. There might not have been any reason for the Fore to think that this particular individual wasn't as detail-oriented as they need to be for everybody to stay safe. If she's a good Fore, she deserves the chance to rectify this on her own, her own way, behind closed doors—to manage her own crew.

I'll have to keep a close eye on them, but that doesn't mean I have to do anything now. And everybody is waiting for my next order. "Everything looks fine up here now. Go ahead and resume positions on the drill."

They spring back to work, happy to be done with this moment. From the way he gestures, accessing something in his interface, Gyu is too—at least, he's no longer paying attention.

I take a second and check the back-right crew member's file. Her name is Na, but besides being new to the crew, there's nothing interesting about her, and no reason to indicate a reason for lying about the coupling. And the Fore's explanation—dirt in the sensor—isn't an uncommon reason for an odd reading.

I sigh and rub my eyes. It's going to be a long shift.

WHEN IT COMES time for a break, Gyu leads me to a small room a few doors down. It's not a real lunchroom, but it does have a table and chairs in it.

I pick a chair. I've been standing still all day, and it makes my body stiff in ways the drill never did. Gyu disappears to get his lunch.

I didn't bring a lunch. I'm not even hungry.

But then Gyu comes back, visor flipped up, and sets a covered bowl on the table. He opens it and sits across from me.

It smells divine, and at once, my mouth starts to water. "Is this for me? What about your—"

He puts a second, identical bowl on the table and smiles before leaning back in his seat.

I don't need a second invitation. I dip a spoon into the soup before sipping at the hot broth. It's wonderful—spicy, salty, with the deep tang of soybean paste. The soup is swimming in actual fresh vegetables, each one laboriously grown under dark-light lamps to induce them to flower and fruit. "This must have cost a fortune."

"I wanted to get you a present. To say congratulations. And by the way, you're doing an amazing job. You realized that the crust-rock in that tunnel would become unstable before the computer even updated the readings. How did you—"

"I guess I have the instinct," I say, and bury my face in the bowl.

"And the loose coupling? That was quite the catch. I think that Fore corrected it to keep her team from getting in trouble."

I nod. Whether from the hot soup or his answer, I can feel myself starting to sweat, because his sentence is flashing in my mind, like the red warning text on the console. Yes, it's a catch for me—but for Gyu?

Like all Pomp trainers, Gyu has a different, full-time job. Pomp classes don't come up every day—and once they're here, they cycle through different trainers with different specialties. I'd assumed the fact that Gyu is training me alone had boiled down to the fact that nobody else was willing to.

But Gyu is an engineer. And if even I, a Pomp with zero engineering training, could sense that something was off about the data—why didn't he?

But then, if he'd figured it out, why not tell me? Gyu stands to gain nothing from my failure. He went to bat for me, made sure CPI gave me this chance. If I fuck it up, it won't just make him look bad. I wouldn't put it past CPI to pin the bad call on him and bill him for the lost productivity and the cost of my training.

Maybe I didn't really sense something in the data. Maybe it was just a gut feeling, more of that *instinct* that Gyu was talking about.

As if in response to the thought, my arm throbs, but it resolves so quickly that I'm left wondering if I imagined it. It's just one more thing I'm not sure about.

Maybe I should focus on the things I *am* sure about. Like how I'd made a promise to myself to stop treating him like shit—and half a shift later, a common problem with an easy explanation presents itself, and I'm mentally throwing him under the bus. I *can* be sure that this is shit behavior, that the heat that burns my cheeks isn't from the soup.

I can do better. I will do better.

RIGHT BEFORE THE shift ends, we've breached the outside edge of my knowledge. I'd only gone so far in the veins during my illicit overnight excursion—could only *reach* so far—and the moment we pass the edge of that journey is like walking into a black room. The vision in my mind cuts away, and I'm no better than any other Pomp, making decisions based off the computer's predictions and guesswork.

I'm sent toppling from the peak of my confidence and careening into the valley of indecision below. For the first time this shift, the probability clouds on the display are no longer reminders to navigate the map inside of my head. Instead, they're all I have—and when it comes time for me to call down and predict a grade change, I don't know what to do.

The Fore repeats the request. I try to breathe, but every decision seems like the wrong one. I zoom in on a mass for the fifth time, examining the margins, looking for some clue as to whether the prediction is right or not. Each moment I spend is time stolen from my crew, money out of their pocket, shifts added back to their sentence—but the wrong call could kill them.

"Hey, are you okay?" Gyu turns toward me. The face display is off, but I can imagine his expression behind it, just waiting for me to have a breakdown. Well, here it is.

I look back at the display, flip a coin in my head, and open the relay to the crew with my fingers. "Let's swing around to the left and dig down. Follow the Cable to the left."

The Fore blinks acknowledgment. The whole team turns, navigating the tight space with the bulk of the drill, swiveling like a great ship trying to dock. They tilt the drill up, and it sprays liquid across the Cable, melting the silvery material away to where it will be siphoned up by a pump in the tip of the drill.

Something catches my attention. I ask the computer for an update while switching the drone's camera between wavelengths, looking for one that will cut through the dust.

Gyu hasn't spoken for so long that his voice makes me jump. "Do you ever wonder where it all came from? The Cable, I mean? Sometimes I feel like—"

His voice dies as he sees it, but I'm already moving. "Cease operations!" I make a fist and rotate my hand fast, an override gesture, and the drill suddenly cuts off.

It's too late, though. The hole above the back-right crew member widens, and down falls a chunk, covered in silvery waste. Right before it slams into her shoulder, everybody ducks.

21

WE BRACE OURSELVES for the explosion. Crew members throw themselves against the walls as the chunk makes contact. It hits Na in the back-right, and she collapses with a high-pitched grunt—but nothing else happens. It was just a piece of rock, then. Not piezanite.

Na isn't moving, though.

I check her suit sensors. All I can tell is that her blood pressure and heart rate are elevated. At the bottom of the screen, the words SUIT BREACH light up in red.

"I'm okay," she grunts over the sensors. Her voice so atonal it's raspy, like someone with a bad sore throat. "It got me good, but I'm alright."

The dust that's been thrown up finally settles enough for the Pomp drone to press in closer to her. The chunk of rock has fallen, sharp edge down, like a stalactite, and embedded its way through her suit and into her arm.

"Really, I'm okay," says Na. "We should just keep going." She pulls at the rock and yanks it out of her arm, before holding open the rip in the suit to show everybody. "See? It's just a scratch."

I zoom the drone in to take a closer look. The abrasion is as long as my thumb, but it doesn't look very deep. It'll need to be cleaned and stitched, though.

"Bullshit," says the Fore. "That's a penetration. We've got to hold operations until you get that taken care of."

Everybody groans. The work stoppage is for my benefit—being a newly compiled crew, nobody knows if I'm the kind of Pomp that gets hung up on a minor suit breach or the kind that demands they move on, as excited for my piece of the cut as they are.

By the time Na gets down to medical and back, the shift will be over. If we call it quits now, people will have made a decent amount—nothing to write home about, but better than most shifts, because I knew ahead of time where all the safe crystal was hidden.

I glance at the probability map's occult dangers. This accident could've have been so much worse. And we've run up to the end of what I saw with my hole in the ground—but I can try again. Push it, see if it will somehow take me farther.

"Agreed," I say over the common channel. "We'll suspend operations until that gets taken care of."

Next to me, Gyu chuckles. I don't have to ask to know he's amused. It's a newbie call.

AS SOON AS I make the announcement that the crew can leave, they start to pack up. They'll take an early shuttle home, then pile off into Rikki's or Willow's or just get on with whatever else they'd planned for the evening.

I'm glad we ended early. For the first time this shift, I realize I'm dead on my feet, as if I've been treading water for hours. I shut my eyes, almost savoring the way they burn, and I'm only vaguely aware that Gyu just said something. "Sorry, what?"

I've still got my projection visor on, muffling my hearing. He lifts it off as if removing a crown. I hate the way the touch seems to come out of nowhere, but then my brain reasserts itself. *It's Gyu. You like when Gyu touches you.*

"I said, I was thinking that maybe we could have dinner together. I know you said that you're okay, that there's nothing to worry about, but after yesterday—"

"No." The word comes out too harsh. I reach for his arm. *I'm going to do better. I will be better.* "I would love that, but I'm dead tired. And I have to clean my house up before I can have visitors. It's still crazy in there." I give him my best smile, but he doesn't look convinced.

I step in, hug him, and tuck my head under his chin. It feels *perfect.* Like the entirety of my life was set up as a preface for this moment. It hurts to rip away, but the veins of Cable are waiting for me. The crew depends on my knowledge, and as much as I don't want to hurt Gyu, I can't let them down.

"Yeah," he says. He turns away, and that hurts worse.

"Unless you're okay with eating late? I just—I want to take a nap, and clean up my place, but you could come over for a bite before we hit the hay?" I blush; it sounds like a booty call—but since we're out early, I might be able to make it out to the mine entrance and back in time. "I didn't mean it like—"

"No," he says, and this time, he returns my smile with a genuine one of his own. "I understand, and that sounds nice." He wraps me up in his arms again. "Thanks for letting me in."

I nod, and then I get going. I'm almost to the door before I remember that I'm not supposed to be limping.

I'VE GOT TO pick up Annie before I can leave the dome. I'm halfway back to my place when I hear a soft, low whistle. I turn toward the sound, trying to find its source, and spot a cafe. Its storefront is set up with cheery imitation Ang-Terre decorations—leaves and flowers and ribbons.

There's a woman sitting at a small, round table, her right leg crossed over her left. Between her white shirt and pants, and her mint green shoes, she's hard to miss—impossibly fresh and clean against the grime. Her top foot bounces, verdant flashes against the lemon-yellow finish of the chair.

She takes a sip out of a delicate teacup, her eyes locked with mine, before putting it down on the table and revealing a crescent-shaped silver charm around her neck.

I hold my breath. The Fore tab is the twin of the one under the fabric of my shirt—of the one at Adda's funeral.

She takes another sip.

Hannah wasn't willing to talk to me—but maybe this woman will tell me what they mean. I turn and limp after her. She waits until I'm just a few body lengths from the table before she stands and briskly walks away.

"Hey, wait!"

She ignores me, but when she gets to the end of the spoke, she gives me another glance and makes a ninety degree turn into a narrow alley.

I need to get to the mine entrance, but she knows something. I can feel it. I can't run on my leg, but I pick up the pace and turn down the alley after her.

It's claustrophobically crowded. Behind Leisure's shops and restaurants are a number of tiny service routes used by people who need back access to the buildings for one reason or another. Sandwiched between those are random sheds—convenient stockpiles of resources crammed into whatever space they could find.

I don't see her.

I venture farther down, toward some little paths that crack off this main strip. As I reach the end, I turn, and there she is, halfway down another side alley.

"Hey, seriously, wait! I just have to ask you something—"

This time, I'm ready for her to bolt. My ankle lights up I sprint after her, but she vanishes around a corner a moment before I arrive. I'm forced to spin, too fast, the pain so bad my vision swims, but I make it around the corner.

She's there, motionless, so close I have to stop short to avoid running into her. "Hi," she finally says. Her voice is soft. Sultry. "You had something you wanted to ask me?"

"Yeah, I just needed to see if—"

In the back of my hearing, there's the slightest *tink*, but I recognize it immediately—the light placement of a foot with a metal sole. Someone sneaking up on me. Before I can turn, though, something grabs my head and throws me backward.

There's no time to scream before the person presses something cold and sharp into the side of my neck. A second later, a soft piece of fabric is jammed between my teeth. "Make a single sound, and I swear to god, I'll kill you." Even scrambled through a modulator, the tinny voice is high-pitched. *Probably female*, I think, the hairs on the back of my neck standing up. *Celeste.*

The woman in the white suit has backed up several steps. "You'll get my money?"

"You know I'm good for it."

She nods and walks away.

"Alright," says the woman with a blade to my neck. "Start walking forward."

Negotiating with her is impossible with a gag. Despite her urgings to speed up, I keep my pace slow, trying to buy time to think—until she cruelly sweeps her foot into my injured ankle. It hurt so bad, I almost pee myself.

"I wasn't kidding. Go faster."

My captor marches me down another alley, one in which a small, open door sticks out like a wing. She shoves me through it and down a series of dark, narrow steps, the knife at my neck never wavering.

This is it. I'm really going to die.

Once we get to the bottom, she whistles, and the door at the top bangs shut, followed by the distinct *chunk* of a key in a lock.

I thought there were no locks on Hib. I guess I was wrong.

"Okay." She finally takes away the knife. Her footsteps recede far enough that I risk turning my head.

She's sitting in a chair. She's wearing an Annie suit, the helmet projection turned off. There's a piece of fabric wrapped around her upper arm, and it takes me a moment to make sense of the blocks of bold color. It's some kind of flag, one I've never seen before.

She gestures at the empty chair in front of her with her knife. When I don't move, she shakes her head. "They're not going to unlock the door until you talk to me. So have a seat, and we can get this over with. And by the way, this room is soundproofed."

Despite the warning, her voice is calm and non-threatening. Even with the modulator, I catch traces of her accent, the way each word pushes softly into the next. An accent Celeste doesn't have. And despite the obscuring bulk of her suit, I can tell this isn't Celeste—too short, no curves.

She leans forward. I pull away, but she's faster than me, striking and retracting in an instant, the flag's colors blurring. In her left hand, she's got the gag. It looks like some padding from an old suit.

That's what she stuffed in my mouth.

I swallow. My mouth is as dry as Hib itself. I should be asking questions, formulating a plan—but I can't think through the shock. It's like pushing the hov with a bad ankle; it's all I can do to stay afloat.

She leans back in her chair, arms crossed, knife hand on top. Maybe she's as nervous as me—but her posture looks perfectly comfortable. At home in the middle of a kidnapping. Although I can't see through the mirror finish of her helmet, I feel the heat of her gaze.

"Maybe I should start," she says. "Why did you kill Adda?"

22

GUILT SLUGS ME, clumsy yet stunningly effective, like a lucky haymaker in a bar fight. Maybe I didn't kill Adda, but it's my fault she's dead, and it feels like my captor knows.

For a moment, I'm here, in this poorly lit, metal-lined room, staring at the mirrored dome of my accuser—but I'm also everywhere else.

I'm arms-length deep in a hole in the sand, warm despite the chill around me, my uncovered skin tapping against the veins of Cable, watching as it drags me below.

I'm crawling down the stairs, finding my parents' bags gone, the fibers of the rug unbending.

I'm walking across Hib, out of air, desperately trying to hook up my beacon.

None of it makes sense. It's like all of the fragments of my life are just patch-worked together—up until the moment that the tunnel collapsed and the piezanite ate Adda and Kola and Oye and Stomp and suddenly, I can't breathe.

I bend over at the waist, fighting until a thin stream of cool air levers through the clenched muscles of my throat. The spring is in my chest again, tightening sharp metal edges against the soft flesh of my heart.

"I didn't kill Adda on purpose," I finally say. "I should've been in the explosion, too."

A long pause. "Who are you working for?"

It's the same as drowning. Confusion, chaos, until a long, unexpected arm drives you up toward the light. I shake—not any particular part of me, and not in any particular direction. All of me, in all the ways. "What the fuck are you talking about? We're all *here*, aren't we? We all work for CPI—"

"So you had no idea that tunnel was going to collapse?"

I deflate. "I'm…not sure."

She nods, light playing over her helmet's surface. "What I want is the *how*, Young. How did you know it was going to collapse? Who told you?" There's a hungry edge to her voice, even through the modulator. She recrosses her arms again, and there's a flicker—no, a *flinch*, so quick that a moment later, I'm not sure if it actually happened.

She drops her hands into her lap. Her fingertip plays with the point of the knife. "I'm waiting."

My brain spins. The truth, or a lie? Best to hedge my bets with a little of both. "Nobody told me anything. I just had a feeling. An *instinct*." The last word is too heavy, too much reverence behind it.

Through the modulator, her laugh is a tinny bark. "That's a good one. So, you just *felt* that the tunnel was unsafe. And when it collapses, your lover coincidentally decides to get you a special exemption to complete Pomp training." She leans forward. "What happens at the end? Do you and Gyu and Celeste all find your way off this rock? Or is it enough to be CPI's dog, licking the sole of the boot that kicks you?"

My skin turns cold as her implication finally catches up with me. "You think that I…killed Adda *on purpose*? For a job?"

She makes a disgusted noise. "You are all pathetic pieces of shit that aren't worth the ground that Adda's boots—"

It hits me. Why this woman feels so familiar. "Hannah?"

She freezes. She relaxes a second later, but it's too late. "Hannah who?"

It has to be her. Even the way she tricked me into the alley, the Fore tab hanging around the woman's neck—Hannah saw that at Adda's funeral, knew how much that would have irked me.

All of this makes sense, now. She needs this inquisition because I've taken Adda from her—Adda, who deserved so much better than to be snuffed out under a pile of rock. *Oh, poor Hannah.*

It's suddenly hard to swallow. "I didn't—I didn't know she was going to die. I had a feeling…that there was something wrong with the tunnel, but…sometimes I think I'm crazy. Like I can't trust my brain. And if I'd gone to her and said, *Hey, I think we should cease operations because I feel like this tunnel is unstable,* despite not having any readings or evidence—"

I shake my head, and my pressured speech slows down to a crawl. "It wouldn't have worked." The words are a revelation. I'd been afraid to unpack this moment, to peel back the rotten skin of my fear and see what lay underneath—and here it was. I couldn't have stopped what happened to Adda. A tiny fragment of the guilt I've been holding onto evaporates out into the air. "It wasn't deliberate—"

"I don't give a shit. And I'm not Hannah." Even through the tin-sounds, her voice catches.

I bite my lip. "I know you are. And look, I'm so, so sorry. It haunts me at night. I couldn't have stopped them going into that tunnel, but if I hadn't been late—" My throat gives out. I have to take a breath before I can keep going. "I'll never escape it. I keep hearing—" And then my voice gives out again, and this time, I can't get it back right away.

"And now you're a Pomp." I can hear the sneer, the rage behind it, the power of the hurt hidden deep within, like crystals inside of a protective metal vein of Cable.

My hands are shaking. "Yes. I'm a Pomp. And I'm guiding a crew, and all I can think about is how dangerous it is. How I have to get it right. You have no idea—"

She's on her feet before I can blink, screaming so loud the modulator fractures her voice. "I don't give a *shit*! I don't give a shit about your feelings. You don't *get* to feel sad right now. You don't get to—"

She slams a fist against her chest before freezing, anguish stretching her whole body into a rigid arc.

And then she stops. She sits. Slumps against the chair. Puts down the knife. The little flag on her arm has a spot of red in the center of it now—somehow, in her outburst, she hurt herself. "You're still alive. There's no amount of feeling bad that'll bring her back. No amount of good deeds that's going to cancel you not being there for your crew."

The weight that had been lifted off me slams down again with bone-shaking force. "I know that."

"Well." Hannah clears her throat. She takes off her helmet. "Adda is never coming back. You don't deserve absolution, but maybe you'll get it, because you're right. There's something I want from you."

I don't know how many moments drip by while I study her face. Part of my brain, the rational part, marvels at her boldness. She's grabbed me, abducted me, kidnapped me—isn't she afraid of what could happen?

But her eyes are like twin stars. Like fission. Grief.

I know that look. She doesn't give a *fuck* what happens next—and even if I did go to Enforcement, it's my word against hers. And the truth is that no matter what Hannah asks me for, I can't imagine not giving it to her. "What do you want?"

Her stare skewers me like a falling stalactite. "I want you to help me finish what Adda and I started. I need you to get me Gyu's credentials."

The ground underneath me shifts. "*What?*"

"Password, key card, all of it. You're going to steal them for me."

"No. That's—that's crazy. I'd be caught in a heartbeat." A thousand explanations for why she'd want them spin in my head. Gyu's credentials give him access to the mine and all of the structures in Engineering. Personnel records. Station data. Nothing she could access would be worth the punishment for getting caught with them, because in the end, you'd still be stuck on Hib, and—

I shake my head. "Hannah. It's impossible."

She smirks at me. "People have done it before. Get me the credentials, Young."

She's so confident, she's practically floating above her chair. There's no reason for her to be so sure, unless…"Holy shit. It was *you*." The unauthorized access that made Gyu barrel out of my training and leave me with Celeste. "You stole Celeste's credentials. Do you realize—"

"I didn't steal them. Adda did. And Celeste owed her, big time."

She glares at me. Her arms are crossed in front of her body, hands squeezing over her upper arms.

"Fine. But you got busted. They know that somebody—"

She throws a hand up in frustration. "They know that Celeste was doing some things she shouldn't have been. Which she was. She dug her own grave on this. And by the time Gyu figures out his credentials are missing, I aim to be long gone."

I shake my head. "This is crazy. Do you understand that? Who do you think you are, Jimmy Kang? Let's say you manage to sneak your way onto the elevator. That you're not discovered and you don't die of lack of food or dehydration over the *ninety freaking circadians* it takes to get back to Ung-Nyeo. Then what? They'll catch you the second they open the container—and even if they don't, you'll have nowhere to go. The elevator ends in the middle of nowhere."

She scowls at me. She knows where it ends, because we all do. We all made our way from prisons in the terminator band to Hib the same way: a vac-train that hauled us below ground to the center of the Desert, where we boarded the elevator. From there, we rode from Ung-Nyeo, through the atmosphere, and then space, all of the way up to Hib's surface—but we had *supplies* then. Technicians minding us. Access to food and water. This, this is completely ridiculous.

Still, she doesn't answer me. "Hannah," I say, trying not to sound incredulous. "There's nothing but sand. And even if you somehow managed to get all of the way across *half a planet* to the terminator band—"

"I'm not going back to the terminator band." She announces it in the same casual way that someone announces they're going blonde.

I sputter. Without the walls to protect it, everything outside of the terminator band has long ago been torn apart by the winds, changed into nothing more than mountains of sand. The Desert bakes. The Ice freezes. Everybody knows that neither is remotely habitable. "Hannah, what are you saying?"

"There are people out there, you dipshit." She rubs the bridge of her nose. "Did you ever stop to think how utterly improbable it is that an entire planet is empty? We're a race of survivors, Young."

"I don't—"

"CPI invests a startling amount of resources into convincing us that the entirety of the planet is completely unsuitable for human life, but think about this. We're on a fucking *moon* right now. Stuck somewhere that is perpetually dark and cold—"

"It's not nearly as cold as the Ice. The gas blanket on Hib—"

"You're missing the point. Human beings, we like to fucking survive. There are people in subterranean enclaves all over Ung-Nyeo, deep beneath the surface, where the frost doesn't reach or the heat doesn't penetrate. The hard part is just getting there. One day, CPI might find them, but it costs them more resources to go looking for these hardscrabble enclaves than it's worth."

Her face turns to stone. "That's where Adda and I were going. Until you fucked it up."

Something prickles at the back of my head. After my parents disappeared, I searched everywhere for them. I put out messages, paid informants, rubbed elbows with gangs. I wanted to know if they'd found a second life, somehow, but it was like they'd just vanished into thin air.

But what if they hadn't? What if they'd made their way to some other place? *If I can find them, I can ask them why they left me behind.*

But the thought winks out. Even for that brief moment, it had the pathetic stink of my adolescent self, reaching forward through the years and asking to be soothed. Real life doesn't happen that way.

"I'm sorry," I say. "I can't steal his credentials." Even if I *could* get Hannah everything she's asking for, once she was gone and the dust had settled, they'd bill Gyu some astronomical amount. And that's not even counting what would happen if I was caught. Both our lives would go up in smoke.

"You're a piece of shit," Hannah finally says. "A piece of cowardly chickenshit."

I think about Adda, pushing me to come to Rikki's. "Maybe. But fucking Gyu over isn't the answer."

She chuckles then, switching off the voice modulator in the middle, the sound changing from tinny to warm right halfway through the laugh. It's eerie.

She whistles, and at the top of the stairs, I hear the door unlock.

"I wasn't sure what I was going to do once I got you down here, you know. I was ready to kill you. Adda told me that you'd been acting strange in the tunnel, and you ran away from us in the bar. I was sure you were a murderer." She snorts, shakes her head. "But you're just a coward."

I almost say something, but she's looking at the floor. Whatever this was, it's over.

I make it as far as the bottom of the stairs when she calls out my name. "Young?"

I tense. "Yeah?"

"Of all the people you could trust, you picked Gyu. You shouldn't've." A long pause. "When you get home, check the light fixture over your bed."

I turn and look back, but she hasn't moved, and I can't see her face. "Why?"

"Press it up and turn," she says.

I wait for what feels like a very long time, and when it's clear that she's not going to say another word, I pivot and go up the stairs.

By the time I make it to the top, my heart hammers. It's the exertion and my busted ankle—or maybe it's the flicker of a memory, a hundred tiny strips of paper fluttering into a toilet bowl.

Gyu is watching you.

But that note had been in Gyu's pocket. Meant for someone else—and if Hannah had written it, how had Gyu gotten his hands on it?

I look down, intent on confronting Hannah for more details, but there's nobody at the bottom of the stairs.

23

I LIMP, TREMBLING, the whole way home, the content of Hannah's veiled accusation against Gyu not half as bad as the soft way she'd said it, as if it didn't require the strength of her conviction to be true.

That's the part that worries me the most, because it'd not only contained surety, but *familiarity.* As if she'd seen the light fixture with her own eyes.

I swing the door open, but the room looks the same as it did when I left for work. Tossed. Violated. I'd thought it was Celeste—but it could just have easily been Hannah.

I step in and shut the door behind me, but I don't feel safer. I'm half-tempted to grab a knife and conceal myself somewhere by the door, but I've lost precious hours to Hannah's quasi-kidnapping. If I don't make it to the mine entrance before next shift, I'll lose my chance to scope out tunnel stability and crystal load. And I'm already running on fumes. I need as much rest as I can get tonight, so I don't fuck up and make some stupid mistake later.

I should just leave now. Hannah was just trying to get under my skin.

But the light fixture is there, attached to my ceiling. Waiting for me.

I drag a chair next to the bed and climb up, before pivoting too fast. Despite the splint, my leg buckles in a flash of pain, and I have to grab the back of the chair to keep from tumbling off. It wobbles under me.

I take a few breaths, the bandages tight around my bent elbow.

I really don't have time for this.

I let go and straighten up. The bandages relax as I try for the light fixture, but my stomach drops—it's too far.

Ugh. I bite my lip and lean into my bad knee until my kneecap taps against the back of the chair. After just missing a tunnel cave-in, after surviving my own suicide attempt—how ironic would it be to die this way, slowly unscrewing a light cover with my fingertips while on the tippy-toes of one foot?

I follow Hannah's instructions. *Press and turn.* Already my shoulders are burning, my arms heavy. The fixture cover slides across my sweaty fingers as I rotate my wrist. An eternity later, it finally comes loose.

I hold my breath as I cup my hands under the light cover and bring it down to my face. It's just a piece of transparent plastic, though. Nothing to see here.

The fatigue catches up with me. My vision swims for a second before clearing. I want to rub my eyes, but my hands are full.

I toss the cover on my bed and reach into the base. I can just barely brush its insides with my fingertips.

There's nothing there. Just the bulb and the metal reflective dish behind it. Maybe if I knew what I was looking for?

I consult the clock. People will be crawling into bed soon. I've burned through a lot of time.

Frustration pricks needles into my forehead. The pain feels well earned. What was the point of this? To make me wonder if Gyu was spying on me? To drive in the point that Hannah had been in my house?

Or maybe her kidnapping was just a ruse to delay me, so that someone else would have time to go through my things again.

The thought turns my stomach. I look around the room at the piles, the mess, but if there's a difference between the ransacked look it held before and the one it holds now, I can't see it.

I have to go, but the idea of leaving my place like this, vulnerable, it ties my stomach into knots. I don't want someone in here while I'm gone. I want even less to return and find the place already occupied.

I put on Annie. As I leave, I take a piece of hair from my head and loop it around both the door handle and a bit of metal that sticks out from the frame, before tying it in a knot. It's probably too much—an intruder will notice it easily—but if they're going to replace it, they'll have to find a piece of hair the same length and shade as mine, so that's something, at least.

I limp to the hov kiosk.

LESS THAN A minute after I engage the throttle, I fall asleep. I dream, but it's just sensations, the feeling of rocking on something moving. I wake up a thousand times between Hib station and the mine, and when the hov engine idles down from a roar to a grumble, I feel more tired than when I started. It takes a monumental effort to drag myself out of the craft.

It's not until I'm right in front of the hole that I remember that I forgot a shovel.

Fuck.

I glance around, but the beam of my headlights doesn't catch any movement. People clear out come quitting time. I drop to my knees, ignoring the little flash of pain—if remembering that my ankle was fucked was the only way to stay alive, I'd be long dead—and start hollowing out the hole with my hands.

It feels like the digging goes faster this time, like I'm a camshaft spinning in a great machine, forcing my arms up and down, up and down, until finally I'm scraping the bottom. I've got my glove off before I can blink. The cold invades my arm as I lay on my belly and push it toward the Cable below.

Before I even make contact, the vein rises up to meet me. I'm catapulted down into the Cable's thick ropes. I fly through so fast it should be dizzying, but instead, it feels again like being lifted up in a river, like riding the great beast through an ocean as it dances and spins. I reach the edge of the place I've seen before, through the Pomp drone, the edge of where the crew has mined this last shift—and there's a trembling wall there.

No, not a wall. More like a membrane, vibrating with the tension of holding back whatever's on the other side.

It's in this moment my awareness splits, my larger mind hyperfocused on my body—the way my breath rustles in and out, the cold that seems to leach in through the helmet, even as warmth invades my arm—but there's another part of me, deep within the earth, listening for something below. It feels like eavesdropping for secrets in hostile territory. More than anything else, it's a question—as if the Cable itself has taken me by the hand and asked: *Are you sure you want to keep going?*

I am. I push my body down into the sand. Grains grind against my helmet as my fingers strain to make better contact with the Cable.

And then, like a bubble popping, the membrane between me and the end of my vision snaps. I pour deeper into the Cable, mapping it in a flood. Vaguely, I'm aware of the way my body grows hotter, the way my pulse pounds faster than the vibrations of a drill. I travel through the next fork, and the next, and the next, and when it feels like I'll set fire to the sand around me, melting it into glass, like I will light up the dark like a thousand red flares—only then does the vein reject me. It hurls me back through the sand, up, up—

I'm dead, I think—

And back onto the surface of the ground.

This time, it's too much. I roll sideways, curl into a ball. The inertia catches up with me, and my stomach contents threaten to empty themselves into my helmet.

After the nausea passes, I lay heaving on my side, my head spinning. It feels like a great fever has burned its way through me, boiling my brain and vaporizing every molecule of water in my body until my cells are dust.

I'm not sure what just happened, or how much time has passed, but I know one thing.

This is power. This is the key to everything.

I BARELY HAVE the energy to kick sand over the hole before crawling into the hov. I blink, and I'm back at Hib station.

Somehow, I manage to drag the craft back and turn it in, to make it down to my house—and there's Gyu, standing in front of the open door. He turns when he hears me approach.

Shit. I forgot. I'd invited him to come over, have a late bite. Sleep next to me.

He gestures at the door. "Young, I'm sorry—"

"It's okay," I say. He can't possibly know what I mean—that *everything* is okay. Celeste, and Pomp school, and Hannah, and us. Everything is okay, because I've been made a goddess, one that has communed with the veins of a moon and been found worthy of its power.

I take off my helmet, hold it up in my palms like an offering.

His cheeks are pale, his eyes haunted. How I must look to him right now—my skin red, covered in sweat and dirt.

"I knocked, and when you didn't answer—"

"It's really okay." I drag myself in. It feels like gravity has quadrupled.

He follows me in, eyes me as I throw my suit into the cleaner. "Did you want to eat—"

"I'm not hungry."

"Ah." A pause. "Where were you?"

I should be nervous. I should feel something, but it's like all of the nerves in my body are scratched, like I'm covered in a gigantic sunburn. My arm aches. My ankle throbs. My thoughts are slowing down, like I'm drunk. Still, I have to tell him something, and I know he doesn't want the truth. Like any normal person, he just wants a lie that *feels* like the truth.

I should do the whole shebang. Validate his feelings, offer a rational explanation for what is going on, attack some piece of his argument.

But I feel like I'll fall over any second. So instead, I say, "I found a little hatch in the sand, a ways from here. I think somebody made it out of junk. And when things get bad, I make my way out there and hide for a while, and it just makes everything better. I'm sorry I wasn't here when you got here, but I'm here now."

It's almost the truth. It's good enough. And even if it isn't, I can't stay up anymore. I crawl into bed.

He says something, but I can't make out more than vague murmurs, like I'm underwater, and then darkness rushes in.

24

I WAKE TO chimes, to trickling water. I'm alone, and it doesn't look like Gyu slept over.

I start with trying to sit up.

My head pounds. I feel desperately hung over, but also jubilant. My triumph at the mine smooths over any raw edges with a certainty that vibrates in my palm like a bird's swift heart. What I've been doing, it's more than instinct, more than an anomaly of my broken brain. Following the veins of Cable boils down to Hibiscus, because the moon is more than a rock. In my journey, I felt give and take. *Communication.* There's something ordered in the chaos in its core, a long-forgotten piece of machinery brought to life by my presence.

It's exhilarating. I can't wait to get to work, to send my crew onto a path as predetermined as a star-crossed fate.

My arm feels achingly full and heavy. The bandages are too tight, and I unwind them, rewind them. I hobble into standing, put on my clothes, and glance in the mirror.

I don't feel rested, a fact clearly reflected in the dark hollows around my eyes, but it doesn't matter. Deep in the shining promise of my next shift, I only feel a few throbs of regret. I wish I hadn't invited Gyu over, because he seemed pissed. And I wish I hadn't told him about the hatch. In that moment of vulnerability, the half-truth felt like an olive branch. I'd given him something of myself.

But he didn't appreciate it. He couldn't see it for what it was. It didn't help anything.

And now, it's time to go to work.

WHEN I GET to Engineering, the ache in my ankle sticks in my mind like an annoying song. Despite my renewed commitment to stop putting so much weight on it, I keep falling into my thoughts and spinning through my discoveries. Each time I stray too far from the present moment, I automatically stop limping, until a flash of pain punctuates the end of my reflections.

Somehow, in the craziness of my journey through the Cable, I'd pushed Hannah out of my mind, but she seemed dedicated. Committed. And if she doesn't let this whole thing go, it could be a serious problem. I should keep my eyes peeled.

Pain.

I wonder what's going to happen to Celeste.

Pain.

I just want to grab Gyu by the shoulders and shake him. I have the entire world in the palm of my hand, but I can't tell him. And his irritation seems so small in comparison, like the bright poke of a mosquito. I know he can't read my mind, but how can he not feel how *big* this moment is?

When I push the button to the intercom, the door opens without a word. I step in, but the room is empty. No Celeste.

The door to the interior pops open a moment later, but Gyu doesn't even greet me before he's back in the hallways, a receding figure I scramble to shuffle after.

Pain. Well, at least I'm sure that he's pissed.

He outpaces me easily. I almost lose him twice. When I finally make it to his office, he's already got his set on and his visor down.

I put mine on, load into the Ice Conduction. My presets for the contrast have been saved, which is nice. Next to me, I can see the mirrored helmet of Gyu's avatar, but not his face.

"So." His voice is incredibly flat. "Let's focus on—"

"Can we talk?"

A tight pause. "I don't think—"

"Just a moment. Please."

His voice raises. "Young, this isn't the place. This is work. And if you could try to be an adult, that would be great."

The words sting, but they also make my chest tighten. Suddenly, it feels important that I resolve this right now—but he's obviously not willing to talk to me.

After the shift, then. I trace down the path the crew will take in my head, surprised and pleased that it's ten times as clear as it was the previous shift. It's like I'm getting better—not only at seeing, but at remembering.

Judging by the length of Cable I have figured out, there's no conceivable way we could make it to the end this shift—and maybe not even the next. Which means that I can delay the trip to the hole at least a whole circadian. "What about after work? We can take as much time as you want—"

"Stop," he says.

"Please." My voice comes out so thin that I wince. I'm embarrassing myself.

"Look, I—" He sighs. "Maybe. Is that good enough?"

I gulp. It's not a yes, but he'll snap if I push this any farther. "Of course. And thank you."

Another long pause. "Listen. There's something we need to talk about."

My throat closes up. It seems impossible that he's about to break up with me now, when I've finally figured everything out—impossible, but also fitting.

But then, it's not a breakup, because we're not anything. I brace myself, will my skin to warm back up. "Yes, sure."

"You were late getting back to your place."

My scalp tingles. Does he know about Hannah? "Yes?"

"Were you with Celeste?"

My head spins. "What? No. What does Celeste have to do with anything?"

He clears his throat, but then he switches his face display on. Something about the avatar's lighting makes him look pale, like a ghost. "Listen, Young. She disappeared. I'm really worried about her."

A cramp of jealousy, but I manage to push it away. He's allowed to be worried about someone. "Okay. What do you think—"

"I'm not sure. I know she's in trouble. I might be able to help her, except that I don't know what's going on. But if CPI Enforcement catches her before I can convince her to turn herself in…"

A shiver steals up my spine. "Yeah."

"And—when I saw her last, she was—" He squeezes his eyes shut. When he opens them, the wetness reflected in them shocks me. "She was not…not herself. And her suit is missing. And I can't stop thinking that she's gone crazy, and she's desperate, and maybe…"

Her face pops into my mind, even as her harsh commands echo in my ears. The way her expressions shifted the last time I saw her—fury, worry, resolve. She feels like the magma bubbling under the surface of a volcano. Not like someone who would kill herself. Not like me.

"Listen. I need you to do me a favor."

There's a brief wiggle in my stomach—less than a shift ago, Hannah was asking me for a favor, one I had agreed to without a thought, until finding out what it was—but this is Gyu. He's safe. "Sure. What do you want?"

"I think you did a fantastic job yesterday. You don't really need me standing over your shoulder as a babysitter. So, if I left you alone for a few hours and went to go look for Celeste—"

"Yes." It bursts out of my mouth, almost joyous, and I have to temper my next words. "I mean, I totally understand."

He hesitates, unsure.

"Gyu," I say. I take a deep breath and put on my most serious voice. "I can do this. Really."

Finally, he nods. "Okay. I'll be back soon, and if you need anything, you can ping me over the com. I'll add an access to your credentials right now that will give you a direct line to me." His hands flicker, fingertips fluttering as he types something.

I feel a twitch of impatience—he could have just spoken the commands out loud—but then a green line of text appears on the bottom of my screen before disappearing. It was too fast to catch it all, although I at least read TOTAL ACCESS and GYU SONG.

"If you need me, you can just flick through serial opposition of all four fingers. Do you want to practice—"

"No. I got it. Really."

"Okay."

He's out the door before the jealousy sinks its fangs into my chest. If *I* disappeared, would Gyu be as worried about me?

CREW SIGNAL flashes at the bottom of the screen. Right. I have things to do right now. Things to prove.

FOR THE FIRST time, I really do the work of a Pomp. I don't worry about someone looking over my shoulder. I don't plan through the words I'll use to justify each decision. The map of the Cable is like a compass, unerring and bedrocked into the back of my mind, and it turns me into a machine.

The shift has all the joy of dancing in circles with the sea creature, water sparkling around me. I make a thousand decisions before the meal break—drill setting, timing of equipment checks, figuring out how my crew is doing and what they need—and each one is easy, and by the time we stop to rest, I know. I am good at this.

I do waver every so often. Stop and think through a problem, make sure I'm not forgetting anything. But the crew and I move together like one organism, and when I get the piezanite tally at the meal break, it's the best kind of proof. We're cleaning up.

I watch through the drone as my crew sits on the ground and unpacks their lunches. My stomach growls. I didn't bring anything to eat.

I shut off the video feed, but even then, I can hear the contented grunts, hear them talking through mouthfuls of food. One of them—Lee Hae-Jin, more affectionately known as "Fifty"—starts a story about hooking up with someone at Rikki's after last shift.

Something itches under my skin. I want to say something, to participate in a way I never did when I was the one behind the drill. Maybe it's because Hae-Jin's life is in my hands, and despite the way I've gone through her file, I feel like I should *know* her—

But then the nasal voice of our third-week instructor floats back into my mind. *Your crew is not your friend.* People feel safer when the Pomp is a lofty, faceless presence, an untouchable god. Everybody knows there's someone behind the drone, but when you can reflect on seeing that person fall down drunk in the bar or break into tears at a sappy movie— it's easier to doubt their calls.

Hae-Jin talks more, her voice muffled by what she exclaims is a truly excellent meal of rice, spicy pickles, and fried fish so crisp I can hear batter crunch over the com-link.

It's too much. I shut off the audio. For the first time all day, I'm completely alone.

Gyu's been gone half a shift. Shouldn't he be back by now?

Maybe Celeste really did take a walk. If she broke her locator beacon, she might not get found for a while.

I check the time. About half the meal break left.

I sit, but the silence is excruciating. I need a distraction.

I bring up the lookup interface, and my fingers tingle with my new access. Lookups for students are preprogrammed with a lot of limitations to keep us on target. Once you're working, you have access to *UPDIN*, the Ung-Nyeo Planetary Data and Information Network, but it's costly. Some people still pay, because they like at least getting the news from back home.

But I'm starting to get the feeling that Gyu's a bit higher up in the Engineering food chain than I originally suspected. One of the perks of working your way into a better position is free access to *UPDIN*, including the news, dictionaries, information lookups, that sort of thing. And when I looked up jungles earlier, there hadn't been any sort of limit or fee indicated.

For a moment, I let myself imagine a dual life. At night, I visit my hole, plot out my course. During the day, I divide my time between Pomping and learning, teaching myself everything I need to know for the job I'll take on once we both manage to get back to Ung-Nyeo. Maybe I'll be a weaver, or a glassblower.

There's fifteen minutes left on the break, which is not enough time to map out a whole new career, so I decide to finish the searches I started before. There was something I didn't get to. I can't quite remember, but it had something to do with the jungle, so I type that in again. A few minutes go by while I follow the path I took before. *Vegetation.* And there is. The *revolving world hypothesis.*

I try to read it, but it's full of scientific jargon so dense that I only manage to capture every other word. Still, the parts I do get make my scalp crawl, like I'm about to be hit by lightning. Like something important is about to happen.

I check the clock. Ten minutes until I've got to start Pomping again.

I open a panel up to take notes on the left side of my vision, and then I chase link after link. I mark some things down as I go, definitions of words, occasional pictures. Slowly, something clicks into place inside of my head, and it's so huge, so ridiculous, that I have to sit down there on the floor of Gyu's office.

It's got to be bogus. Out of all of the things I've ever heard, the idea that Ung-Nyeo *used to be* like the planet in that ghost girl book that Gyu loaned me that I never read—what had he called it? A spinner? No, a *turner*—it's impossible. Other planets, maybe. But not *ours.*

I try to envision it. To imagine my view from the aerie—the roof I used to frequent, before I was pushed off—brightening as the sun casts it in the same light as the Desert. The storefronts and leaning apartment buildings darkening to a complete blackness, like the Ice. A world in which there is no temperature differential to breed the fierce winds that have ripped away every living thing outside the wind-walls before crushing the earth into sand. Where the Ice has melted into something… what? Habitable?

A world where there is no tether between Ung-Nyeo and Hibiscus. Without it, maybe we'd have never come to Hib, because there'd be nothing for the elevator to rest on.

My stomach rolls as a sick sensation steals across my limbs, as I realize how much of my world isn't as solid as I thought. After all, I haven't seen any part of the elevator but the inside of a cargo container, and it's not like it had windows. I haven't seen the tether, either. As a protection against "potential terrorism" (and to protect CPI's investment in the elevator), the planet-side anchor is fenced off and heavily guarded—not to mention being protected by its location in the middle of the Desert, a place so hot that the only way to access the elevator from that side is via underground tram. And when we arrived on Hib, our cargo container was loaded onto a vehicle and brought to the colony bubble without being opened.

I could've taken a hov over to the elevator facility since, maybe, but other miners have told me that the security checkpoints make it hard to see much because you can't get close enough.

I type in *elevator*, and a number of entries pop up, but the one I want is close to the top. *Ung-Nyeo to Hibiscus Transport Elevator*. The second heading in the article is *Construction*.

Perfect. The elevator exists, which means the tether exists, and for some reason, knowing that at least these parts of my world haven't changed makes it easier to breathe.

I choose the *Construction* subheading with a gesture to read more. Maybe there will be some photos—they're banned planet-side, for the same reasons that approaching the anchor isn't allowed, but maybe with Gyu's credentials?

RESTRICTED ACCESS flashes across the screen, and then: ENTER PASSWORD.

Which I don't have. After a few moments, I blow out a breath and check the time again. There are three minutes left until the break.

I'm paralyzed by all my choices. I could look up something else. Something about the terminator band, or see if there's anything about the enclaves that Hannah mentioned. But what I *should* do is check the prediction cloud against the map in my head, and then maybe review my crew's personnel records and—

Oh. Personnel records.

I didn't have to put in a password to use some parts of the lookup, which means things low priority enough are freely accessible. I can, of course, see my own crew's personnel records, but I'm curious about people outside of my crew, too. Especially Celeste.

I feel guilty, but only for a moment. I flick my hand, and the lookup closes. I load into the administrative panel and scan the headings, click the one I need.

I definitely shouldn't do this.

I type in CELESTE, before realizing I don't know her last name—but once I expand the filter to all of Hibiscus station, only one match comes up. CELESTE HADARI.

I click on it, but PASSWORD REQUIRED immediately appears.

I type in my own name, and I'm able to start poking in my own file immediately. It only takes me a moment to determine it's about the same as the one I saw in the interrogation room with Gyu.

Okay. So Gyu can access mine without a password, but not Celeste's. Probably because Gyu and I are in the same chain of command or something. Just to be sure, I should look up somebody else—and after what she did to me last shift, Hannah is the obvious choice. I have already decided to avoid her at all costs, but more information about her can't hurt.

I type in HANNAH.

The computer thinks for a second, and then returns: NO MATCHES.

I try HANNA. HAENA. HANAH. I try every combination of letters and sounds I can think of that resembles *Hannah* at all, but nothing matches.

Great, a girl dragged me into an alley, put a knife to my neck, and asked me to steal Gyu's credentials, and I don't even know her real name.

A light flashes on the console: INCOMING TRANSMISSION. I open the feed, thinking it might be Gyu, but it's just the Fore. "Hey, everything alright up there? I mean, we like the break and all, but if we're not drilling, we're not making money."

"Yeah. Sorry about that. Let's get to work."

By the end of the shift, Gyu still hasn't come back. I wait at home, hoping he'll take me up on my offer for us to talk it out, but he never shows up. And the next shift, when I go into work, he's not there at all.

<h1 style="text-align:center">25</h1>

TWO MORE SHIFTS pass by without Gyu. I think about messaging him through the emergency line he set up, but I don't have a good reason. Besides—when he *does* come back, I want him to see how great it's gone.

Before going to bed, I take the hov and go back to the mine—this time with a shovel—and dig my own hole. The Cable welcomes me the same.

When I get back, I check for Gyu, but he's still not there. The need to reach out to him makes my skin crawl, but I don't want to piss him off.

Despite my resolution to leave Gyu alone, by the end of the my third shift, I'm starting to feel insane. In an effort to keep myself focused, I've taken to filling my time with studying the materials Gyu's credentials have provided me access to: reviewing Pomp training documents about tunnel stability predictions and piezanite formation, looking up details about the planet, trying to calculate how much I'll likely earn per day on average. At some point, I pull up the personnel files and review them again, searching for any information that will make me a better guide for the crew. But when I pull up Na's file, and see her name at the top—NA, SKY—something wiggles in my memory.

I can't put a finger on it. Almost as an afterthought, I pull up the lookup and type in the word SKY. I scroll down to the bottom. Usually, there's a section with a translation of the term into each of the four major languages of the terminator band.

CIELTRO. ORU. MA'NGU. HA-NEUL—

And there it is. Sky's name, translated into Hangan, would be Na Ha-Neul.

Ha-neul Na.

Hannah.

When Hannah kidnapped me, I'd noticed the little spot of red on the flag on her bicep. I'd assumed it had been from her whipping around the knife she'd been holding, but it could have just as easily come from a stalactite falling from the ceiling.

I scan through her file, but when I go to bring up her picture, the words FILE CORRUPTED flash across the bottom of the screen.

My heart pounds.

If Na is Hannah—then, why the *fuck* is she here, on my crew? There are only a few possibilities, and none of them make sense. Maybe she *requested* a change to this crew—but Pomp names are kept confidential, so how did she find out I would be Pomping in the first place? And she was here from my first day, which meant that she'd had to have applied for a transfer before I even told Gyu about my decision.

And more than that, why would she want to be on the crew of the woman she thinks killed her girlfriend—unless this is in some way linked to trying to get Gyu's credentials?

If Hannah *didn't* request to be placed on this crew, then somebody assigned her without her knowledge. Which *also* doesn't make sense. What would anybody stand to gain out of making us work together, when neither of us knew who the other person was?

Fuck. I need to think, and I don't want to do that in Gyu's office. I go home, but I can't even hear myself. Instead, there's just a tap-tapping in my brain, the knowledge that the door could open any time. And I can't stop thinking about Hannah telling me to check my light fixture. Feeling like she'd been in here.

Eventually, I put on my suit and head out the door. I haven't been to my hatch in a long time, and the need for a space that locks—one where I can take a breath in the dim lights and be dead to the world—it's so bad I almost consider getting a hov, but I can't justify the cost, not now that the swelling in my ankle has started to go down, so I just go on foot.

The journey there passes by so quickly I don't remember any of it, save for the occasional moment where I step wrong and feel warning pang of soreness. It's like I just wake up in front of the hidden button. I press it and raise the hatch's metal beastliness out of the ground before jumping in and locking the door behind me.

Inside, finally alone, I collapse on the floor.

Something next to me rustles. "I was starting to think you'd *never* make it here."

My heart stops cold. Out of all the voices I expected might join me, the last one I would have ever guessed was Celeste's.

26

"WHAT THE FUCK are you doing here?" My voice rings inside of my helmet, but I can't seem to stop shouting. I scramble backward on my hands and knees. "Gyu has been looking for you for—"

Celeste takes a few rapid steps forward, and now she's between me and the exit. The light green glow of the hatch bounces off her skin, highlighting her sharp cheekbones. "I'm hiding from Gyu. And whatever you do, you can't let him know you found me. He's dangerous, Young."

Shit. Gyu was right. She's mentally unstable, and although I can sure empathize, that doesn't mean I want her to chop me up or some shit. And right now, I'm fucking trapped.

Except that this place has an emergency exit. There's the little crawl tunnel—maybe if I can distract her somehow, I can make it through the tunnel and out to the surface before she catches me. I crawl backward, like a crab, but she dances to the side, before reaching down and offering me a gloved hand.

I stare at it as if it's a snake about to strike.

She rolls her eyes. "Look, it's awkward crawling up from the floor in one of these suits, and we don't have a shit-ton of time, so maybe you could get up and we can get this explanation over with."

When I don't answer, she sighs and leans forward, faster than I can move. Grabs my hand and hauls me to my feet. "I want to be here even less than you do—"

"I fucking doubt that—"

"—but I just need a minute of your time. If you decide to throw me to the wolves, so be it. But a lot of fucking people are depending on this moment, and if you give a shit about the fate of humanity, you'll shut up and give me a chance."

The fate of humanity. *Wow. She really has lost it.* I take a small half-step sideways toward the crawl tunnel.

"I need your help."

I snort. "Even if I gave it to you, it wouldn't be worth very much."

"I'm inclined to agree. But everything has gone straight to crap, and as much as I tried to keep you out of it, you decided to stick yourself in. And now, you're what's left."

"I have no idea what the fuck you're talking about." I still haven't figured out if it was Hannah or Celeste who broke into my house, although the needle has definitely just swung toward the latter for me.

"Pomp training. As soon as I figured out you had the touch, I—"

The blood rushes in my ears. "The *touch*?"

"Like your parents."

I stumble, as if from a hammer blow. "I don't…What do my parents have to do with this?"

Celeste nods. Her face, once lined with tension, has gone slack. Like all the life's just left her. "Everything. I know I just helped you get up, but I've reconsidered. I think you'd better sit down."

I sit. Celeste takes up the position furthest from me, right up against the doorway that leads to the exit tunnel, and when she starts talking, I keep my mouth shut.

"When CPI started to mine piezanite on Ung-Nyeo, they didn't give people protective equipment, like the full body suits we use now. People started to get sick almost immediately. They all developed a kind of fast-growing cancer that rooted in the axillary and cubital lymph nodes, before spreading like wildfire through the body."

Celeste shuts her eyes. "CPI did tests and found out there's some kind of off-gassing that occurs when Cable is broken down by the son-chem drill. They kept it quiet while they looked for alternative ways to extract piezanite, but everything they could come up with was astronomically more expensive than having people suit up. So they did, and to avoid a panic, they didn't tell anybody why."

I bite my lip. Despite how little reason I have to believe anything Celeste says, the greed, at least, is plausible. And the idea that the Cable itself could make people sick—something cold slithers through my belly.

Celeste doesn't seem to notice. "One other thing they discovered is that a few of these people, before they died, told some wild fucking stories in their delirium. Stories about journeying through the Cable and seeing the payloads—but we didn't have the technology, at the time, to determine how accurate they were. We didn't have special radar calibrated to sense piezanite or the algorithms for tunnel stability or the prediction clouds. But someone at CPI thought, you know, what if this is possible? And they put together a team and radioed back to someone in a fucking hospital bed that guided them through, and of course, they were right."

Her face grows stony. "Their guide died that night. But the scientist gave these people a name, and it stuck. Pomps, from the concept of a psychopomp: a mythical being that guides the dead into the afterlife. And they exposed as many people to the Cable as they could to try to find more Pomps. Poor people. The disabled. Prisoners. And what they found was that the first batch had been a lucky batch— that this ability was exceedingly rare, although it tended to run in families."

She lifts an eyebrow at me. She's talking about me, which means she knows what I can do. How did she figure it out? Had she known while bullying me in training? *I* hadn't even figured it out yet.

"Everyone exposed died, of course. They found just enough people with the ability to develop some of the computer models by using their predictions to help shape the way we interpret the data from ground-penetrating radar. But it was a small mine, and it tapped out fast, and then everybody forgot it for a while." She lowers her eyelids a bit, as if staring at a lover. "Until?"

She wants to see if I've made the connection. I feel like I'm floating outside of my body. "Until Hib."

Her cold smile is as sharp as a nail. "That's right. They sent the crews up, along with the last two true Pomps they had. Both of them had previously developed cancer during mining on Ung-Nyeo, but when that mine was tapped, CPI pulled out all of the stops for treatment. Removed a bunch of their lymph nodes, injected stem cells, the works. When it took, I imagine they thought they were free. That they'd finally survived, but—"

Horror fills my guts like acid. "CPI was saving them."

She nods, as if impressed. "That's right. Just in case something like Hib happened. And your mother was one of those Pomps."

It's like my chest cracks, right down the middle, sternum pried apart by a blade made of secrets. "You're wrong. My mother wasn't on Hib. She was—"

"Your mother *escaped*. She and your father were part of Hib's very first crew." She gestures at the walls around her. "They, and the rest of that first batch of escapees, helped to build this hatch."

"That's impossible. How could they possibly—"

"Down the elevator. Although there was no elevator yet— just the tether. It's fascinating, you know—the way Ung-Nyeo and its moon orbit. They're like a single body."

This is too much to process.

"The tether is why removing piezanite from Hib is so cheap. There are wheels in the elevator car that cinch around it, motors that turn them to roll the car up and down. Once the elevator is far enough away, it doesn't even have to contend with gravity, so the amount of power it uses is minimal. But before the elevator was built, there was just the tether, and somehow, a small crew of people managed to spirit themselves down its length without getting caught."

"That's impossible. The distance alone—"

"It's not impossible, because it happened. That's the point. Over half of them died in the attempt. They're legends now, in the right circles. They went underground the second they got back. Nobody that's not connected with the right data at CPI even knows their names. But I knew from the second I saw you in Pomp school that your mom was one of the ones who made it. Your face looks just like her picture."

Her picture. What picture? What in the ever-loving fuck was Celeste talking about?

She covers her helmet visor for just a second, but then she pulls her hands down, and her expression is like iron again. "So. I tried to get you to quit. And once you failed out, I figured I could forget about it—but your suicidal detour into Medical invited more scrutiny into your file. And pretty soon, I wasn't the only person who recognized you. They assigned Gyu to keep eyes on you."

A snake wraps around my liver. "I don't believe you."

She curls her hands into fists. "I tried to warn you. I left you a note, even, in one of your dresser drawers, letting you know that he was watching you—"

A chill spreads, up my chest, down my neck. I can't feel my face or my fingers.

"And then you started showing up in my hatch. You nearly caught me the first time—gave me a fucking fright. I barely had time to get out of the escape tunnel."

"Why are you telling me all of this?" My shout bounces around my helmet. "Why the fuck would you do any of this?"

She bites her lip. Brings up her fist and opens it, and inside the palm of her glove is a small, black square of plastic. A memory drive. "Because of this. I'm part of an organization that believes that what CPI is doing is slavery. People don't deserve to spend their lives sentenced to prison because of a debt—especially not one CPI so skillfully engineered in the first place. They've reshaped our entire society to benefit only a few rich people at the very top. We don't have to live like this."

"I…" My voice dies. I get what she's saying, but the idea that anybody can stand against the goliath that is CPI is patently ridiculous. "How, exactly, are you going to change that?"

"The entire terminator band is completely dependent on piezanite, and that's by design. Long before CPI became the government itself, they paid a number of politicians to make other forms of energy generation and distribution illegal. They say it's because piezanite is so much safer, because it doesn't cause environmental pollution, but that's bullshit. They bought the remaining solar farms, the wind farms, the reactors—everything we had to make power—and shut them down and destroyed them. And people aren't willing to go back to a dark age. The people with power aren't going to give up the comfort of their current living circumstances to help overthrow this system. We have to take away the incentive for things to just stay the same."

"I still don't understand what it is you expect me to do."

"I've been sending drives down the elevator. This was supposed to be my last delivery—but then someone compromised my credentials. And when CPI investigated further, they found the switched manifests." She rubs the back of her helmet. "A one in a million chance. I still don't know how the fuck that happened. If it was just bad luck, or maybe Gyu—"

It was Hannah, I think, but I don't say anything out loud. "What's on the drives?"

Her gaze finds mine. Her eyes hard, impossibly deep. "Schematics. For the elevator."

"Why would you need to—" My blood goes cold. *Remove the incentive for things to stay the same.* "You're going to fuck up the elevator."

"No, not fuck it up. We're going to *blow* it up. We've figured out how to reverse engineer our own elevator car. We're going to send up a payload of explosives, timed it so it deploys halfway up the tether. It's not perfect—CPI will still be able to get the piezanite down with shuttles—but compared to the elevator, it'll be astronomically expensive. There's no way that's tenable for long."

"And everyone on Hib is going to, what, float down to safety? Everyone on Hib will *die*."

"And their deaths will start a revolution."

"You're fucking insane."

"Desperate times," says Celeste, and then she shakes her head. "But I can't do it anymore. I can't get within half a planet of that elevator. Gyu and the rest are looking for me. This hatch is shielded, but they'll still find it eventually. And when they do, they *can't* find the drive. There's over a generation of work waiting on this."

She locks eyes with me. "Which is why you're going to get off this moon, and then you're going to deliver it."

"What?" I snort. "I'm not helping you—"

"You *are* going to help me, because Gyu has already sent a message down that he thinks you might be a true Pomp. They're going to send you down to the surface—possibly treat you, if you've already got the cancer—and then they're going to study you. Use you to refine their models. When that happens, all you have to do is bring it down the elevator with you. Someone will contact you with a drop location."

My head is swimming, my heart lifting and falling like it's floating on the top of angry waves. "They're going to take me off of Hib? How long—"

"I don't know. Last I knew, he was still waiting to hear back for details, but of course, I haven't been to work in a while. And I can't hide out here, not forever. The food and water is limited. And the truth is that I'm near cracking. I'd rather go out on my own terms, because once they find me, they're going to fucking torture me to find out everything they can about our organization, and I can't let that happen."

"That's crazy. *You're* crazy."

"I thought you'd think that. That you'd need proof. So I added some extra files to the drive. Take it somewhere safe— don't check it in your bedroom, and don't check it at work, either. Look at those files, and then you can decide if I'm crazy or not. You don't need my credentials to access the drive. Just a password: RESURRECTION."

She grabs my arms. "I'm leaving now. You won't be able to follow me for two minutes, so don't try."

"Wait, I—"

Celeste grabs my helmet, throws it backward with impossible force. I slam into the floor, so hard my ears ring and my stomach turns, so hard that all of the air goes out of my lungs.

I'm seeing double of her as she climbs up the ladder. I can't let her get away. It takes me too long to find my feet, and she closes the door after her. I hear the lock engage.

No. I somehow make it up the ladder, try to push on the door, but it doesn't open. I struggle with it, mash the button over and over, but it's dead to me.

I'm going to die down here.

I'm suddenly taking huge breaths. *I'm trapped down here, and I'm going to run out of air—*

I check my oxygen tank. An hour, maybe, if I don't breathe too hard. An hour until I—

She said two minutes. Maybe the lock is on some kind of timer. Okay. Two minutes, and then I'll—

Oh fuck, I'm an idiot. The tunnel.

I crawl out the emergency tunnel until I make it to the surface. I haul myself up through the sand, push through the last few blind body lengths, and then I'm panting in the dark, on the surface of the sand.

I sweep my headlight beam, but Celeste is nowhere to be found. After a few moments, I push the button, and the hatch retreats into the sand.

27

I MAKE MY way over the sand, push through the darkness back to Hib station.

But once I'm back in the dome, I don't know where to go. I turn circles for a bit. Go to Rikki's, but I never make in the door. Double back, and eventually, I'm on my way home, which is not the right place to be. Celeste even told me specifically not to check the drive in my bedroom—but there's some part of my brain that's trying to connect these things together, and it's pushed my brain offline. Instead, my feet just drag me back to my door.

I push it open. My room is still a mess, of course. I take the light fixture down again, but there's nothing under the cover. I start to put the chair back, before I reconsider and wedge it up under the door handle instead.

Someone could be watching me right now, and that would make this the exact wrong thing to do, but it's better than somebody just walking in on me. At the very least, it will give me a second to pull the drive and destroy it, if I have to.

And then I take my tablet into the bathroom. Into the shower—if I'm being watched, if there's some kind of recording device, this seems like the least likely place. I shut the small door. The shower blinks on, asking me if I want to use real water or just have a standard cleaning, but I just ignore that.

I turn the tablet on. I hesitate before sticking in the drive. Celeste could still be lying to me, could be upset about me and Gyu and be trying to give me some kind of virus—

I jam the drive in before I can finish that thought. I type in the password and access its contents.

It's just a few folders. There's one called SCHEMATICS, which makes sense, but there are others. ACCESS KEYS. A folder called PERSONNEL RECORDS. And there's one at the bottom that just says YOUNG.

I swallow, but I open it, and there are two files inside.

The first one is actually a shortcut. I check its pathing and see that it refers back to a file inside of the PERSONNEL RECORDS folder, which is interesting.

I open it. It's a kind of spreadsheet, separated by columns. The left column has names in it. The one after that has some kind of digit and letter-based identifier. There's a column for dates—although some have one date on them, and some have two dates. There's a link to an attachment on each one, which turns out to be a picture. A few of the columns have notes after that, but they seem to be all over the place. On a whim, I type in my name, and it comes up immediately, toward the bottom. There's nothing in the notes section, but the single date in the third column is familiar. That's the date I arrived on Hib.

I swallow and type in my mom's name, and then my dad's, but there are no matches.

If there was something Celeste meant me to find here, it's not working.

I turn it over in my thoughts, my hand absently trailing up to the charm around my neck—*of course.*

I type in the code from the front of the charm, and almost immediately, the computer scrolls to the matching column. There is the number, next to a stranger's name—KIM, MI-HEE. Both dates are right before I was born, so this person wasn't on Hib for very long. In the notes column, it says MISSING, DEAD OR ESCAPED.

I click on the attachment, and I suddenly can't breathe. It's my mother's face.

Celeste had said my father, too. It only takes me a few moments to check the attachments of the people who left on the same date as my mother—and there it is, my father's face, even though the name is foreign to me: ALASA, JUN.

I spend a few more minutes in the spreadsheet, but if there's anything else in the roster I was meant to see, I can't find it. So instead, I go back to the YOUNG folder and open the other file in it. It's a very short snippet, and from the language, I think it's part of some kind of medical report.

```
CABLE LYMPHOMA:
KEY SYMPTOM PRESENTATION


> FATIGUE, OR ALTERNATIVELY, INSOMNIA

> SWELLING OF THE AFFECTED LIMB

> DELIRIUM, PARTICULARLY MANIFESTED
  AS  DELUSIONS  OF  GRANDEUR  OR
  DELUSIONS OF PERSECUTION

> TINNITUS,   HEARING   IMPAIRMENT,
  DEAFNESS
```

I close my eyes. I can't read this anymore.

I SIT ON the edge of my bed, the drive folded tight into my palm. It's proof that my entire life is a lie. I was born to parents with a hidden history and fake names, parents who abandoned me— but knowing what I know now, I have to wonder if there was more to the picture, things I never dared dream about. If their leaving had something to do with the long arms of CPI or maybe the bandages my mother always had to tightly wrap around her arm, a way of combating the swelling from the cancer. Once treated, cancers can come back, can't they?

I have her cancer; I know that now. When I dig my fingertips into my armpits, I can actually feel the hard lumps under the surface, a variety of sizes like a ration of mixed nuts. Were they already there, after the explosion, when I went to Medical? Or had they not manifested until later, some time before I showed up for my broken ankle? The technician had acted strange, and I'd chalked it up to his general distaste for the circumstances that CPI had put him through, for the decisions he'd had to make, trying to deliver care while keeping costs low. But I saw a pearl-like lump on the x-ray, one that he'd called an artifact. So, he must've known.

And *Gyu*. Questions about Gyu whip through my mind like storm winds. Because if Celeste was right, Gyu is the axis on which the gyre spins. And as much as I want it to be a lie—as jagged as the rip in my heart feels, the edges peeling apart and coming together with every breath—I have to acknowledge that it fits.

He showed up *right* after I tried to kill myself. It had weirded me out, the way he wanted to connect with me, the kindness he'd extended, like a handful of coins to a beggar, even as I desperately wanted him to get closer. And quickly, very quickly, he'd placed himself at the center of my world.

I'd thought it was a symptom of my mental illness, the fact that I let him in so fast. The way I clung to him. It never occurred to me that my response was what he'd *wanted*.

The dream he espoused, the two of us, making a future together somewhere on the fringes of the terminator band. The way he'd pulled strings to get me into Pomp training. As far as I knew, nobody got further training once they were dropped—and yet, *I* did. And I'd had the gall to consider that it might be because I was special—if not special by myself, then to Gyu.

Is he really angling to get me back onto Ung-Nyeo to be tested by CPI? And if so—what am I going to do? Maybe I *should* just make my way out into the sand, spend my last days in the hatch—*the hatch I told him about*, I realize with horror—trapped but somehow free. And if I don't, if I comply and get brought down planet-side—should I take the drive and try to give it to Celeste's people?

The inside of my mouth tastes like bile. I curl my fist around the drive so hard it presses sharp corners into my hand, so hard I can almost feel the plastic shifting, warning of its impending break.

I let go. I scoot backward until I can lean my back against the wall and pull the covers around me. The last thing I remember is staring at the ceiling, trying to make sense of it all.

I WAKE UP, still seated, with my legs folded to my chest. My knuckles ache. In my left hand, the sharp corners of the drive press into my palm. Somehow, I've worked my right hand under the collar of my shirt and grabbed ahold of my mother's Fore tab.

I open my eyes, turn my head, and freeze.

It's Gyu. Despite it only being a few circadians since I saw him last, it feels like an eternity. My heart betrays me with a quick flutter—but maybe the organ isn't traitorous. Maybe everything Celeste said was a bad dream, a lie, just part of a plan to get the drive off Hib.

His eyes look bloodshot. He's been crying, maybe. "They found her. Celeste."

Celeste. Had he heard her name in my thoughts? I try to keep my voice casual. "Oh? Where was she?"

"Nobody knows." There's something in his glance, a flicker of interest that he's trying to hide. "But she's in Medical now. She tried to kill herself. They're not sure if she's going to make it."

It feels like he knows more than he's letting on—but then again, isn't that what Celeste said she was about to do? Walk out and let *them* discover her, no matter what the consequences?

If someone dies for a cause, can you really call it a suicide?

"Okay," I say. "Thanks for telling me."

He looks at me. Turns his palms up, as if asking for help. "I came to walk you to work. I'm sorry I've been gone for so long—I was just worried about her."

"Right."

He hasn't blinked the whole time he's been talking to me. I realize how I must look—sleeping sitting up. Like I'd been keeping vigil by a grave.

"Are you going to hit me?" He cracks a smile and points to my hands, still balled up in fists.

I can't even feel them anymore. I let go of the charm and push my hands down my sides and under the covers. "No. I just—"

"Let me see." He crosses the room before I can stop him. I barely have time to cram the drive under my leg.

He picks up one hand, and then the other, before winding his fingers between mine. He lightly kisses me on the cheek. "Really," he murmurs. "I'm sorry I've been gone. It was wrong of me."

His touch makes my senses go haywire: lights blinking, electric shocks zapping my skin. My body begs for him to hold me. My mind urges me to pull away. Finally, I do, just enough to see his face. "Gyu. I have to ask you something."

He searches my expression, but he nods. "Okay."

"What you said before. About us together, on Ung-Nyeo— about our little homestead in the terminator band, the kids—"

"—only if you want them," he says hastily, as if I've forgotten my own feelings on it.

"Yeah. Did you mean that? Is that really the future you see for us?"

His eyes widen. I sputter out an explanation before he can ask questions. "It's just—this thing with Celeste. You up and left, and you didn't even bother to drop me a note." It sounds plausible enough.

"Oh, Young." He heaves a sigh. "Yes. I know. That was—that was the wrong thing to do. I just…I feel like I've lost so many people lately. I didn't think I could lose anybody else. Surely you understand."

I do understand, but that makes it worse, more confusing.

"And—" He clears his throat. "I absolutely mean what I said."

There's a depth in his eyes, and it buoys my heart up in a warm, liquid current. It feels like the truth, this. I'm still afraid, but it's not like I can trust Celeste. I feebly start to extend toward him, a blade of grass unfurling up toward the light.

"In fact, we might be able to have the dream sooner rather than later."

My pulse, my breath, the flow of blood through my veins—it all stops at once. "Oh?"

He nods. "Yes. I—well, I was going to wait to tell you this, until we'd had a few days to put this all behind us, but… CPI is really impressed with how you bounced back. They're thinking that they'd maybe like to start a program that looks at people that showed promise but failed out. They'd like to use our experience as a model." He takes my hands. "They're asking for us to come down and share our experiences with a big group—and there's the chance that they might pay us *a lot* for it."

It's strange, but I'm almost certain I can hear the sounds of metal screeching. Of glass breaking. "Wow. I don't know what to say."

"Yes. Seven circadians, maybe, and we'll be on our way down to see Ung-Nyeo again."

Ung-Nyeo. My heart sings the name of our planet, but for the first time since I made it to Hib, I don't want to go home.

He leans in again and embraces me. His heart beats so loudly, I can't hear anything else.

28

IT'S NOT UNTIL we're both standing in his office that I realize what our mutual presence means. After abandoning me for that long, Gyu intends to pick up where we left off, with us working side by side.

I don't buy that CPI is going to start some kind of program. He must think I'm dumb, must know what I can do—or at least, he suspects. Maybe he's even followed me to my hole by the mine or out to the hatch. For all I know, he's been tracking my hov rentals, my lookups, watching my actions as a Pomp from a distant screen. The idea that he's been there all along, an audience, it shoots ice into my veins. I wish I'd never met him.

For the first time, I feel something new. Something righteous, like glass blown into its final form. There's always the chance that he's innocent, that Celeste parlayed all the doubts and unsaid spaces between us into a neat story—but I don't think so. And if she was telling the truth, then Gyu is a *liar*. He lied the moment he met me, right up until the moment we're in right now, waiting for the Conduction to finish loading.

Every kindness, every softness, every fuck, every meal—all of it, lies.

I feel violated. I want to rip his arms off of his body. And instead, somehow, I have to get through this circadian, and the next, and who knows how many more until CPI turns me into a lab animal. There's no way out, no escape.

Escape. I spend hours meditating on that word. After being kidnapped by Hannah, being ambushed by Celeste, after everything that's happened on Ung-Nyeo and here—the concept's taken on a different gravity.

We're almost at the quarter shift when Gyu finally gets a message and the general channel freezes.

"Gyu!" I make my voice high-pitched, hiding my excitement behind a veil of frustration. "Put the Con back!"

"Just give me a moment, I—"

"Gyu, I have been directing this team alone with *zero* interference on your part, and I don't feel particularly like risking someone's safety because you want to take a *call.*"

He's quiet. I've gone too far, tried to balance looking like an overzealous newbie and an estranged girlfriend. It's tense, too tense—but then he nods and waves a hand. "Okay." The Con springs back to the normal overlays. "I'll just be a minute."

"Thank you," I say, but he's not listening.

I open the crew general channel. "I'm getting a funny reading. I'd like to do a quick equipment check."

The crew moves into position without hesitation. After the last several shifts of working together, I've finally earned their trust. I ask about the pressures and other measurements, and they report back that everything's within tolerances.

I'm sweating. I wish I had Annie and her blowers. "Okay. I guess it was nothing then. I swear, sometimes I wish I could take the people that designed this thing and bury them underground. Maybe under the Desert, or in the Ice. Just put them in a nice little enclave."

It looks like Na stiffens—but it's hard to tell through the drone. And I'm not actually sure that Na Haneul and Hannah are the same person. I want to say something else, a better clue, but I can't be any more obvious without attracting Gyu's attention. And when I look over, his fingers twist in the motion that means he's ending a call.

"Alright," I say over the crew channel. "Let's get back to work."

AT THE END of the shift, Gyu gives me a hug. He's remarkably inconsistent about his concern for CPI's eyes and ears. "Let's have dinner together. I'll make you something."

"No." The word is reflex, almost violent in the way it tears out of me.

His face falls. "I know things have been weird between us."

I've got to smooth this over. I don't want him getting suspicious—and even though I know he's a liar, I so desperately wish I could believe this was a misunderstanding, that maybe he was on my side all along. It aches in a way that makes me disgusted with myself.

I exist outside of Gyu, I think, but it feels like a lie. Like I died out there, somewhere on the sand, leaving behind a single cell he saved in a petri dish and grew into something new. "I just…I just need a little bit of space. I'm trying to not be jealous of Celeste, and I'm glad you're good, but I think I just need a circadian to get my head on straight. Is that okay?"

His expression is sour, but he nods. "Yeah. Of course."

And then he's gone. Evidently, he didn't want to wait for me.

He leaves me with a raw ache that I know is my body desperately trying to cling to the feeling of him in my presence, his scent, the traces of warmth that must have been left behind in the air molecules bouncing off of his skin.

But behind the ache is just relief he's gone.

THE KNOWLEDGE THAT the drive is still under my covers, that my house has already been broken into multiple times—it makes me want to go straight home and find a better hiding place for it. But there's always the chance that I'm being watched, which makes what I'm actually about to do stupid— but I feel like if I don't find Hannah now, there's no way I'll talk myself into it later.

I make it out the door of Engineering and take the spokes that will lead to the cafe where I first saw the woman with the charm around her neck. The tables are crowded with people socializing and enjoying drinks, hot and cold. I catch a sweet, warm-pepper tang—spiced milk—and over it wafts the acerbic, clean scent of a green tea. Some people hold clear glasses with single washes of color inside, so bright I can almost taste the fruit juice.

The woman's not here. I try to think. I meant to pull up Na's personnel file again before leaving, but that hug rattled me. And I have to assume Gyu's already looking at every move I make, inside the Con and out. Which means that finding Hannah right now is dumb—but besides Celeste, who is likely dead, she's the only other person who knew he was watching me. I need to find out more.

I decide to try to locate the little bunker she dragged me into. The woman I followed there moved too quick for me, limping as I was, and I didn't do a good job of marking my way through. I stumble down a side street and find a flyer advertising that CPI is temporarily reducing prices at a fish-fry restaurant. Five minutes later, I find the same flyer. I think I've turned a circle, but no—the flyer is *everywhere*.

It's not until I turn a corner, almost at random, that I find out why—two even stacks of flyers on the ground, work that somebody started but didn't finish. CPI likely offered them a debt reduction to distribute and post them, and whoever it was just left them in the alley. Pretty clever, if it worked.

I turn more corners. I keep seeing things that I think I saw last time: a cracked piece of imitation stone. Two cigarette butts that have fallen to make an "x." A stain shaped like a kidney.

I realize I also don't know how to get out of this place, and panic burbles up in my throat. You can't actually get lost on a space station—if you just go one direction, without quitting, you'll eventually hit the outside bubble—except that I keep running into dead ends. I can see myself, dead of dehydration because I couldn't find my way out of the maze of storage alleys. Nobody would ever find my body.

"What the hell are you doing?" It's Hannah's voice. No modulator.

"I—" My breath comes in gasps. "I was trying to find the entrance—"

Hannah snorts. "I saw you come in. Every time I managed to get kind of close to you, somebody walked up, and I had to act like I was going in a different direction, but I've been following you for like, five minutes straight. I can't believe you didn't notice."

My cheeks burn. Despite how carefully I'd looked behind me, despite being afraid of Gyu or a spy, she'd tailed me easily.

Hannah could be Gyu's spy, though. That seems like the kind of sneaky shit CPI's dog would do. My throat closes back up.

"I don't think we should talk here," she says, despite the fact that I've been silent. "Follow me. Try to act nonchalant about it."

It blows my mind how well she navigates through the narrow alleys between the different buildings. She knows her way around like it's a second home.

Despite her telling me to act like I'm not following her, I can't help but say something. "What kind of idiot would design something like this?"

She looks back and gives me a glare, as if to say, *shut up*, but she also answers my question. "It's storage, mostly. A lot of it is stuff the station needs only for emergencies or periodic maintenance. Stuff we can't *not* have on Hib, but that we don't have to access regularly, which is why it's jammed so tight. CPI didn't plan well enough for the amount of growth the station was going to experience."

She shrugs, still walking. "It's also a good place if you want to shoot up or something, although you have to be careful. Enforcement is wise to it."

I think about my Brin, his lips blue. "Can't people just do that at home?"

"Depends on what you're shooting up," she says, before turning down an alley.

And just like that, we're there. She looks both ways before inserting a thin piece of metal in a hole near the doorjamb. There's a groan as she turns her hand—some kind of homemade key.

We both step inside, and she locks the door behind her. I follow her down the stairs. "What is this place?"

Her eyes look distant. She's buried somewhere in her own mind. "Adda and I found it," she finally says. "It was full of spare parts that Hib was never going to use. We reprogrammed the inventory so that on the next audit, this space would kind of disappear from the mainframe. It doesn't exist anymore—at least, not to the computers."

"Spare parts." I parrot the words, but my mind is flying. Adda and Hannah are some kind of programmers. That explains how Hannah's picture could wind up missing from the file—maybe even how Hannah managed to get herself reassigned to my crew.

"Don't worry," she says. "We were careful. The chances of us needing those exact parts are pretty low."

"Right," I say. "Who was the woman that—"

"I paid her. She thinks I'm pissed about what happened to Adda, that I planned to just fuck you up a little."

"I see."

Hannah sits. Her foot bounces, and she drums the table with her fingers, her pink nails flicking like signal lights. "You know, I assumed from your not-very-cryptic message about enclaves over the com that you wanted to meet with me."

"Yes," I say, but my nerve has evaporated. I have no way of knowing if Hannah is Gyu's spy, or a sellout, or if maybe she just wants to get me in trouble for what happened to Adda. And despite being the wedge between us, Adda is also the only strand of trust between us. Hannah's grief for Adda feels like the twin to my own guilt. "I guess before I say anything, though, I've got some questions."

"Are you going to help me or not?"

Only if I get what I want—and only if I think I can trust her. "I don't know yet. You're asking me for something huge. Something that could fuck up or even end my life. Before I help you, there are some things I want to know."

It's one of the boldest things I've ever said—we're literally in a soundproofed bunker, and there's no doubt in my mind that Hannah would willingly kick my ass or worse.

She looks furious for a moment, her cheeks twitching with anger she bites back, but she nods and leans back in the chair. "Your life is already fucked," she says. "But, shoot."

"The light fixture."

She waves a hand in the air. "Found it, did you? I figured that's why—"

"I didn't find anything."

Her intake of breath is harsh. "Oh, fuck?"

My heart hammers. "What do you mean, *oh fuck*."

"I discovered it when I was tossing your room." She glances at my face, and it's clear from her next words that she misinterprets my expression. "Don't worry. I was wearing a mask—I don't think anybody can identify me."

"When you were *tossing my room*—"

"Listen! After you fled the bar, Adda and I were getting tucked into bed, and she said that there was something fishy going on. And then everything blew up. It seemed too big to be a coincidence." She pursed her lips. "I went through your stuff for clues. That's when I saw your crew assignment and decided to get closer to you, to figure out if you were guilty. What makes you tick. I'm shocked my request for transfer went through so fast."

An alarm rings in the back of my mind. "You didn't ram it through yourself, with the computers or something?"

She shakes her head. "No."

"But…you can't just *request* a specific crew."

"No, but you can go to Medical and say that you're feeling incredibly bereaved and hinting that you're possibly suicidal, and that you're sure you can keep it together, but only if you get a fresh start, because everything keeps reminding you of your girlfriend that got blown up. And then, when they move you to the crew with the next available opening—"

"You got lucky," I say, and this time, I'm the one who leans back in the chair. "There wasn't an opening on my crew, except that someone got injured and opened up a slot."

"Yes." She smiles, the arc of her lips thin, tight, and cold. "He fell down a flight of stairs and got a head injury. He got to Medical quickly, and he's going to be fine, but it's not like they can give you an injection that makes your brain heal faster. He's going to be out of commission for another twenty circadians, at least."

I bristle. *Out of commission, and he'll owe almost a lifetime's worth of debt to CPI before he's ready to go back to work.*

Hannah reads my mind. "Don't worry about him. He's dying, anyways. Some kind of liver disease. He's been dosing to get through the day, and it hasn't gone unnoticed by his Fore. If CPI was willing to bring him down the elevator, they could probably treat him in time, but they won't."

It's heart-stoppingly cruel on both CPI's *and* Hannah's part.

She makes a frustrated sigh at my expression. "Look. I also sent a bunch of money to his family. He's got a kid. He consented. He *thanked* me for the opportunity. At least this way, he leaves them something."

I nod, but I can't tell if she's lying or not. Her eyes have gone hooded and cold. Haunted.

I can't do this. And even if I could, she never answered my question. "What did you find in my room?"

"A listening device—or maybe a recording device. I thought maybe it was yours, trying to protect your stuff—or Celeste's. We were already watching her, trying to see if she'd caught on yet about her credentials. Right before." She closes her eyes, shakes her head briefly, as if trying to dislodge a memory. "We could tell Celeste was taking an awfully large interest in you. We were thinking that maybe you were working together, and she was trying to make sure you weren't going to stab her in the back. Especially given what she was mixed up in."

"Which is what?"

Her mouth becomes a hard line. "Fanatics. Zealots, it sounds like. The kind of people who would blow the station to hell and back to make a point. She tends to get real talky after a roll in the hay."

"I don't…You were sleeping with her?" First Gyu, then Hannah. Was anybody not sleeping with Celeste?

"No, you dumbass. Adda. They used to date, back on Ung-Nyeo. Adda was even wrapped up in Celeste's little group for a while, before realizing that they wouldn't accomplish anything useful. They're zealots, but their convictions are far stronger than their ability to get anything done."

I didn't bring the drive with me. I'd left it in my room, under the covers. Now, that feels like a mistake. What would Hannah think if she saw how detailed the schematics were? If she knew the exact details of Celeste's plan? Would she try to stop it? Or would she just…let it go?

"Anyways, I'd be careful. If the device isn't there, and you didn't remove it, then somebody took it out. Which means they were worried about getting caught. Now, do you have any other questions, or can we get on with it?"

Gyu, Hannah, and Celeste. I can't trust any of them.

But I *know* I don't trust CPI. Whatever they want with me, it's not going to end well, and if there's a way out of here, I have to take it.

I bite my lip. "I am willing to help you—but I have two conditions."

Hannah narrows her eyes. "Which are?"

"First, I want you to use your computer skills and find out everything you can about two people that disappeared on me a while ago. I want to know if there's any record of what happened to them or where they are now."

Hannah cocks her head to the side, appraising me. "Who are they?"

"That's not important. Can you do it or not?"

"I can try." She produces a food wrapper and a pen. "Write down their names."

I write down my parents' names, both the ones I know and the ones from Celeste's file, fold the wrapper, and hand it over to her. I try to act normal, but the moment feels both momentous and painful. Like saying goodbye.

"What's the second condition?"

"You have to take me with you."

"What?" Hannah's mouth falls open. "No. There's no room, and there's no way—"

"I'm dying," I say, and the finality of those words, spoken

aloud, it's like a cold coal settling in my gut, waiting to be lit. "I have cancer. It's bad."

Hannah's face goes grim. "How long do you have?" I can see the math playing behind her eyes, calculating the odds of getting what she needs from me in time.

I have no idea how long it will be before the cancer kills me. Despite the sinking feeling, the artifact on the scan, I'm not even sure it's cancer—maybe Celeste was lying about that, too.

But I don't think so. And I'm not going back to Ung-Nyeo's surface with Gyu, under lock and key. "Not very long. I may not even survive the trip down the elevator."

"You don't look very sick." Hannah narrows her eyes.

"Come here."

Once she's close enough, I grab her hand, press it into my armpit. She pulls away, a reflex, but not hard enough to break my hold. Her fingers writhe like worms before going still. Then they prod, slowly, exploring my armpit like a soft tongue. "Holy shit," she finally says. "That's…They're huge."

"Yeah," I say. "But if I can get back to Ung-Nyeo—"

"They won't treat you," she says, her brow lifting. "Not without money."

"They won't," I say. I'd hoped she was going to fill in the blank a different way. "Do you think—do they have doctors in these enclaves?"

"Maybe." Hannah runs her gaze over me, her eyes crawling up and down my bandaged arm with the prickling touch of spiders. "What's with the wrapping?"

"My arm swells. Something about the lymph nodes."

"It's the Cable, isn't it?"

My insides freeze. "How did you—"

"It's a rumor that floats around certain circles. Certain *orga-nized* circles. But I didn't think…How were you exposed? Was it the blast?"

I shrug. "Maybe. Or maybe it was the day before. My glove ripped, and I accidentally fell and touched a bunch." It's close enough to the truth.

She absently rubs at her upper arm before dropping her own hand down again. She's probably thinking about the rip in her suit, the rock buried in her skin. Probably nothing, but maybe something. Maybe we're in the same boat. "I should say no. Even if the plan requires two people."

This hurts. "I'm a sorry substitute for Adda."

"Yeah," she says. Another long pause. "We'll need some supplies. Suits. A place to hide. Some water and food if we can find it. It's all easy enough to come by, but—" She bites her lip. "We need Gyu's credentials, too."

I swallow. "Why Gyu's?"

Hannah's expression betrays nothing, but I understand the implication beneath the poker-face: There's a limit on what she'll tell me before I commit.

"Right," I say. "I'm willing to get them, although I'm not sure how." It's the truth, on both counts.

"Well," she says, and she smiles that awful smile again. "I sort of have a plan for that."

29

IT TURNS OUT that as escape plans go, Hannah's is pretty elementary. We go down the elevator the same way we came up—as cargo.

I've never seen the elevator from the outside. Other miners on Hib station have tried, have told me about journeying over the sand to make it as far as CPI's perimeter fence, an automated checkpoint that requires credentials for entry. The checkpoint is so far from the elevator you can't see the tether, although I imagine it's like an ethereal wisp of smoke rising straight into the sky, far too unbending to be anything natural.

On the Ung-Nyeo side, the elevator facility isn't inside of the terminator band, which means it's outside of the wind-walls, so there's no way for someone to access it without CPI's permission. To get us to the elevator's location in the middle of the Desert, they loaded us all into cargo containers, each one the size of a small market square. We sat on hard seats with odd projections that stuck out like tree branches, and they allowed us all one box of belongings that stowed underneath the seat. The projections, we found out, were to chain us to our seats.

The guard who chained me down had done so with a smile. "It's just to keep you from getting nervous and hurting someone. It's to keep you safe."

"Thank you," I said. I didn't feel safe.

Once we were all loaded, they hitched our container to some kind of giant engine that rumbled like a factory—a truck, I thought. It towed us for a while, and then I felt the axis of gravity shift beneath me. All at once, it cost me effort to sit up, to keep from folding over. We were going down a steep slope.

"I wish I knew some prayers," I said to the man next to me.

"I doubt they'd do you any good." He pushed his glasses up his face with his unbound hand. Rich people generally opted for more permanent correction, but something in the way the man spoke, each syllable carefully articulated and crisp, his vowels singing and gliding—he was from somewhere else in the terminator band, somewhere far away. Maybe things were different there.

He regarded me for a long time before speaking again. Under his constant gaze, I looked down at my feet, my back aching with the strain of keeping me upright. Around the container, others had given up and let themselves sag against the chain. One woman in front of me was even sleeping, somehow, her arm behind her and holding her up like a tent-line. I marveled.

"We're going down to the vac-train," he said, finally. "The elevator is a quarter of a planet away, and between the windstorms and the heat of the Desert, we'd never make it over the surface."

After feeling creeped out by him, I didn't want to talk anymore, but I was curious. Around us, some people had that stiff, unmoving posture that meant they were straining to listen. "What's a vac-train?"

"It's a kind of fast transport. It runs inside of a sealed, pressurized tube that's a little bit bigger around than this container. We'll get loaded onto a floating floor that levitates on magnets and then launched a quarter of the way around the planet at six times the speed of sound."

"Is it going to hurt?"

"Does it hurt when you go fast in a vehicle?"

I squinted at him. "I've never ridden in a private vehicle."

He shook his head gently. "A train then."

I considered. "No. Although I can feel when it first starts to move."

"This will be the same. We'll feel it accelerate, but once we're at speed, your brain will adjust, and it will start to feel normal. We'll cross out of the terminator band and under the Desert. If you were outside, up there, it'd get very hot, but it won't bother us down here.

"The end of the elevator is actually in a small area of shadow cast by the moon. It's cooler there, and that's where we'll decelerate and stop. They'll load us onto the elevator, and take us up to space, and we won't see a thing."

"How do you know all of this?"

"I helped designed it," he said, pushing his glasses up his face again.

When I first got to prison, I quickly discovered that most of my compatriots were just debtors—and that it was rude to ask the reason someone was here. But him, I asked.

He didn't answer. He didn't talk to me for the rest of the trip—not even after we were on the elevator and ascending up the tether, not even after they unchained us from the seats. We discovered that our cargo container was actually broken into two rooms: the main room we lived in, and a narrow strip of a side room that just held a tiny bathroom stall and a water cooler. Once we were far enough away from Ung-Nyeo, there was no gravity for a while, and using the toilets without making a mess of yourself involved holding down a button that sucked your pee and shit through a tube, although someone invariably fucked this up at least once a day. The sinks had dry sanitizer. The only water available came out of a cooler that sat in the corner, part of a pressurized system that somehow brought it all of the way up from Ung-Nyeo. It always tasted like shit, too, some relic of the chemicals that were squirted in to lower its friction coefficient and make it easier to pump up.

Every so often, the flow of the water stopped, meaning the tank that immediately serviced the cargo container had gone empty. At that point, one of the guards would hit a button, and pumps all the way up and down the elevator's main shaft would activate. We were ascending so fast that when they turned on the pumps, we'd hear ourselves pass them, the banging growing louder, then quieting to silence, growing louder, and quieting again.

Guards were posted around the perimeters of the room at all times, stun guns at the ready—at least, we hoped they were stun guns. I'm still surprised that none of us were stupid enough to find out. There were videos projected on each of the four walls, with subtitles in all four core languages, so that if you could read—and you could see, which wasn't a given in prison, although this crew seemed to have fewer obvious physical disabilities than the crowd I was used to—you could watch. There was no sound.

Guards periodically entered and exited from a door on the side to bring us food. The door led out of the container into the other parts of the elevator car, but we never got a chance to see what was out there.

The circadians all blended together. The only sign that time was passing at all was when we hit the halfway point of the journey, and the guards came in and turned pairs of cranks at the ends of each row of seats. Each row detached itself from the floor before revolving 180 degrees, ascending to the ceiling, and locking in place with a loud click.

It was strange, but it also didn't really matter. Almost as soon as you become fully weightless, you lose all sense of up and down.

So, it was an eternity later that we arrived on Hib, the moment forecasted by a sense of increasing gravity that at first felt imaginary—until we realized our ability to stay rooted to the floor had more to do with planetary forces than the magnets in our shoes, and the guards came, once again, to chain us to the sides of our chairs.

Our cargo container was loaded onto another truck, driven to Hib station, and dropped off inside. Opening it anywhere else would have exposed us to Hib's gas composition, and without being connected to the elevator's utility system, there was no way for us to get air or water until we were safely in the station.

So I never saw anything of the elevator except for the container that had served as our holding cell—which meant that while Hannah's plan *sounded* simple, there was no way for me to check.

Hannah claims to know when the next shipment of piezanite will go down and wants us to sneak into the elevator facility after the end of the previous shift. Given the high security, this seems impossible—unless you have the right credentials from someone in the right department, like Engineering.

Once inside the correct room in the facility, you would have to work fast. Open a cargo container with the credentials and stow away. If Hannah is right, once the container is in motion, if you have the right credentials, you should be able to sneak into the bathroom. If the cooler is working, you'd have access to water. She is less sure about our ability to sneak into the guard rooms, where the food is, but she is optimistic.

When Hannah and Adda were testing their hypothesis, they put a small bug inside a package they knew was going down in a container soon. It sent a brief but strong pulse of radio waves in a specific pattern when the lid of the container was opened and the bug eventually exposed to light. Before I'd even arrived on Hib, they'd discovered that the container had made it all of the way to the terminator band before being opened—which meant that if you were clever enough, you *might* be able to find a way to escape while it is still in the underground tunnel in the middle of the Desert. You *might* be able to then traverse the tunnel's length until you find yourself on the outside edge of the moon's shadow, where the temperature would be similar to the terminator band—if you could somehow avoid being hit by a vac-train moving several times the speed of sound. And then, still, you'd have to find some way out of the tunnel, up to the surface, where the wind would tear your body apart.

Where there'd be nowhere to go—except that Hannah is sure there is an enclave there, somewhere on the rim of the shadow of the moon. There would be no dome or wind-walls, which meant that navigating around the circumference of that shadow would involve crawling with your face covered and your eyes closed, trying to avoid having sand shear off pieces of your flesh as you rapidly dehydrated.

After their first test had been successful, Hannah had been ready to go. Adda, though, had wanted to wait, to do one more test. They sent down another bug, not realizing that on that particular shift, Celeste's credentials had accessed the shipment and the facility twice already.

Once, for the standard checks and protocols that Engineering is supposed to do with every shipment.

Once, for an after-hours project of Celeste's own—a drive. I know the details of it, even if Hannah doesn't.

So, when a guard in a control room somewhere saw Celeste badge in *yet again* in the system, he got suspicious. Twice made sense: Maybe the Engineer had come back after realizing she forgot something. But after the third time, Gyu was alerted— and given that, at that exact moment, Celeste had been standing in front of me, Gyu had realized that Celeste's credentials had been compromised.

He'd stopped the shipment and combed through its contents for clues. He'd found one of Celeste's drives, and Hannah's bug, and he'd enacted a new protocol until everything could be sorted out. Gyu would be the only person who did the final inventories before a shipment. And once a container has been visually inspected at the mine and sealed, nobody could access it but Gyu—which meant that his credentials are the only ones that mattered.

GYU'S CREDENTIALS.

It makes sense, now, why it has to be Gyu. Why Hannah was willing to risk so much to reach out to me, despite the way she must feel about me.

After she gives me her plan to get Gyu's credentials, we work out the few details we can. We need a safe phrase that we can drop into communication during a normal work shift—something that will let the other person know we need to meet.

"What about 'I'm going for a walk'?" Hannah gives me a cold smile.

I don't get it, not until I see that her eyes aren't smiling with the rest of her face. She's making a morbid joke about how I tried to commit suicide. "I feel like that doesn't make sense— like we can't just mention we're about to go for a walk."

"Fine, then. 'I *need* a walk.'"

It's sufficiently innocuous. "Okay. I guess that works. But where will we meet?"

"What about here?" She tilts her head, indicating the wall of her hidden bunker.

I don't know. Even with the coordinates, I'm not sure if I can find it in an emergency. "Wouldn't it be better to have it outside of the station? That way, nobody can see us."

"So what? A set of random coordinates or something?"

I want to say yes. I don't want to tell her about the hatch—not after Celeste. But the hatch makes the most sense. Celeste even mentioned it was shielded, whatever that means. "I have a place."

I pull up the coordinates in Annie and hand them over to her. I don't tell her how to get in—that much, maybe, I can keep to myself until the last second.

When I get home, I wedge the chair under the door. Balance a cup on top of it, so that any movement will send it hurtling down. I don't want to be surprised while I get the drive.

The cup won't do anything about recording devices, so I try to look nonchalant. I kick off my outer clothes, my shoes, yawn far too many times for any normal person. I sidle up to the bed, before flopping over on it. The feeling that someone is watching me, right now, peels away at my skin.

The room is sweltering, but despite that, I rub my arms like I'm cold. Yawn again. I slip under the blanket and slowly fish around with my fingers.

I can't find the drive.

My heart beats faster. Somebody must have been here— it can't have been Hannah; she was literally right in front of me for almost the entire time. And Celeste is…what? Gone? Disappeared?

It was Gyu. I feel like vomiting. Because if Gyu has the drive, he has Celeste's schematics—and now, he's going to think I was involved. I should have come straight home and recovered it. The password won't stop him. He'll see the files Celeste earmarked about me. He'll know I know.

Can this really be happening? It's not too late for Celeste and Hannah to both be liars. For Gyu to be innocent. As certain as I felt in the moments after going through the drive, after seeing my mother's face—I am also sure, now, that it would be easy for Celeste to pull a con on me. The best cons all have enough truth in them to be convincing. It's a bonus if they pull hard enough on a person's heartstrings to make someone look past their own interests, past what is rational. It would be easy for Celeste to tell the truth about the drive—but not about Gyu and his involvement. It would serve her ends well.

There, on the bed, I give up. Press myself into the cover, sink down, down, as if the weight of my muscles is enough to flatten my bones. Did I really think that Hannah and I could get Gyu's credentials and somehow sneak onto the elevator?

Everything seems so hopeless. Everything has been hopeless, right back to the moment my parents left. Back to the moment I walked into the kitchen to see the pictures upside down, the pillow in the oven. Back, even, to the moment I was hauled out of the water, almost drowned—only then, it felt like my fate had turned. Maybe I *did* drown. Or maybe I was *meant* to, and all the suicide attempts, the bad luck, the near-brushes with death, were just the world trying to set things right.

I don't know how much time passes, but eventually, the basest functions of my body intervene. I'm hungry. I have to pee. And I'm sweating.

And worse, lying like this feels like it did before, when I was little, sick in bed, listening for the sounds of my parents below, wondering why our stolen house had gone so incredibly quiet.

They abandoned me. Maybe they had a good reason; maybe they didn't. Either way, I had gotten up, crawled out of bed, and made it down the stairs. And in all the things that happened after, I made it through.

I don't believe in deeper meanings. I don't think surviving this long *means* anything, other than the fact that I have the ability to do that. To get out of bed.

And I am still hungry, and I still have to pee—because those are the demands of a living body. Not a dead one. I am still alive.

It doesn't feel good. But it doesn't feel bad, either. It's a fact, and one I can't just ignore by lying here and hoping it will go away.

I have a packet of poison from Hannah in my pocket. Odorless, tasteless. Easy to stir into a drink or mix into a meal—as soon as Gyu gets close enough. As soon as Hannah gives me the signal that we're ready and they're about to send a load of piezanite down. All I have to do is get Gyu's password before I poison him.

I'll have to get close to him to use it. Have to share a meal with him.

Gyu could still be innocent. He might deserve this. He might be telling me the truth.

I'm calm—calm enough to see how disordered my mind is, cluttered thoughts in a destroyed room I still haven't managed to clean up. The next step seems simple, almost.

I pull the blanket off. Roll to the edge of the bed. I find my feet, walk to the desk, start picking up the pile on the floor, sorting everything into neat stacks.

I do the kitchen next. The rest of my room. When everything is done, I clean, really clean in a way I haven't since…since before water became expensive. Before I was homeless. Before my parents left. I clean the way I did when I was a child, a bowl full of water and a shirt for a wash-rag. I wipe the walls. I wash the floors, squatting and crab walking forward.

When I get to the edge of the bed, I make out a dark patch underneath.

The drive. It fell off my bed, somehow. Probably when I flopped over onto it.

Out of the view of any devices, I palm it. Somehow, I finish cleaning, and when everything in my room is finally in its right place, a small, ordered forest that has been bent to my will, I look for a place to store it. Nowhere feels right. I'll have to bring it to the hatch later.

I eventually fake using the bathroom, dropping it behind the tank as I do, and when I stand up and go through the pantomime of flushing and cleaning my hands, it's out of sight.

THE BREAK PASSES by without incident, but the next shift, Gyu comes to get me as if nothing has changed. As if the shifts he spent looking for Celeste and my request for space were both imaginary.

I already figured out he would. Before falling asleep, I ran through every interaction we ever had, only to come up with one certainty: Gyu always gets the upper hand. If we split up, it will be on his terms, and not mine. I hoped I was wrong— but here he is. Here's the proof. Despite my volatility, it's Gyu, really, who calls the shots in this relationship.

"I'm glad it's finally all cleaned up in here."

I nod.

He steps in without an invitation, without asking. He bustles around the kitchen—apparently, some things are in the wrong place—but I don't pay attention. I can't get over the fact that, in a way, he might be more fucked up than me. Despite all the lies I've told, I've never faked an entire relationship—and when he's opening my cabinets, making it hard to breathe, I can't believe how dumb I am. I really believed in his affection. His warmth. His kindness.

It will be a delicate thing, maneuvering this situation to go the way I need. He'll get suspicious if I push too hard. "Hey Gyu, I think we should talk."

"I see," he says, his face falling into a scowl. Then, the expression melts away. "Look. I get it. I'll go." He turns to leave, his shoulders slumping.

It shakes me, his contrition. How much he looks every inch the picture of a dejected lover. I step forward, place my hand on his shoulder. "Wait." I steel myself. My voice can't be too pathetic, too loud, too commanding. I have to hit this just right.

He pauses. It's a moment we've had before, but now, everything is different.

My chest burns. *Careful.* "I was thinking about your offer."

"My—"

"To have a meal together. After the shift."

He still hasn't turned around, but his shoulders relax. "Of course. I can bring—"

"No," I say. "We always eat here." And despite the fact that I'm acting, despite the fact that every word I say is a lie, designed to get us close enough for me to figure out how to get what I need from him—his password, access to the schedule, his credentials—the truth of my lie stings. We *do* always eat here.

"I'm sorry," he says, so quick that I can't help but forgive him a little, and I have to heave up on the stone walls around my heart. "We could go out—"

"I feel like your pet, sometimes. Like…something kept. It's not equal. You never let me in." It burns, holding myself back, but I've got to let it come from him.

"I'm sorry," he says.

I wait, but the invitation doesn't come. "Okay," I say. "It's fine. But…we'd better get going. I don't want to be late."

This time, he's the one who grabs my wrist. "Wait," he says. He swivels me around, until we're eye to eye. His gaze darts back and forth, as if reading the lines of my face. "Does it really bother you that much?"

"Yes." The word burns on its way out. I can't take the way his eyes unpeel me. I look down at the floor. "No. It's fine. I'm fine." And then, I look back at him, and I smile, as forced as I can make it.

I know exactly what it looks like. I've spent hours in a mirror, perfecting different smiles. Taking photographs to reflect the image I need in the moment. This one says, *Stalwart martyr bravely defending herself against the world.*

Or maybe it doesn't. It doesn't matter, though, because the next thing he says is, "Maybe you're right. Let's do my place instead." His smile says, *I'm cute, because I'm self-depreciating.*

I kiss him, because that's what a girl who'd just gotten what she wanted would do, and not in the least bit because I miss his taste.

30

I WAS YOUNG the first time I ever stole anything. I hadn't quite figured out the trick to hiding in plain sight. And it was shortly after the house's owners came back and called for someone to haul me out. I could have fought it, maybe, chained myself to the front door in protest, but I didn't. By then, the dark cloud that always seems to follow me was already swallowing me up in its mist.

I hadn't yet started to roam new neighborhoods like a stray cat. Instead, I stuck close, still clinging onto the hope that my parents would come back.

It was a big mistake, they'd say, their hands fluttering like wings. *We got lost. We got detained for something we didn't do. We came back, but you weren't here, and we'd thought you'd run away. We've been looking for you this whole time.*

The day of my first theft, I'd woken up fighting a wicked cold. My head buzzed like crazy, and I needed a nap. Despite how exposed it was, despite how hot it was, I plopped right down on the side of the road, the air like a stifling blanket, full of rain.

The sun felt sharper, somehow, which was impossible. The twilight never got brighter, only dimmer, like when a bank of clouds moved across the sky, or we were the victim of one of the terrific storms that forms from the winds running into the wall. But the light felt unconscionably bright, and that was the sign that I was in trouble.

I tried to get up, but I couldn't. Instead, I just fell asleep. I eventually woke up to the sound of something clinking.

Two coins had landed in my lap. And when I looked up, there was a man there, standing clean in fresh robes, his nose curled up at me. "Get a job."

I wanted to throw the coins at him, but instead, I curled them up in my palm.

It was the first money I'd ever made on my own.

After some effort, I managed to stand. My legs protested at holding my weight and the ground felt like it was rocking underneath me, but I was dying of thirst. Now that my fever had broken and my head was starting to clear, my brain recognized the danger.

I wobbled to the store with the intention of buying water. I'd gone to this store ever since I was a kid. I knew well the weight of the door, the clatter of the bells that were wrapped around the inside handle.

Hye-Gwan was behind the counter. The shelves had just been restocked, filled with packages of nuts, roasted seeds, candies, and small pots of lip stain. Her mother was nowhere to be seen—maybe busy with something else. Or maybe she just wanted her daughter to mind the store, to keep her out of trouble. I'd seen the circles Hye-Gwan was starting to run with, the guys that cooked drugs using the heat of running engine blocks.

I went down the aisle that had the water. Grabbed two jugs as big as I could carry, and then a smaller bottle I could refill later. The coins I'd brought with me would just about cover it.

Hye-Gwan wrinkled her nose at me, clearly disgusted with my appearance. "Did you touch anything?"

In my addled state, the question didn't make sense. Touch what—the bottles? The ground? "I don't—"

"Did you steal anything?"

I felt my face grow hot. I'd never stolen anything in my life. I'd been the kind of kid who, despite all of my problems, couldn't lie about anything. I'd once broken a small toy in the market and hid it from my mother, and the shame of it still burned in me like a hot pan. And worse, Hye-Gwan knew me. We were close in age; our mothers were friendly.

I would have exploded on her there and then, but the water was so close I could taste it. Clean, sweet, and unlikely to leave me with a fever. "No," I said, the word sand in my already parched throat. I tried to meet her eyes, but my gaze only got as high as a jar of bright red lip stain before it fell again. I hadn't done anything wrong, but I could already feel shame snaking fingers around my guts, the man's voice—*get a job*—staining everything around me with its hate. I put the coins on the counter.

"If you're lying, I'm going to call 'em in—although I doubt a stint in cus' would straighten you out."

I couldn't understand it. Hye-Gwan was a few grades above me, but we'd gone to the same school, until I couldn't attend anymore. She *knew* me.

If I'd been a little older, a bit smarter, I would have asked why she was treating me like this—but I hadn't yet learned to wrap my words around me like armor. "I didn't take anything," I said, with force. It felt like there was a great pressure building in my chest, a boil that threatened to rupture and spread infection throughout my whole body.

She grumbled, but she grabbed my coins and turned around. In the few moments it took her to key in the total, to put the coins in and extract my single, smaller coin of change, my hand lashed out like a snake. I took the jar of lip stain, palmed it, and put it straight in my pocket.

Hye-Gwan turned back around. I held out my hand, palm up, but she put the coin on the counter. "I'm not going to touch you," she said. A sentence whose only purpose was to wound.

"Fine." I took the water out with me, feeling her gaze on my back the whole time. Even as I walked down the street, and down the next, it felt like the eyes of the world were on me. It was terrifying. It was exhilarating.

I'm sure it was just my thirst that made the water taste so sweet—but there was also the feeling, for the moment, that I'd somehow beaten back the black cloud that followed me.

GYU ISN'T HYE-GWAN. He isn't one of the rich bastards like the one who threw the coins at me and told me to get a job. Those people are all the same, a kind of overclass formed by suckling at CPI's teat. They park their vehicles however they want, yell at kids for walking on the sidewalk too close to their building or for laughing too loud. The kind of people who have a private beach at the top of an apartment building, while people in the street are dying for want of water.

And they knew it, too, and they didn't care. My parents had taught me to always read the news, because everything that mattered to them, by extension mattered to us. A production failure of one of their favorite condiments half a world away could turn these people into something vengeful or deadly. They just didn't have empathy for people like us.

Those people, I stole from willingly, greedily, happily. Those people I stole from *without exception*, once I figured out that Hye-Gwan, despite the way she treated me, was not the orchestrator of her own hate.

Gyu isn't those people. And yet, with Gyu standing next to me during my shift, I can't help but feel the same way I did during each of those thefts. The pressure inside of my chest, the vibrating wire strings that always come when it feels like the whole world has turned to watch you, all-knowing about the sin you're about to commit. Every theft is different, but every theft is the same, and this tension won't go away until I either get away with it or I'm caught.

It's hard not to feel like I've gotten away with it already. My calls to my crew are impossibly fast, so fast that I have to consciously slow down, make it obvious that I'm checking the probability cloud, the data readings, even though I don't need them. Every time I've communed with the Cable—and after breaking through the membrane, that's the word I've come to use, because whereas before it felt like I was journeying through it, this time, it now feels like I've taken part of it with me, like I've learned to speak a new language that has sunk in so thoroughly I am dreaming in it—each time I've communed with it, my skills as a Pomp have gotten immeasurably better. This shift, I'm so in my element, it almost feels like the Pomp technology is more of a hindrance than an asset—but Gyu's here, watching me, and so I have to pretend.

I take extra-long to read each message. I ask for more frequent checks on the Cable status when none are necessary. I try my hardest not to talk to or look at Hannah, before realizing that, too, could raise questions. From then on, I count the number of words I speak to each person, the number of times I look at each person, and I make sure to assign everybody the exact same amount. I take deep breaths and stay as calm as I can, no matter where I look, so that my visor doesn't pick up on my stress.

Every so often, I make small talk with Gyu, and it's this, more than anything else, that makes my heart race. I could give myself away at any second. I feel impossibly alive.

By the end of the shift, we've gotten through only a quarter of the information I picked up on my last visit with the Cable. I have at least two more shifts before I need to get back out there—two more shifts to work on Gyu.

"Are you ready for dinner?" His voice is just the right amount of nervous. I want to hate him for it, because if he's lying, he's tremendous at it—but there are a thousand possibilities swirling through my head like butterflies. Maybe he thinks he's doing things for the greater good. Maybe he thinks he's protecting me, somehow. Maybe this is all Celeste's trick.

I refute each of these possibilities, not with facts, but with will, driving pins through them to stick them to the table. "I'm ready," I say, and I follow him out of the office.

IT SURPRISES ME when we go back to Lodging. Having never set foot in Gyu's place, it feels like it should be somewhere distant, but instead, it's a stone's throw from my house. *Close enough that it would be easy to do surveillance.*

It's set back apart from the others, in a cluster of slightly larger buildings that are for people of some import. I can't believe I used to think Gyu was just an engineer. I'd thought he was just *Gyu*, the awkward guy that came over to have sex and make food and nuzzle up next to me. Instead, he was someone to be afraid of.

He pauses outside of his door. "Here we are."

I feel like storming the place. I don't know what I'll do when I get inside—burn it to the ground? Collapse for a nap? My thoughts are swirling with the glinting fever-pitch that heralds a breakdown, but it's one I can't afford right now. I can't always push that energy away, but this time I do, packing it deep inside of my core.

He's obviously expecting me to say something, but when I don't, he removes a key from his pocket. His cheeks are pale as he unlocks the door and steps aside to let me in. I almost stumble. I hadn't counted on his place being locked. I'd counted on exploring this place when he was out.

I've tried my hand at picking locks in the past, only to give up in frustration. It's a skill that results in complete failure unless everything is perfect. Your knowledge of the lock, having the right touch, the right tools on you—and the kind of time alone that's going to be hard to come by in Lodging.

Maybe Hannah can create some kind of distraction, I think, but I already know that's unlikely. The easiest way to toss his place will be if he lets me in himself.

"You look lost in thought," he says, and I realize that I've been standing, facing his bookcase, staring without seeing.

Fuck. I'm having a hard time staying in the moment. I have to get a hold of myself. "Yeah," I say. "You have a lot of books." I turn back to him, careful to make my face look slightly awed—soft, relaxed eyes, mouth gently parted—and then the rest of the room suddenly comes, if not into view, then into *mind* for the first time, and my expression becomes real.

Gyu's space is nothing like I would have predicted. I'd assumed it would be boring. Beige. Instead, it's a riot of colors, of textures.

There are decorations packing every square visible inch of the walls, tagged with the imprint of different cultures around the terminator band. Dyed cloths with geometric imprints that, when viewed from afar, assemble pictures of large game animals and bending trees with palm fronds. Wooden masks from Hangan interpretive dances, used eons ago as a vehicle for the poor to criticize the nobility. A beautiful, yet grotesque sculpture of a man made out of wood, his skin embedded all over with tiny nails.

"What is all of this?" I reach out to touch one of the nails, its flat head cool and slightly rough under my hand. It doesn't have the smooth, machined surface of something on the station, laser-cut or injection molded. It's imperfect. Uneven. Handmade, maybe.

"It's art." Gyu's voice has gone a bit high-pitched, and when I look up and catch the way his glance darts around the room, it takes me a breath to understand his pallid complexion. Despite the tension, the only reason I can come up with makes me laugh.

He's afraid. Afraid that I'll see all of this and judge him. Think he's crazy. Instead, I can't breathe at the thought that there are hidden layers to Gyu, secrets I don't know or understand.

I knew that already. I push back on the doubts that have suddenly crept in at the corners of my mind. I'm dying, and I can't afford them. "Where did you find all of it?"

Gyu's pale face reddens. "I made it."

It doesn't compute. "What?" I get closer to the Hangan mask, pull the string up off of the nail that holds it into the wall. Up close, I can see the marks of true artisanship—the smoothness of the lines in the wood, the evenness of the paint. There are two red circles, one on each cheek, and a hairpin and head covering on top that have the bright colors of a bride from a historical drama. "What do you mean, you made it? I thought you were an engineer."

"I am," he says, and he sighs, evidently giving up on skirting this train of thought. "I mean that engineer is my job, but it's not—it's not *me*. It's what I do because I have to."

"You don't have to," I say, but he shakes his head tersely, warning me not to go down that road. He's right. I was about to protest, to tell him that he could always take a different position within CPI's system, one of lower rank—but that's stupid. Anything other than the one that gets your debt paid off the fastest is stupid.

I think about how hard he had to push me to finish Pomp training. *I'm a hypocrite.* But then, if Celeste can be believed, that was all a setup. Fake.

I try to hold on to the…not certainty, exactly, but it's as close as I've been in a long time. I can feel its tug as it slips through my fingers. "This is really amazing," I finally say. "How did you make all of it? What does it mean?"

Gyu shrugs. "Where do you want to start?"

I hand him the mask. "What about this?"

His face brightens immediately, as if his expression had been buoyed up on a warm zephyr, one of the soft breezes that sometimes stirs inside the walls of the terminator band when the heat of the storm has broken. He points to each feature of the mask, using it as an anchor to launch into a story, and each time I catch his face, I can't help but notice how much younger he looks, how joyful. His words blend together, but his face beams and his eyes shine.

It's addictive. I hand him another piece, and another, and it's like the light within him grows, like there's a warmth in the room that builds and builds until everything around me is shining with the glory of his details.

And yet, as much as I want to see more of it, it stirs something in my gut. It makes me—unsettled. Angry. It makes me think about being sick, about being a child.

It's not until I lift one of the hangings up to examine the stitching—until I use it to hide my face—that I suddenly realize what his expression is. *Love.* I haven't seen it for so long, that I almost wasn't able to identify it.

And just like that, everything in me falls, as if down a tunnel. I don't know what it is that Gyu feels for me—if anything—but it's not this. And whatever my strange, aching fascination for him is, it's not this, either.

31

AFTER WE'VE PICKED the last bit of food off our plates, the moments hang between us, turning as if in a gyre.

I feel hot, almost feverish, although I think that's the wine. I only drank a glass—just enough to seem polite, sociable, just enough to take the edge off the fever-pitch of my anxiety, but I can feel it winding its way through me, lighting fires in its wake.

Then again, my arm is throbbing, so maybe it's not the wine. I could be imagining the way the ache seems to descend from inside of my armpit, the way my eyes burn every time I close them, but there's also a drowning fatigue that clutches at my skin, my hair, trying to drag me into the depths of sleep below.

So maybe I'm sick. Maybe I'm just stressed. Every shift since Adda died has been a fight that I've had to drag myself through—often on little sleep, and always on a heart that bounced like a toy boat in a river. Adrenaline can only buoy you for so long.

I should make small talk. I should *definitely* not fall asleep here, in my chair, in front of Gyu—but I'm so impossibly tired that time seems to pause in between blinks, *light, dark, light, dark*, like the piano-key lights in the interview room.

Vaguely, something in the back of my head stirs, but I'm already slipping into unconsciousness.

I WAKE UP in a bed that isn't my own. For a second, I panic, but then I hear Gyu's breathing next to mine. There's a brisk flood of warmth, one that has me turning and reaching for him—and then the memory catches up with me. The knowledge that Gyu is someone I need to be afraid of.

I freeze in midair. Drop my hand back to the bed, try to breathe. I watch him lie, his eyes closed, his chest rising and falling, as my questions crash together.

I am sure—*sure*—that he drugged me. There's no natural explanation for the way I just collapsed in my chair after eating, is there?

Except that I'm sick, the tumors slowly eating their way through my arm.

Except that I've always been sick, even if it wasn't the kind that would show up on a scan.

And why would he drug me, and then put me to bed here in his place?

I check the time. I haven't been asleep that long. If he *did* drug me, whatever he used was weak. And a drug doesn't have to be *nefarious*—maybe he saw how ill I was and gave me something to help me sleep.

I don't know if that makes sense. I creep to his bathroom, shut the door, and flick on the light. My face looks feverish, and my eyes are rimmed with dark circles. Like a person dying.

I've had moments of anger, of grief, ever since I found out about the tumors—but not like it should be. Not the all-consuming knife that sends you to your knees as your voice wails to the wind for your soul. Instead, the more I think about it, the less I feel. The less real it becomes.

If Celeste has told the truth, then Gyu knows I have cancer, and he hasn't said a thing.

I almost start laughing—but instead, I shut off the light. Crack the door open and listen again for Gyu's soft breathing. When I'm certain he's asleep, I slink away from the bathroom, toward the farthest wall.

Clues, I think. *To his password*. It's got to be some kind of esoteric, meaningless pattern of letters and numbers. CPI's security would demand it. Something impossible to guess— and things like that, people write down.

It used to start with "G," but he's probably changed it by now.

I search his desk. His clothes on the floor. His bathroom. I open each of the boxes of dried food in the kitchen, silently running my fingers through grains and noodles and dried fruits. I check each of his cups, his bowls, underneath each piece of furniture.

Is this what it was like for Hannah, when she tossed my place?

I push that thought out of my mind, the way it makes my stomach roll. I crawl under the bed. I turn over every piece of art, leaf through every book in the bookcase. When I'm flipping through one of them, a line catches my eye, because it's underlined.

<u>NO MATTER HOW FAR SHE WENT, SHE'D NEVER ESCAPE.</u>

I shudder, shake it out, and stick it back. Something about the spine makes my memory tingle, but I can't place it, and I don't take the book back out.

Minutes go by. The tiredness comes back, an aching pulse in my eyes. I'm running out of places to search.

I debate sneaking out, but it feels suspicious. The last thing I can afford to do right now is hurt him or make him wary of me. I need to draw him close, so that I can find clues to his credentials.

My eyes sting. I settle into a chair for a moment. I'm tired enough that I could nod off here, but I don't want him to realize that I got up, just in case I didn't put something back right. In case I made a mistake.

I creep back into bed. Despite his sound sleep, the motion is enough that he stirs, rolls to the side. His snores stop. He reaches out for me, gets his hands around my shoulders.

His touch burns. I can't breathe.

He grabs me tighter and pulls me in, an instinct despite his sleep, cocooning me with his body.

The minutes tick by. I don't think I can fall asleep, but I do.

I WAKE UP before his alarm, but he's already up, getting ready.

I lay there for a moment, but I can't put off facing him forever. So I turn over, sit up on the edge of the bed.

"Hey," he says, and his voice is warm. He comes close, kneels in front of me. "You were right. This is—I've been afraid to open up to anybody, but it feels so nice to let you in like this."

In the back of my mouth is a dry tang, like sour wine. "Yes," I say, and I look down, as if I've suddenly gotten shy, but the truth is that my skin is crawling. Why can't any of this make sense?

His movement is sudden, and before I can parse its meaning, his lips are on mine, hungry. Searching.

I hate it. I hate him. I hate myself more for wanting it. Hate the way the thought of destroying myself like this—destroying myself with him, *in* him—sends shivers down my back. Before I can stop myself, I'm leaning into the kiss, dragging my fingers through his hair.

Destroy me, I think. Make me into something that won't have to worry about anything anymore.

He sweeps me up in his arms, pushes me back on the bed. It's like the sudden change in position rights my mind.

This is a fucking mistake. I could have let the kiss just lie, corralled it into something sweet, instead of feeding it like a flame, but now, it's too late.

I do my best to abandon myself to it, but just like last shift, I can't feel anything. I'm just dead inside.

When I go to the bathroom to clean up and catch my reflection, my eyes fill up with tears.

What are you doing? I ask the girl in the mirror. Of course, she doesn't answer.

32

THE NEXT FEW circadians that pass float between worlds, strange. I change my mind a thousand times a shift.

Celeste was right. Gyu's evil, and every time he reaches for me is just cruelty. Every one of his mannerisms and movements is an elaborate form of torture.

Celeste's a liar, and Gyu's innocent. He's just trying to get close. I'm the snake that is slithering up to bite him in his sleep.

Work grinds by, impossibly slow, the effort required in keeping up the act as uncomfortable as being dragged naked through sand. Sometimes, I close my eyes and lose myself in the tunnels, touch the veins of Cable in my mind.

Sometimes, I look up to catch him staring at me. When his helmet projection is off, I imagine his face, full of anger, waiting for me to slip up so he can tear me apart. Mocking how stupid I am, at how I let things go this far. But when it's on, his expression is always blank and sort of shining, a pale reflection of the way he looked at his crafts.

It looks real. It looks fake. I'm starting to develop a cough, one that costs me to suppress. I feel hot all the time, and there's a buzzing in one of my ears that won't go away. I have to wrap the bandages tighter and tighter, and even so, my arm swells, like a fat sausage in a casing.

I'm falling apart. If I don't figure this out soon, I might not be able to get off Hib after all.

Every so often, when we're not working, I send him encrypted messages. I try not to imagine the cost, the credits adding to my debt.

Just once, I figure, *he'll open one up in front of me*. I just need a chance to see some part of his password, to have some idea of where to start.

But each time, he turns away before entering it. No matter how fast I move, I never catch so much as a glimpse.

AT THE END of the next shift, he pulls off his helmet, smiling. "Can we do your place tonight?"

"What?" We've reached the end of my knowledge of the Cable. I'm in the middle of planning my trip to the mine's exterior when his words catch up with me.

"Sorry," he says, and he grabs me around the waist, brings me in closer. He's done this a hundred times over the last few shifts. Each time, it's the same, a jangling mixture of longing and disgust, one so odd that I know there are no words for it. You'd have to be crazy to feel something like this, and even crazier to keep walking down this road, knowing how it's going to feel.

"Sorry for what?" I force myself to lean into the embrace.

"For making you uncomfortable, if I did. This has just been—really great. Like you've finally let me in. I know we've been doing my place lately, but I guess I just miss your bed." He chuckles softly to himself.

I almost laugh in his face. Despite our proximity, there's really an entire planet between us. "Sure."

It'd be better if it was his place, so I could look for clues again, except that there aren't any clues. I've gone through it, top to bottom, more times I can count, always on a knife-blade as he slumbers in the bed. I'm exhausted. If we stay at my place tonight, maybe I'll sleep through the whole night—except that

I need to go to the mine. "It sounds great, but do you mind if I swing by Medical first? I've got a headache."

It's not an untrue statement, I do—and maybe that bastard in Medical, the one who knew I was sick and didn't tell me, maybe he could've given me something to take the edge off, if I were actually going.

"Oh. Young, are you okay?" He pulls away from me, brings his eyes to mine. They shine like dark mirrors as his eyebrows pull together with worry. "I can go with you."

"No," I say. I bite my tongue, and the voice that comes out is smooth. Not like mine. "Why don't you just relax for a bit, and then meet me at my place later? I love the time we've spent together, too, but I just want like, to decompress for a bit."

"Oh," he says, and then he tilts his head to the side. "Are you going to your hatch?"

"What?" The word *hatch* hits me like a thunderbolt—but of course, I'd told him about it myself. "No."

"It's okay if you are, you know. I am so happy for what you've given me, lately, but if you need something to yourself, I understand. I really do."

I nod. It's hard to breathe, like the room's gone unbearably hot. "Thanks," I say. "I'll meet up with you in a bit."

"Okay." He gives me a swift hug, and then he's gone.

I nap in the hov on the way to the mine, the dark and the engine lulling me to sleep. Despite all of the secrets between us, *I'm* the one who revealed to Gyu the location of the biggest hole in my armor.

In my dreams, I'm a giant lizard. Gyu reaches in and pulls out my heart before discarding it to one side. He sticks a finger in the hole, levers up one of the scales around the edge. He peels it off, before working his way down my stomach, one peeled scale at a time.

I PUSH THROUGH the membrane between me and the consciousness of the Cable. This time, though, it's more than a communion—this time, it's so quick and tangible that it's almost a *conversation*. Something deep within Hib's core echoes through to me, as if asking me questions. I try to answer.

Time passes by, me deep in the bowels of the moon, and when I come to myself, the map is there—but not the rest of it. It's like my memory has been wiped away, and I'm not really sure what happened in the gaps.

After it's over, it takes me a long while to peel myself off of the ground. I want to just lay there forever, but in the back of my mind is a dim heartbeat, a pulsing quasar that blinks a message in code: *Gyu's waiting for you.*

I shift, and some feeling bubbles up—a half-memory of a moment inside the Cable—but then it's gone, like a scent I didn't identify in time and now can no longer smell.

I climb into the hov. As soon as I'm moving, I'm asleep—something dreamless, or if there were dreams, I don't remember them when I arrive at the station. I drag myself across the spokes, to the door that Gyu is already standing outside of. He looks nice. He's done his hair, put on a nice shirt.

I want to leave the helmet on, but I take it off.

"You look beautiful," he says. "Radiant, almost—are you sure you're not pregnant?" His voice is almost giddy. His words are like a punch to the gut.

I haven't used any protection the last few times. I don't remember when my last cycle was. Anxiety flickers in my stomach: a baby, a nest of lies—until I remember. It's far more likely that I'm just dying. "Thanks," I finally say, "but I don't think that's an issue." I open the door and trudge in, before throwing the suit into the cleaner.

When I turn around, Gyu is staring at me.

Fuck. I was supposed to go to Medical—which means I wouldn't have needed a suit in the first place.

He gives me a conspiratorial wink. There's a brief flash of confusion, but then I catch his meaning. He thinks I've been to the hatch.

The anger is irrational. I have to turn away so that he doesn't see the way my nose flares, the way my eyebrows pull into a line. The bookcase is in front of me, and just for something to do, I run my hand down the volumes.

Hopefully, he just thinks I'm embarrassed. It's actually to my benefit for him to think I'm going to the hatch. It gives me a chance to go to the mine. But even knowing that, I still wish I could take back telling him about my secret.

The title on one of the spines leaps out at me: GHOSTHOOK. Gyu loaned me this book. He either loved it so much he had two copies, or he bought one just for me—at great expense—and had it shipped up the elevator.

I pull it out as I remember again the terrible lines about how the girl can never escape.

"Did you read it yet? It's great, isn't it?"

"I—I'm not done with it yet."

"Oh." He's disappointed. And then he takes in a breath. "I need you to look at me."

I turn. For the first time, I notice that he's holding his hands behind him. "What—"

"I have some really good news," he says, and his voice gets high. He pulls his hands out from behind his back, and there's a bottle in one. Some kind of wine. It looks expensive. Two glasses held in the other hand by the stems.

He sits down at my small table, somehow dwarfing the room with his presence, before patting the other chair.

A suspicion grows in the back of my mind, but I'm not going to panic. Not yet. *This could be anything. This could be...*but my mind won't fill in the blank. "What's going on?"

"So," he says. He draws it out, as if that one word could deliver the entirety of his message. "I got the approval to bring you down to the surface. We're going on the next elevator shipment."

My heart hammers. "When's that?"

"First thing next shift. Just think—you're so close to getting on the elevator. To getting off this rock. I just got back from doing the final checks—all the containers are sealed and ready to go." He smiles, and his teeth look sharp.

This can't be happening. The plan isn't ready yet. I don't have his password or his credentials. I haven't spoken to Hannah. I don't know if she's even ready.

"Oh," I say. My swallow is audible.

"Hey." His voice goes soft, and he's on his feet in a flash. "Don't worry. Everything is going to be okay." He holds me by the shoulders. "You don't have to be scared. This is a *good* thing, remember?"

"Right." I fake a smile. "Of course." He's still got the glasses in his hand, and they sparkle like chunks of piezanite. "Let me open this bottle."

"I can—"

"I want to help."

He cocks his head to the side. He eyes me strangely for a moment, but then he nods again. "Okay."

I bring the bottle over to the desk and open the drawer. I keep my back to him, so he can't see me take out the piece of cloth I used to wrap the powder that Hanna gave me.

"What are you doing?"

"Looking for something to open this with."

He stands up, and I palm the powder a moment before he comes into my view over my right shoulder. "Are you sure you're okay?"

"Sure I—"

"It's a vac-container, Young. You just twist it off."

He's referring to the wine bottle. "Right." I laugh, as if embarrassed. "I guess I'm just nervous." I turn to look at him, and he's got an eyebrow raised, clearly not believing me.

"Really," I say, nodding. "I'm fine."

"Okay." His gaze lingers on me.

I need a reason not to do this in front of him. "I like mine chilled."

"It's already chilled."

It *is* chilled. It's so cold it's starting to burn my hand. "I know. I mean, I want it on ice."

"Young—"

I stride over to the kitchen. Press the button for an ice cube, tap the screen display that asks me to confirm if I want to add the charge to my debt. The cube dispenses into my glass, but before I can figure out what to do with the powder, he's next to me, pouring out his own glass.

Fuck. I'm fucked. I'm completely fucked.

His tablet chimes. "Hang on." He walks across the room for it, leaving his glass on the counter, and it's like the heavens have opened up to pour light through, like Hib itself has deemed me worthy of something impossible.

There are a thousand questions I should have asked Hannah—would have asked her, once I'd gotten the password and we'd communicated on the plan. For starters, I have no idea how much powder to put in.

I drop the whole packet into his glass. It dissolves the second it touches the wine, a burst of milky fog that turns white and then red again. I look up at him.

He's got his back to me, but over his left shoulder, I catch the first letter of his pass code. *G.* So he hasn't changed it—which tells me nothing.

He turns toward me. "Sorry about that."

"It's okay." I smile.

He walks back across the room and raises his glass to me. "Let's toast."

We clink our glasses together. He takes a big sip. Smacks his lips together. "Hmm," he says. "It's a bit sweeter than I remember."

"Is that bad?" I can barely force out the words.

"No. Might have been a better year for grapes—they update the technology in the grow rooms all of the time."

"Right." I take another small sip. "This is pretty good."

"It's my favorite." He gulps down half the glass. "Well, I'm sure you must have a ton of questions about the journey—" His face contorts. He shakes his head, as if dizzy, before swaying on his feet. "Young?"

He looks at me. Down at the glass in his hand.

And then, like a tunnel collapsing, he smashes into the floor.

33

THERE'S A VIOLENCE to it, one that brings me back to another moment: a hovel, screaming, crying, throwing my shoulder against the locked door, watching it break open a second before I find Brin, needle still in the vein.

But this isn't then. This is now. This is Gyu, not Brin. His glass crashes into the floor, impact converting its singular body into a rain of clear fragments and red fluid. Gyu follows before I can catch him, a second of unfocused eyes before the thud.

I'm on my knees. I scramble close. Glass cuts into my skin.

His lips are turning blue already. I've seen that before. I hold my hand in front of his face. He's breathing, shallow whispers I can barely feel.

I don't know what to do. I have to call Medical, have to tell them everything. I've poisoned him. He's dying, his heart and lungs shutting down as a depressant steals over him. I don't even know what I gave him, how much.

But then, what was I expecting?

If I leave him here, he'll probably die. And if I don't, I will. It's him or me.

It feels like it takes me a long time to stand up. *I'll call for help*, I think, but I know I won't.

I have to figure this out. There are cameras, maybe—but if there are, they're Gyu's, right? He's not going to be checking them. If I'm lucky, nobody else knows about them.

I drag him into the bed—limp as he is, he's impossibly heavy. His head is bleeding. I wrap his wound the best I can with a piece of cloth, but my hands are shaking. He already feels cold.

I go through his pockets, find his key cards, his tablet, and his electronic credentials.

I clean up the glass on the floor. The stain doesn't look like it can be fixed. There's blood—his or mine, I can't tell, we're both cut up—and wine all over my shirtsleeves.

Gyu doesn't look like he's going to wake up, but if he does, he'll see me missing. People will come looking for me, and as long I'm somewhere here on Hib, they'll find me.

Fuck. I need a plan. I send Hannah a message: NICE NIGHT FOR A WALK. Our emergency phrase, so she'll know to meet me at the hatch. I can't get over how grim her humor is, how she thought a suicide joke would be the ideal—

It emerges. A plan.

I pull out the drawer and dump it upside down on the table. I root for a pencil and something to write on. The pencil is easy, but I can't locate any paper, not until I turn and rip one of the pages of out of the book he loaned me.

Dear Gyu, I write, and then I take a deep breath.

> *By the time you find this note, I will be dead. I appreciate the opportunity you tried to give me with pomp training, but it's just too much. I was never made to do this kind of work. I can't handle being on Hib anymore. I can't handle what happened to Adda. I'm sorry I took your stuff, but I don't want you to try to follow me.*

I read it over once. It's trite and half-baked, but there's no time. And if someone comes into my place, and Gyu is really dead, and I'm gone—I'm hoping they'll assume the worst. That

I killed myself, and that he killed himself after me, like two star-crossed lovers.

Ugh. It's disgusting.

I've got a hand on the door when I remember Celeste's drive. For a second, I think about just leaving it—but if investigators toss this room and find it, it will fuck everything up. I should have destroyed it. I should destroy it now, because no matter what happens, I'm never going to let Celeste send a cargo hold of explosives up the elevator and strand everyone on Hib. It's murder.

I kneel by the toilet and reach down into the space between the tank and the wall, searching for the drive's sharp corners. It takes a few tries to wiggle it between my fingers far enough that I can scissor them together and pull it out.

I stick it in my pocket, and I run.

I WANT TO rent a vehicle, but I can't take the risk—if my credentials are used to rent something *after* Gyu overdosed, it'll unravel everything—so instead, I hoof it out to the hatch on foot.

They could be tracking me right now, watching my beacon. I want to crush it with every breath in my body, but I still need it to find the hatch. The second I get to the button, I unplug the beacon, open the top of the hatch, crawl in.

I almost die with relief when I find Hannah waiting there.

"Young, what the shit? Have you lost your mind?"

I collapse, breathless, on the floor of the hatch. "Speaking of shit, we're in it. Deep shit."

Her eyes flare wide. "What *kind* of deep shit?"

"The next shipment's this next shift."

Hannah laughs. "So what? We can't be ready that soon. We'll just have to go on the next one..." Her voice dies as she studies my face. "You're kidding, right? You want to go *now*?"

I unzip my suit. Pull out Gyu's credentials, his key card, his tablet. "It's all Gyu's. I drugged him. I... I used the whole packet."

She lets out a low whistle as her eyebrows draw together. "Stone cold, Young."

I can tell she's thinking, weighing the same things that I've been. Gyu's been drugged, and his credentials are missing—which means that we don't have that long to get on this shipment. And once it's discovered, the credentials will be disabled—and Hannah will have to find a way to get close to someone new.

Finally, her lips become a tight line. "Do you have his password?"

It's hard to answer, but I do. "No."

She slaps her forehead. Her fingers drag down her face hard enough to leave marks. "Why the *fuck* would you drug him without the password?"

"I didn't have a choice! He's sending me down to CPI on this shift, which means—"

"What do you mean, sending you down?"

I swallow. "I'm…" I close my eyes. I don't know how I'm going to explain any of this to her. "The Cable-sickness," I finally say. "CPI wants to study it. They're going to kill me. Cut me open. Torture me." For all I know, it could be true.

"You didn't tell me any of that before." Her voice is flat.

"I didn't trust you before."

She snorts. "And now, you do?"

I shrug, helplessly. We both know I don't—and yet, I'm trusting her with our escape.

"Fine," she says. "But we can't do this without his password."

"I—I brought his tablet. Maybe we can…maybe we can guess it?"

"That's the dumbest thing I've ever heard."

"Do you have a better idea?"

Her eyes grow so cold I shudder. "No," she says, and she sighs. "I don't."

An hour later, Hannah and I are no closer to Gyu's password than we started. I've tried every possible combination of words and letters—his birthdate, my birthdate, his prisoner number, my prisoner number—but I know before each combination they won't work, despite the "G" I paste onto the beginning of each attempt.

At one point, Hannah and I list words that start with G. I type in permutations of Gyu's name. More than once, I bang my head against the hatch's metal walls.

Hannah shrugs. "Maybe it's just a random combination of numbers and letters. Maybe it's uncrackable."

A snake coils in my guts. Despite having had that thought myself, I hate her for it. "No," I say, more vehemently than I feel. "Gyu isn't that kind of person."

She stiffens. "What kind of person is he?" Her voice is measured—neither light nor dark, believing nor disbelieving.

I can feel her thoughts—or maybe those are just my own thoughts, amplified a hundredfold, shouted off a mountain's peak and echoed back. Gyu has deceived me, all this time— what right did I have to those words?

I shut my eyes. It hurts to comb through my memories of him, dredging between their grains, as if searching for something buried on Hib's surface. "He's really smart, in a lot of different ways. He likes equations and math and sometimes, I get the feeling that he honestly enjoys working for Engineering. Enjoyed, I mean." I try not to think about how blue his lips were, the way his skin already shined against the backdrop of my sheets.

She shrugs. "If he had a secret, what would it be?"

It's a meaningless mental game, and we both know it, can feel the failure slowly filling up this room like gas hissing into an airlock.

My throat hurts when I can finally formulate an answer. "He was an artist. That's something he didn't share with me until the end. He made things."

"An artist." She makes no effort to hide her disdain. In a world governed by CPI, there's nothing more useless.

"He liked books," I say, defensively—and then a volume swells to occupy the space in my mind, the worn corners of the paper. A copy on his shelf, the twin on mine.

Picturing the book awakens a slumbering beast deep inside of the earth. That first bridge between us—the story he used to illustrate his own anxiety and despair. A girl with a hook in her chest, one put there by a ghost. *And no matter how far she traveled, she could always feel it, pulling her back.*

I take the tablet from Hannah. My fingers are shaking as I type in the word: GHOSTHOOK.

The screen unlocks.

"Shit," says Hannah.

"Shit," I say. "But this means—we can do it?"

She nods. "Maybe." She checks something inside of her suit, and then she shakes her head. "We don't have any supplies, and there isn't enough time to get any. Everything is closed right now. The shift's going to be starting soon, which means that we can't exactly be seen running around Hib—"

"Supplies? What kind of supplies?"

"Food. Water."

"It's... It's like ninety circadians. Even if we only bring the bare minimum of water to keep ourselves alive, it'd likely fill the entire cargo container. We'll have to just get it from the cooler—"

"I don't know if the cooler will be active on a return journey. And even if it is, we need to be careful. If it's drained, it'll activate the pumps, which is noisy, so the only safe time to get water from the cooler is if the crew in the rest of the elevator has just drained a tank and the pumps have already kicked on. And I think there's only five or so people that crew the return trips, because there's nothing but the piezanite itself in the containers."

"And if the cooler isn't even active?" My heart is beating hard. I hadn't considered any of this.

"Then we'll have to sneak into the general bay while the crew is sleeping and hope we don't run into someone who's still awake. And that's assuming we can even get the container open."

My blood goes cold. There are a thousand ways for this to go wrong. I imagine Hannah and me, trapped in a container, slowly dying of dehydration. How long before one of us killed the other for survival? Does drinking blood stop dehydration?

I know without a doubt that in a fight between Hannah and me, I'm not the one who would be the victor. And the truth is I'm already dying. Ninety circadians down the elevator would be cutting it close. Maybe I'd make it all of the way to the bottom, only to be too weak to escape from the container itself. "So, what are you saying, exactly?"

"We need to keep some stores with us. If three circadians pass where we can't figure our way out of the container, or if there's a guard we didn't predict, and it takes us time to work out the schedule—we need enough food and water for these contingencies."

She's right, but given the alternative of not getting out of here, her resistance strikes me as flimsy. For the first time, I wonder if Hannah is afraid.

And for the first time, I'm not.

I walk toward the lock on the side of the room. I slide around the black and white pieces, the old puzzle my mom showed me a long time ago. It takes me a while to solve. Did she learn it before she came here? Was the puzzle some kind of code between the escapees that eventually made it off of Hib?

It feels like she left it for me.

The last piece slides into place, and I pull the door open. I step in and pull out boxes, covered in dust. Silver-wrapped packages that I'm pretty sure are food. The odd bags of water. "Will this work?"

I try not to think about Celeste. She must have been living off these supplies. Must have wanted them for her own escape.

"Yeah." Hannah cracks a smile. "They just might."

34

WE'RE NOT HOME free yet, by any means. I rehearse Hannah's plan as I hoof it after her through the sand. We have to get to the facility. Use Gyu's credentials at the first checkpoint to get in and find our way to the final shipment. Break into the cargo container. Remove some crystal, maybe, and stash it where it won't be found. Change the manifest so that it reports that Gyu and I are not supposed to be going down. Sign off on the final checks with Gyu's credentials. Finally, we have to seal ourselves in the container. And that's all before even leaving Hib, before we have to start thinking about things like food and water.

Hannah is the one who takes the credentials. "I'm taller," she says, which is true—she's taller than me, but only barely. She's a good hand's length shorter than Gyu, and anybody who isn't asleep on the job is going to know she's not him, credentials or no, but she doesn't seem fazed. "Just follow me," she says. "Follow my lead."

Ninety circadians is a long time. We carry as much water and food as our arms can hold, wrapped up in a wadded thermal blanket—but it isn't much. Enough for a few shifts, if we're lucky. Almost all scenarios point to us being fucked, but I try to ignore that.

As soon as we make it back to Hib station, we wind up grabbing a hov with Hannah's credentials. I'm tempted to use Gyu's, to see if they're still valid. He'll be found any moment—although we're lucky in some ways. Gyu doesn't have to wear an Annie suit, which means that there's no annoying alarm that will give his position away when he doesn't show up. If someone goes to his house to check on him, he won't be there. I've also never seen Gyu report in to anyone, although between the calls and messages, he seems to be in pretty constant contact.

And since he's the person who would report me missing from my shift, there's the chance that nobody will come looking for me, either.

If just a few circadians pass before he's found, it might be long enough that people can't calculate if his time of death was before or after the final inventory adjustments. I don't know if they'll do a blood test or not, although they certainly have the equipment for it judging by the testing they did on me after the explosion.

That thought, combined with the memory of him falling to the floor, ignites a spark within me. "Hannah," I holler, tapping on her shoulder, and she brings the hov down to an idle.

We both have our suits on, so she has to turn on the speaker for me to hear her, and in the odd composition of gases on the moon's surface, her voice sounds ridiculously high-pitched. "What?"

"What was in it? The packet?"

"Are you serious? We don't have time for this—" She turns the hov engine back up, but I grab her hand, crank the tiller back down, and we float back onto the sand.

"Tell me."

"It's just a general soporific. They give it to you in medical if you haven't been able to sleep—bill you an arm and a leg for it, of course. Adda picked it up a long time ago."

A soporific.

I know that word. It was on the report that Gyu had when I was being interrogated about Adda's death. SOPORIFIC.

"Hey, Young? If we could get going?" Hannah pulls at my arm.

Gyu had said the traces of the drug in my bloodstream was from the explosion, the report's neat, tight font backing up his assumption. But I was late in the first place because I'd overslept the night before. Gyu had come by to make dinner, and we'd had noodles, and then I'd overslept.

To be fair, I'm no stranger to sleeping in. When the past dragged me down into its depths, I had to fight to get out of bed—and the day before, I'd ripped my glove. Exposed myself to the Cable, which always wore me out. And Gyu had no reason I knew of to make me late for a normal shift at the mines.

Yet, if I hadn't been late that day, if Adda hadn't died, I wouldn't have gone back to Pomp training.

There's a cold, steel rod in my belly. "Hannah, how easy is this stuff to get?" My voice is ragged.

"What, Sleeping Beauty?" She searches my face—and for a moment, I think she's hiding something—but no, she's *looking* for something. A clue. It's obvious that she has no idea what I'm on about. "Young, I don't know. Easy. All you have to do is go to Medical and tell them you haven't been sleeping and that it's affecting your productivity. Are you…are you okay?"

I nod, but I'm so sick that I can barely stand. It could have been Gyu—he'd easily have access, and he'd made us a meal the night before. It could have been Hannah or Celeste, who'd both admitted to sneaking through places that were supposed to be mine. It would've been easy for any of the three to leave some powder for me, in my food or a glass.

And the truth is that Celeste is dead—I have no proof, but I can feel it, deep in my guts. And Gyu is probably dead. So that just leaves Hannah, alive, which means that regardless of *who* gave it to me, Hannah's the one I have to follow, because she's the only one who's left.

She purses her lips. "Young, what the hell is going—"

"Let's go." I flip the switch, and the hov roars back to life, lifting us from the sand like the giant dancing sea beast from my dreams.

WE ABANDON THE hov a long walk from the checkpoint to the elevator facility. The ground here is mostly flat, without the soft dunes and rocky, finger-like peaks that mark so much of the moon's surface—at least, the part I can see, before even that rapidly fades into Hib's eternal darkness—but despite the distance between us and the checkpoint, I can make out the line of a security fence from the glow of the spotlights that must run down its entire length. The fence snakes across the terrain, left to right, like a brightening horizon, and I wonder if the sight resembles what the ghosthook girl saw every morning.

Hannah ties a bundle of supplies to her back with the same method my mother used to hoist me up when I was a child. The technique left her arms free to clean houses and gave me a safe spot from which to view the world. I've never longed for safety so desperately, never felt it so far away.

We strip and disable the GPS, the computer, smash anything that looks vaguely electronic. When the hov's not returned at the end of the rental window, they'll be able to tell it was checked out with Hannah's credentials. If they can't send out a locator for it, it'll buy us some time—but even so, it'll be found eventually. We're hoping we'll be well down the elevator by then—and even though she's not sure if the signal will reach that far, Hannah takes a moment and disables the BANS in both our suits with a couple small flicks of her fingers…and an ease that makes me wonder how many times she's done that before and where she gets off to when she's supposed to be starting her shifts.

We kick as much sand over the hov as we have time for and hoof it in the direction of the elevator facility's outer gates. Before long, the terrain under us shifts—becoming flatter, the passage easier. Not a road, exactly: That would be unnecessary, when all the vehicles in this place have treads or hover over fans to tackle the sand, but the change in grade channels us forward—an invisible, inevitable force.

Did we come this way when we arrived, shepherded blind in that cargo container? Or does the fence have another gate? No way to know, but it feels like I've come this way before. Like I shouldn't be coming this way now.

From a distance, the only feature of the fence is the length of its brightness as it stretches across the horizon from left to right, but as we approach, textures and dimensions emerge. The fence grows skyward until we're finally close enough that I can understand its height—at least four times as tall as me, looming over us mockingly, even as its surface coalesces into the recognizable and mundane: a thick metal weave. The fence would be see-through were it not for the gloom behind that even the spotlights don't penetrate.

And then we're standing right in front of the gate: a vertical seam of two side-by-side panels large enough to permit the passage of large vehicles or laden cargo containers, ornamented by a few bays of electronics I take to be readers, speakers, sensors, and intercoms.

I lean down until my face is even with some of the diamond-shaped openings, trying to catch a glimpse of the facility in the darkness beyond, but Hannah pulls me back. "Electrified," she whispers through her speaker, and then she pats her helmet visor twice with her fingertips, right over where her lips would be if she didn't have the face projection turned off: The sign between thieves to keep your mouth shut.

I'm shocked. Where did she learn that? What else don't I know about her life?

She swipes Gyu's key card in front of the readers. The gate rattles open, its two halves springing to each side as if chased apart by magnets, though my vision of what lies behind is still murky, obscured by bleed from the spotlights around us. The back of my neck tingles as she steps through. I hesitate, but she proceeds without looking back.

I can't be left behind. I bolt through, trying not to panic as the gate closes behind me. This time, the rattle sounds like laughing, as if the gate knows every step will take us deeper into a place of no return, with no way to tell if we're making a mistake.

The terrain we can see still hasn't changed. I glance at Hannah. "There's nothing here—"

She turns swiftly, her hand flying up to her helmet in the double-tap again, an emphatic warning to *shut up*.

And then she's edging over the sand, the bundle on her back marking her as an ancient traveler. I have no choice but to follow. Before long, we're in the full dark again, our headlamps barely cutting through the gloom—but this time, we don't have to walk far before I catch a brightening in the distance, though unlike the fence's illumination, this one coalesces around a single point, like a lighthouse.

After five minutes, it's consolidated enough that I can catch a shape highlighted against the forming gray, a sense of something tall and thin, like a skyscraper. Something metallic that reflects light back as it stretches up above us. It's taller, even, than the fence was, though I can't tell *how* tall, because the top of it quickly fades into the same black that presses in on us.

That is always pressing in on us. For the first time, I realize the truth—darkness is the universe's default. Only the smallest slivers of the world ever make it out into the light.

I shiver and focus instead on the structure we're approaching. It has to be the elevator and the tether. As I try to pick their forms out of the black, it fills me with a strange energy, as if they could invigorate the electrons in the air inside my suit and send them hurling into my flesh. For once, the choking anxiety—the feeling that this was the wrong course, that I've come this way before, that I'm not supposed to be here now, all of the fear that's plagued me since we stopped the hov—ebbs.

Instead, in its place, I can taste something different: a yearning, a call I don't know what to do with. It grows as we get closer. *I've never felt anything like it*, I think, but that's wrong. Because I *have*, even if I can't place it yet. The song it makes in my head—a constant soft drumming like rain, overlapped with a tinnitus-like ringing—clouds my thoughts, until I'm cutting in and out of time. Spots flicker in the corners of my vision.

I blink, and we've traveled far enough that I can just make out the borders of the elevator facility—a tower that looks like it fell too fast from the sky and smashed into the ground, its bottom levels fattening as they folded in on themselves, their deformation leaving the building shaped like a dog's lower leg.

I blink again, and we've commuted half of the distance, Hannah still ambling slowly in front of me like that ancient traveler. We're close enough that even with the scene blurring around me, I can separate the shape of the building into discrete sections. The bottom part, the paw, is actually an angular ring that encircles the tower. A hexagon—no, an octagon, I think, though it's hard to tell from this distance. It's red and silver, no doubt made of plasteel. For a moment, I think of a snake eating its own tail, but then my gaze stretches up and I catch a glimpse of the building as it ends, something *silvery* on top—

Another blink, and I'm closer, but still staring up, up, though my vision is swimming worse, squirming like bacteria under a microscope. My whole body fills with a ringing drone. A song begging me to commune with it, to ride it deep into Hib.

It's the tether. Calling to me. As soon as I have the thought—as soon as that word, *tether*, picks itself loose from the strings of my brain—my vision clears, the scene in front of me solidifying into distinct, sharp edges. The ring at the bottom, the one that looks like a paw—that must be the elevator car, encircling the cargo facility that supports it. And stretching up from the building's crown: a single silvery thread that shoots straight up like a beam of light until fading into the darkness.

My skin tingles in recognition. *It's Cable.* The tether the elevator rides, the strand that unites my world and its moon—it's a gigantic, braided vein of Cable.

My knees go weak. I stumble, but Hannah doesn't notice.

No wonder I could hear it. Even now, I can feel the Cable begging me to ride it, to chase its vein straight into the sky, all the way to Ung-Nyeo.

I suddenly understand why CPI doesn't let anybody near either end of the tether. It's not just the need to secure the elevator and the valuable piezanite it transports. It's because seeing this, even here on the moon, surrounded by darkness—it's a religious experience. What would it be like if I were, instead, bathed in the eternal light of the Desert, taking in the way the tether stretches, endless, into the sky, a vertical so massive and infinite that only gods themselves could've built it?

CPI's security would never be enough. People would die by the thousands, the millions—braving the heat of the Desert, making pilgrimage for that single moment of awe.

To know the tether is to understand *control*—moments before you lose it completely.

35

FOR THE NEXT few minutes, I hold my breath. I feel like there should be activity here—guards, technicians, people loading and unloading—but the facility seems abandoned. We stroll up to the ringed elevator car, Hannah's gait so nonchalant, it's almost criminal.

There are doors here, embedded into the side of the car, giant doors large enough to accommodate cargo containers, each built next to one of the obtuse corners formed where two walls meet. It takes me a second to work out the angles: if the door swings open wide enough, you'd be able to drive a container straight into the elevator ring, filling up one of the massive sides. The elevator car is too big for me to be sure of the exact shape—septagon, octagon?—but assuming that you filled the entire thing with containers, you could haul a *lot* of piezanite. Or people.

Hannah doesn't seem to care about the elevator car's odd shape or its massive size. Instead, she approaches a much smaller door—six feet tall, if that—and swipes Gyu's credentials across a reader. At the same time, something moves in the corner of my eye. My heart catches in my throat as I spin, but it's just our reflection; there's a smooth spot on the elevator car to our left that somehow hasn't been buffed dull by the sand, one that's trapped our blurred reflections.

We look pathetic. Like we don't belong. All of the calm that hearing the song of the Cable brought deserts me in an instant.

The door cracks open an inch, revealing pitch darkness behind. I hold my breath, waiting for a guard to address us, as Hannah works her fingers into the crack and pushes but again, there's no one.

She steps through, but I hesitate. I'd feared the shrill blare of alarms, a swarm of guards. It feels too easy to just float into the building—but deep inside of me, I can still sense the Cable's presence. It pulls me forward, through the door, and for a moment, I have the vision of my feet falling in the exact spaces that Hannah's have left behind, because each step draws me closer and closer to the Cable. In my armpit, a second heart throbs. The fluid that fills my arm, making it swell, seems to ripple in acknowledgment.

A light blinks on above us, anemic but welcome, revealing a tiny, featureless room no larger than my bathroom. It has two doors: one in front and one behind, shotgun style. Hannah shuts the door behind us, and the air fills with a pressurizing hiss. It makes sense—we weren't wearing suits on the way up, so either the cargo container or the elevator itself would have to maintain an atmosphere somehow.

But we don't remove our suits. After a minute or so, there's a soft chime, and a green light flashes on the door in front of us. Hannah pulls the handle, and it opens easily.

We step into a dim hallway, just barely lit by a series of emergency lights. The space in front of us feels crooked, and it takes me a moment to realize it's because of the shape of the ends of the hallway—the angles of each corner are far greater than 90 degrees, revealing a peek of what lies beyond.

I catch a glimpse of a panel of switches to our left, some of which would no doubt provide better illumination, but Hannah ignores those. Instead, we proceed down the hallway in the semi-darkness, though I can see enough to know that I'd been mistaken—from what's in front of me, at least some parts of the elevator ring don't get filled with cargo containers.

I was mistaken in other ways, too. Although I hadn't

articulated it in my mind, from the moment I laid eyes on the tether and the elevator facility, I had formed a prediction that the inside of the car would be shiny and impressive. Gleaming, like the insides of that giant tower my parents snuck me into to experience the ocean. But the only thing impressive about this place is the height of the ceiling and the width of the hallways. Everything else is strangely utilitarian: gray, cheap-looking, a mess of visible rivets and exposed wiring, handwritten signs pasted up to the wall with warnings like *FIRE HAZARD* and *WAIT TEN SECONDS BEFORE ACTIVATION.*

It makes sense, I suppose. Why spend money on something only CPI's employees will see? Still, to have something so shoddy strapped to something as wonderful as the Cable-tether—it feels like an outrage. Like the miracle of the elevator car is nothing more than a cash-grabbing pimple. I hate it.

My attention bounces back to Hannah. Not once has she even paused on her trek into the eye of the storm, which makes no sense—except that Adda and Celeste were lovers before Adda and Hannah were. Maybe Celeste gave Adda the schematics or at least walked her through them.

The schematics. I stop, but only for a moment—I don't need Hannah turning back around.

The drive is still in my pocket. It makes the inside of my skin itch. I want to dig my fingers in, tear out the signs of its presence.

You've gone nuts, I think, and it's like a cold bath. *Something is wrong with you. You need to keep it together.*

I know it's not me. It's the Cable's song. I want to burrow into my hatch and sing it until tears fall from my face, until the spring in my chest unwinds so far it snaps. *Free,* it seems to wail. *Free. Free. Free.* The Cable is alive, and it wants to swallow me whole, to push me up like a depleted cell through a vein, to drive me up to Ung-Nyeo's beating heart.

I glimpse a restroom sign on the wall to my left. It swings into full view as Hannah pushes the door open and pulls me through. A light comes on automatically, blinding after the dark halls of the abandoned elevator facility.

My vision clears to reveal a bog-standard bathroom that nevertheless fills me with anxiety. *Why isn't there anybody here?* My mind bounces through conversations with Gyu, with Celeste. Aren't they about to send a container down? Shouldn't this place be *swarming* with people—

I watch in the bathroom mirror as Hannah grabs me by the shoulders and swivels me around to face her. "What the fuck is wrong with you?" With our helmet projections turned off, I can't see her face. She's whispering, but still—anybody could walk by and hear this.

I shake my head, and the fog rolls back slightly. "What?"

"You're swaying on your feet. Are you even going to make it into the container?"

"I'm—I'm sorry." My heart is pounding again, and that clears my head some more. Being so close to this much naked Cable, not sheathed by the dampening presence of the earth—it's like being suddenly exposed to a loud noise or a bright light: jarring, though I can feel that over time, I'd get used to the Cable's influence. *Maybe.* "I think I'm just nervous."

"Well fucking *un-nervous* yourself."

"Yes. No problem." Before I can say anything else, she turns and leaves.

She's got Gyu's credentials. I have to double-time it to follow her or else risk getting stuck, but the more I move, the better the dazed feeling gets. Soon, the song of the Cable is nothing more than annoying buzz in the back of my mind, like a mosquito's hum.

WE WRAP AROUND the elevator ring. With the drone in my head and the way time squiggles around me, it's hard to estimate how much of the car we've circumnavigated. Half, maybe, which included a small workspace with computers and desks, some kind of mini cafeteria hall, and an exercise facility.

But the entire point of the elevator is to move cargo—which is why I'm not surprised when the next door that Hannah badges open reveals a sign on the wall: *CARGO BAY 1.*

The small room we enter, though, doesn't match the sign. It's tiny, though there are three doors branching off from it: one to the left and one to the right, which are both open, and a closed door straight ahead, in the back. This one is reinforced metal, with a security panel with a reader to the side. Whatever is behind there is *clearly* more valuable than everything else.

Hannah moves confidently toward the metal door, but I still catch flashes of the other rooms in the sweep of my headlight beam as I follow. The one to our left holds a living area, with a couch, a table and chairs, a small bookshelf, and a few random pieces of exercise equipment—free weights mostly, though there's also a bike. In easy view of the couch, a number of screens hang on the wall—for entertainment, or monitoring the contents of the cargo containers?

The door to our right is only cracked a few inches, but I can spy a bunch of beds through it, softly backlit by a pleasant glow. It finally hits me what this area is. This must be a kind of crew quarters for whoever is assigned to the cargo container. All of us prisoners had been packed in like cattle. The guards might not have had all the creature comforts of home, but I sure would've preferred staying in this part, sleeping on one of these mattresses and—

My thoughts freeze up as my headlight bounces off something unexpected. I lean toward the crack, bringing the wall on the right side of the bedroom into better view.

The whole right wall, the wall facing the inside of the elevator ring—it's *shiny*. In fact, it's *clear.*

It makes no sense. Why would the designers of this car feel the need to make one of the bedroom walls into a *window* for the crew, given that they would be staring at the black nothingness of space for the majority of the ride. Not only that, but it's facing the *inside* of the ring—

Oh. Understanding rolls into me like a wave. I push the door the rest of the way open and move forward into the bedroom, shutting off my headlamp as I do. I'm suddenly aware that I'm holding my breath, that some part of me is dumbstruck by my own boldness for there could be someone in here, catching a nap before the container gets sent down—but with each step, I can hear the Cable singing louder. Because it's getting closer. Because—

Because that, I think, as the window fills my vision. There's plenty of light coming through from the spotlights outside, and I can make out everything: the supply lines for air and water, a curved nub I think must be a housing for brakes. Once we re-enter Ung-Nyeo's gravitational field, we'll need to slow our descent.

But behind all of that is the fat, silvery braid of the tether, so close that if I was strong enough, I could punch through this window and touch it.

I lean against the window, my helmet thumping against its hard surface. When I close my eyes, I can feel the Cable, can feel its silvery fingers reaching through everything between us and caressing my hot face.

And then, behind me, I hear a whispered curse. "Shit."

I suddenly remember Hannah. Why we're here. I rip myself away from the window and back out of the room, away from the sterile beds with their perfect white sheets.

Hannah is on her knees in front of the metal door.

"What is it?" I whisper.

"New lock," she says, and even through the speaker, her voice sounds impossibly sad.

My heart races. I swallow. In the back of my mind is the drone of the Cable. It's faded to a mosquito whine, a quiet idle, as if it's watching and waiting.

"What kind of lock?"

She steps aside and points to a word on tiny panel: BIOMETRIC.

"What does that mean?"

"It means it needs DNA."

"DNA," I say, and I almost start to laugh. I have plenty of Gyu's DNA. I have a whole body's worth of his DNA. It's dead, cooling in my bed and worthless to both of us.

"I don't suppose you guys just fucked."

Crass. "We did, but he didn't come inside of me."

"Fuck," says Hannah, and the need to laugh gets stronger. It's the first time I've ever been upset that someone pulled out.

Maybe he knew were going to try this. That we would need some part of him. "Now what?"

"Now we go back to the hatch and hide. Now we wait for them to come and get us. Either way, we're dead."

We stand there for a moment. I don't know what to say to her.

I suddenly go blind as the lights come on.

36

WE SWIVEL AT the noise of footsteps behind us. The door opens to reveal a man in a gray CPI security uniform. "Gyu? I saw you badge in—is there something wrong with the shipment?"

He studies Hannah, then me. I can see his mind doing the calculations. He can't see our faces, but there's Hannah's frame. Hannah's height. Something is wrong.

He suddenly swivels toward the door. I reach out and grab his arm. If I can just stop him for a moment, if I can just hold him up long enough to explain—explain that Gyu's double-crossed everyone, that I'm dying, that I have to get off of Hib—then maybe, maybe we can convince him to let us go. There has to be something we can offer—

We go tumbling together to the floor, pinwheeling like a thrown bola. The man tries to scream, but Hannah stomps on him, somewhere center mass. She kicks him in the throat, and everything—the scream, the man, my hope—crumples easier than a crushed snack-wrapper.

She's looming over him like a black-hatted reaper, waiting to take a soul.

I'm the first to speak. "Hannah, you can't—"

The man struggles abruptly, flailing like a fish. One of his arms knocks into me, and I fall over backward, my helmet clunking against the floor. Before I can sit up again, I see the flash of movement out of the corner of my eye—Hannah's fist, striking down, as swift and sure as an arrow. Something glints like Cable in the palm of her glove.

Hannah twists and yanks with both hands, as efficient in her movements as she is on the drill, and his cry ends in a gurgle.

There's blood spatter on my helmet. I don't know where she got the knife. I watch as she grabs its hilt and pulls it out of his chest. It's a cheap plastic thing—the kind of knife you don't trust to peel an apple. She waves it in front of the reader, but there's no change.

"Crap," she says, her voice clearly exasperated. "Even *this* guy doesn't have credentials for the cargo container?"

"Hannah. You killed him."

She grabs my shoulders and drags me to a sitting position. She's strong, incredibly strong—she'd have to be, to cut a man up with a blade that flimsy. My gaze falls to his face, his horrified expression. I'm suddenly not sure he's a *guard* at all— he could've been an engineer, an admin. Just some worker bee that noticed Gyu's credentials badging in at the wrong time.

"We need to go, Young. *Now.*"

"Hannah, you *killed* him!" It feels like there's a wave inside of me—like it wants to lunge full force at her, crash over her—but I'm afraid of her, too. She's still holding onto the blade. Both of us are covered in blood.

"He would've killed us," she finally says. "He's CPI, and CPI would've killed us. They're going to, anyways. I wasn't going down alone."

She reaches down to help me up, but I can't take her hand. It's covered in blood. Blood is everywhere. On the floor. On the man. On my helmet, like tiny stained-glass raindrops covering a window, making little runnels down the front of its curve.

A switch clicks in my brain. Blood, spread all over my floor like wine, sparkling with broken glass.

I struggle to my feet and unzip my suit.

"What the fuck's wrong with you?" Hannah backs up a bit.

I can't see her face, but from the wary stance of her shoulders and the way she's pulled her arms in front of her, she's bracing herself for a fight.

I pull out my sleeve, stained red. Through the mess on my helmet, I can't tell if it's blood or wine.

If it's blood, where did it come from? Me, sinking onto my knees, the shards cutting into my shins like angry fangs? Or the wound on Gyu's head—

Oh, *stars*. Why would anybody believe he tried to kill himself? He's got *a head wound*.

A head wound, because *I* killed him, just like I killed this guard and Adda. I didn't mean to, never acted with anything like Hannah's knife-point intention—and yet, everybody is dead all the same. Everything I touch turns to ash.

I'm the worst kind of murderer. Does Hannah know? Logic says she'll be next.

I jam my sleeve under the reader. After a moment, the screen changes, a green light flashing. ACCESS GRANTED.

Hannah's in motion before I can take a breath. "Help me with this body," she says. And because I don't know what else to do, I grab the body where she tells me, and drag him into the container.

But once the door closes behind me, I have to stop. Too many images are flashing in my mind, memories of my trip up to Hib that lay themselves over the scene in front of me, a game of spot the differences. There's obviously a modular aspect to these containers—the seats, the chains, the view screens on the walls for entertainment, these are all now missing, no doubt removed to make room for non-human cargo—but the corrugated brown sides, the matching ceiling and floor, the door that leads to a tiny bathroom with a water cooler, these are the same. Except for the removed items, the container is identical to the one we rode up in, large enough to contain a small market square with ten or so stalls. About half the floor space is taken up by crates stacked floor to ceiling against the left wall. Stacking them that way keeps them from shifting after the journey's halfway point, when gravity switches.

For a moment, I want to take off my helmet. To see if this container still holds the smells of rust and unwashed sweat.

"Good thing it's only half-full." Hannah sounds pleased. "CPI must be in a hurry for this shipment. There's plenty of room for us. Let's set him down here."

We put the body down. Hannah reaches behind her and pulls off the blanket, dumping the supplies on the ground. She wads the blanket up into a ball and passes back through the door behind us, leaving it open. It's not until she crouches down on her hands and knees to wipe at the blood that I realize what she's doing.

"People could get here any second," she snarls. "Help me."

I pull off my own blanket, but I can't just leave the man like this. I close his eyes and turn away. Was he a prisoner, one that had earned his way into CPI's good graces? I'd resented the guards, standing over us, all of the way up the elevator—but now I wonder if anybody ever gets sent to Hib of their own accord.

Hannah's mopped up a lot of the blood trail that connects the spot he died to his body in the container, but her blanket is saturated, so now she's just making red-streaked circles with each motion of her hands. She's not doing a very good job of cleaning up. Even she should be able to see that.

Maybe this wasn't as easy for her as it looked. Maybe she's kind of cracking up, too.

I take my blanket through the door at the back of the cargo container, the one that leads to the small bathroom and water cooler. I wet the blanket and wring it out a bit until clean water dribbles on the ground like an offering.

Then I return to Hannah in the small crew quarters. I wipe, turning the blanket as it gets dirty. A song comes to my lips, but I don't hum it, even though it feels right. It's not until we're done that I realize my mother used to sing it every time she washed the floor.

ONCE WE'RE DONE, Hannah and I take our blankets back to the cargo container and stash them behind one of the stacks of crates. Then she uses the panel on the outside of the container to log in as Gyu and delete his and my name from the manifest. There's an extra password check, another biometric scan. I try to press the exact same spot of my sleeve to the reader, and then a confirmation message appears: CHANGE ACCEPTED.

Hannah disables both of our Annie alarms before queuing up the command to seal the container. TEN SECONDS, the display reads. She turns off the light. We head back to the stacks of crates, sit down, and before I have a chance to get settled on the floor, there's a hiss and a click, the container re-sealing itself.

We'll just have to hope that the small tablet interface on the *inside* of the door still has access. Which is something that we probably should have checked before sealing ourselves in.

A thrum of nervousness fills my belly, but then my gaze falls onto the guard's body. It's too much. I can't look at it.

I grab my blanket, still bloody, and cover him. Somehow, this lump, this shape—it's easier to convince myself it's not a real person when I don't have to see the contours of his face, the sweep of his dark hair, the crook of his elbow.

We'll have to find some way to get rid of it, I think. He'll start to stink—maybe not as bad as the time I broke into a burnt-out apartment building and found a man's body in the skinny bathroom—

that day had been so hot that his smell was like a tangible thing, a wave that pushed you angrily for violating its space.

—but once it gets bad enough, it won't be something that any crew on this trip will ignore. The question is, of course, where to put him.

Before long, we make out faint echoes in the room next to us. Spatters of conversation. Doors opening and shutting. Hannah crawls up to the wall, puts her ear against it.

"I can't tell if they're still there," she whispers. "My information wasn't clear on how many people to expect, but if they're just shipping piezanite, they don't need a lot of crew, and they probably won't stay in the crew quarters for much more than leisure time and sleep. As long as we're quiet, we should be good. And I think we're running full atmosphere in here, even though there's no human cargo. Maybe the electronics need it."

Tension hums in my belly, but I don't say anything. I'm frozen to my spot on the floor.

A long time goes by. The ground around us lurches, filling me with panic again.

We're moving, I think, and I really can't believe it. *We actually made it this far.*

Then there's the feeling of rising, a slow acceleration that seems to quicken as we ascend. There's no doubt in my mind as to what's happening, because I can hear the Cable. It's a chorus of singers that pulses in the background of our journey, individual voices fading and getting louder again as we pass them on the way up.

"Do you hear that?" Hannah cocks her head sideways.

"Yes," I say, and my heart lifts. If she can hear these voices, then they're real. They're not just my sick brain or the influence of the tumors growing in my armpit. They're—

And then I hear the groans and rumbles of the pumps kicking on, all of the way up and down the elevator.

Before I can say anything, she's dashing through the door to the little bathroom. I hear the cooler bubble, hear her taking draft after draft after draft. "Come drink and use the bathroom while it's safe," she says, and for a moment, I don't want to.

But the truth is that Gyu is dead, Adda is dead, Celeste is dead, the guard is dead—but me? Despite my best efforts, I'm still alive.

I crawl over to the cooler, remove my helmet, and drink my fill, and I have to admit that although it tastes *horrible,* it's also pretty good.

37

HANNAH HAS THE knack for napping—the ability to just curl up in any spot and doze off, not quite asleep and not quite awake. We've both got our helmets off, now, and any movement on my part makes her open up a single eye and stare at me like a cat.

I've seen that behavior before. People who are used to sleeping rough. Women accustomed to being exposed to every terrible thing in the environment. Old soldiers—there isn't really a military anymore, in the traditional sense, the conflicts between the city-states resolved when CPI established dominance over everything left in the terminator band, but the remnants of that time still remain.

And, of course, prisoners, although I'd largely forgotten that, because I'd been in prison for such a short time. I'd been shipped off to Hib almost immediately, free to sleep alone in my single-room house, free to descend down into the privilege of sleeping like the dead. I'd been lucky that I'd been able to flip that switch so fast—but Hannah, apparently, has never come back from what I call watchful sleep.

I shouldn't be able to sleep at all. Not after what happened to the guard, not with the knife-blade of being discovered forever hanging over our heads—but as soon as I lean against a wall, I can feel my fatigue pressing in on me. I'm sick enough that I might not make it all of the way to the bottom of the elevator.

I've stayed up for so long, hiding from Gyu, running to the mines, trying to piece together Hannah and Celeste and CPI, and now that there is nothing to do but sleep, I embrace it.

Well, I almost do—except there's something kicking around in the back of my mind, a stone I forgot to turn. "Hannah," I whisper, and she opens up her cat-eye. "Do you remember our agreement?"

"Remind me. A lot's happened lately."

My stomach turns. I push that away. "I said I'd help get the credentials, but you had to try to find out what happened to two people—"

"Oh, *that.*" Even whispering, she sounds almost exasperated. She straightens up some, stretches her arms. "What is this, anyways. Some kind of research project?"

"I don't know what you mean."

"I *mean* that you seem to have a real interest in some of the original escapees off of Hib. I'm surprised you didn't just throw Jimmy Kang into the mix—"

"*Hannah.*" The whisper comes out too loud. We freeze and wait quietly for a moment to see if anybody has heard. But at least she understands now that I'm serious—I can tell from the way she brings her finger up to her mouth, shushing me, the intensity of her stare.

After a moment, she slides closer to me. "Okay, Young," she murmurs, her lips inches from my ear. My skin tingles from her warm breath. "Here's the deal. There's not a lot of info on them *after* their escape, but I managed to chase down a few rumors. They didn't go to an enclave, if that's what you're thinking. The group they were with chose to separate, and they must've slipped back inside the wind-walls somehow."

I blink, not understanding. "Why would they do that?"

She shakes her head. "I don't know—looking for someone, maybe? A family member they didn't want to leave behind?"

For a moment, I think it's *me*—and then I realize that no, this would've been before I was even born. "Is there anything else?"

She nods. "Yeah, but it's fuzzy. I guess over a decade later, CPI got wind of their location. They sent out a team to pick them up and intercepted them in a market…I forget the name. Jang-dam? Jang-mun?—"

My breath catches. I suddenly remember standing in Jang-mun market, picking out the suitcase with the flowers, my parents arguing about its practicality.

"—and took them to a holding facility. They were there a while, although I'm not sure how long. This was…years ago. Three? Maybe five? A lot of what I could find was just notes about interviews, so the dates aren't in there."

I don't need the dates. I know *exactly* when it was. "And then what happened?"

She shakes her head. "I don't know. The records of them being there just stop. It's possible they were moved to somewhere else, and the transfer wasn't recorded for security reasons, or they could've died." She snorts. "Or maybe they escaped, and CPI erased the records."

It was obviously a joke, but my chest suddenly fills with hope. I don't know how to feel, how to process what I've just been told. My parents didn't just abandon me. They were *captured*. They'd likely spent *years* wondering what happened to me, hoping that I got away safely.

But I didn't get away. The thing they were trying to avoid— them and me being studied by CPI like test animals—it had come to pass, anyways.

"Sorry," Hannah whispers. "That's all I could find."

I sag against my corner of the room. "Thank you."

Some time passes before sleep overtakes me, but when it does, it's the dream of the sea creature again. We rotate like two orbiting planets—only this time, my parents are there, floating in space like two errant moons.

I WAKE UP when Hannah claps a hand over my mouth. She must have expected I'd start screaming, but instead, it's like trying to drag myself out of sucking mud that clutches for me every step of the way to consciousness.

"You look like shit," she whispers. She's got her suit off.

"I'm alive," I whisper back. My arms are aching, no doubt from sleeping in the suit's weight. I pull myself into a crouch, unzip it, and pull it off.

The drive skitters onto the floor. It must have come out of my pocket while I was out.

"What's this?" She picks it up, but doesn't hand it to me.

I consider lying, but it's hard to do with a dead body sitting next to me. I've seen her kill someone. What kind of secrets can we really have between us? "Celeste gave it to me before she disappeared. I put it in my pocket when I was running out of my place—I didn't want to leave it there. And then I kind of forgot about it. We had a lot of shit on our minds."

She looks skeptical. I can almost read the calculations on her face—like she's trying to figure out if I can do her any harm with a piece of plastic. Finally, she hands it back.

I wish I could get rid of it, but there's nowhere to put it at the moment. I stick it back in my pocket.

She goes to stand in front of the door and presses her ear against the metal. "It sounds like everybody is asleep. This is a good time to get supplies. We have to be careful, though. They could still have a guard."

My heart beats in my throat. I nod. I take off my boots, and she does the same. We'll be quieter that way.

Hannah activates the panel on this side. The biometric lock flashes back on. "Shit, I forgot. Give me the blood again."

I raise up my sleeve, but nothing happens. My stomach sinks.

"I should have fucking disabled it when we had it open, but there wasn't any time." She scrunches up her face. "Maybe the blood's too dry."

I don't know if that's how it works, but I go into the bathroom and sprinkle some water on my sleeve—it is the same spot? It's hard to tell. When I raise my sleeve up to the reader, I can catch the sour-sweet notes of old wine, and a copper scent that has to be blood.

The lock changes—ACCEPTED—and we both let out long breaths.

Hannah works fast. She flies through menus with a practiced hand, barely bothering to read them while moving from one to the next. She disables the biometric lock, using the little wet swatch again to confirm. It takes the computer a second, but it accepts the instructions. And then, she types in the command to open the door.

This click is impossibly loud. I hold my breath as the door retracts into the wall.

We wait five seconds, ten, and then we creep out. The bedroom door is now shut, but I hold my breath as we pass. We progress slowly forward, feeling our way through each step, never putting weight on the foot until we're sure the floor won't creak or groan.

When we get back out into the main hallway, I expect we'll turn left and go back to the cafeteria room we passed on the way in, but Hannah immediately veers to the right. Her steps are purposeful but silent, like a cat stalking its prey. It's again clear to me Hannah is a much better thief than I ever was.

Once, we hear someone coming and duck behind a box of what looks like spare parts and tools, but other than that, we're unimpeded as we proceed to Hannah's final destination: a large room full of shelves and cabinets. Some kind of pantry.

We look through a few cabinets and find individually portioned dried fruit, canned meat, rice, grains, all of it. There's even a fridge, although we leave that alone. Anything that needs to be kept cool will spoil quickly in the cargo container.

I grab a clear bin of dried fruit. Hannah gives me a look and gestures at all the other food, and I shake my head. I put the container down. I point to her, the meat, mime holding as much as my arms can carry, before grabbing the bin again. It's so wide that when I lift it, my arms have to stretch to their fullest, and it renders me half blind. Which is dangerous, but I'm sure that I want it.

When I was first homeless, I lived off noodle packets. Loaves of bread. Things that were easy to store, easy to transport. After about sixty circadians, I started to get weak. I bruised easily. It wasn't until my mouth started bleeding that I realized something was wrong. I asked an old hand under a bridge for advice, and he told me to eat fruit.

I stole some fruit from a convenience store, canned peaches in syrup, oranges I had to peel. The scent of the citrus in that moment was like nothing else I'd ever experienced. It was transportative—a communion, like riding through the Cable. I ate so much fruit I got sick, but my mouth stopped bleeding.

I don't know if Hannah knows this. We should have discussed it beforehand, what to take. That we'd need vitamins, fats, protein. But we'd kind of been in a hurry.

It looks like she's going to try to argue, so I just leave. I can't see my feet, and every step feels treacherous. All it will take is one piece of furniture I hadn't accounted for, one moment of putting my foot down in the wrong position to send me tumbling down and alerting the sleeping skeleton crew that they're not alone.

When I make it back into the cargo container, I quietly dump out the clear bin, scattering the multicolored fruit pouches around me. It takes everything in me to turn around and leave it, to go back out to the pantry, but I do. I pass Hannah on the way back, her arms stuffed full of canned meat—she got greedy, took too many, and she's barely got hold of them all.

I stop her by waving my hand at her. Take two cans off the top, the ones that look most precariously balanced, and nod. She continues on her way, and I make it back to the pantry.

After a few more trips, our journeys sync up so that we're both in the container at the same time. "I think we should stop," she whispers. At some point, she's grabbed her blanket, filled it with boxes. She carefully lowers the blanket to the ground and unpacks each box, one by one. "They're going to notice if we take too much."

I shake my head and quickly explain some of the tricks I've picked up. How you can take a lot when there's a lot to take from, and people won't notice—but later on in the trip, several shifts from now, once their pantry is starting to slim, they'll notice every missing can. Especially if they were eyeing the last of something. And right now, they've only seen the configuration of everything inside once, which means that they won't be hit with that feeling that *something is off* when they open the cabinet door and are confronted with a patchwork of things missing.

She doesn't protest. Instead, she just follows me out. The fridge taunts me once more on my last trip, daring me to try the noise, the light inside, but I manage to avoid it.

When we decide we've pressed our luck enough via a series of quick nods to each other, we seal ourselves back into the container. I press my ear up against the wall and wait, the sounds of the blood rushing in my head like underwater echoes, but there's no sign that we've been heard.

ONCE WE'RE SETTLED, I grab the clear fruit bin again, now empty, and I wave at Hannah while pointing to the body. He's already starting to bloat, and we've got to get rid of him soon.

She stands and follows me as I go over to the guard. We turn him over, making him belch. The container fills with a horrible smell that sends us both gagging. If we were on Ung-Nyeo, he'd already be covered in flies.

It takes both of us straining as hard as we can to center him over the open bin, his arms and legs splayed out. As soon as he's in position, it's clear that he's not going to go in. The bin's just big enough, maybe, but his body has gone all stiff, his arms and legs as hard as wood. "Fuck."

"It's okay," Hannah says. "It'll go away."

I look at her. "What do you mean?"

"It takes about a circadian for the body to hit peak stiffness. Another for it to go away, and he'll be floppy again."

"How do you know that?"

Hannah retracts inside of herself like a turtle. Some things are not meant to be shared.

"Look. In the absolute best of circumstances, we're going to be together for a long-ass time. Maybe it would be better if we got to know each other a little bit better."

She shakes her head, an emphatic *no*, and then she turns her back on me.

I look back around the rest of the container, the food laid in piles. I've counted all of it—a hundred and two cans, boxes, and jars. It would take three or four objects to make even a full meal, which means we'll likely have to make some more trips to the pantry—but we have bags of water we can refill every time the pump runs and a store of food that could last us half the journey if we're willing to keep our belts tightened. We have a way to use the bathroom. If it wasn't for the dead body lying stiff over the container like a plank over some sawhorses, I'd almost believe we could make it out of here.

Part of me recognizes that this is a human being, that a moment ago, I was galvanized by shock and grief. But a numbness is rapidly stealing over me, sealing my insides up like an airlock. Little by little, he just becomes a puzzle to solve; even the way Hannah looked as she stabbed him is already fading in my thoughts.

What does this mean for me, if we survive this? Are there parts of me that, once lost, I can never have back?

"Let's assume he softens up," I say. "We get him into the bin. Where should we put it? Even if we seal it and wrap it as tight as we can, it's going to stink. He's going to rot."

"Maybe," says Hannah. She's got a can of meat in her hand, and it occurs to me that I'm suddenly impossibly hungry.

I kneel down next to her as she yanks the pull tab open. She pulls a striated, gray-pink chunk of unknown provenance out with her fingers and hands me the can.

"Where does the trash go?"

She shrugs. "There's a storage room a few doors down. I don't exactly know where, though, and I don't think it's a good idea to just start opening doors at random."

Trash stinks. It probably doesn't stink as much as a dead body—unless it's the trash of over a hundred prisoners, accumulating. Even in food packets alone, a pile like that had to have been considerable.

"We could try to cut him into pieces," she says. "Try sucking him through the bathroom hose one bit at a time."

I gag, another piece of meat halfway to my mouth. Despite my hunger, I've lost my appetite. I put the can down.

"Then again," she says, thoughtfully. "Skulls are kind of big."

"We're not cutting him up," I say.

"I mean—"

"It's not fast enough. And slicing him up with your tiny knife would make more of a mess than it would fix." There's nothing to wipe my fingers with—another thing we'll need to grab—so despite my disgust, I suck them clean. I fiddle with the drive in my pocket. "Do you know how to read a schematic?"

She cocks her head at me, her eyes narrowed. "Why?"

"It might help us find the trash receptacle, or figure out somewhere else to stow—"

She shakes her head. "No good. There's no access to the schematics through the panel. I've already checked every—"

I pull out the drive and hand it to her. "On this," I say.

Her eyes narrow. Her warm fingers brush my palm as she grabs it. "Let me check."

38

HANNAH PLUGS THE drive into the door panel. She navigates its contents, paging through and reading things so fast I can't hope to follow.

After a while, she looks at me as if she's seeing me for the first time. "Seriously, Young, what the fuck? Why do you have this?"

"I told you. Celeste gave it to me—"

"Why would she do that?"

I shrug. It sounds nuts. "She wants to blow up the elevator." I realize, too late, the right verb was probably *wanted*.

"Huh." Hannah leans back against the wall. I wonder if she can hear voices on the other side. "It would hamstring the shit out of CPI." She shakes her head. "You can't do that, though. Everyone on Hib would be stranded—"

"Yeah, I know. I told her *no*."

"But you kept the drive." Her eyes narrow.

"It's lucky I did. We wouldn't have the schematics."

"Right. Well, I found something."

I lean in close, watch over her shoulder as she taps at the screen. I can smell her, a soft sweetness that's also just a bit spicy, like vanilla. It's covered over with the tang of sweat, overlaid again with the dead body in the corner. It's too many smells, too confusing, and so I just focus on the motion of her fingers.

"Right here," she says, and she zooms in on a section of the car. "There's a door around the back of the entertainment area that leads to trash overflow storage."

"That's really close to everybody. I feel like they're going to notice a rotting body before long, even if we do stick it in a container."

"Yeah," she says, "but there's a protocol to make it dump into space. We could either set it on a timer so it happens at night when everybody is asleep, or we could just not activate it unless the smell starts to get really bad."

"Maybe we should just leave the body in the pantry or something."

Her jaw falls open. "What?"

"I just mean—think of it this way. If you were on a crew, and then a body showed up in the morning in the pantry, would your first thought be that some prisoners snuck on and are living in the cargo container? Or would it be that one of the other crew members did it?"

"Yeah," she says, "except then they'd probably start combing through the place—especially since the body wasn't there a few days ago, which means that they're going to be looking for clues."

I think it over. "You're right. And if we put it in the trash room and it's discovered, there's always the chance that people will think that maybe the murder happened before the trip started. It'll be hard to do time of death. They probably don't have the equipment here for that kind of thing. So, it'll raise more questions, and maybe they won't search everything as thoroughly."

"Maybe," she says.

"It's a risk either way, but I don't think we should dump it into space. There'll be a record. They might try to figure out where the command came from." I bite my lip. "Let's assume that eventually, this body is going to be found. That the only questions are *where* and *when*. I think the best approach is to leave it in the trash room, bundled up as much as we can to cut the smell. We'll just have to hope that they either don't realize it in time, or that maybe the smell is so bad they just decide to dump it themselves, or…"

I'm reaching. But the only way to know which plan is the best one is to predict the future, and no matter what, we have to move the body.

"Okay," she says, finally. "I agree. We'll just leave it there. Maybe they'll start accusing each other. Maybe we'll get super lucky and they'll kill each other off, and we won't even have to worry about escaping inside of the tunnel. We'll just walk the hell out. We'll have to wait for the next time everyone's asleep, though. I think we're pushing our luck for time."

"Yeah," I say, thinking of the footsteps we heard in the hall. "There's at least one person awake, for sure."

She shrugged. "There's supposed to be multiple guards up at all times. But like, they're not really guarding anything. Nobody is going to steal a load of piezanite on a mostly deserted elevator, not when there's nowhere to go with it."

BEFORE I FALL asleep, I think about everything that had to pass for us to find ourselves on this elevator. I have some answers, but more questions—and the thing I want to know most, about who this person is I'm sharing this ride with—is the one thing I probably won't get any answers to.

It makes me think about something else, though. About Adda. "What was Adda like?"

She sighs. "What kind of question was that? You knew her."

I swallow. "We never got very close. I was just…afraid of irritating her or something. Getting myself kicked off the team." I want to laugh. It sounds stupid, now, of all the things I could worry about.

Hannah doesn't say anything for a long time. Sleep starts to pull me down into its clutches. When she speaks again, I break free. "She used to be a farmer."

"What?"

"Yeah. Her whole family is farmers. Her parents worked on one of the giant rotating disc-farms."

I close my eyes and imagine it. Before scientists had figured out all the ins and outs of hydroponics, crop choices were severely limited to those plants that could grow in a constant twilight. Unless you were rich, of course. CPI wiped out an entire city to build a giant, oblong disc, going so far as to cut away slits in the bottom of the wind-dome, before expanding the plasteel enough to bubble over the disc's surface. Twice a circadian, the discs would rotate, exposing plants to a covered piece of the brightness of the Desert, before swirling them back into the twilight of the terminator band. I'd only seen pictures of the food, the fat ripe tomatoes, the citrus fruits, the leafy greens—until normal people figured out how to crudely ape the method with lights.

My mother used to do that in our basement. Lights on like the Desert. Lights off. She felt they grew better when the dark time was true dark, like the kind you'd see in the Ice.

I'd never thought about it until this moment, how dumb it was that plants grew better when they only had things the rich could afford to give them. "A farmer. I never would have guessed."

"Yeah." Hannah turns her face away, so that I couldn't see her expression. "She really loved to grow things. She moved in with me right after we started to knock boots, but she'd go back to her place every day. I thought she had someone else. I went over there to confront her, and she'd rigged her entire house up with grow lights and water. There were plants everywhere. It must have cost her a fortune. Maybe that's why she decided she was going to escape—she couldn't stop herself from the plants, which meant she'd never pay the debt off."

I want to ask more. About what Hannah and Adda were going to do in the enclave. If she'd grow things, there, too. But there was a little hitch in Hannah's voice on the word *never*, and she doesn't seem to want to keep talking, so I just stay quiet until we both fall asleep.

HANNAH WAKES ME like she did before, a hand over the mouth. She's not taking any chances.

I stretch. I feel impossibly stiff. Part of me wants to steal a pillow, soft blankets, a bed—but that kind of stuff will almost certainly be recognized as missing.

She's right, the man's body has softened enough that we're able to squeeze it into the bin. Then we stand, frozen, as she keys open the door. We'll drop this body off, take some more food from the pantry on the way back—and then I think we should maybe just stay in the container. Every time we leave, it increases the chances that we're going to get caught. That tonight will be the night that someone can't sleep. It's too much of a risk.

She ties a blanket around her waist—for transporting food, probably—and we haul the bin with the body up, the plastic bending under his weight, before we finally manage to get both sets of our fingers under it. I start out in the lead.

We creep across the floor of the cargo container. This close to my face, the stink is unavoidable, and I worry that it's going to wake people up as we waft it by.

Creep, creep, creep. I feel like our steps are impossibly loud.

By the time we get to the first door, my back and arms are screaming. I'm not sure how we'll make it all the way to the trash facility. We set down the container so she can operate the panel to open the door—a click, and then both of us wait, frozen, to see if we've been discovered.

We peek through. Like before, the doors to both the bedroom and the leisure area are closed. We stoop down again. Pick up the container. Our progress to the trash facility takes an eternity, and by the time we make it and bring the bin inside, sweat is running down my back. Finally, though, we set down the bin.

Hannah unties the blanket from around her waist and lays it in the far back corner. She mimes picking the bin up to me, dumping it out on the blanket. We heave, my arms and legs trembling, and then once our load is safely delivered, Hannah pulls the sides of the blanket up and ties the corners into a little bow on top. It looks like an oversized version of the bundles that old grandmothers are always carrying around.

Hopefully, by the time the stink is unconscionable, enough trash will have been heaped in front of it that nobody will think twice about pushing the button and ejecting it into space.

We retrieve the bin and return to the pantry to load it with more supplies. When we make it back, though, as soon as we step into the little transition room between the main hallway and the cargo container, the door to the bedroom suddenly opens. I know this, because I can hear the swell in the song of the Cable.

"Hello, Young," says a voice that stops my heart in my chest. The bedroom light flicks on, and there, highlighted in the doorway, is Gyu.

39

HANNAH LUNGES FOR Gyu before I have a chance to react.

Everything happens in slow motion. He steps backward into the bedroom and raises a gun. She makes it to him before he can fire and slams into him, and they tumble backward together.

I sprint forward, following them into the bedroom. Before I can understand the scene in front of me, I hear two blasts—*pop, pop*. The first goes wide and smashes into the plasteel window. It fractures, a chunk half the size of my fist breaking free, and the room fills with a sucking noise, wind whistling through its surface.

With the barrier between us damaged, the intensity of the Cable's call strengthens, as if the molecules of gas between us are delivering small bursts of an addictive substance. *Free, free, free.* For a moment, I'm paralyzed, as if held in a thrall, but then somewhere above us, blowers kick on. Alarms blare. The elevator car engages its brakes and screeches to a halt. The vibration, like an earthquake, jolts me off of my feet and shakes me back into reality, even as metal rattles and food packages rain down around us.

There were two shots. *Shots.* As I struggle back onto my feet, I repeat the word, again and again, because its meaning has finally caught up to me. *Shots*, because Gyu is here, and he's got a gun.

The first shot missed his target. But the second?

I look for Hannah, and she's face-down on the floor, a red bloom spreading on her back.

And Gyu—he's dead, which means he can't be here—but Hannah's dead, which means he is.

I can't move. There's too much happening here, too many sounds pulsing inside my head. My heartbeat. The Cable's voices, singing almost in time, begging me to touch it. And penetrating from outside is the rhythmic blare, a groan as the car begins to slowly shift direction, back toward Hib's surface.

The alarms stop. The sudden silence is almost worse.

Gyu speaks first. His voice is dead calm. "You tried to kill me."

I look up at him, really seeing him. The way he's standing, as perfectly straight as the tether between Hib and the planet. The way not a single muscle on his body twitches.

"No," I say. I shake my head. "It was just supposed to be a sleeping draft, I didn't realize—"

"Do you expect me to believe that? You staged my body to make it look like a suicide. You lied to me, over and over." He taps one end of the gun against his own temple before centering it again on my chest, a movement too fast and fickle for me to react to. "You're a bitch, Young. Do you know that? Do you have any idea how that felt? I really cared about you. I tried to keep you a secret for as long as I could. I can't believe you were working with *Celeste*—"

"I'm not." My protest is too angry, too vehement, like a match that could light the tension in this room. "I'm not working with her." It's hard to stem the flow of anger— he's upset with *me* for lying—but I do. "I can explain this. I'll explain everything." I need a second. I have to think. "Just—let me check on Hannah? Please?"

He waves at her body with the gun. I show him my palms while I edge over to her, closer to the vein of Cable. With each step, the force of its pull increases, begging me to reach up and touch it.

Hannah's heavy. Still warm. I flip her so that she's face up, putting my whole body into it. I put my fingers on her neck to take her pulse, but it's obvious from her stare, already glassy, that she's dead.

Free, sings the Cable. *Free, free, free.* When I stand, the hole in the plasteel draws nearer still, so that my face is only an arm's length away from it.

I don't know how Gyu can't hear the song of the Cable. The way it cycles, around and around, like a wheel—it makes something spin inside the gyre of my mind.

"Tell me something," he says. He narrows his eyes at me. "Let's say your stupid plan somehow worked and I died in your room. That I never found your message to Hannah. That you somehow managed to subvert detection, get to the planet, make it into the tunnel—then what? You'd never make it all of the way back to the terminator band without being discovered. Even if you escaped at some point, there's nowhere to go. There's no—"

"There're enclaves," I say, suddenly defensive. It's irrational—but there's a stream behind me, singing my name, and it's hard to hold on to that and this moment and also be rational. I'd have to tell myself the singing isn't real, and I can't, because it's more real than me, more real than my body—I feel like my skeleton will come apart. Like I'll fall to the floor in a pile of bones and muscles and sinews and organs.

"Enclaves?" He laughs, a series of short barks, honestly amused. In another time, another place, I would have treasured that laugh, maybe. "There aren't any enclaves. That's a rumor that CPI spreads to root out resistance. If you'd asked me, I could have told you that."

I sag. *No enclaves.* All of this had been for nothing, an attempt built on a foundation of clouds. My insides sink, faster than the elevator's whistling descent. I press the heels of my hands into my forehead. It's only when I pull them away that I see that they're wet with Hannah's blood.

It's like her blood has gone into my eyes. Changed the way everything looks. Maybe it's because everything is blood, all of the time—Gyu's blood, the guard's blood, Hannah's blood. I wonder how they killed Celeste. If she bled a lot. If I will, when Gyu kills me.

"Tell me something," I say, turning his own question against him. "Why seek me out? Why make me think you care? You could have just thrown me into a cell—"

"I do care," he growls. "I cared about you, right from the beginning." He raps the heel of the gun against his chest. "Do you think it was easy? Buying you more time? Knowing what you were doing? Did you think I didn't notice the note missing from my pocket? The way your suit needed constant cleaning? Did you think you could keep meeting with Celeste alone in that hatch?"

He shakes his head. "I found the drive in your sheets. We intercepted her first shipment, Young. None of the schematics ever made it down. We faked transmissions, messages up, so that she'd think she'd been successful, dredge herself in deeper. We used every single thing she sent down to find more of her people. As for her resistance, I doubt there's any left."

There's a painful lump in my throat. It doesn't matter that some of the details are wrong. He's got things right enough. "Did you bug my apartment? In the light fixture?"

His silence is all the answer I need.

I bite the inside of my cheek so hard that the pain is a bright flare that centers my mind, removes it from the trance that the Cable wants from me. "Did you drug me? Is that why I overslept that day, the day that Adda—"

"I didn't have a choice," he says. His voice has gone impossibly quiet. "CPI has my family. My wife. My kids. If I hadn't complied, if I hadn't come up here, they would have been turned out into the Desert. My debts were—"

The world goes silent. Even the Cable's song fades away, so that there's nothing in my ears but a buzzing whine and the passage of my breath.

I snap out of it, and to my surprise, I'm *laughing*—laughing so hard I double over and there are tears coming to my eyes.

"What the *fuck* is so funny?" Gyu roars, but I can't stop. I'm on my knees, laughing so hard I might just throw up on the floor.

I'd gone through his pocket, torn apart the note and flushed it. I'd spent nights awake, sure he was cheating on me. Sure that he was lying to me. Fearing the whole time—torturing myself with my doubts. With my insecurities. With my surety that I was worth being abandoned, traded for a better model.

And all along, I'd been right about so many things—not the details, but the *nature* of things. Every time I thought I was crazy, that my mind was broken again—the Cable, Gyu's dishonesty, Gyu's cheating, not with someone else, but with *me*, because *I* was the other woman—I was *right*. I'd been thinking straight. My worst fear—that my mind was unraveling—hadn't been true at all.

It doesn't matter that I'm going to die today. At least I die knowing all the things I am, and all the things I'm not. And looking at Gyu now, at the way his body trembles like a branch in a windstorm, cracking and cracking, getting ready to snap off, everything is crystal clear.

I'm not a chosen person, but I was chosen. Not by CPI. Not by Gyu. Not by my parents, but by the Cable, the veins that run deep into Hib, into Ung-Nyeo. The tether between the two, holding our planet and its moon stationary in some great counterweight, never letting either turn.

Because I've felt that, too. Felt it in my dreams, where I danced on the back of a great creature in the sea. In my journeys through the vein. In the dizzy, spinning feeling I get each time I broke away from the communion and had to lay on the sand, as the world slowly tilted around me.

Celeste was right. I can see that in the shake of Gyu's gun as he points it at me, in the silent movement of his lips, forming words I can't hear. There is no life worth living while we are owned by CPI.

I reach my hand through the window's hole, out for the Cable. The world fades to perfect silence as my hand lands, and I can feel the smooth belly of the silver braid slithering under my palm. My mind splits again—half here, in the car, half screaming up the Cable. In my bones, I feel its agony—the agony of the planet, the agony of a moon. The pain of a balance that longs to be restored—who were these first people, so bold, so arrogant as to tether a moon? To shoot a silver thread into the deepest layers of its mantle, to do the same to its planet, knowing the pain it would cause? They bound a child to its mother, forever, making sure it could never be truly born.

I remember something I'd long forgotten. A moment, out of air, moving into darkness.

I found you out there in the sand, says the Cable. Its voice is warmer than the bright light in my dreams, and I know, now, that it's more than just the Cable. It's the voice of a moon. *I didn't want you to die. I remembered your mother.*

Will you remember yours? I think. *After you are parted?*

I hope so, says the voice. *But I'm ready to be something else.*

The part of me still in the elevator car looks back at Gyu. He's gesturing frantically, waving the gun like a pennant.

He gives up. Centers it on me. Raises it from my chest to my head.

I let this half of me find the other. Together, we find the center, the point exactly halfway between the two sides of this travesty. We grab this problem by the middle. We pull, and pull, helping the moon and the planet that cannot help themselves.

Somewhere in the space between Hibiscus and her shadow, there really is a perfect darkness. And in this darkness, the tether snaps.

An angry energy roars away from the middle, driving down two lines of Cable like a whip-crack, ripping both ends of the elevator's tether free from their moorings. That force is transferred down, down, to the cores of both heavenly bodies.

Somewhere above Hibiscus, a gun shoots.

On either side, two giants turn.

EPILOGUE

THE TEMPERATURE READINGS coming in from the weather station of Enclave 12, more affectionately known as the Ear of the Desert Rat, didn't make sense.

Jimmy Kang knew this, because he had spent most of his waking life in the Ear watching the screen. Desert Rat's inhabitants rarely came up to its surface, but there were some who needed to be alerted when the winds died down. It was during these brief periods of detente that intrepid scientists, engineers, and mechanics would venture up to look for those things that were only accessible in the flash-flood moments where nature bloomed, where water collected, where the surface was exposed.

The things they scavenged were many: pollen samples. Insects that had waited long, only to hatch, mate, and die within the ethereal window of semi-stillness. Minerals. Raw materials. Seeds, flower specimens, tadpoles—for as much as those outside of the enclave believed that the Desert was a desolate, barren place, the people of the Rat knew better. Life always found a way. Even if the way meant spending the majority of life underground, safe from the wind and the prying eyes of CPI satellites. Even if the way meant waiting in chrysalis for the next time the winds went soft, waiting for a chance to riot into life and flame out just as quickly, embedding the next generation in suspended animation until their own soft wind finally came.

But in all his time as the Watcher of the Ear, Jimmy had never seen anything like this. The wind had not only gone soft—it had blown weaker, circadian after circadian, until it just died. More than that, the readings from the instruments were all over the place—the temperature had gone down, down, down, and then up, up, up, a swing so wide it rivaled half the temperature of a human body—and now it was starting to fall again. Precipitation readings were off the charts. The magnetic readings had all gone haywire, the needles all suddenly swinging in the same direction. It was like every instrument had broken at once, and after waiting a few days, Jimmy Kang decided that for the first time in a very long time, he was going to head up to the viewing dome on the surface and figure out what the heck was going on.

On the way to Up, the tongue-in-cheek moniker they'd given the core-to-surface transport elevator, he felt suddenly pensive. Jimmy was getting old. A while back, his right knee had started to hurt in intervals that at first felt random, and he'd tried everything—stretching, sitting more, sitting less—until he'd realized that it seemed to correspond to when the Ear told him it was about to rain. Since then, his left knee had joined in on the fun. He wondered what joint would be next.

At least he was not in his parents' generation. They were the ones who had seeded Desert Rat in the first place. They'd come in waves, like flocks of migrating birds, somehow drawn to this exact spot.

Desert Rat was underneath an anomaly in the wind—for some reason, the currents in the air here were much stronger than other nearby spots in the Desert, which meant that the area was subject to a cacophony of unending rain. Between the wind and the rain, it was often cooler than you might expect—incredibly hot, but not so hot that exposure caused immediate death, and the rain dripped below the sand and into the aquifers they'd built.

Jimmy boarded Up and set his lantern on the ground. He hauled on the rope, hand over hand, again and again, and slowly the basket started to rise. Almost instantly, his shoulders broke out into a sweat, and his lower back began to ache. *So, that would be the next to go, maybe.*

About halfway up, he had to lock the brakes and stop. He leaned back against the wall of the car and wheezed—the truth was that although he'd *like* to blame his lack of stamina on age, being the Ear Man couldn't have helped his position. While others broke their backs making food, building tunnels, hauling themselves and entire crews Up so that they could maintain the wind farm, he'd sat on his ass and watched a screen, and now he was paying the price for it.

His breath was coming easier now, and he was only halfway there. It was time to get back to work. Hand over hand, Jimmy climbed. He had to stop twice more for breaks before he finally made it to the platform near the surface. His legs and arms wobbled as he hauled himself over the platform's edge, and for a brief moment, he imagined himself plummeting backward, down, down into the hole, all twelve stories to the very bottom—but then his leg decided today was in fact not the day that it would be giving up on him, and he stabilized on the edge.

Well. That had been shitty, but it was over now. At least the fear had sapped the ache out of his knees and back.

Jimmy made his way to the end of the platform and walked up the short grade that led to the observation bubble. It wasn't until he made it halfway that the light grew dim, and he realized all at once—he'd left his lantern in the basket.

He could've certainly used it, as the hallway was dimmer than he'd remembered—but of course, it was. He was a lot older than it had been the last time he'd come up, and he'd already passed the halfway point. But if he could just make it a little further, the tunnel would start to lighten again as sunlight filtered in through the clear plasteel of the observation dome. He kept on, making a concerted effort to ignore the ache in his knees. Partway through, he had to find the edge of the tunnel wall with his fingers to continue the climb, and he set his foot down wrong once or twice. Right as he was about to give up, the tunnel got lighter again.

He climbed and climbed, until he made it to the final stretch. And there, cast through the clear plasteel window into the dim at the end of the tunnel, were soft blades of golden light. The beams caught errant dust motes that glistened like water.

Jimmy had never seen anything like it. The light from outside was always harsh, the sun over the Desert white and merciless. This was something else.

Something moved inside of Jimmy's chest—an aching pull, half grief, half joy, although he couldn't say why. He sped up, tripped, fell on his hands and knees, but even then, he didn't want to stop long enough to stand. Jimmy crawled the final length and looked up through the bubble.

There was no sand in his view. The wind really had died, died so completely that it had left a portal straight into heaven. In that clear circle was a light-show of colors, as if the clouds themselves had been set on fire. Rust reds, bruise purples, yellows more intense than any he'd ever seen before. There was even a series of streaks he couldn't quite place at first, a color halfway between yellow and red that he hadn't seen in so long the word refused to loose itself from the tip of his tongue—*orange*, that was it.

After beholding it for a moment, Jimmy couldn't help it. The world was obviously ending. He was old, now, and he wanted to see it come. He found the hidden door that allowed exit from the observation dome and crawled out.

The sand had fallen almost completely still—a few errant grains wove their way across the top like dancers, but the rest of it lay in unmoving peaks and valleys, a mountain range in miniature. The entire sky was the same as it had been in his bubble—painted, the colors somehow blazing brilliant against the darkness of the horizon. And right above that line of darkness was a single, golden disk, one that Jimmy somehow understood wasn't good to look at straight. He watched it from the corner of his eye as it sank toward the dark, and he marveled that his life had been so good.

And yet, when the air started to grow cold, Jimmy found that he was still alive. He recognized that his obligation was probably to go back down and let everybody know that the sun had died. They deserved the right to choose how they wanted to spend their last circadian on this planet.

But then he looked up at something impossible. There, in the dark sky, was a dense blanket of stars.

Jimmy knew about stars in a factual sense. But to *see* them, to have them unveil themselves in front of him like a swirling sandstorm made of light and frozen in time, it was enough to bring tears to his eyes, and he couldn't break himself away. There was one in the distance, brighter than the others and steadily growing brighter, a trail streaking behind it. It grew, and it grew, and at some point, Jimmy realized it was actually getting *closer*. That it was coming *right for him*.

But it didn't hit him. Instead, quick as a blink, it plummeted into the ground in the distance, kicking out a cloud of dust so bad that he had to stick his face into his sleeve and cough.

Hours passed before the dust settled again. But finally, it did, leaving behind a bright, silvery chunk, roughly the size of Jimmy himself, half-embedded into the sand.

He approached it carefully. It was shiny, and almost certainly made of metal. A rare find, a gift from the sky. The kind that could've made quite a few wind-farms from its pieces, if they could've figured out how to melt and shape it just right—

It cracked down the middle, just like an egg.

Jimmy backed up, certain that its inhabitant was an alien, because who else would fall from the sky?

The two halves of it rolled down onto their curved sides, and the occupant fell to the ground.

It was human-shaped and face-down. Its clothes were old-fashioned.

And then it coughed—once, twice, and it took a great, gasping breath. Jimmy almost pissed his pants, but he forced himself to stand there and wait.

The thing rolled over. It was a woman. She had a pleasing face and bright eyes, but she looked like she'd just been worked over by a gang. Or fallen out of a space rock.

When she saw him, her eyes went wide. "Who are you?"

How did one talk to an alien? He decided on being as casual as possible. "I'm Jimmy Kang. Kang Jimmy, if you go by things old-style. I work in the Ear, and you're at Desert Rat, and—"

Her face looked impossibly confused. "Kang? Jimmy Kang? Are you crazy?" She glanced around herself. "Where in the Band—"

"Not the Band," he said, shaking his head. "An enclave." And then he remembered that that wasn't the kind of thing one usually volunteered to a visitor, although Desert Rat hadn't had a visitor in a very, very long time. Still, maybe this person was some kind of CPI technology, some kind of—

"An enclave," breathed the woman, and she smiled a beatific smile, and Jimmy Kang knew it was going to be alright.

She looked him over, and then she turned and took in the oceans of sand all around them, the stretch of stars in the sky. At those, she stopped and held her breath, her face clearly filled with awe.

"They're beautiful, aren't they? Stars," he said, in case she didn't know. "I was just watching them. Would you...would you like to sit and watch them, too?"

They took up two spots, side by side on the sand, and watched as the stars faded. The sky grew gray, and then soft pink. They bore witness as the disk of the sun blazed into rebirth, washed the world in its light, and rose in an arc to its apogee.

"I guess the world's not ending," he said, his heart full of wonder. And then, because that was sorted: "Are you hungry?"

His guest nodded, and they stood, to make their way back to civilization.

ABOUT THE AUTHOR

 **MARIA DONG** is the author of *Liar, Dreamer, Thief* and *Psychopomp*. Her short fiction, articles, and poetry have been published in dozens of magazines, like the *Best American Science Fiction and Fantasy, Lightspeed, Augur, Nightmare, Khoreo, Fantasy, Apex,* and *Apparition Literary Magazine,* and her story, "In the Beginning of Me, I was a Bird," was a finalist for the Theodore Sturgeon Memorial Award. She is represented by Amy Bishop-Wysick at Trellis Literary.

Also Available or Coming Soon from Dark Matter INK

Human Monsters: A Horror Anthology
Edited by Sadie Hartmann & Ashley Saywers
ISBN 978-1-958598-00-9

*Zero Dark Thirty: The 30 Darkest Stories from Dark Matter
Magazine, 2021–'22*
Edited by Rob Carroll
ISBN 978-1-958598-16-0

Linghun by Ai Jiang
ISBN 978-1-958598-02-3

Monstrous Futures: A Sci-Fi Horror Anthology
Edited by Alex Woodroe
ISBN 978-1-958598-07-8

Our Love Will Devour Us by R. L. Meza
ISBN 978-1-958598-17-7

*Haunted Reels: Stories from the Minds of Professional
Filmmakers* Curated by David Lawson
ISBN 978-1-958598-13-9

The Vein by Steph Nelson
ISBN 978-1-958598-15-3

Other Minds by Eliane Boey
ISBN 978-1-958598-19-1

Monster Lairs: A Dark Fantasy Horror Anthology
Edited by Anna Madden

ISBN 978-1-958598-08-5

Frost Bite by Angela Sylvaine
ISBN 978-1-958598-03-0

The House at the End of Lacelean Street
by Catherine McCarthy
ISBN 978-1-958598-23-8

When the Gods Are Away by Robert E. Harpold
ISBN 978-1-958598-47-4

The Dead Spot: Stories of Lost Girls
by Angela Sylvaine
ISBN 978-1-958598-27-6

Grim Root by Bonnie Jo Stufflebeam
ISBN 978-1-958598-36-8

Voracious by Belicia Rhea
ISBN 978-1-958598-25-2

The Bleed by Stephen S. Schreffler
ISBN 978-1-958598-11-5

Chopping Spree by Angela Sylvaine
ISBN 978-1-958598-31-3

Saturday Fright at the Movies: 13 Tales from the Multiplex
by Amanda Cecelia Lang
ISBN 978-1-958598-75-7

The Off-Season: An Anthology of Coastal New Weird
Edited by Marissa van Uden
ISBN 978-1-958598-24-5

The Threshing Floor by Steph Nelson
ISBN 978-1-958598-49-8

Club Contango by Eliane Boey
ISBN 978-1-958598-57-3

Free Burn by Drew Huff
ISBN 978-1-958598-94-8

The Divine Flesh by Drew Huff
ISBN 978-1-958598-59-7

Disgraced Return of the Kap's Needle
by Renan Bernardo
ISBN 978-1-958598-74-0

Haunted Reels 2: More Stories from the Minds of Professional Filmmakers Curated by David Lawson
ISBN 978-1-958598-53-5

Dark Circuitry by Kirk Bueckert
ISBN 978-1-958598-48-1

Soul Couriers by Caleb Stephens
ISBN 978-1-958598-76-4

Abducted by Patrick Barb
ISBN 978-1-958598-37-5

Cyanide Constellations and Other Stories by Sara Tantlinger
ISBN 978-1-958598-81-8

Little Red Flags: Stories of Cults, Cons, and Control
Edited by Noelle W. Ihli & Steph Nelson
ISBN 978-1-958598-54-2

Cold Snap by Angela Sylvaine
ISBN 978-1-958598-55-9

The Starship, from a Distance by Robert E. Harpold
ISBN 978-1-958598-82-5

Dark Matter Presents: Fear City
ISBN 978-1-958598-90-0

Shiva by Emily Ruth Verona
ISBN 978-1-958598-93-1

Neon Moon by Grace R. Reynolds
ISBN 978-1-958598-96-2

Part of the Dark Hart Collection

Rootwork by Tracy Cross
ISBN 978-1-958598-85-6

Mosaic by Catherine McCarthy
ISBN 978-1-958598-06-1

Apparitions by Adam Pottle
ISBN 978-1-958598-18-4

I Can See Your Lies by Izzy Lee
ISBN 978-1-958598-28-3

A Gathering of Weapons by Tracy Cross
ISBN 978-1-958598-38-2